FOUR RUINED REALMS

BOOKS BY MAI CORLAND

THE BROKEN BLADES

Five Broken Blades
Four Ruined Realms

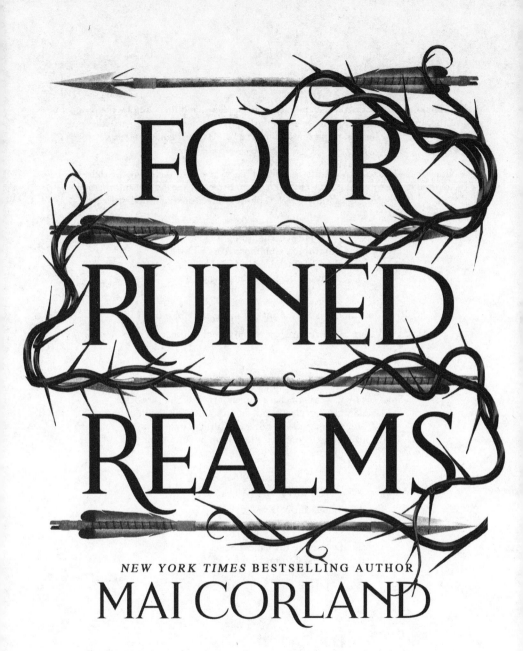

FOUR RUINED REALMS

NEW YORK TIMES BESTSELLING AUTHOR
MAI CORLAND

RRED TOWER BOOKS™

Entangled Publishing, LLC
644 Shrewsbury Commons Ave., STE 181
Shrewsbury, PA 17361
rights@entangledpublishing.com

Red Tower Books is an imprint of Entangled Publishing, LLC.

Visit our website at www.entangledpublishing.com.

Edited by Liz Pelletier
Cover art and design by Elizabeth Turner Stokes
Stock art by Cover boonchai sakunchonruedee/Shutterstock,
MagdaSurgiewicz/PixelSquid, and Karamaz/PixelSquid
Interior map art by Elizabeth Turner Stokes
Deluxe Limited endpaper illustration by Juho Choi
Interior design by Britt Marczak

HC ISBN 978-1-64937-750-0
Ebook ISBN 978-1-64937-675-6

Manufactured in the United States of America
First Edition January 2025

10 9 8 7 6 5 4 3 2 1

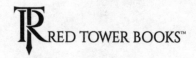
RED TOWER BOOKS™

*For my heart, my sunshine,
and my man of steel*

Four Ruined Realms is a dark adventure fantasy full of sharpened blades, poisoned lips, and a new power rising in the realms. As such, the story features elements that might not be suitable for all readers, including depictions of violence, blood, death (including the death of family, incarcerated people, and animals), imprisonment, poisoning, drowning, evisceration, torture, classism, sexism, graphic language, and sexual activity. Indentured servitude, assault, child sexual abuse, colonization, and genocide are discussed. Readers who may be sensitive to these elements, please take note, and prepare to risk it all for the Golden Ring...

Main Characters

AERI (*AH-ree*)… A Thief, Princess of Yusan, King Joon's Daughter

MIKAIL (*Mick-ALE*)… The Former Royal Spymaster of Yusan

ROYO (*ROY-oh*)… A Strongman from Yusan

EUYN (*YOON*)… The banished Crown Prince of Yusan, King Joon's Brother

SORA (*SOAR-a*)… A Poison Maiden from Yusan, formerly indentured to Count Seok

TIYUNG (*TIE-young*)… Count Seok's only Son, sent to Idle Prison

Other Characters of Note

KING JOON (*King JUNE*)… The King of Yusan

QUILIMAR (*QUILL-i-mar*)… The Queen of Khitan, King Joon and Euyn's sister

GENERAL VIKAL (*VY-cal*)… General of the Khitan Armed Forces

COUNT SEOK (*Count SEE-ock*)… The Southern Count of Gain who holds Daysum's Indenture

DAYSUM (*DAY-sum*)… Sora's Sister and Count Seok's Ward

COUNT BAY CHIN (*Count Bay Chin*)… The Northern Count of Umbria

~~COUNT DAL (*Count DAHL*)… The Eastern Count of Tamneki~~ (deceased)

GENERAL SALOSA (*General Sah-LOW-sa*)… General of the Yusan Palace Guards

ZAHARA (*Za-HAH-ra*)… A Yusanian Spy

FALLADOR (*FAL-lah-dor*)… The Exiled Prince of Gaya

AILOR (*ALE-or*)… Mikail's father

GAMBRIA (*GAM-bree-uh*)… Fallador's Cousin

UOL (*OO-ul*)… Priest King of Wei

Previously, in The Broken Blades Trilogy

Five of the most dangerous liars in the land came together with one mission: to kill the God King Joon of Yusan. Aeri, a gem thief, approached strongman Royo, offering him a fortune for his protection as she journeyed to steal the Immortal Crown. Sora, a poison maiden owned by the Count of Gain, was guaranteed her and her sister's freedom in exchange for murdering the king, but she was forced to travel with her longtime enemy, the Count's only son, Tiyung. Euyn, once the crown prince of Yusan, was banished in exile. His former lover and royal spymaster, Mikail, found him and gave him a chance to usurp the throne from his brother. Through narrow escapes and hidden motives, the group learned to trust one another, only for their alliances to be shattered when it was revealed that King Joon was behind the plot the entire time. His real goal was to have his daughter, Aeri, assemble the killers so that they would bring him the Golden Ring of the Dragon Lord, worn by his sister, the Queen of Khitan.

But our five blades have other plans...

AUTHOR'S NOTE

Korea has a rich mythology and vibrant culture all its own. And as a Korean American adoptee, I drew on my own personal story and experiences to fashion the world of *Four Ruined Realms*. However, it is worth noting that this story is neither historical fiction nor fantasy based on the real world; it takes place in a unique setting that is inspired by my research of Korean myth, legend, and culture. Creative license has been taken throughout, but it is my hope that readers will leave the story with their lives enriched, as mine has been through the writing of this book.

—Mai

CHAPTER ONE

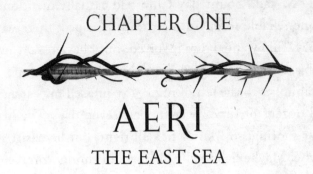

AERI
THE EAST SEA

I'm so sick of being on this ship—the rocking, the closed-in space, everyone wanting to kill me. It's been exhausting.

Still, my week on the East Sea hasn't been nearly as bad as Euyn's. His room is to the right of mine, and I've caught the echoes of him retching day and night. I think he's just seasick, but I'm not sure. I would've checked, but I'm kind of worried about him shooting me with his crossbow.

By "kind of," I mean seriously concerned.

I guess that's what happens when everyone finds out you're the king's daughter—and you were planning on betraying them from the very start.

Footsteps sound outside my room, and I freeze, gripping my book. Someone is coming. I glance at the furniture wedged against my door. There's a lock on the cabin, but I doubted a little bolt would do much on a ship full of killers. So, the second we got on board, I barricaded myself in with every free piece of furniture. I've only left to sneak some meals and to empty my chamber pot.

The noise fades, and I let out a slow breath. I'm about to return to my book when there's a knock on my door.

My heart skips. Royo?

I've hoped for and dreaded seeing him again. I want to tell him that I didn't know he was part of the king's plan to bring in Sora,

Euyn, and Mikail. Count Bay Chin had casually mentioned Royo as someone reliable to guard me. I didn't suspect there were other reasons Bay Chin wanted him involved. But I haven't said any of that to Royo because, in the end, I don't think he'll believe me.

His cabin lies to the left of mine. I've pressed my ear against the thin wall dozens of times over the last seven days. I've heard him stirring or snoring, so I know he's all right, but he hasn't spoken a word to me. Maybe he's finally changed his mind, forgiven me. Or maybe he's here to kill me—the same way he murdered his girlfriend years ago.

I sigh and bite my lip, remembering I'm not the only liar. Maybe I should avoid him, too, since I learned in the throne room that I'm the worst judge of character.

A second knock pulls me from my thoughts. I hesitate, but curiosity gets the better of me.

"Who is it?" I ask. My voice sounds weird and raspy from not speaking for a week.

"It's Sora."

Relief and a little disappointment rush through me as I get up and push the furniture out of the way. Finally, I get the door open a couple of inches.

Sora stands there looking stunning as always. Her violet eyes shine, her clear skin is dewy, and she's in a luxurious green dress. I give a heartfelt sigh. Even her black hair is perfect—and no one has had a proper bath since we left Yusan, so how?

"Yes?" I ask.

"We're approaching Quu Harbor," she says. Her voice still sounds like wind chimes. "Come above deck with me? We all need to talk before we reach Khitan."

Sora gave a really nice rallying speech when we were sent on this deadly mission to steal the Golden Ring of the Dragon Lord. While the rest of us were reeling from all the betrayals spilling out in the throne room, Sora gathered us together with a plan. She wants to persuade the vicious Queen of Khitan—my aunt—to start a war with Yusan in order to force King Joon to leave Qali Palace again. That way we'd have a second opportunity to steal the crown and actually kill the king.

My father.

I have mixed feelings about this, but it's not time to think about him—Sora is waiting. I get it together and nod. Then I throw on my red, fur-lined cloak over my dress and slip out of the door.

Sora gives me a small smile as we take the stairs. She's the only one who seems to care that I double-crossed my father, that in the end I chose *them*.

I shiver as the cold wind whips around us when we step above deck. I squint at the daylight. Somehow, the sky is both gray and painfully bright. The East Sea rises in white caps and the deck is slick, but the fresh air feels nice after being cooped up in my cabin for so long. The waves have been rough for the last few days with the monsoon season starting any bell now. We're lucky the rain has held off—otherwise, this voyage would've been worse.

I shake my head as I glance up at the heavy clouds. Hard to believe it could've been worse.

My gaze shifts to Mikail and Euyn on the bow of the sleek, wooden fleet ship. Mikail casually leans his tall, athletic frame on the railing, his teal eyes scanning the horizon. Euyn stands to his right, but farther away than normal. The prince's beard is unkempt, and his lean figure has become a little gaunt, but they're still two of the deadliest men I know.

I swallow hard and continue closer.

I spot Royo off to the side, brooding in a fur jacket. Gods, I missed him. His head is now covered in thick black hair that's grown in since we met. My foolish heart flutters the moment he meets my eyes. It was torture to have him just a thin wall away. I want to run to him, but I shouldn't for any number of reasons, the biggest being he might toss me overboard. And I can't swim.

He pretends to not see me, but he sets his broad shoulders back as I walk closer. His hands ball into fists, the muscle in his jaw tightening. I look away, acting like his reaction doesn't make my chest hurt. That's when I notice Euyn and Mikail haven't spoken a word to each other.

I guess it makes sense. After what we've all been through, we're bound to be leery and angry, but now we have to work together. To be honest, though, I'm not sure we can manage a conversation, let alone start a war.

Sora glances at each of us and purses her lips, her face all resolve. "We have too much to lose to not come together. I understand no one wants to trust anyone again, but I refuse to give up on my sister. I refuse to let Tiyung rot in Idle Prison if he's even still…"

She trails off and then shakes her head. She gathers a pained breath, her delicate hands running over her dress. My father had Tiyung thrown in Idle Prison, the dungeon under the palace lake. It's impossible to say if Ty is still alive, and we all know it.

Sora raises her chin. Her hand trembles, and she hides it behind her back. "I refuse to die before I watch Count Seok beg for his life at my feet. I'm not exactly thrilled with you all, but we have to do this. King Joon thinks we are going to steal the ring, but we need to persuade Queen Quilimar to help us lure him out of Qali Palace. We need to kill him and finish the job by putting Euyn on the throne, or we'll all die and better people than us will suffer." She stares at each of us, driving home the point. "Our loved ones hang in the balance. If it can't be trust, let vengeance bind us."

I study her sincere expression, her determination. It must be exhausting to be Sora, to always be the better person. It's so much easier to sink to the level of everybody else. But maybe the good naturally rises above like curds and whey.

"How do we know she isn't still working for Joon?" Euyn vaguely gestures in my direction.

I bite my lip as my stomach twists. I'm now certain they've all considered killing me. Before it had just been a theory.

"Because she betrayed him in the end," Sora says with a shrug. "And he sent her on a suicide mission."

The urge to defend myself and, to some extent, my father rises inside me, but there's no denying that he doesn't care if I live or die. Yes, he promised to acknowledge me and make my mother his posthumous first queen, but promises are cheap to lying lips. He never cared about me, not once in nineteen years. Then again, I wasn't too concerned with his safety and well-being, either.

A year ago, he swore he'd be the father I deserved, that he'd changed from the ruthless young man he had been. In hindsight, it was foolish to believe him, but I was so broken from losing my mother, so desperate to not be alone anymore, that when he poured honey in my ear, I drank it down. My mother had always said all we needed was Joon's love, and I thought she was right. Poison can taste like candy when you're starving. But while traveling to the capital on the mission to bring him these killers, I realized they cared more about me than he ever did. More than he ever will.

But that was all before they found out that I am Joon's daughter. His only child.

"We need to get an audience with this queen, is that what we're doing now?" Royo asks. His voice rumbles, and I strain toward the sound.

Mikail runs a hand through his wavy brown hair. "It's easier said than done. Ever since Wei attempted to assassinate the King of Khitan fifteen years ago, no one has been allowed within a hundred feet of the throne. They call it the Rule of Distance. And we can't exactly shout our treasonous intentions in front of the Khitanese court. There are always Yusanian diplomats and spies present."

The deck falls silent other than the waves crashing against our bow and the call of gulls. I twist my now shoulder-length hair into a spiral. The birds signal we're close to the northern realm of Khitan, and there's a new wrinkle to an already knotted plan.

Sora taps her chin. "There has to be a way to get closer than one hundred feet. Euyn is her brother. And Aeri is…"

"A princess," Royo grumbles.

He doesn't mean it nicely.

"We're both supposed to be dead," Euyn says. "And my sister has no love for her bloodline. No one in my family does." His brown eyes narrow on me even as he turns a little greener from the rough sea.

I let that shot land because he's not wrong. My father ordered Euyn's execution, my uncle tried to murder me, and I conspired to assassinate my father. I've heard that my aunt tried to kill my father more than once. It's a bit of a Baejkin family mess. The more power a bloodline has, the more problems.

"Queen Quilimar must have an inner circle of some sort," Sora urges. "No one can rule alone."

"A captain of her palace guard, or ladies in waiting. Maybe generals?" I ask.

Mikail eyes me with disdain, and I shift my weight to be ready. This is not great. I might be able to get away from Euyn, especially since he doesn't have his bow, but Mikail slaughters with a speed I've never seen. I have throwing knives hidden in compartments of my cloak, but that's little comfort. I'd be dead a second after I released one.

I do have the amulet as a last resort. Without thinking about it, I place my hand by the neck of my dress. The Sands of Time of the Dragon Lord lies where it always is, hidden on a necklace under my clothes. I thought about using it to flee before we boarded the ship. I could've done it—frozen time again and disappeared. But I had nowhere to go, and more than that, I knew they'd fail without me. I can't help but love them all. Even if they distinctly don't care for me now.

"Vikal," Euyn says, wiping his brow. "She is the general of the Khitanese armed forces. She must have Quilimar's ear. I recall them being close."

Mikail wavers. "They are, but if it were as simple as talking to a general, Joon wouldn't have gone through the trouble of bringing us in. He chose us for this mission for a reason. What unique traits did he mean? What is the catch? We're missing something crucial, but I can't put my finger on it."

Everyone turns to me. Royo pretends not to look, but he's waiting for me to answer. The problem is: I have no idea.

"I really don't know," I say. They stare at me with various amounts of belief. "I wish I did. All he told me was that you were dangerous to the throne and he wanted you taken in alive with minimal casualties."

It's silent on the prow of this ship, the tension crackling. I wince. "Minimal casualties" was my father's term, not mine, but it hangs in the air, sounding worse and worse as the seconds pass.

"Well, let's think about it," Euyn says. "Sora poisons. I shoot." He pauses and stares at Mikail. "And you're a spy. And a liar. And a manipulator. And a traitor."

Mikail's lips curl up into a fake smile. He just stares at his lover and slightly raises his eyebrows.

It's super awkward.

The rest of us look anywhere other than at the two of them. I guess they haven't spoken, either. I didn't hear anyone else in Euyn's room, but I'd assumed they made up. It doesn't look like that happened, though. My chest tightens. The failed assassination attempt broke all of the bonds in our group—even the deepest ones.

A large wave crashes against the ship, rocking the vessel. We all look for something to steady ourselves. I grab at the thick rope hanging off the mast. I'd rather hang on to Royo, but he's far away in every sense.

Once the sea calms, Sora's lips part. She looks ready to try to smooth things over, but Mikail speaks first.

"We can discuss being secretive, if you like, but I'll remind you that you're not innocent," he spits. "You weren't exactly forthcoming about hunting Chul for sport."

Euyn looks away, but Sora's head snaps to his.

"Chul? Did you just say Chul?" she asks.

She's breathing fast, and her eyes are locked on Euyn. The ocean is calmer after the last wave, but I've never seen her so intense. What is happening right now?

I glance at Royo and then Mikail, but they also seem thrown. Mikail's teal eyes dart between Euyn and Sora; Royo's brow furrows.

"I did..." Mikail begins, hesitant.

"Chul what?" she demands. Silence greets her. "Chul what, Euyn?"

"Sora..." he says softly. But he won't look at her. He's pursing his lips—whatever it is, he doesn't want to tell her and that can't be good.

"Was it Inigo, like the village? Was it Chul Inigo?" she asks.

Royo takes a step closer to her. I'm still not sure what's going on, but she's looking increasingly unhinged. Who in the world is Chul Inigo?

Euyn shakes his head. "Sora, I..."

"Were you hunting my *father* like a wild pig?" she shouts. "For your sick entertainment!"

Oh shit.

Euyn blanches as white as the sails, and that's confirmation enough.

Everything around me slows down. If I didn't know better, I would think I was gripping my time amulet. Mikail's eyebrows rise in surprise. Royo's jaw drops. But it's Sora whose expressions change like lightning. Shock, humiliation, and something else I can't name flit across her face before her beauty contorts in anger.

Sora lunges forward, but Mikail grabs her just as she's about to reach Euyn's neck. Royo rushes in to help, wrapping his muscular arms around her waist. They pull her back as she reaches out, her nails scraping the air. She's desperate to get her hands on Euyn even if it's just her fingertips.

I've seen her kill, but I've never seen her *want* to—it's a fearsome sight.

Unable to reach him, Sora lets out a wail more desperate than anything I've ever heard. I shudder from head to toe at the pure animal sound. It's fury and heart-wrenching grief, wrapped up in one.

"You should've died in exile!" she screams.

Royo and Mikail pull her away. Mikail looks over his shoulder at Euyn, complete disgust written on his face.

He didn't know Chul was Sora's father.

They half walk, half carry Sora toward the back of the ship as she wails in anguish. The crewmen rush around and pretend not to see anything, but everyone notices Sora.

It's just Euyn and me at the front of the ship, and he stands with his back to me. His shoulders go rigid as his hands grip the railing. I brace myself, thinking he's about to speak. But he leans forward and vomits hard.

We're almost to the port. The Palace of the Sky King gleams through the mist at the top of Oligarch Mountain, and the harbor comes into view.

Good gods, we're screwed.

CHAPTER TWO

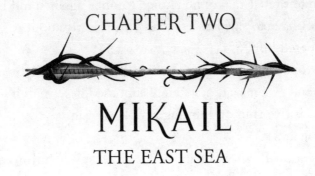

MIKAIL
THE EAST SEA

I'll be honest: this isn't great.

Euyn knew. My shoulders sag, and I breathe out my disappointment, along with my utter lack of surprise. Of course he knew. He recognized Sora the night we met her in Rahway—that was the look on his face when he asked her full name at dinner. He'd put it together, and yet he said nothing.

There are times, like this, when I wonder if I can really love a man like him. Is this love, or am I merely addicted to the highs and lows like a laoli addict? Will he ever be a good king, or will he be the same as or worse than his brother?

I push my doubts to the side. Right now, I have more pressing issues than the future of Yusan.

Sora was the glue holding all of us together, and she's in pieces. For once in my loquacious life, I don't know what to say. She wants to hurt him, and she's not wrong to, but I can't let her. In the end, I'm not that much of a hypocrite. I accepted that Euyn hunted people, and it's hard to be upset with him for keeping secrets from me when I lied to him about any number of things, including Joon's assassination plot coming from Quilimar. Really, I've kept more secrets from him than he could ever keep from me, including the fact that I'm not Yusanian.

It's a bit too much for me to be self-righteous about honesty.

Just like that, I make the choice to once again stand by Euyn. Although I have to say, I'm less than enthusiastic about it.

"He spared him, Sora," I say.

She stops crying long enough to flip her black hair over her shoulder and give me a death stare. I suppose I deserve it. It's difficult to put a positive spin on hunting people for fun.

I try again.

"The reason Euyn was banished was because Chul lived," I say. "Because Euyn let him go."

"He doesn't deserve the throne. He deserves to die," she says.

She holds my gaze, challenge in her pretty eyes. This is that side of Sora, the one fiercer than any warrior I've known. She'd slaughter him right now without hesitation or regret.

"Sora, we all deserve to die," I say.

Her face shifts, her expression surprised. An understanding passes between us. Regardless of our motivations, we are both mass killers. We steal souls and hope Lord Yama doesn't come to collect. By most measures, we deserve death.

With a breath, Sora softens just a touch. She won't kill Euyn— not at the moment, anyhow, and I'll take it.

"We all made choices that can't be undone," I add. "But it's Joon we need dead."

"If we bring him the ring, though…" Royo begins.

"He'll double-cross and kill us," I say. "Or make us steal the Water Scepter from Wei, which is tantamount to certain death. It would be so unoriginal to let Joon outsmart us a second time."

"He was never going to spare Hwan?" Royo's broad brow wrinkles, his expression confused.

Hwan is the man in prison for killing his daughter. The one Royo has been fighting to free. I'm surprised Royo hadn't figured out that while Joon had promised us great rewards—title, properties, mercy—he has little to no intention of keeping his word. A god king doesn't care about promises to the likes of us.

Royo, however, is a man of honor, and people like him can't fathom someone like Joon. Royo and Sora are guided by absolute right and wrong. They don't possess the flexible morals of those with power. So Joon will eliminate them. Joon eliminates everyone he can't control.

"No," I say. "Not unless it suits him. The king has never worried about a commoner unless it served his end goal. He might have Hwan brought to Idle Prison, but only to torture him if need be."

Royo rubs the old scar dividing his face. "Then King Joon has to die."

Sora sighs and nods, her anger ebbing. Her back curves, her posture failing. Without burning anger, all you're left with is the embers of grief. In many ways, fury is better because at least it's something to cling to. Sadness is a barren expanse.

"You're bleeding," she says.

She's looking at my neck. I touch my skin, and my fingers come away wet with blood. She scratched me while trying to get to Euyn.

"I'll live."

"You're certain Euyn let my father go?" she asks.

Tears swim in her eyes, along with a little hope. It's nice that I don't have to lie to her this time.

"Absolutely certain. It was your father who told the palace that Euyn had been hunting convicts in Westward Forest."

"Which you knew about," she says.

She searches my face, and Royo eyes me, too. I want to lie, but it would only be to save face. In order to get through this new mission, I'll have to start telling the truth—as much as I can, anyhow.

"I did," I say.

She holds my stare. "Did you know he was my father?"

"No. I swear and I vow it. You look nothing alike."

She sighs and looks down at her hands, at the nails that drew blood. We'll have to spill a lot of it to save the people we love. I made my peace with that a long time ago, as did she.

"You really think Euyn'll be a good king?" Royo asks.

I draw a breath. Do I?

"I think we've all done things we aren't proud of," I say. "I think a person is more than the strikes against them. At least I'd like to believe we are. I think Euyn has changed and continues to evolve. And if nothing else, he will be better than Joon."

"Or maybe you just hope," Royo says.

Both of them stare, waiting for a response, so I shrug. "All the same."

Bells ring out on the ship. We've reached the capital of Khitan.

"Quu Harbor!" the captain calls out, walking the deck. "Quu Harbor!"

Just in time for me to forget Royo's words.

I glance at Sora, her spine straightening again as she pulls herself back together once more. I forged papers for her because she has an indenture mark on her real ones. Although indentures and slaves are free once they cross into Khitan, the country has to at least pretend they snuck in. I also created papers for Aeri and Euyn, as they are both technically dead. And I, of course, never enter any foreign realm under my real name. I never use my real name at all.

It's not an auspicious beginning, bringing dead liars into Khitan, but I will outsmart Joon. We lost the battle, but I will win the war.

First, I need to meet with another technically dead spirit—Fallador, the exiled Prince of Gaya—to see how we can get to the queen. And how we can finally free our homeland.

CHAPTER THREE

ROYO
CITY OF QUU, KHITAN

We got to Khitan without killing each other—so that's
something.

The capital sits right on the harbor like how Tamneki squats on
the sea, but Quu looks nothing like Yusan. There's a huge mountain
towering over the city with villas carved into the sides and a golden
palace at the top. The castle shines like a lighthouse, even in this rain.

I adjust my hood over my hair. I thought about shaving it on the
ship, but I dunno, I've gotten used to it. We trudge through the soggy
streets of Quu. Cobblestones wind in every direction, and the painted
houses are stacked up next to each other. We pass homes painted
apple red, evergreen, deep blue, or mustard yellow. It's a mashup, and
the people are, too. Some are Yusanian, a lot are Khitanese. There's
a few Weian, and some must be from the Outer Lands. It's all a wet
hodgepodge of familiar and foreign. Especially the women, who dress
like men, with weapons on their belts and pants on their legs.

I knew we were going to another place, but I didn't think Khitan
would be this different.

It is.

We make it to the Gray Shore Inn after a confusing series of
turns. We didn't actually go that far, though. I can smell the salt of
the harbor and see the ship sails from the lobby as Mikail checks us
in. It's a nice enough spot, despite Euyn bellyaching about it under

his breath. It's no palace, but it's dry and warm. That's all you need in a storm.

Mikail hands me my key. The girls went to the powder room as soon as we walked in, and they're still in there. I think about waiting for Aeri even though I shouldn't. I got nothing to say to her. Or too much. Sometimes, it's all the same.

I go up to my room and toss my bag onto a patterned chair. Weapons clang inside, but the gold bars and the million-cut diamond are gone—taken by the palace before they sent us on this trip. All of the money I saved to buy Hwan's freedom. All of those years of blood work. All of the screams and death and close calls for no coin. I never let it in, the shit I've done, because it was what I had to do. But now that it was all for nothing, everything rushes back.

The pleas for mercy, the cries and death throes echo in my head. The ghosts of past wrongs stand over me. The men who ain't did nothing to me but I made bleed. My shoulders fall, the weight too much. The gurgling, the begging, the tears. I put my palms over my ears to make it stop. Doesn't help because the sound is *in* me.

No. I shake my head and stand up straight. Everything I did can't be for no reason. It all led me here. I'll free an innocent man. And by killing the king, we'll save a bunch of prisoners who don't deserve to die. Maybe it won't balance my scales, but it won't hurt none either.

I throw off the memories and strike a match, starting a fire. We've got a job to do.

The dry wood in the hearth sparks to life, the flames dancing on the logs. Fire is the best comfort when you're wet and weary. The only thing better is the arms of someone you love.

Aeri.

No. Not *Aeri*. Princess Naerium.

She was a princess this whole fucking time. And she said nothing.

My chest squeezes. I've got no money and no girl, all because she was playing me from the start. And even knowing all that, I still couldn't help myself. I listened at the wall on the ship, making sure she was safe in her room. I patrolled to keep the others from killing her. Because what I had with her felt real. Because I'm lonely. Because I am the king of fucking chumps.

I groan, tipping my head back. I stare at the tin ceiling. I gotta stop. I gotta turn cold. I can't care what happens to Princess Naerium. Aeri is dead to me—I have to accept it.

But I can't.

I keep going back to the fact that Aeri stole the crown in the arena. She did her part for us. She chose us and double-crossed the king.

No, she double-crossed her *father*. She had talked about them as separate people, and I fell for it. The same way I fell for her— hopelessly, stupidly. It wasn't real.

Except that after we were captured, she begged for my freedom. Only me.

I run a hand down my face as my thoughts loop around for the hundredth fucking time. My scar hurts, my face aching. The week on the ship allowed me to heal and for my headache to fade. This is the best I've felt physically since I left Umbria and the worst because of Aeri.

And Bay Chin.

As confused as I am about her, the only thing I want with the northern count is to watch him bleed. He was the one who told Aeri to look for me. He was the one who set up Hwan. I don't know why—I'm not smart enough to figure it all out. But I am strong enough. I will make it out of Khitan and watch Bay Chin breathe his last gasp in front of me. I will be the last thing he sees before the light leaves his eyes.

There's a knock on my door, and I'm halfway to answering before I realize I'm only racing there because I think it's Aeri. Chances are it's not. She didn't look for me on the ship. Not once. Not to apologize. Not to explain herself. Nothing.

Because she doesn't care. Not really.

I let the sting of that settle into my bones. I need to let it hurt— pain is the only thing that's going to make me wise up.

I turn the doorknob, and it's not her. Disappointment sits heavy in my chest, but I shake it off. It's Sora, and her eyes are ringed with sadness from missing her sister and Tiyung. Or because Euyn hunted her father. Or for any other shit reason we're here.

"We need to go over the plan now that we're in Khitan," she says. Her nice voice sounds weary. She's the best of us, though. The only one who hasn't lied. Well, I guess I haven't, either. Except to myself, but that don't count.

"Okay." I grab another blade and tuck it into my belt.

Sora wants to start a war. I still kind of think we should give Joon the ring, but if what Mikail said is true, Sora's plan is the only shot I have at saving Hwan.

That's a big if, though. The spymaster could just be lying. I don't get why everyone always believes him.

She knocks on the door next to mine. Aeri's room. Furniture creaks and groans, and the door opens a crack. A sliver of Aeri's face appears before she swings the door wider and steps out. She pauses when she sees me. Her big brown eyes meet mine—a little afraid, a little hopeful.

I look away.

It was easier to hate her when I didn't have to see the worry in her eyes. She seems guilty, sorry, but if she were, she would've said it. Nah. She has the same amount of remorse as the rest of her family—none.

Next, we go to Euyn's suite. After a while, he answers, too. He shrinks back, his shoulders coming forward when he sees Sora. He's thinner than when we left Yusan, his cheekbones sharper. I think he got seasick. Pretty sure I heard him puking as I patrolled.

"Where's Mikail?" I ask. There's nobody in the room with Euyn.

"In his room," Euyn says. "One over."

He points to the left, then shuts his door. The bolt turns with a snap. The three of us look at one another and then walk away. The hallway has ugly red-and-white wallpaper. I'm staring at the walls, the floors, anything to avoid looking at *Princess Naerium*. Still, I can feel her next to me. Still, I want to reach out for her.

I shove my hands in my pockets.

Sora knocks on Mikail's door, and there's no answer. She glances at me. I bang on the wood in case Mikail fell asleep.

Nothing.

"Must be gone," I say.

"What if something happened to him?" Aeri asks. She plays with the hem of her mid-thigh dress. I look away from her legs, which is harder than it should be.

"Let's ask Euyn," Sora says.

Once again, Euyn takes two lifetimes to answer the door. I thought he'd changed, got less paranoid, after facing off with his brother in the throne room. Guess not.

"Did Mikail say he was going out?" Sora asks.

Euyn shakes his head, and his eyebrows come together. "No, he should be in there."

"Well he ain't," I say.

Euyn strokes his beard as his eyes dart around. "That's odd. Come in or go, though."

He grips the doorknob. I don't know what he thinks will happen or why he thinks a closed door would stop it. One kick and the wood would be in splinters. But I don't say it.

"Maybe I should pick his lock?" Aeri says.

All of us turn to her.

Right. She's a thief. A pickpocket. A con artist. Plus, a princess.

Euyn's mouth slants. "Be careful if you do. He could have trapped the room."

Great.

"Should we wait?" Sora asks.

Aeri shakes her head. "We need to check. If he's not okay, we have to find him. Without him, we have no way of getting to the queen."

Everybody realizes she's got a point. Euyn can speak Khitanese, but Mikail is the one with real knowledge about how this place works. He's the only one who can get us to the throne.

"Can I borrow your hairpins, Sora?" Aeri asks.

Sora's eyebrows knit, but she takes out her two silver hairpins and hands them over.

We go back to Mikail's room, and Aeri studies the door. She gets on the ground and puts her cheek to the worn carpet. There's just a crack of space under the door. I don't think it's wide enough for her to see, but she takes out a dagger from inside her cloak and slides the blade under. I wonder what she's doing until I realize she's trying to spring traps.

"I think it's clean," she says.

She sits up on her knees and peers into the keyhole before putting the pins in and fiddling with them. In seconds, the door unlocks. Weird for royalty to be able to pick locks, but she did say she had to make it on her own for a while. Then again, that could just be another lie.

Aeri turns the handle. As the door opens, I yank her to the side in case there was a trap she missed. She falls against me and lands with her back to my chest. Memories of Rahway, of hiding in the alleyway, flood my head. That smell of flowers fills my nose.

She turns and looks at me with those beautiful eyes. Her lips part.

"Thank you," she says breathlessly.

My heart swells, and I want her. Still.

But it doesn't matter. In Rahway, we ran so the king's guard wouldn't recognize her. So I wouldn't find out she was a princess.

I force myself to take my hands off her and step away. I really gotta stop touching her.

The room's now open, and we peer inside. I don't see any traps, but you can't be too careful with someone like Mikail.

Step by creaky step, we make it all the way in—the room ain't large. Bed, chair, dresser, nightstand, washroom.

The bed is made, and Mikail's bag sits on top. It only takes a second to realize there's no one here.

He's gone.

CHAPTER FOUR

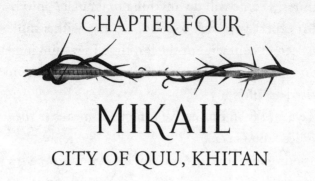

MIKAIL
CITY OF QUU, KHITAN

Fallador is more attractive than I remember, which is saying
something. He's about six inches shorter than I am, but just as
solid. His posture and manner are regal and relaxed, but he's sharp as
a tack. He's my age—maybe a month or two different. And neither
of us should be alive.

Allegedly, we both died in the Festival of Blood nearly twenty
years ago. Like me, Joon made him an orphan, but Fallador didn't
have to depend on the heart of a stranger. His royal connections
hid him and spirited him away to Khitan, where he's entertained
the court ever since. Every realm adores former royalty—especially
someone charming like him.

Most importantly, he's been a source of information for me since
I became a spy.

Fallador's villa is halfway up Oligarch Mountain. The closer you
are to the top, to the golden Palace of the Sky King, the higher your
status.

Interesting, in a country of supposed equals.

We sit in his parlor. He placed tea and custard buns on a tray
between us. Rain pours against the glass balcony doors, but it's well-
lit in here. Fallador occupies the couch; I'm across from him in one
of the plush armchairs. His green eyes sparkle like the gilding around
us. This country is obsessed with gold the same way Tamneki loves

water features. People will do anything to emulate power.

"I didn't expect you back so soon," he says with a smile.

We've been in contact, but the last time I saw him in person was over a year ago. What he means is he never expects me to be alive. I'm surprised at times myself.

"En Gaya," I say in our native tongue. It means *to the homeland*.

He smiles. "En Gaya."

We lift our porcelain cups and sip. It's a good strong tea from the island. The smell reminds me of home. Everything about Fallador does. We speak in old Gayan when we are alone, which is a comfort I never remember how much I need.

"Not that I don't love making small talk with you, but to what do I owe this pleasure?" he asks. "I assume you already know about the rather sudden regime change."

I nod. "I've come as part of an envoy sent by King Joon to welcome the new queen regent."

I try out my first ruse on him. It makes the most sense—to be here with Euyn as part of a diplomatic scheme to greet the new ruler of Khitan. The king of Khitan conveniently died a month ago, leaving Quilimar as the regent for their young son.

Fallador grins. "Except she already received Yusanian dignitaries last month."

No dice.

"There's no way to arrange for an audience?" I ask, leaning forward.

He mirrors me, ready to whisper a secret. His skin is also a warm brown like mine, in sharp contrast to the white of his shirt. When he gets closer to me, there's a feeling of longing that hits my core. But Fallador and I have never been lovers. It's the desire for home.

"There was an attempt on Quilimar's life a week ago," he says. "She sees no one now."

I sit back and sigh. The timing is hardly a coincidence. But why? Why would Joon send us to fetch the ring, yet at the same time make it more difficult to get to Quilimar? The monarchs are always trying to eliminate each other, so assassination attempts are nothing new, but what is his ultimate goal? And how far does this plan extend? Is it possible there is another player involved? Or is that wishful thinking?

"Any chance the general was behind it?" I ask.

General Vikal is as ruthless as they come. In some ways, women have to be in order to be respected, whether here or in Yusan. Especially Yusan. Mercy is seen as weakness when it's doled out by a feminine hand.

Fallador shakes his head. "Doubtful. The rumor is the general shares Quilimar's bed. And perhaps helped her dispose of the former king. However, the attempt was carried out by Vikal's second in command."

"Perhaps Vikal wants the throne for herself," I say.

"It's possible," he admits, stroking his dimpled chin. "But after the assassination attempt, the general publicly chopped up her lieutenant, starting with the toes. It ended with her throwing his head into the sea. Hardly speaks of a coconspirator."

Stars, the Dasseos Continent loves a brutal murder. Piteua is a horrific way to die and the Khitanese equivalent of lingchi. It means "death from the feet up," and it's exactly what Fallador described. You're alive to feel most of your body being hacked away. It's saved for the worst offenses—attempted regicide being one, of course.

"I'll probe my sources for a way in for you," he says.

"Thank you, my friend."

I rest my cup on the table, hiding how disheartened I am. I was hoping for an easy and fast way to Quilimar's ear. But nothing is going to be quick or simple now. Not after a conveniently timed assassination attempt.

I stand, and Fallador does as well. He shakes hands with me. His palm is warm, his hand strong. We lock eyes, and there's a spark, a distinct energy between us. But I look away. I always do, because some doors can't be closed once they're opened.

"Before I forget, this came for you this morning." He reaches into his satchel and pulls out a sealed envelope. It's still coated with intact clay and stamped with the seal of Qali Palace.

I examine the envelope.

"You can imagine my surprise at receiving eagle post meant for you," he says with a soft smile.

I arch an eyebrow. He already knew I was coming, and he didn't bring it up until now. Of course. Fallador would never show his hand early.

"I didn't think Joon would miss me enough to write," I say.

I smile and open the letter, using a hidden dagger in my sleeve. I'm careful to control my breathing, giving nothing away, as I read the simple message. It's coded, but it translates to:

GONE

Just one word sent by eagle post to reach me quickly. No signature. But I know Zahara's handwriting and her code. She was my second-in-command and now must be the acting royal spymaster. However, she is telling me that Joon is no longer in the palace and she is unsure of his whereabouts.

But she knew where I would be and whom I would contact. Also, just as surprisingly, she is still loyal to me.

Unless it's all a ruse.

I crumple the note in my fist as though the message is of no real importance. What is Joon up to? Is he actually out of the palace, or is that simply what he wants me to believe? He would need something compelling to put his life at risk outside of Qali. What could that be?

"Another friend in the palace?" Fallador asks, raising a thick eyebrow. He, of course, knows about Euyn. It's hardly a secret.

"Something like that."

I toss the letter and envelope into the fireplace and watch them burn. The papers disappear as I grip the mantel. Why would Joon leave? And why would Zahara say either way? She came to me through him. She is loyal to him. At least on the surface—anyone, including a royal spymaster, can have other allegiances.

Zahara told me "safety in death" before the Millennial Celebration. At the time, I thought it meant to kill the traitors rather than bring them in alive. But if she knew the plan all along, perhaps she was telling me to take my poison pill before I could be used by the king.

Why, though? Who can tell me more?

"Adoros," Fallador says.

I shift my gaze from the fire to his face. He'd been speaking, and I missed it until he said my name. My real name. I haven't been called Adoros since I was a child. But we knew each other as little boys. We used to run through the charm fields together, a lifetime ago.

I meet his eyes.

"The empire will never understand us, no matter how much you love him." He places his hand on my shoulder and gives me a meaningful look before smiling.

It's as much as he's ever said about Euyn or my connection to the palace. When I first learned that Fallador was alive and living in exile, I worried he'd judge me for surviving, for living with the enemy, but he never did. Instead, he said: *if you are devoured by an iku, it does not make you sprout gills.* But perhaps his feeling has changed. I'd like to say it doesn't matter, but it does.

After our traditional cheek kisses goodbye, I walk out of his villa and into the heavy rain. The monsoon season started today, giving us twenty-eight days, two sunsaes total, to return to Yusan. I hope it's at the head of Khitan's army.

Either way, I swear on the stars that if Joon touches a hair on my father's head, I will cut away everything he's ever cared about. Including his daughter.

Sora may trust her, but I do not. She's still hiding something. I'm not sure what it is, but I will find out.

With my collar up, I take the narrow, winding side road that leads back to the harbor. Oligarch has a main passageway that circles the mountain as well as smaller, connecting side streets that snake down the hillside. I decide to take the latter.

Most people carry umbrellas once the rains start, but I never do. I need to be able to see in every direction. A lined raincoat would be a good purchase, though. I'll buy one soon. Khitan uses paper money, and Fallador gave me a thousand marks before I left. It'll be more than enough to cover everything we need, but there are always other means of getting money.

I make it down one street before I confirm I'm being followed. I caught a shadow as I left Fallador's villa, and I just heard a noise. I let out a sigh. Whoever is watching me is plain sloppy. The lack of effort is offensive.

A single block later, I'm surrounded—three spies, all Khitanese. Someone tipped them off. Another traitor in our midst.

I sigh. Yet another lie to sniff out.

"Spymaster," one says. "We are here to bring you in."

"I'm afraid I already have plans," I say.

Thunder claps overhead, and I grab ahold of my dagger. I turn so my back is to the wall of a yellow villa, leaving a spy to each side of me and one in front.

The woman steps forward. She must outrank the two men, but all three seem younger than me. No wonder they're sloppy—they're low level. They even look like spies, wearing dark, drab clothes. Although one does have a nice raincoat.

"Drop your weapon," the woman says.

I smile. "Now, why would I do that?"

She is just far enough away for me to get a running start. I take one step. Two. Then on the third, I launch into the air and aim my dagger. I don't slit her throat so much as lodge my blade into her neck.

I pull out the dagger just as swiftly. She falls, gurgling to the ground. The second spy moved to strike while my back was turned. Not a bad play, but he's not nearly fast enough. I swing my arm back and stab him in the gut. Then I pull the blade upward until I hit his breastbone. He doubles over in pain and lets out a howl so loud it can be heard over this thunder.

Stars, die with dignity.

I yank the dagger out and slit his throat so he stops screaming. I don't need nosy passersby or innocent, helpful people to join us in this alley. Thankfully, most sought shelter from the storm.

The last spy is still trying to get his blade out. I shake my head. He should've been a fisherman instead.

He stills when I walk up to him, too scared to move, despite being my height and maybe a little more muscular than me. My arm and dagger are dripping blood. I drop the blade as I get within a few feet of him, letting it clatter onto the wet stone. He stares at the ground, confused for a moment. It's long enough for me to reach out and take his head in my hands. With a hard twist, I snap his neck.

All three lie dead or dying. I take the raincoat off the last spy, then rifle through each of their clothes. I help myself to another five hundred marks, two daggers, and three poison pills. It's not like they need any of that now.

None of the spies carry identification, so they at least knew that much. There's no indication of who sent them, but I'm fairly certain this welcome party came from General Vikal herself. I might as well send back a reply.

I wait for a full minute, folding my new black raincoat, and then I set it on a barrel down the street. It's still raining hard, but I leave it off because I'm about to make a mess—blood work, of a sort.

I grab my dagger off the ground and then I kneel. I slit the woman and the last spy open from their necks to their navels. Conveniently, I already cut open the other one. But this is why I waited the extra minute—to ensure they were dead. The spies were incompetent, but they hadn't wronged me. They didn't deserve to be alive to feel this. This isn't lingchi.

With all of the bodies open, I stick my hand into the first man. The organs steam. It's all blood and a hot, squishy mess because this is the one I gut stabbed, but I'm far from squeamish. It takes a little fishing around. I'm a killer, not a healer, but I find his spleen. I cut it out and toss it to the side.

It's kind of like gutting a fish.

Then I do the same to the other two bodies.

Khitanese people traditionally believe bravery comes from the spleen. They might as well believe it comes from the big toe for all the sense it makes. Bravery is in the mind being stronger than the body, more powerful than logic. But my message is clear: the demon is alive and well in Khitan, and if you come for me, you'd better have more nerve than this.

Once I'm done, I walk down to the barrel. I rinse my hands in a nearby puddle, then drape the raincoat over my shoulders to hide the blood soaking my clothes. After all, what's another secret?

CHAPTER FIVE

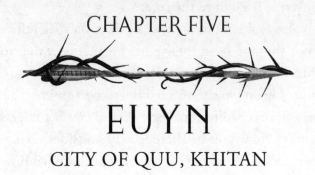

EUYN
CITY OF QUU, KHITAN

I pace by the window, my spine rigid, my pivots as sharp as when I served in the king's guard. Where could Mikail be? Why leave without saying a word? Tension crackles through the suite as we silently wait out another bell.

We are staying in a traveler's inn that's on par with the one in Fallow—meaning it's a hair above a donkey stable. I am here under the name Donal again because of Mikail's terrible sense of humor. And now he is missing. I had the feeling we were being followed earlier, but he, of course, dismissed it.

"He didn't say nothing about leaving?" Royo asks, leaning by the fire.

I shake my head, and his eyebrows slash down.

I eye the door and consider arming the traps again, but I don't need them as much with Royo here. He has remained loyal to me. Regardless of what Bay Chin said, I don't think he killed his girlfriend, or if he did, I'm sure he had his reasons. Either way, I trust him the most.

Naerium paces by the window, nervously doubling back and shaking out her hands. She's my niece...of sorts. There's not much resemblance between her and Joon, which explains how I missed the connection. They're both built on the slight side, but she's lanky and must take after her mother. But with how she murders, lies, and betrays…Aeri is Baejkin to the core.

Sora is also in the room, waiting by the table. She refuses to look at me, and I suppose I can forgive her for that now that she knows about Chul.

In truth, I hadn't meant to keep the secret from her, but we had a mission, and that had to come first. As she taps her fingers and her hand trembles from poison aftereffects, I consider saying that her father never stopped looking for her, that Seok forged his signature and forced the illegitimate sale.

Sora must feel me staring at her, because she meets my gaze. I open my mouth, but her eyes harden with hatred. I swallow my words. It's too raw a subject to bring it up now.

I will tell her later.

Turning, I move the drape to peek out the window again. Where is he? There are few situations Mikail can't fight his way out of, so I doubt he's in trouble, but his disappearance is unsettling and begs a million questions. We just arrived at port late this morning. What could be so urgent that he had to sneak out before midday? Why did he leave the rest of us in this horse stall?

And why did he try to destroy the crown?

I wish I had answers, but I never receive them when it comes to Mikail. I'd resolved not to speak to him until he told me the truth about why he sliced the decoy crown in half and why he looked so pale when Joon mentioned he'd take good care of Ailor. I know it was a threat against someone he loves, but who even is Ailor? I waited for seven days for Mikail to come to me, but all I wound up with was a week of silence and sea sickness.

Perhaps waiting was foolish. We've known each other for so long that apologies and explanations are pointless—or at least that is what I tell myself. Plus, we have a new mission.

Sora wants to tell Quilimar about Joon's plan in hopes of waging a war against Yusan, but if we bring my brother the ring, he will reinstate me as crown prince and Aeri as princess. He will raise

Mikail to be the Count of Tamneki—an elevation second only to being king consort. It is worth considering. Joon has his flaws, but he keeps his promises. And if we give him the ring, I won't have to risk being exposed as a fraud, turned to ash by the Immortal Crown because I'm not Baejkin. It's the best outcome for everyone, whether they realize it or not.

But for now, I need to pretend to go along with Sora's plan. Our goals align, as both stealing the relic and starting a war require face time with my sister.

I *would* speak to Mikail about all of this, but that would require his presence.

I stew in my lonely thoughts until there's a knock at my door. Two knocks—Mikail. I hate how joy bursts in my chest at the thought of him. My standards should be higher, but that's never been the case with the royal spymaster.

"It's him," I say.

Even though I'm certain it's Mikail, Royo still brandishes a blade at his side as he answers the door. He doesn't trust Mikail, and maybe he's right to be leery.

I'm wondering if even I can fully trust him when Mikail waltzes in with that easy confidence and swagger. I fall for that face every time I see it. But then I notice that his clothes are absolutely soaked in blood.

Gods on High. What happened now?

CHAPTER SIX

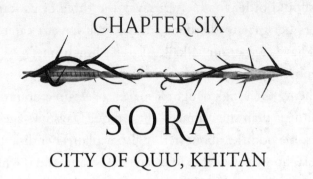

SORA
CITY OF QUU, KHITAN

I put my fingers over my lips. Kingdom of Hells, Mikail is covered in blood.

At first, I thought it was water darkening his blue shirt, but then I noticed his pants. They were cream-colored this morning. They are crimson now.

"Oh good, you're all here," he says, looking at the four of us in turn. "I'm going to bathe and change. Do keep the door guarded until I knock again."

I sigh. He's so cool and casual. The thing is, it's not even an act. I scan his face for a tell, but being soaked in blood truly doesn't bother him.

Mikail turns to leave, and I take a step closer. "Wait, are you hurt?"

He shakes his head. "Only my feelings. I thought I was on better terms with the spymaster general of Khitan."

The side of his shirt is torn, but I don't think he's injured. He isn't favoring a leg or holding any wounds. On second thought, I don't think any of the blood is his. It's not a surprise, of course—we've all seen him fight—but that much blood is shocking.

My stomach twists, and I grip the back of the chair as Mikail leaves. I knew this mission would be dangerous, but I didn't think we'd be attacked the second we stepped foot in this realm.

"We should order food," Aeri says. The three of us stare at her. She lowers her gaze to the floor. "Euyn, you haven't eaten in days, and we'll have to wait on Mikail. Also, it's lunchtime."

I suppose it is.

Aeri being the king's daughter makes a certain amount of sense. She is younger than she claimed—just about Daysum's age—which explains some oddities about her. It also explains her disappearance in Capricia, how she was able to escape in Oosant, and the murder of the assassin in Aseyo. The palace assassin must have been protecting her and mistook my window for hers. And then she killed him to keep the secret.

Of course, there are still things that don't quite add up. I don't understand how she is such an experienced thief when she is a princess. And why, in the end, did she betray her father?

Mikail, Euyn, and Royo continue to stiffen in her presence, hands moving toward weapons whether they realize it or not. They distrust her for setting us up, but I can't be too angry about that. I would've betrayed everyone if it had helped Daysum. But the men aren't as forgiving of the binds put on women. Ty would understand, but he's…not here. My shoulders sag, and my breath catches. He is in Idle Prison. I hope. At least that would mean he's still alive.

I inhale and push him from my thoughts. It doesn't do me any favors to think about what must be happening to him—or to worry that he's dead. But I can't seem to help myself. I thought about him every day aboard the ship and doubly so since we arrived in Khitan.

I force myself to shrug. "Lunch would be good," I say.

Aeri's lips turn up in a small, grateful smile.

"I'll get a boy to fetch it." Royo finally unfolds his arms, and he begins to lumber toward the door. He must be hungry, too. That or he wants to get away from Aeri.

"Here, tip him well." She holds out a silver mun. They use paper money here, but gold and silver always translate.

Aeri's fingers brush Royo's palm as he takes the coin from her. He stares at their hands for a second too long, then recoils and leaves without a word. Aeri visibly wilts, and my chest tightens. She must truly care for him.

Around half a bell later, there's a knock at the door. We all exchange glances. Royo returned a while ago, and Mikail's signal is two knocks close together, so it's not anyone we know. There's another knock. And then again, louder. Euyn carefully takes the traps down, creeping toward the door with a loaded crossbow in his right hand. I shift the dagger hidden up my sleeve to my palm.

"Who is it?" Euyn asks in Khitanese.

"Your lunch, sir," a boy's voice answers.

Royo's broad shoulders fall away from his ears; Aeri takes her hand away from her cloak. I return my dagger to the hidden compartment in my dress.

The boy comes in, puts the food out on the table, then leaves. Euyn immediately begins to help himself.

"Wait," I say. "Let me check for poison."

He drops his hand so fast his knuckles smack the table. Aeri and Royo pause, blinking at me.

I wouldn't normally suspect poisoning, but someone already attacked Mikail, so I take small bites of each dish in between sips of water. Although I wouldn't be devastated if Euyn died right now, the others will be eating the food as well. We can't be too careful in a foreign land.

The noodles, steamed pork buns, chicken thighs, and soup dumplings all seem fine, but some toxins are slower acting, so I wait for aftertastes, running through my recollection of dozens and dozens of poisons. I roll my tongue, but there is nothing—just traces of soy, peanut, and honey.

"Lunch is clean," I say.

"But...wouldn't you be all right no matter what?" Royo asks. His brow is lined as he waits with his empty plate.

"I wouldn't die," I say. "But there are still effects from the stronger toxins no one can escape. Plus, nearly all poisons have tastes or smells that give them away."

Hence poisoned, perfumed lipstick being most effective.

They all fill their plates. I suppose my ability with poisons is the unique skill King Joon was after. I just don't understand how it's needed in Khitan—not when there's a Rule of Distance that doesn't allow anyone within a hundred feet of the throne. I won't be able to get close enough to have a private conversation with Queen Quilimar, much less kiss her. So why have Aeri bring me in? Why involve the southern count?

We've just started eating when Mikail knocks twice. Euyn's face brightens as he removes the traps, and Mikail saunters inside. He's freshly bathed and clad in gray slacks and a fur-collared shirt. With his new clothes, he looks like a local. I admire how he always blends in. I never have that luxury.

"Oh good, there's lunch." He grabs a plate and sits, straddling a chair. "I would be careful with picking my lock in the future. I didn't have time to set up traps, but I will."

I look at Aeri and Royo. How did he know we broke in? I made sure not to touch anything, and Royo locked the door as we left.

"What happened to you?" Euyn asks as Mikail selects a pork bun.

"Nothing I couldn't handle," he says.

Royo's eyes track him. "Why were spies after you?"

Mikail shrugs and spoons soup dumplings into a bowl. "I'm one of the most wanted men in the world. It was due to any number of crimes, I suppose. But in fairness, they wanted to take me in for questioning, not kill me. I just had other plans."

I take a sip of water, both glad he is here and disturbed by how casual he is about slaughter. We are both killers, but the lives I take weigh on my soul. Mikail doesn't seem to have that guilt. And guilt creates balance and limits.

Aeri studies him, her eyes sharp. "But how did the spies know you were in Quu?"

Mikail smiles. "That's the better question. Someone tipped them off. Or they've gotten much better under Quilimar's reign. Based on their tailing skills, I suspect it's the former."

He doesn't seem to be accusing anyone in the room, but without trust, conversation doesn't exactly flow.

Euyn keeps glancing at him as if he's trying to piece together a puzzle. "Who did you go see?"

Mikail washes his bite down with some ale. He chews slowly, stalling. My stomach sinks—he's hiding something again.

"A source. I was hoping they would have a lead on how to get close to Quilimar."

"And?" Royo asks.

"Nothing yet, but I'm working on it. The new complication is that there was an attempt on the queen's life a week ago. No one is allowed to see her now."

Forks drop, and we all stop eating.

I shift my weight in my chair. How does this mission keep getting worse? The Rule of Distance was one thing, but the palace being closed to outsiders makes our plan impossible. I put my spoon down and sigh as I try to regroup.

"So, what do we do now?" Aeri asks. "We only have four weeks."

The meal sours in my stomach. Four weeks. King Joon gave us until the end of monsoon season to return with the ring, or he would torture and kill our loved ones. A month does not seem like enough time to figure out how to get into the palace, arrange an audience with Queen Quilimar, convince her to start a war, mobilize troops, and defeat the immortal king.

But Daysum hangs in the balance. Tiyung, too. The likelihood is slim, yet a small chance is still a chance. I'll take it. I have to.

My heart pounds in my chest as I work through all that needs to be done. I try to slow it down and think through one step at a time.

As soon as we arrived in Quu, I sent eagle post to Count Seok informing him that the plan failed and Tiyung was captured, but

I can't be sure if the messenger birds will land or be shot down, especially when crossing the border. All eagles fly to Tamneki, and then new birds are sent to farther cities like Gain. The whole process would take weeks on horseback, but with eagle post it takes less than two days. Which is why a two-eagle post costs ten silver mun.

I also sent a message to the Countess as a backup, but I had to guess at her location. It was probably all money wasted, but I will try anything and everything to save my sister and help Ty.

"Our first order of business is paying a visit to General Vikal," Mikail says.

Euyn raises an eyebrow. "Vikal is not your biggest fan."

Mikail wipes his mouth. "Nor yours. That's why we'll send Sora and Aeri."

I'm not sure I like the sound of that. What does "pay a visit" mean? Do they expect me to poison the general? For Aeri to kill her?

"I don't think—" Royo starts. All eyes turn to him. He closes his mouth and colors red.

He still cares about Aeri, no matter what he says. Beneath his hard exterior is a soft, gentle heart.

Royo shoves food in his mouth as if no one noticed. Everyone did. The same way I saw him patrolling while we were aboard the fleet ship. The only reason to be walking the passageways was to protect Aeri. Everyone knew that.

I dab a soft napkin against my lips. "Why would we see General Vikal?" I ask.

"To get information," Mikail says. "Perhaps build a connection to bring us close to Quilimar."

I exhale. It's not poisoning or stealing something. He wants me to charm the general, which is also a unique skill set I have, I suppose. Women are typically harder to win over than men, but anyone can be seduced.

"All right," Aeri says, "and what if we're captured?"

"There's no reason to capture you as long as you don't reveal that you are Princess Naerium. And you kept that secret well." Mikail pauses and stares at her, anger flashing in his eyes. "Sora is an indentured servant who is now free. You were and are free."

Aeri seems to accept that, twirling and slurping her noodles.

Mikail turns to Royo. "I don't imagine your blood work brought you across the border, correct?"

Royo continues chewing but shakes his head. His thick black hair is an improvement over the shaved look he had when we first met—it softens him a touch.

"Then you can go with them if you want to keep them safe."

Royo's amber-colored eyes dart to the side. I hope he does come with us. It would be nice to have his protection.

"What'll you be doing, Mikail?" Royo asks.

"Meeting with the Yusanian Ambassador. There has to be a way to get close to the throne. Something I'm not considering. I'm hoping Zeolin will know."

"And Euyn?" Aeri asks.

Mikail barely glances at him, despite Euyn giving him his full attention from the moment he stepped inside. "Euyn has a bounty on his head. He should stay as hidden as possible."

Aeri's eyebrows come together. "I thought Quilimar hates the king. Wouldn't she want to help Euyn?"

"Her reign is new and tenuous," Mikail says. "She is not of Khitanese royal blood or Khitanese at all, and ostensibly, she is only a regent. It is hard to say whether she'd give Euyn's head to Joon to broker better terms with Yusan, especially after the attempt on her life." He shifts his gaze to Euyn's, and one corner of his mouth tips up. "And she's not exactly a fan of Euyn."

I wish Ty were here. The politics goes above my head, but he would be asking the right questions. He understands power and the nobility.

I close my eyes, reliving how he said he'd wait for anything in the throne room, how he bravely stood knowing he'd be hauled away to a sunless dungeon. Tears prick my eyes, but I push them back. I don't have the luxury of giving in to emotion right now.

"We should check their Temple of Knowledge," Euyn says. "If the Rule of Distance was put in place fifteen years ago, their Yoksa will have a record of it, and they will also have documented any exceptions. Even with Quilimar seeing no one now, the exceptions should hold."

"The Yoksa?" Royo asks.

"Priests of knowledge," Euyn answers. "Historical records of all kings are kept in the Temple of Knowledge by independent priests called the Yoksa. There is a temple in each kingdom, and they are always in hidden locations. That is how they stay true…for the most part."

I roll the idea around in my mind. An exception to the Rule of Distance is exactly what we need. A little spark of hope lights inside me.

Mikail sighs.

"What?" Euyn asks, his gaze searching him. "You don't agree?"

"No, I do. But the Temple of Knowledge in Khitan is under a frozen lake this time of year."

I tilt my head so my good ear is toward Mikail. I'm not sure I heard him correctly.

Royo's eyebrows shoot up. "Under?"

"It's surrounded by a glass dome, but yes." Mikail speaks as though it's nothing unusual. When we all just continue to blink at him, he chuckles and adds, "It was built by the gods."

Another impossible riddle. How do we get inside an underwater temple?

I sit back in my chair and run my hands over my hair. I spin the long, thick strands. There's yet another complication. There's always another. Too many. Every time I think I have my head wrapped around something, I don't.

Euyn wipes his mouth with a napkin and then tosses it down.

"Are we going to talk about the person who betrayed all of us, or are we planning to just let it go?"

I'm...honestly not sure if he means Mikail or Aeri, the latter of whom has paused with her fork halfway to the kimchi.

Mikail finishes his ale, then says, "You're awfully bold now that *your* secrets are out."

Euyn pales but lifts his chin. "Why did you try to destroy the crown?"

All of us are silent as we wait for the spymaster to respond. I've wondered the same thing since I saw him slice the replica crown in half in the arena.

"You didn't need it to be king," Mikail says, waving his hand.

It's not really an answer.

"But why try to break it?" Euyn presses. "Joon said you destroyed the decoy."

Mikail stares into his lover's eyes. "Because no person should be immortal. Even you. Especially not you. The power of the crown allows your brother to hide behind the walls of Qali without a care for how his rule affects the people of Yusan, the people of Gaya, or Khitan, or Wei. And you once felt invincible, as did Omin. What did the two of you do? You hunted and murdered for your own amusement, while he assaulted young girls. Nothing good comes from the Baejkins having unlimited power."

The tension in this room is so thick, it's suffocating. There's not a sound until a chair scrapes the floor.

"We'll see Vikal tomorrow," Aeri says, and then she rushes out of the room.

I'm not sure what has upset her, but it's enough to know she's near tears. I know exactly what it feels like when your chin quivers because you're fighting so hard not to cry out. I push my chair back and follow her, not only to check on her, but because I need to leave the room as well. I'm aching to wring Euyn's neck at the mention of him hunting people like my father.

As I reach the door, I have a moment of clarity. Euyn won't be any better than King Joon, and I refuse to trade tyrants. Someone else will have to sit on the black serpent throne, and I have an idea.

CHAPTER SEVEN

TIYUNG

IDLE PRISON, YUSAN

I'm not certain how long I've been in this dungeon. It could be only a few days or maybe a full sunsae. I rub my growing beard. From my scruff, I think it's been at least a week.

There's no sunlight in here, which is to be expected in a prison under a lake. But there are also no bells. No normal routine. No way to mark the passing of time.

It's maddening but better than death. So far.

When the guards pulled me from the palace and walked me to the water's edge, I thought maybe I wasn't going to prison at all. As I waited, I feared I'd be fed to the iku—the monstrous creatures that inhabit the deep water of Idle Lake. I prayed to the gods to save Sora and to have mercy on my soul.

I hope they answered the first prayer because they didn't seem to hear the second.

As the guards held me by the shore, stone walls rose through the surface of the mirror lake. The water receded and a black staircase came into view, leading all the way down to a door in the lake floor—the entrance to Idle Prison. The most secure place in all of Yusan.

It looked like the gateway to the Ten Hells.

With my head high, I forced myself to walk down the steps and not suffer the indignity of being dragged. I looked up as I descended, trying to savor the purples and oranges of the sunset, to remember the daylight, but it hasn't done much good. Sunlight and hope are now distant memories. I promised Sora I would make it through anything, yet I've learned it's far easier to spout brave sayings than to live them.

Not that I've had to be brave. Not exactly. I thought I would be tortured when the prison doors closed. Instead, I've been left to rot in a circular, smooth stone cell. It's a different kind of torment—to be completely alone with nothing but my thoughts. I haven't spoken to another human being since I was placed inside here. Sometimes, I hear the wails of other men. I have called out, but I must be too far away for anyone to answer me.

Or no one cares.

My cell is large but dark and dank. There's a transom window around thirty feet off the ground, but it casts almost no light in here. The only light I do have is from the oil torches in the hall, visible through a six-inch meal slot.

Meals are served at random times, but the uncertainty doesn't matter much when the food is infested. I ate the first tray I was served, and I was sick for days after. The ten skulls lining the ledge at the top of this cell watched as I retched and nearly soiled myself. I stick to the stale bread and water now. My stomach twists and growls in constant hunger, but I won't touch the other food again.

The walls around me suddenly shake. It happens from time to time as moaning causes tremors. The moaning is not human, though; it's from the iku calling to each other in the lake. Sometimes it's mournful. Sometimes it's excited. I suspect the higher-pitched, sharp sounds occur when they hunt. I always hope it's an animal and not a person, but there's no way for me to know for certain.

Still, I tell myself stories. About the iku, about anything to keep my mind occupied. I'm twenty-two and have lived a full life with a variety of memories to recall, but I wonder how long I can hold on to sanity. There are no books. No ink and paper with which to write and not enough light to do so. Being alone isn't new because my father felt friends were a liability, but I always had my studies. Here, I don't even have that.

All I'm left with is wondering how long I'll ultimately be in here. By now, my father must know his plan failed. How many days will they keep me hostage? How long before they no longer need me as leverage and execute me?

As the thought enters my head, noises resound outside of my cell—murmuring and footsteps. The metal cranks turn on my door, and I scurry to my feet. The room spins; the sudden movement makes me dizzy. I shake my head and try to stay alert.

The hinges creak, and I back up, my heart frantically racing as the door opens. I put my hands up, my mind filled with both fear and hope. Maybe my father has ransomed me and I will get to leave. Or maybe it's time to die.

Either way, it seems my time is up.

A flaming torch enters the darkness. The light sears my eyes. I fall backward onto the stone floor and scramble away as I put my hands over my face. There's a sigh and some mumbling before the door slams shut again.

But I'm not alone. Someone is in here with me. I can hear them breathing.

When the pain subsides, I slowly move my fingers so I can try to adjust to the bright light. It takes longer than expected for my vision to return at all, but then I can see again…somewhat.

Instead of the fire torch, there's now a small oil lantern on the ground, as far from me as possible. Before I was in this cell, I would have called the light dim, but now it seems like broad daylight.

Once my eyes fully adjust, I get a look at the person next to the lamp. I shake my head. So much for clinging to sanity. Standing there, in my cell, is Hana—one of the girls my father trained as a poison maiden.

And Hana died years ago.

CHAPTER EIGHT

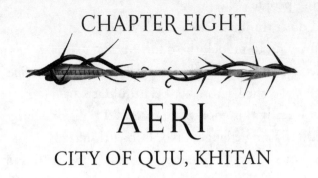

AERI
CITY OF QUU, KHITAN

I race out of Euyn's suite and back to my room. For the past week, I've thought about how my father knew his brother, Prince Omin, was assaulting and murdering young girls and he did nothing to stop it. No one did.

And I was almost one of his victims.

Mikail mentioned it as just another scandal. Another in a long line of Baejkin misdeeds. The thing that has haunted my nightmares for years. The invisible scars I bear. The stealing of lives from countless girls who had the misfortune to be powerless in the presence of someone like Omin. Just another character flaw.

My stomach turns and my throat burns, the meal threatening to come back up. Innocence is a cheap flower to be plucked and torn apart by powerful men.

Before I can get my room unlocked, Sora comes up behind me in the hall. Because of course she'd follow and check on me. Of course she cares. She's *Sora*.

"Are you all right?" she asks.

Tears sting my eyes. I try to blink them back, but I know my face is red. My nose and mouth feel hot and flushed, my throat tight.

"I… I'm sorry. I'm sorry for all of it—for lying, for trying to bring you in—but I am *not* the same as my father or my…family."

Sora remains quiet for a moment. She has a way of listening, not just hearing people.

"No, I don't think you are," she says plainly.

I stop trying to unlock the door. My hands shake too much to get the key in, anyhow. I look over my shoulder at her. She stares at me, sympathy etched across her beautiful face.

"Are you really this good of a person?" I sigh, slouching.

She utters a single laugh. "No, I don't think so."

It's an honest answer. She moves to take the key from me, and I let her. She opens the door. I step inside and wave her in.

We don't talk. Instead, I go over to the fire and busy myself stoking it back to life. She stands quietly—because she knows I need a minute to collect myself, and she's nice enough to give it to me.

"Don't you find it exhausting to care about everyone all the time?" I ask. "To always take the high road?"

She closes her eyes and smiles slowly. "Aeri, from the second I realized King Joon wasn't a god, my plan was to steal the Immortal Crown and give it to my sister. Tiyung talked me out of it by saying that Daysum would just end up dead. But there's only so much high road, and I'm not walking it."

I turn to her, my mouth falling open in shock. It didn't seem like she wanted the relic or had any desire to be royal. "Why would you give the crown to your sister?"

"Because she may be dying."

She says it without emotion, but pain twists in my chest for Sora and a girl I've never even met.

"Oh, Sora. I'm sorry."

She nods and inhales deeply, her chest rising. "Anyhow, it's hard to be too upset with you for keeping secrets when I had my own. And, in all honesty, I need you now."

I blink. "For what?"

She steps closer to me, stopping at the other end of the mantel. "To take the throne of Yusan."

I laugh, then look at her face. She's not laughing or even smiling.

She's dead serious. "Wait, you're not joking?"

"You're the daughter of the king," she says. "That gives you a birthright to the throne, above Euyn."

I shake my head. If I were a boy that would be true, but I am not. "Yusan has never had a queen."

"I remember in school there was a rumor that there had been queens in the past," she says. "That there's evidence in the Temple of Knowledge. I hadn't given it much thought until Euyn mentioned the Yoksa."

I chew my bottom lip and worry the hem of my dress. Even if there had been queens, it was so long ago that no one remembers it outside of rumor. And although I am Joon's daughter, I wasn't raised to rule. I wasn't even brought up in the palace. "But Euyn is…"

She stares at the fire, her expression grave as her hand curls into a fist. "It can't be Euyn. It just can't be. Your father can't keep the throne, but Euyn will only be more of the same."

"What makes you think I'll be any better than him? I'm Baejkin." I shake my head, then smile a pained grin.

"You aren't your family. Ty…" She trembles as she exhales. I've noticed it before—her right hand shakes a little sometimes. She balls it in a fist before releasing it. "Tiyung made me realize that people can grow to be different than the soil they were raised in."

"Or sometimes they are the same." I think about my father, Euyn, and Omin murdering without conscience. The story goes that my aunt is just as bad or worse—but that's a tale told by killers.

"It was true, then, that Prince Omin…" Sora begins.

I tense, but she doesn't say any more.

"They thought he killed me when I was twelve." I smile even though there's nothing to smile about.

"You don't have to tell me," she says. "There's an old expression in my village that sometimes the tongue isn't ready to speak what the eyes have seen. I believe that. But I'm listening. And I know a thing or two about cruel men."

She stares into the distance. I know she does.

"He was charming," I say. "Much more so than Euyn or my father. He charmed my mother so easily. Then again, all he had to say was that the king had made a mistake throwing out a woman like her. That was all it took."

Sora nods.

"Omin courted her for a week, maybe two, and she was so excited to move into his villa," I say, wringing my hands. "She was so ready for the life promised to her that she didn't think twice about it. It was the happiest I'd ever seen my mother. For the two weeks we lived in his villa, we had servants she ordered around, great food from the kitchens, expensive gifts and lavish surprises. Anything she wanted, Omin gave her. Including his carriage to go visit with her sister."

Sora frowns. "Powerful men can often appear charming until their masks slip."

"He attacked me the night she left," I whisper.

Sora inhales sharply.

"And then I...um... I killed him."

She exhales. "I'm sure you didn't have a choice."

Did I? I guess I could've let him take what he wanted and then butcher me instead. I would've gone to the Ten Hells with a clean soul and spent my three years in Elysia. But I hadn't meant to murder him. I just wanted him to stop touching me. In my nightmares, he watches me sleep. Sometimes the sewing scissors aren't on my bedside table. Sometimes they are, but I miss his neck. I've relived a hundred different versions of the same horrific night. Same beginning of him waking me and pulling down his trousers.

I shudder and stare at the fire, remembering the flames of his villa rising into the night sky. All I wanted was for people to think I was dead and to be unsure of how he died. That's all I was thinking when I broke the oil lamp under the bed, but I learned that three servants died in the blaze. I think about them all the time—how they did nothing wrong but died all the same.

I killed four people that night, and I will be judged by Lord Yama for all of them.

"After he was dead, I was on my own," I say. "I knew I wouldn't have been believed. I knew I couldn't go home."

"You did what you had to in order to survive," she says softly.

I look away, the heaviness in my chest nearly unbearable. She understands, and I'm not certain whether that makes it better or worse. I'm not even sure why I told Sora all of that. I've never told anyone.

Still, I don't mention the amulet I found on his wrist. Prince Omin wasn't even supposed to have the Sands of Time of the Dragon Lord, but somehow, he did. And now, I do.

I didn't know what it was when I took the relic from his body. I just saw a gem and stole it. I had to figure out on my own that it stopped time. The price I paid was aging four years in the minutes it took to clean his blood off me. The curse of the amulet was the reason I couldn't see my mother again. I couldn't explain suddenly looking sixteen when I was only twelve. I thought I would see her again one day when I was older and the age difference wouldn't matter, but she died last year. I was too late. My only family was gone.

"You aren't your bloodline," Sora says, stepping closer.

I sniffle. "I know."

But I *am* a killer. Unlike my family, though, I've suffered consequences. I paid for the murders with loneliness, with never seeing Mama again, with constantly worrying that someone might find out that I killed Omin, with staying awake wondering if I'd die of old age clutching the amulet while I dreamed, with no one caring if I lived.

All of it hits me—all of the things I don't think about.

I died, and no one mourned me.

Tears stream down my cheeks, and I can't stop them.

"It wasn't your fault." Sora takes another step.

"Sora." I put my hands up to defend myself. Not because she's hurting me but because she's getting close to me. And no one, other than Royo, has been close to me. And now he hates me. He hates to even look at me because I can only hurt or abandon the few people who love me. I am doomed to live this life alone.

"You were a child trying to survive," she says. "And you are not your family."

She opens her arms, and I lean on her shoulder and cry. A really ugly, gasping cry while she strokes my hair and lets me ruin her dress.

As I cling to her, I get it. I would do anything to keep this feeling of being cared for. And Sora feels a hundred times stronger than this for her sister. She will do anything for Daysum, even if it means sacrificing everything and everyone else she loves.

Which makes her the most dangerous killer in the world.

CHAPTER NINE

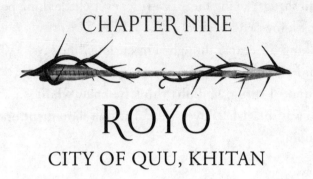

ROYO
CITY OF QUU, KHITAN

Aeri just ran out of the room. I can't be sure, but I think it was because of what Mikail said. About the dead prince who was touching and killing kids. And wasn't that the same guy who King Joon thought had killed her? Would that mean…

"You don't need that," Mikail says.

I look down to where he's pointing. My fist is curled around a steak knife. I drop the blade on the table, and it lands with a clang. I just told myself I wouldn't care about Aeri. I have to keep my word for more than a minute when it comes to her.

"How are the girls gonna get in to see the general?" I ask, needing a new topic.

"General Vikal used to see petitioners at dawn each day in Trialga Square," Mikail says. "I'm not certain that she still does. After I meet with the ambassador, I'll know more."

He pushes back from the table and stands.

"You're leaving?" Euyn asks. He looks kind of confused and hurt.

"Yes, I don't think it's wise to invite Zeolin here," he says.

"Why's that?" I ask.

"For starters, he's the one who tipped off the spies today." Mikail stretches, cocky, like it doesn't matter.

"You're gonna go see the guy who just tried to have you killed?" The grooves in my forehead deepen.

Mikail shrugs, facing me. "I can't let every little thing bother me."

I don't know why I asked.

"Speaking of setups, though, I'm curious," he says. "What does Bay Chin have against you?"

"I dunno." I shrug. "I didn't think he knew who I was."

"Who was the girl?" Euyn asks. "The one Joon mentioned in the throne room."

Lora.

The memory knocks the air out of my lungs. That son of a bitch Bay Chin said I killed Lora, that I let Hwan, her father, take the fall. The man who'd treated me like a son. The one I've tried to free for nearly a decade. The only girl I ever loved. Aside from... Never mind.

"Royo, I'm going to give you wooden cutlery if you can't stop that," Mikail says.

I look down and see I'm brandishing the knife again. I let go and push it out of the way. It skitters toward Euyn, and he catches it and sets it by his plate.

"I didn't hurt her," I say.

"I didn't think you did," Mikail says. "I'm trying to piece together what happened and why the northern count was involved."

"She was..." I go to say her name, but I can't. Grief makes the word stick in my throat. And that's not what they're asking anyhow. They don't care who she was. They care what she was to me, but more what she was to Bay Chin. "She was the daughter of a merchant. I took the wrong job and killed a gang member, and then two gang members tried to kill me but got to her instead. But her father was the one arrested and jailed."

Euyn and Mikail exchange glances. I don't know what those looks mean, but I doubt it's good.

Mikail nods. "That makes sense, then."

"What does?"

"Bay Chin is the head of the gangs in Umbria," Euyn says.

My heart lodges in my throat. The gangs. The ones who ran the city. The ones who stabbed her to death. I'd never figured out the connection before.

Mikail frowns. "You were a dead man once you killed a gang member."

No need to tell them about the two I left in pieces.

"Why set up Hwan?" I ask. "Why not take me down?"

Mikail shrugs. "He certainly tried to by having Aeri bring you in. But it could've been any number of things. Bay Chin has a long memory and bides his time. I suspect this Hwan person either took something precious from him or became a threat to his interests. The counts do not tolerate competition from commoners."

Hwan had two successful gambling houses. After he was arrested, they were given to the gangs. But that couldn't have been it. I shake my head. It couldn't have just been money.

Then I remember the sanctions on the city—a quarter of all revenue went to the throne because the count tried to kill the king. Eleven years of tribute nearly ruined Umbria. Then Bay Chin risked his own neck to bring in the most dangerous killers in Yusan, just to get the king to lift the sanctions. All to line his pockets with more gold. So yeah, it could've all been money.

"I'll slice him apart in lingchi myself," I say.

"I don't doubt it," Mikail says. "I hope you get the chance, truly, because it will mean we've won. Now, if you'll both excuse me, I have to drop in on the ambassador."

"Don't kill him," Euyn says.

Mikail pauses and looks surprised. "Why not?"

He walks out the door before Euyn can answer.

CHAPTER TEN

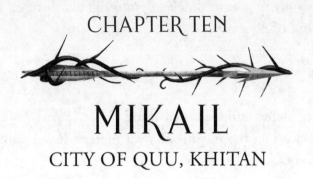

MIKAIL

CITY OF QUU, KHITAN

Ambassador Zeolin is a tall, thin man with dignified gray hair who I currently have hanging from his office window.

"It was a rather cold greeting, Zeolin," I say as I lean on the sill. I'm getting wet, but the cold rain is rather refreshing.

He's screaming. Well, he's trying to scream, but he's gagged. His fingers are constantly slipping on the slick stone. I tighten my grip on his wrist, but only slightly. I don't want him to feel safe from falling. The picture window of his office is high up on the mountainside. It's easily a hundred-foot drop to the rocky ground below.

Khitan does love its views.

"Your villa has scenic vistas," I say. "You can see nearly all of Quu from here, but I find it hard to believe you spotted me arriving at port today. Are you ready to cooperate?"

He tries to speak, but he can't because of the gag.

"Afraid I'll need a yes-or-no headshake," I say.

He vigorously nods yes.

"You'll tell me everything you know?"

Another enthusiastic nod. He, of course, wound up out the window because he claimed to know nothing and then had the nerve to order me out of his office.

I let his wrist slip. "Are you sure?"

He's screaming so loud that I can hear it even with the gag. The rain causes my fingers to slide as I go to tighten them on his wrist. He slips out of my grasp.

Fuck.

Diving forward, I reach out and grab his shoulders, then retake his arm.

Stars, I almost dropped the bastard.

But I don't let the surprise show. I pretend it was another part of this game.

"This is what is going to happen," I say, my voice even. "I'm going to pull you inside, and if I don't think you are being fully truthful with every answer, I will skewer you slowly to your desk. You will wish I had let you fall. Do we have a deal?"

More nodding.

Coward.

I'd take my secrets to the grave with me, but I am a different type of man.

With a sigh, I heave him inside. I toss him into his leather chair and take down the gag. Down, not off. The second these men feel safe, they believe they're in control again.

I stab his fine wood desk with my dagger, then lean against the side of it with my arms folded.

"All right, I'm listening."

He's shaking and crying, and he might've soiled himself. It's hard to tell with the rain. Really, for a man in his late fifties, this is a rather pathetic display. He's a nobleman, a diplomat, a patriarch. He should have *some* dignity. But the nobility live soft lives. They are at a severe disadvantage when status doesn't matter.

I look around as I wait for him to calm down. Everything in his office is expensive and designed to impress. Sculpture, awards... Is that a medal of valor on his wall?

I yank the dagger out of the desk and walk over to the glass case. Stars, it is a Yusanian medal of valor. This couldn't be more out of place. I smash the glass with the hilt of my blade, grab the medal, and toss it out the window.

He gasps at my lack of decorum.

"Zeolin," I say, "I'm getting bored. If you don't start talking, I will find a way to entertain myself."

I spin the dagger in my hand.

His eyes widen, and he sounds like a large dog, the way he's breathing and whining. There are advantages to being thought of as a demon. He believes every word I'm saying despite the fact that I really don't intend to kill him right now. Too many people saw me come in here. He would be replaced by the week's end by another self-important noble anyway, so it wouldn't be worth the mess.

At the moment.

No one is untouchable. You just have to be willing to deal with the fallout. And I have other things to do.

"General Salosa said to eliminate you," he cries. "That you had betrayed the king—tried to kill him. I didn't believe the part about you trying to kill King Joon. You know as well as anyone that he's immortal with his crown. But I believed you'd changed allegiances."

"And Salosa also told you to eliminate Quilimar," I say.

It's a guess, but I suspect between Zeolin tipping off the spies and the incredible timing of the assassin that Yusan was behind the attempt on Quilimar's life a week ago.

A look, just a fraction of a second long, passes over the ambassador's face. A bead of sweat begins to roll down his temple.

It was him. General Salosa is the head of the palace guards at Qali, which means Joon was behind the attempted regicide. Stars, we are never going to get close to the throne with Yusan to blame. The question is why the double effort? Why go through all of the trouble to assemble and send us and at the same time try to kill her?

The sweat drops off his jaw. Maybe Zeolin's motivation will shed some light on this.

"What was in it for you?" I ask.

He swallows hard, the lump in his throat bobbing. "H-he told me that if the queen dies and I help bring him the Golden Ring, I will be made regent for the Count of Tamneki."

I smile. "The king seems to be recruiting quite a few people for the same job opportunity these days."

Once a snake, always a snake. He was never going to give me Tamneki, very simply because he can't make both of us counts and he would inevitably choose this sniveling diplomat. A dog is an easier pet than a jaguar. Joon's plan had to be for me to die first. So why not just kill me then? I was at his mercy in the throne room. A flick of a blade and it would've been done. He needed me alive for some other, more important purpose.

"What else do you need to tell me?" I ask.

The ambassador shakes his head.

I turn and stab the armchair, splitting the leather. I purposely miss his right hand by the width of a hair.

Zeolin shrieks and then whimpers.

I lean closer to him. "I asked nicely because I am a patient man, but you are testing the limits of my benevolence. Let me point out that you are still alive after plotting against me this morning. I've been more than fair. I can be less polite if you draw this out."

The whimpering continues.

"Zeolin. Zeolin…" I tsk. I straighten up and draw back my blade to strike.

He lifts his hands to shield himself. "There's a rumor…"

"Fantastic. I love rumors. Do go on." I perch on his desk, facing him.

He looks bewildered, blinking hard. The baggy skin around his eyes crinkles.

Switching interrogation modes quickly is a favorite tactic of mine. Your subjects can never get a sense of your true mood and intention, which prevents them from feeling at ease.

"The rumor is that Joon left Qali," he says.

Zahara was being truthful. Or they are spreading the same lie—

but to what end? "And where did he go?"

He blinks. "I don't know. I swear and I vow it!"

He's telling the truth.

"All right then. How do I get an audience with Quilimar?" I ask.

He shakes his head. "It's not possible."

I sigh and stare meaningfully at my dagger. I butchered three people with it today and yet it's clean—amazing how the most gruesome acts wash right off steel.

"It's impossible!" he insists. "No one has gotten an audience with the queen since the assassination failed. She must have used the ring, though, because the assassin's shirt was solid gold during the piteua. The only person she meets with now is Vikal."

He's being truthful, and the answer is angering me more. Vikal being the only way in is not great. The general is as competent as she is clever, not to mention that she's in love with Quilimar. She won't let people like us get within a hundred yards of the throne.

"Vikal is still meeting with petitioners?" I ask.

"Not since the attempt. But there is the Banquet of the Sky King tomorrow. She will be there. Quilimar is supposed to be there, too, though I doubt she will attend."

That's right. Khitan celebrates the arrival of the monsoons as a gift from the Sky King. In Yusan, we say Sun King. Same shit. The gods abandoned Gaya long ago.

"What else?" I ask.

"Nothing else."

I silently stare at Zeolin. He's back to playing dumb, and he needn't try this hard.

His eyes dart all around. "There... It's nothing."

I spin my blade again. "You know, a less patient man would've taken your head clean off by now. Do you think your body would still run around like a chicken? I think it would. At any rate, it would be amusing to find out..."

"There's a rumor that Count Seok is in Khitan!" He says it so eagerly he spits. A glob of saliva lands on his fine shirt.

I nearly raise my eyebrows. Nearly. I never show my surprise when talking to sources, but that *is* interesting. If the southern count is here, he likely doesn't know that Tiyung is in Idle Prison. Or he does, and that is why he is here. Either way, I can't let Sora find out. She'll lose focus. We'll deal with Seok later.

"Why?" I ask.

"I don't know. I thought he fled the realm when the eastern count died before the celebration. He arrived a few days ago."

It's possible. He might've seen the writing on the wall. I would think Seok was involved in Joon's plot, but he wouldn't have put his only heir in harm's way.

I decide to change subjects.

"Have you ever heard of Oosant?" I ask.

His brow wrinkles. "You know I have—it's a city in the old borderlands."

"The very one."

"What about it?" he asks.

I study him for a moment. He doesn't know. A million mun of illegal drugs in a shitty warehouse, and no one has heard about it. My gut is telling me that the drugs are somehow tied to all of this, but I haven't found the right source yet. I switch gears and ask my final question.

"What do you know about the Temple of Knowledge?" I don't expect miracles, but he may have heard something about accessing the temple.

He looks to the side and then shakes his head. "No one knows who killed him."

This is news. Someone killed a *Yoksa*?

"Why is that?" I ask casually.

He shrugs. "It's hard enough to figure out who the Yoksa are—you know how secretive the priesthood is. Figuring out who murdered a secret priest in Trialga Square is nearly impossible. All three realms claim to have had no hand, and the Outer Lands wouldn't care. It violates all their edicts, though, to harm a priest of the God of Knowledge. Someone must not like what was written. Quilimar has ordered piteua of anyone involved and has offered a hundred-thousand-mark bounty."

A hundred thousand. A fortune for the capture of someone who killed a commoner is awfully suspicious. But the priests aren't ordinary people. Even in Yusan, the Yoksa are left alone. The treaties and edicts guarantee their safety. A war of the realms is supposed to occur if any ruler sanctions the murder of a priest. I don't think Joon is behind this, although I don't put it past him. With a bounty that large, it was likely Quilimar herself. I simply need more information, and the ambassador has nothing left to give.

"It's always good to see you, Zeolin." I slap his shoulder, and he cries out like I stabbed him.

He will miss that medal of valor, I'm sure.

I put my dagger away. "You'll be bringing two guests with you to the banquet tomorrow. I suggest you keep them safe."

He nods so hard I'm surprised he doesn't snap his own neck.

I walk out of his office with more questions than information, but with a lead I just stole.

CHAPTER ELEVEN

TIYUNG

IDLE PRISON, YUSAN

Hana stands in front of me, her curves covered in a fine dress and cape. She's illuminated by a lantern, but she doesn't say a word.

"I'm losing my mind," I mutter.

"That tends to happen in Idle," she says.

It is Hana's raspy voice, but it cannot be Hana. She died two years ago while trying to murder a nobleman for my father. But this woman has the same thick brown lashes and thick brown hair. Her skin tone is the same shade of brown, and she's tall, nearly as tall as myself. Of course, she's not Hana, but she could be Hana's twin. She has the same extraordinary beauty that my father looked for in all of the girls he trained to be poison maidens.

All that to say, I am currently imagining a lantern and a dead girl. Perhaps I'm not doing as well as I thought.

I run my hands over my beard.

"Hana," I say.

She stares at me and then looks around. "They held Prince Euyn in here, you know. You have royal accommodations. No chains, no torture, a private cell with a latrine—it's practically a villa compared to the other places in this dungeon. I suppose your status matters even in the tenth hell."

"Hana, are you really here?" I ask.

"My name is Zahara," she says. But she meets my eyes and gives me a small nod. It really is Hana. I gasp. Somehow, she's alive and standing in front of me. "You look terrible, Tiyung."

"How? I thought…"

"Your beard doesn't suit you," she says.

"No, I mean…"

"Neither does prison. I could slip poison into your water." She casually eyes my full tray. "End this internment for you."

She speaks like she's bored, and it's in the same tone I remember. It really is Hana.

Or I'm having a very detailed hallucination.

"Why don't you, then?" I ask.

"Why should I be kind?" she says. "Not to mention that Seok wouldn't know it was me, and what is the point of that?" She pauses and shrugs. "Besides, you are the king's captive—I am to leave you alive for now."

She looks at me with hate in her eyes, and then I remember that we never did recover her body. I saw a girl who resembled her burn on a funeral pyre, but we were too far away to check for details. Hana must've struck a deal with the nobleman she'd been sent to kill. She faked her death with his help, then fled to the capital and somehow met the king. She isn't wearing all blacks, but I bet she's an assassin for the throne.

Or a spy.

"You have nothing to say?" she asks, one eyebrow raised.

"No, because you're correct," I say. "You have no reason to be kind to me. I benefited from your suffering, from the torture of the other nineteen girls. It's only right for me to suffer some of what you did. As Sora did."

She lunges toward me and stops herself. Barely. Her muscles strain, her fingers spread, and she's so close I can smell her rose perfume. But she takes a breath and regathers herself. Then she stands straight and exhales, smoothing the skirt of her dress. "Do not speak that name."

The realization hits immediately: Hana loved her. I wonder if Sora knew, then remember Sora saying something about it being too much to even think of your loved one, but desperately wanting to honor their memory. I thought she was talking about her parents, but that never really made sense.

She was talking about Hana.

My gut twists in a new way.

"You were in love," I say, my voice weak and raw.

Hana resumes her casual air, even as her gaze burns into mine. She must've studied Mikail to act the same way, to be so casually lethal. That shouldn't surprise me, though. Hana was the smartest girl in my father's school. I am positive she would make an excellent spy.

"I *am* in love with her," she says, and my chest tightens. "True love doesn't end just because of death."

She bangs on the door once, and a guard opens it.

Even if her words hurt, I wish she'd stay so I have someone to talk to, but she is done with me.

Desperation takes hold. I try to think up something, anything that might interest her, might make her stay, but my mind is slow from however long I've been in here. I stand with my mouth open, but no words come.

Hana is almost out of my cell when she tosses an envelope onto the stone floor. It lands on the dirty ground near my feet. Then she walks out like it never happened, leaving me with a lantern, a message, and a million unanswered questions.

CHAPTER TWELVE

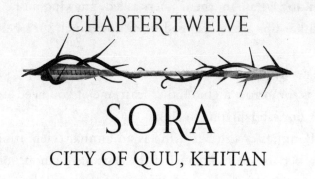

SORA
CITY OF QUU, KHITAN

With so much hanging in the balance, it feels strange to be getting ready for a ball. Yet for the last three years, I've done this same routine to prepare to murder, so I suppose it's normal for me.

I make up and perfume my face, arrange my hair, and don my heavy silver-and-blue dress as if it's armor. I slide on my rings, necklaces, and earrings. All of the gems are owned by the southern count. All make me something different—a courtesan instead of a scarred girl desperate to save her little sister. Last, I put my fur cape over my shoulders. I debate for a second, then decide to apply poison lipstick, just as a precaution.

Beauty will be my only weapon tonight, as we won't be able to bring in blades.

Aeri and I will attend a banquet while Royo, Mikail, and Euyn head to the Temple of Knowledge.

Mikail came back last night suspiciously soaked again, but at least this time it was only rain. He had a new plan for us: divide and conquer. We don't have much time for a variety of reasons, but no one was comfortable with splitting up.

"I thought I was going with the girls," Royo said, crossing his thick arms.

Mikail shook his head. "We may need your muscle."

"Shouldn't we all go, then?" Aeri asked, gnawing on her lip. I'm surprised her lips aren't chapped from how much she's been biting them.

"No," Mikail said. "Unfortunately, both events are pressing. The banquet is tomorrow night, and at least one of you needs to attend. I'd rather not send anyone in alone."

The Banquet of the Sky King is an annual celebration of the rains that occurs one full day after the start of the monsoon season. Mikail wasn't sure when we could meet the general, but the ball is the perfect excuse. Even in my border village, we used to celebrate the monsoons and the life-giving water they provide. The rains also cause floods that destroy and kill, but life surges after destruction.

Hundreds of Khitan's elite will attend the ball in the armory. I thought the men would stay at the inn, but someone murdered a Yoksa recently—a holy priest. As shocking as that is, Mikail feels certain it's related to our mission here. Someone wants to alter history before we can read it. Which means there's something to find, and we have to discover what it is before the information disappears.

The three of them already left for Lake Cerome. Aeri and I will try to probe the general for information tonight. And then we'll meet back here.

I knock on Aeri's door. She comes out in a high-necked forest green dress made of lace and satin and a heavy white fur cape, both of which we purchased this morning. She looks stunning, but her head is low and her eyes dart around. Without Royo, she's nervous, I'm sure. I don't blame her. I've grown accustomed to the safety of having Mikail nearby.

But we are on our own tonight.

"You look lovely," I say. Her hair is swept up in the fashion of Khitan. It must grow very quickly, as it's noticeably longer than when we first met.

She smiles. "You always do."

We go downstairs and hire a private carriage to take us to the armory. In Khitan, the armory is not inside the palace. Instead, it's a building across Trialga Square. The Khitanese kings are the Trialgas, the same way Yusan has the Baejkins. But Khitan has also had queens. Queen Quilimar is the sixth female ruler in their history.

We are nearly to the summit when the carriage stops. The view is breathtaking, even in the dusky rain. The villas on the hillside are lit up. Below that are the colorful houses of the harbor. And then there's the vast, dark expanse of the East Sea.

Valets with umbrellas meet every carriage as it arrives, and we are escorted to the portico of the armory. I say thank you in Khitanese, and the valet stares. I'm not sure if it's my language or my face. My village was close to the border of Khitan, so I learned quite a bit when I was young. Not as much as Mikail or Euyn, but certainly enough to be polite.

We pass through the arched entryway and follow the crowd into the main hall, and my eyes widen. The military headquarters is decked out in gold with gilded weapons hanging all around the walls and golden chandeliers illuminating the space in twinkling light. Even the ceiling is painted with gilded decoration.

There must be pounds and pounds of gold in here, but I suppose that's what happens when you can create it with the touch of a ring.

In the center of the room hangs the purple flag with the golden eagle of Khitan, and long, linen-covered tables line the walls, creating a wide dancing space in the middle. There is no head table, but directly in front of us is where the general will sit—right in the center of the table facing the entry.

For all its similarities to a lavish banquet in Yusan, the atmosphere is markedly different—I could feel it from the second I stepped in the room. Women are not only attractive decoration here but active participants. They hold court—not just among themselves, but with men. Some wear suits and have their hair cut shorter than Euyn's. They laugh and talk boldly and help themselves to the passed food and drink.

It's very odd.

Is this the difference when women can hold their own money and title? Does it matter to this extent? Then again, we are still among the nobility. Who knows what life is like for women of low birth? Khitan is called a land of equals, but some are always more equal than others.

An older man, tall with gray hair, approaches us. He's Yusanian and wears the decoration of an ambassador with a small red flag hanging from the pocket of his suit jacket and a medal decorating his neck. The medallion is a black snake wrapped around a blade.

"You must be Yunga," he says, extending his hand. "I am Ambassador Zeolin."

I smile and curtsey. Yunga was the name Mikail forged for me. "How did you know me?"

"Mikail said to look for the most beautiful woman in the room." He smiles and his eyes are kind, but he is Yusanian nobility, so appearances are just that. "So that *must* be you. And who is this?"

"I am Narissa," Aeri says.

He inclines his head to her as she curtsies, but then his eyes are on me again. "What brings you to Khitan?"

"I was an indenture in Yusan," I say. "I recently escaped my binds."

"Ah," the ambassador says. "I can understand a man being unwilling to let you go, my dear. But you will find the freedom you dream of here. And what about you, Narissa?"

"I'm here to make my fortune," Aeri says. "One I can own."

It's close to the truth, I suppose.

"Very Khitanese thinking." He sniffs through his pronounced nose. "Well, you arrived just in time for the monsoons. Unfortunate weather, but that does allow you to be here for this banquet with the high society of Quu tonight."

"And you are at the top as an ambassador." I stare like I'm in awe and then look away demurely as if he caught me.

He raises his chin higher, puffing out his thin chest. These men can't resist flattery, no matter how thick. "One of, but outside of the palace no one ranks higher than the general."

"An army general?" I ask as if I'm confused by the concept. Noblemen like beautiful women to be smart enough to follow conversation but nowhere near as clever as themselves.

"General of the Armed Forces. That is General Vikal in the center behind the main table." He turns his head because it's rude to point in any realm. "It is different here than in Yusan. They value their military the most. And they allow *women* to serve, if you can believe that."

I follow his line of sight. I'm not sure what I expected, but the woman in front of us is not it. For one, she is not in a military uniform. Instead, she has on a form-fitting silver dress and a zaybear fur cape fastened by a thick gold chain. She is a little taller than Aeri, which makes her quite tall. I think she's probably forty years old, maybe a few years younger but battled-hardened. Her dark, curly hair is swept up and likely shoulder-length when it's down. Her features are Khitanese, which is a mix of the indigenous people of the continent and the descendants of those who came over long ago from the Outer Lands. And there's probably a touch of Yusanian in her lineage, too, judging by her cheekbones.

"I know… It is odd to have a female general, but that is how they do things here," Ambassador Zeolin says with a sigh.

"Would you do us the honor of introducing us?" Aeri asks.

"Of course," he says. "Our seats are at the same table."

Pride and status ring in his voice. Aeri rolls her eyes when he can't see her. I suppress a laugh.

We follow the ambassador as he glad-hands everyone we pass. Aeri and I look around. Because our cover stories have us just arriving in Khitan, we are free to gawk. The fashion here is far simpler than what I wear, so I am stared at more than usual. But it feels different. It's hard to explain, but there isn't the hunger, the same feeling of being prey that I've grown accustomed to in Yusan. Instead, the crowd is simply curious.

The ambassador relishes the attention. He is Yusanian through and through. They adore attractive courtesans they can use and discard at their leisure. Mikail told me there are no courtesans here in Khitan. Because women can inherit, there's no need to produce male heirs. Just one rule has shifted an entire society. It makes me wonder what else is possible.

"General," Ambassador Zeolin says. "May I introduce Yunga and Narissa, both formerly of Yusan."

She gives us a small smile. "It is nice to meet you both."

She speaks in perfect Yusanian, although it's clear from her stiff posture and delivery that she doesn't love these social events. The general is sharp, too direct for this kind of flattering ball. From far away, she looked slight, but up close, her arms are defined. She's a woman of action. Mikail said she was the daughter of their naval commander. She rose to outrank her father and relieved him of his duties when she became general of the Khitanese armed forces. Her aura speaks of quiet but unquestioned power.

I part my lips to ask about the queen when someone else calls for her attention.

"I hope you both enjoy the banquet. And I wish you welcome to Khitan," she says. "Please excuse me."

Aeri and I bob our curtsies.

That…was it.

We didn't accomplish much, but we still have the rest of the night. I turn and smile brightly at the ambassador as if I'm thrilled to have met someone so important.

We sit and dine on a meal of goose, califer, which is like caribou, whole spit-roasted boar, and other delicacies. Ambassador Zeolin talks about himself the entire dinner, but I am accustomed to that. Aeri isn't. She keeps glancing over at me as if to say *will he ever be quiet*, and it's all I can do not to laugh.

I'm glad she told me about what happened to her years ago.

There are scars we display, and then there are the ones we don't want anyone to see. Aeri trusted me with the darkest parts of her story, the deep, ugly wounds, and I think she's more beautiful for surviving them. The darkness makes me appreciate her light.

Yet as the time passes, I'm getting more and more anxious. I look down the table at the general several times, but she is five people from me and constantly occupied in conversation. There's no good way to get her attention, no means to get to know her.

After dinner is cleared, desserts are wheeled out and ice wine is distributed in gilded goblets. The musicians start—the instruments, of course, are gilded as well—and dancing begins.

My stomach drops. I still haven't found a way to have a private conversation with the general. I don't want to tell the others we failed, but as the night wears on, it's clear that we'll need to find another time to speak to General Vikal. Every single person in this room wants her ear.

I try to listen in on her conversations, but the ambassador is on my hearing side and constantly speaking. I catch bits and pieces, though. The nobility inquires about the queen and the prince, and the general firmly reassures them of their good health and safety. The queen is popular, which is surprising, given what Euyn and King Joon think of her. But General Vikal speaks with love and admiration in her tone. I can't tell if it's genuine or not.

After dessert, we rise from the table for air, and the ambassador excuses himself to use the bathrooms. I stare out the windows toward the palace and sigh. It would be so much easier if we could just arrange for an audience with the queen directly.

I spot a figure at the top of the palace stairs. Two, actually, protected by the portico and a cadre of guards. I squint because there's a dash of purple. In Yusan, only the royal family can wear imperial red. Here, it's any shade of purple.

My heart races in my chest as I realize that must be Queen Quilimar. She's so close, but also a world away.

She holds the hand of a young child who must be her son. He leans into the skirt of her dress, and she picks him up, raising him in the air. Just from that gesture, that second of affection between them, I suspect that what we were told about Quilimar is wrong—at least about her stealing the throne from her son. This is a woman who loves her child.

So, what else was incorrect? People have a peculiar way of believing the worst about powerful women.

"Come, my dear," the ambassador says, striding up to me. "Do me the honor of a dance?"

"Of course, my lord," I say, because he isn't really asking.

I glance at the palace again, but the stairs are now empty. Disappointment and frustration flow through me, but I smile them away.

The ambassador leads me to the middle of the room and puts his arm around my waist, holding me tighter and closer than necessary.

Music starts again, and the steps are easy enough to follow. Madame Iseul taught us many dances in poison school, as we might need them to charm our victims. We learned to dance in the same way she taught us to be good conversationalists and better listeners. To be knowledgeable about the world, in case more than a pretty face was required.

There were very few instances where more was necessary.

I spin around the room with the ambassador. He leans down so we are nearly cheek to cheek, but he wears so much cologne, I think I might faint. He must've applied more in the bathrooms. I breathe through my mouth.

"You should see the view of the city from my terrace once the rains end," he murmurs. "My villa is not far from here."

What he means is: I am important, and you should sleep with me soon.

"I'm sure it's spectacular," I say.

It's noncommittal but not a rejection—rejecting this sort of man is dangerous. However, it's not the enthusiastic yes I'm sure he expected.

"I—" he begins.

"Zeolin," a familiar voice says behind me. The sound makes my blood run cold. Without even turning, I know exactly who it is. I just pray I'm wrong. Perhaps I'm hearing things, because there is no way the southern count is here in Khitan.

I keep my back to him, my spine rigid, as if I can change the stars by avoiding them.

"Ah, Seok! My old friend!" the ambassador says. He speaks louder than necessary because he wants people to know he is friends with one of the most powerful men in Yusan. "I thought I might see you here."

"And here I am," Seok says.

My heart hammers my chest, my dress feeling too tight. I want to tear it off and run. Instead, I plaster a placid expression on my face, because I know I'm about to be face to face with Seok. And I refuse to shudder or cringe.

"Yunga, I'd like to introduce you to Seok, the Count of Gain." The ambassador smiles, wildly oblivious to the tension between us.

"Your Grace," I say, turning. "It is a pleasure."

I curtsy to the southern count, not taking my eyes off him. He looks handsome as ever in a black suit and white tie, especially when he's smiling. And he is smiling as if he's just met me. His coal-black hair is styled, and his dark eyes glitter as they drink me in. As I told Aeri, monsters can wear such charming masks.

"The pleasure is all mine," Seok murmurs. "May I cut in?"

"Of course," the ambassador says. He grins and gestures to me, although his smile doesn't reach his eyes. He was probably going to try to tempt me with more than a nice view. Jewels were likely the new offer in exchange for bedding him.

Seok puts his arm around my waist and pulls me close. My skin crawls and my breath comes in shallow sips, but I do my best not to show it. I don't want to make a scene here. But I press my lips together, glad I wore poison after all.

"You're looking well, Sora," he says as we begin to dance. "I must admit, though, I'm surprised to see you here. You had me fooled."

"Fooled?"

"I always thought Daysum meant more to you."

The mention of Daysum sends chills careening down my spine. At the same time, panic floods my mind. I don't flinch, but I want to. I want to flail and scream like I did as a girl.

"Where is she?" I whisper. My nails dig into his suit jacket. My breathing is rough, my heart thundering. The ringing in my ear is absolutely chiming as I wait for him to answer.

"Ah, you've forgotten the terms of our deal," Seok says. "That's unfortunate." He frowns for a moment and then goes back to his unaffected demeanor.

"Where *is* she?"

I stop dancing, and another couple bumps into us. We all mutter apologies.

Seok pulls me into him, forcing me to keep moving. The way he's forced me to dance through my entire life. But I don't even care about him touching me right now, because where is my sister?

"I imagine she's working at this point in the evening," he says. "But I don't keep track of my brother's affairs."

The realization hits me a moment later, just as intended. It's a dagger to the gut, yanked straight up to my heart: he sold her. He sold Daysum to the brothels.

My sister, my only joy, the only good thing I've been able to protect in my life, is now fresh meat for wolves.

My face tingles as blood drains rapidly from my cheeks. My pulse thuds like it's trying to break my neck. My vision spins.

No. Please, gods. Not Daysum.

This is worse than any poison I've ingested. Worse than anything I had to watch and endure in a dozen years. Because it is my sister.

Because it is my fault. Just as we had freedom within our grasp, I failed her. I was supposed to save her, heal her, protect the only family I have, but I didn't kill the king, and now she is a brothel indenture. Now she is alive in the deepest hell.

"You should've thought about her welfare before you fled," Seok says. Then he smiles. Actually smiles.

Fury I've never felt before builds up in me until it burns. I've hated and feared Seok since I was a child, but this is something else. This is molten. Nothing matters more than hurting him. I would burn down the three realms just to see him singed.

I smile, but it's more of a lioness baring her teeth. My lips shake because I want to kiss him so badly. But I wait. I make myself wait. If I killed him now, I'd doom the others. And a fast death would be too kind for Seok. He will suffer. He will plead to deaf ears.

"And you?" I say, staring into his eyes. "Have you thought about the welfare of your own?"

Seok falters a step—just one. He doesn't know. He didn't get my eagle post because he was here and not in Gain. No one has told him about his son.

"You wouldn't dare." He's all bravado, but there's a hint of uncertainty in his eyes.

Suddenly, I wish I had killed Tiyung. My feelings for him be damned. I wish I could tell Seok that his only heir died by my lips or at the end of my blade. I wish I could watch him crumble.

"He is rotting in Idle Prison," I say. "*If* he is even still alive. For all your schemes, you were outplayed by the king from the start. Tiyung will be tortured to death in there. Or maybe he's been eaten by the iku." I force myself to shrug about the fear that's been torturing me since the throne room. "Either way, I wish you a long life, Seok, now that your title and your bloodline will die with you."

With that, I walk away.

I make it three feet.

CHAPTER THIRTEEN

TIYUNG

IDLE PRISON, YUSAN

As soon as Hana leaves, I dive at the envelope, scrambling on my hands and knees across the dirty floor. I'm so eager to get to the message that I have to stop myself from tearing the paper.

The letter was already opened, but strangely, it is my seal on the envelope. Puzzled, I turn it over in my hands. Why would Hana give me a letter I wrote? Then I realize that Sora must have my seal. It is a message from her.

My heart overflows to the point that I think it will burst. I feel happiness for the first time since being thrown in this cell. And more than that—the light of hope is rekindled inside me.

I slide out the paper, ready to read her words, but the letter isn't addressed to me. It's to my father.

Seok,

It was his plan. Tiyung is idling the day away. Within a month I will keep my word. Keep your word.

Disappointment hits. It's not exactly the heartfelt message I hoped for, but I still feel bolstered having something written by Sora's hand. She must've penned this within the last day or so and sent it by eagle post. Which means she survived the throne room.

This is proof she is alive and free.

I read it again and revel in how clever she is. Sora wrote expecting that the letter could be intercepted and read. There is nothing incriminating in the note, but she is telling my father that our assassination plan failed because it was the king behind the plot all along. She is also letting him know that she still plans on killing King Joon within a month. And she wants to ensure her sister will be safe in the meantime.

But all I can focus on is the fact that she is trying to tell my father that I am in Idle Prison—*Tiyung is idling the day away*. She is warning him and trying to help me. The same way she begged for my life in the throne room of Qali.

She cares. Maybe it isn't love, but she is still doing all she can to free me. She still believes I can make it out of here.

Tears fill my eyes, and warmth spreads down my chest. She doesn't have to care. I wouldn't blame her if she walked away from my suffering the way I walked away from hers many times as a boy. But Sora is better than me—she always has been. I won't let her brave efforts be in vain. I will make it through this for her. Even if she may love Hana, not me.

I draw a breath and sigh, holding the letter to my chest. But soon my smile fades. Something is off about this whole thing. Namely, the fact that I have it. This message never reached my father, so why did Hana give it to me? She hates me and my family. Why did she leave me a lantern and the letter?

Maybe she is trying to get me to trust her. But to what end? I don't have a lot of options in here.

I puzzle over it for a long while, trying to solve the riddle. I would think that it's just kindness, but Hana isn't Sora. She has no reason to be kind; therefore, she is not.

Eventually, I give up. In whichever way Hana meant it, the letter and the lantern are a gift. One I will remember.

I stare at Sora's letter until the oil finally burns out.

And then I'm alone again in the dark.

CHAPTER FOURTEEN

EUYN

THE NORTHERN PASS, KHITAN

We are around a bell outside of the city walls of Quu when the rain turns to snow. Not a blizzard, but constant large flakes. The fresh snow is pretty, covering the country in a blanket of pure white, but it does make travel trickier. Our horses are halibreds—fast, normally, but not sure-footed winter horses built for trekking through deep snow.

Half a bell later, we find a trading post and exchange our mounts. They don't have winter horses, so instead we take a sleigh large enough for us and our gear. It is dark wood and around twelve feet long with two benches—one in the front, one in the back. Four califers are tied to it. Califers are a cross between caribou and horses. A team of four will still be slower than winter horses, but they were our only viable option, so we will have to make do.

With Mikail taking the reins, we head directly north to Lake Cerome.

"It's fucking freezing." Royo blows a breath into his bare hands.

He's complained numerous times since we left the Gray Shore Inn. The conditions aren't that bad—he is just in a foul mood. He'd rather be at the ball with Aeri, and I can't say I blame him. Between the snow and wind, it's not a pleasant journey. I'd also rather not risk traveling through the night, but we have to reach the temple before the information disappears, and we need him with us. Someone willing to kill a priest means there's danger, so the more men we have, the more muscle, the better.

No one knows who the Yoksa are, generally speaking. Of course, spies constantly follow the known Yoksa in Yusan, but they change often. All records have to be brought to the repository by scroll, book, or person, however, and that makes them trackable. The Yoksa are known as independent, and their records veritable truth, but with enough blades and power, history can be malleable.

The old king Theum invaded the Yusanian temple and changed the records not long after he took the throne. I am not certain what he altered—I doubt anyone living knows. But my supposed father is not the only one who has forced his spin on history. The written atrocities of Wei are far milder than what Yusan endured.

And now, someone is trying to alter history in Khitan at any cost. If I had to guess, it's my sister.

Quilimar is ruthless and more than apt for slaughter. As a teenager, she killed a chambermaid she found fault with. She murdered multiple fencing opponents, despite the fact that those matches were supposed to end at the touch. She claimed all those fights were legal, her competitors agreeing to gamble their lives. And the rumor is she murdered her suitor, the western count's brother.

When Joon signed her marriage certificate to the King of Khitan over her pleas for mercy, she attacked our brother. She tried to slit his throat, and it was one of the few times I actually saw fear in Joon's eyes. If I had to guess, Quilimar knows we are in Khitan and she is destroying the exceptions to the Rule of Distance so that no one can reach her again.

"It's still a day and a few bells to get there?" Royo grumbles, adjusting his coat. He's seated between me and Mikail, a buffer in our stalemate.

"Normally," Mikail says. "But we can sleep in shifts, and with the four califers pulling us, I think we will make it there in less time."

"Great." The scar on Royo's face moves as he scowls.

"Royo, maybe you should sleep first," Mikail suggests. "There's room in the back of the sleigh for you to lie down."

I'm not sure if Mikail wants to speak to me privately or if he's tired of Royo's sour attitude. Either way, Royo takes the hint and climbs into the back. There are blankets along with weapons and our bags on the bench. None of us were comfortable leaving our things at the inn. I wasn't comfortable there at all, between the poor quality and the feeling that we were being watched.

Mikail and I sit in silence as he steers the sleigh through the dusky snowfall. The sun sets, but the monsoon moon is huge and illuminates the white snow. The effect creates so much light that it's easy to see across the open fields. I wish conversation glided as easily as the sleigh.

I look at his handsome profile and wait for him to say something, anything, but the only noises are the wind and Royo's snoring as we travel toward the moon. The night is so still, the moon so close, it feels like we could reach the lunar goddess. The snow has a kind of magic that makes it difficult to remember that we're on a dangerous mission to the Temple of Knowledge.

"I think it's Quilimar," I say.

Mikail finally looks over at me. He has barely spared me a glance since we reached the harbor, and not many on the ship, either. But his attention still causes the same stirring in my lower stomach, the same pull in my chest.

"I think my sister ordered the murder of the Yoksa," I add.

He nods. "I'm nearly certain of it, but Joon has a greater plan in motion than just the ring, so he may be behind the murder. It could also be both of them."

"Both?" I shiver and adjust the hood of my coat as the temperature continues to fall. The wind hitting the open sleigh makes it worse, although Mikail seems unbothered. Then again, he never seems fazed by anything as ordinary as the elements.

"Working together," he says. "I have been trying to figure out why

Joon would keep us alive—specifically me. I am a commoner and a threat to his rule. Surely it would have been easier to kill me in the throne room than to send me on this mission. Yes, the country needs gold, but why break the peace to steal the ring? Why risk another war? Maybe it is all a ruse. Maybe he's not plotting *against* Quilimar, but with her."

I consider the possibility of Joon and Quilimar working together. It would be a formidable alliance if it were possible. But it is not.

"I doubt it," I say. "Joon and Quilimar genuinely hate each other. When he forced her to marry, it turned from dislike to bad blood. The ring is likely just part of his plan to acquire all the relics of the Dragon Lord."

Mikail's eyes shift. "All of them?"

I nod. "You know we constantly try to take the Water Scepter from Wei. And he already acquired the Flaming Sword."

"Stolen from Gaya during the Festival of Blood, yes," Mikail says, his jaw tightening. "But the cost to acquire all of them is enormous. Not to mention that the amulet was lost long ago. Joon is pragmatic to the core, and I don't think he would believe it's possible to get all five."

"Since when has a king worried about what is possible?"

Mikail's eyes narrow, and then he nods. "Fair point, but these relics are invaluable. Khitan will do anything to protect and keep its ring. And the Water Scepter is Wei's most prized possession. It has never seemed worth the blood price to try to steal it, because even though Wei uses the scepter to magic their waters, their nation would still function without it. They just wouldn't have an unsinkable navy."

"You really don't know the reason?" I ask.

He glances at me, arching an eyebrow, and I can't help the rush of warmth in my cheeks as his gaze darts to my lips for the briefest of moments. But then he seems annoyed.

"I'm just surprised," I say. "I figured you knew, as you usually have better sources than I do."

Mikail smirks and turns back to guiding the sleigh.

I rush on, eager to capture his attention again. "It's the myth that once a king unites all of the relics on his body, he will become the Dragon Lord on earth."

Mikail purses his full lips as he stares into the distance. I missed him. I missed just talking with him this past week. My heart feels lighter, better when he's speaking to me. Even if he won't get physically close to me ever again, at least I can savor this moment.

"In other words, he will possess *all* the powers of a god," I add.

"How is that even possible?" he asks.

"Etherum." I shrug. But he eyes me. What he meant was that he hasn't heard the rest of the legend. I clear my throat. "The myth is that as he ascended back into the Heavens, his powers were sealed into the relics. Some versions have the god bound to do the king's bidding once the relics are reunited. Others have it as more of a merger of a celestial and human being. The result, however, is the same."

"Stars," Mikail whispers and snaps the reins to urge the califers into a trot. "With that kind of power…"

"He could do absolutely anything. Reshape the entire world."

We both sit in the horror of that thought. The realms have not seen that kind of power since the Dragon Lord walked the earth. I can only assume that a man can't survive becoming a god, but we both know that Joon would do it. He is the most ambitious king Yusan has had in centuries.

Mikail eyes me. "Reshape the world, metaphorically speaking?"

I shake my head. "No, he would use the power to sink Wei into the East Sea."

Mikail laughs, the sound ringing out into the night. "His goal, with all of that power, is genocide? Of course it is."

"His goal is to eliminate a centuries-old enemy," I correct.

Even though it happened years ago, I still remember Joon telling me bedtime stories when I was a boy. Due to the death of King

Theum and our twenty-two-year age difference, Joon was like a father to me when I was young. And I used to love him like one. He'd sneak me treats when I couldn't sleep and tell me how all of Yusan would cheer when the Dragon Lord returned and pushed the isles of Wei back into the sea.

"Correct me if I'm wrong, but didn't he provoke Wei in the War of the Flaming Sword?" Mikail says.

He's not wrong. "After he took the sword from Gaya, Joon thought he could conquer Wei, but we were outmatched due to their navy. There was also a rumor that he couldn't wield the sword, though I don't believe that."

"Nor do I," Mikail says. "Joon is of royal blood, or the crown wouldn't work."

I nod, pretending like I haven't lived in fear of disintegrating to ash due to the Immortal Crown. I'm glad that's one of the few secrets that didn't spill out in the throne room. Mikail is disgusted enough that I didn't tell him about Chul. I can't imagine how far he'd slip away if he knew I wasn't Baejkin.

"Regardless, ever since we lost the war, we've had to pay Wei an unreasonable tribute. If we didn't need to send that money, a lot of the problems could be fixed in Yusan, from poverty to laoli addiction. And with Wei eliminated, we would finally be safe."

"By 'Wei eliminated,' you mean hundreds of thousands of people murdered," Mikail says. "Killing off nearly an entire race. Sinking islands full of innocent men, women, and children into the sea. Those who had nothing to do with the War of the Flaming Sword or the scepter."

He smacks the reins, and the califers speed up even more.

Mikail's posture stiffens, his face full of hate. I'm not sure why he is so disgusted. He calls the people of Wei innocent, but they are not. They had no issue slaughtering untold numbers of civilians in Yusan and Khitan over the last thousand years, and no qualms about taking just as many back to their islands as slaves. Even the Yoksa don't know how many people they've killed and tortured.

During the War of the Flaming Sword, they used Yusanian children and babies for arrow practice. They emptied the brothels in Tamneki and put the indentures aboard their ships to entertain their soldiers. Then they drowned them before they reached the shore. All of them. Noblewomen and first sons were brought back to Wei as prizes, treated as concubines or common pleasure slaves. Wei committed acts never heard of before once they arrived on our shore. Weians are many things, but they are not innocent. At best they are complicit, benefiting from atrocity for generations.

"You know how Joon thinks," I say with a shrug.

Joon, like all the Baejkin kings, puts Yusan above all else. It is one thing I can say in defense of my family: they truly love our realm. Mikail seems to think there is an issue with not being shepherds of the entire world, when no nation does that. Each realm cares for its own. Each reign stops at the borders.

"And you?" he asks. "Do you believe it would solve our problems, too? To sink the three islands of Wei?"

Technically, it's more than three. Wei is a hundred islands, but over ninety percent of the population lives on the three main isles. Without Illiyo, Song, and Wal, Wei wouldn't have any power.

Mikail holds himself casually, relaxing his shoulders, but he stares at me out of the corner of his eyes.

I shrug. "I see his logic. We need to stop the tribute, and I doubt Wei will just agree to forfeit millions of mun. And without the sizable threat of Wei, we would be safe on our continent. As would Khitan."

Mikail smiles. "I see."

His gloved hands curl into tight fists, and his jaw ticks. He's furious, but I don't understand why.

"What's wrong?" I ask.

He doesn't respond. I stare at him and wait, but he remains silent. Minutes pass and still nothing. I suppose that was all he wanted to say.

I hate how I wait on him. How desperate I am for him to talk to me. How much it throws me when he's upset. It should be the other way around. I should be the one sought after. But that has never been the case with Mikail.

"Who is Ailor?" I ask after a few minutes.

More silence greets me.

He doesn't speak another word. A bell later, I try again to get Mikail to talk, but he simply ignores me. The insult slaps my face harder than this biting wind. No one would have dared ignore me when I was a prince of Yusan. Servants could have been thrown into Idle Lake for that kind of offense. But I am not a prince anymore.

Unless I bring Joon the ring.

With the distance growing between me and Mikail, it seems more and more tempting to regain my old position than our old love.

Yet my skin prickles with an uneasy feeling. I truly don't know why he is upset. I know he is angry with me for not telling him about Chul, but that doesn't seem like enough to drive this large of a wedge between us. Plus, the distance started in Tamneki. It has to be something…or *someone* else. My stomach sours at the thought, and I swallow my conspiracies. Perhaps it *is* just Chul. I soothe myself with the thought that Mikail is just being stubborn, even though that doesn't seem quite right.

Either way, it's going to be a long trip. I hope the girls are doing better than we are.

CHAPTER FIFTEEN

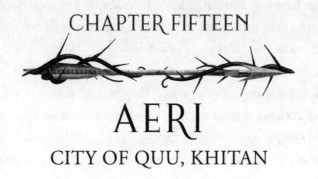

AERI
CITY OF QUU, KHITAN

Tonight was a total failure. All I learned is that the ambassador thinks he is excellent at everything, beloved by everyone, and likes to ice fish. Not really the realm-shattering secrets we were hoping to uncover.

"But how do you keep from freezing?" Sora asked during dessert. No idea how she had questions when the ambassador spoke nonstop.

"There are warming huts by the shore," he said. "Or you can make a fire right on the ice."

"A fire on the ice?" Sora gasped. "How incredible."

She looked at the ambassador as if she hung on his every word. I don't know how she did it.

The meal ended without us getting a second chance to talk to the general. We'll have to find another way. If Mikail can get ahold of the blueprints to her office, then I can sneak in. Or maybe they are doing better than we are. I hope so. It would be hard to do worse.

Dancing begins, and I wish Royo were here for the hundredth time tonight. Yes, he'd hate this whole thing, and he'd refuse to dance with me. He'd probably stand by the map on the wall with his arms folded, refusing to enjoy life. But I would try, and he would soften. And then eventually, maybe he'd hold me like the couples spinning around the floor.

It's almost like I can feel his hands on my waist, but then I remember he hates me and a knot forms in my throat.

The moment the music starts, the ambassador takes the opportunity to paw at Sora. They make their way toward the center of the room, and I wander closer to the general while admiring the golden weapons on the wall. The part of me that will always be a thief considers stealing one. My fingers itch to take the jewel-encrusted throwing knife, but I leave the blade alone. The last thing I need is to cause a scene or alert the many guards in this room. We are only here to gather information.

Instead, I move toward the enormous map of Khitan. I find Lake Cerome. It's not far from Vashney, the original capital of Khitan. Quu itself was once part of Yusan. Khitan invaded during a war centuries ago and battled Yusan until they gained this warm-water port.

"The queen remains sequestered," a woman says in Yusanian. I think she's speaking to me, but then another voice answers her.

"For her own protection and the prince's, I'm sure," a man's voice says. "It was a terrible event."

My heart races, but I stay still with my back to them, studying the map. I hope they'll gossip freely in a room that can't understand them.

"They blame Yusan, you know. The people of Khitan clamor for war, having already accepted her." The woman sounds not entirely thrilled by either fact.

"Of course," the man says. "The queen opened the coffers for a widows and orphans fund and built housing for the poor. She increased the realm food subsidy and allowed the gambling halls to reopen. All within the month since the king died mysteriously. All shrewdly popular moves. The queen may have murdered her husband, but she is brilliant."

I wonder if these changes are as calculating as these diplomats believe, or if Quilimar has helped the people because she cares. If a ruler is doing good for the people, bettering the lives of thousands, does it even matter?

"The ambassador has a new favorite," the woman says.

"I hear he's to be made regent for the Count of Tamneki," the man says.

"Then he'll be able to afford such splendid company," the woman says. "Unless, of course, Seok gets there first."

I bite back a gasp at the mention of the man who holds Sora's indenture.

"To the courtesan or to the young Count of Tamneki?"

"Both."

They laugh.

I look back at Sora, and something is off about her. Her spine and movements are rigid as she dances, and she's never rigid. She flows like water. So that's weird.

But then I see *him* and forget to breathe.

Shit. It took me way too long to realize who Sora is dancing with. She'd been dancing with the ambassador and then a handsome, older guy cut in. I didn't think anything of it because nearly everyone wants to meet Sora. But I should've kept a closer eye on her. This one looks a lot like Ty. Which means that's Seok—the count who owns her and her sister. The one the diplomats were just gossiping about.

Shit. Shit. Shit.

She walks away from him and makes it a few steps before her knees give out. Her palm smacks one of the tables as she tries to steady herself.

I race to her and catch her before she falls. She's pale as snowfall, and her lips quiver. Sora doesn't even flinch. She certainly doesn't break down. So, something terrible must've happened.

I put my shoulder under her arm to try to help her walk out of the room. Seok stares and then shakes his stupor.

"Guards! Authorities! There is an assassin in the room! Protect the general."

Great. His words cause pure chaos. Guards shift to alert, and people begin to scream and run. The general is spirited out by a squadron of guards.

"Run," I whisper to Sora.

She can't. Sora can't move. She's falling apart in a way I haven't seen, which can only mean something happened to Daysum.

I eye her with sympathy, but we need to get the hells out of here. And it would be good if she could help.

She can't.

Fuck. What do I do now? I'm not strong enough to carry her, and Royo isn't here.

I had the same problem on the Sol River when the pirates attacked. I couldn't move someone as big as Royo. But at least I could cut the lifeboat, get it beneath him, and let him fall into it as I froze and unfroze time. I can't do that in the armory. There's no lifeboat here.

I look around and spot a dessert cart. That'll work. I run over to it.

Once I'm within a foot of the cart, I reach into my dress and grab the amulet. With the Sands of Time in my palm, everything instantly stops. The sands of the golden bell glass freeze mid-fall. Sora looks ready to faint, but she stops breathing. People are mid-stride, mid-scream, but everyone is suddenly still. There's not a movement or a sound. The quiet is the oddest part. Well, the whole thing is weird, since it's god magic. But the quiet of etherum always throws me off.

I push the desserts off the cart and then shove Sora onto it. It's not dignified, but I have to move fast. With every second I hold time, I lose about a day, then a sunsae, then a month. The longer I hold, the quicker I lose my life. And the toll has only gotten worse. The cost seems to be increasing, the fatigue and aging hitting harder and faster with every use.

Once I have Sora on the cart, I wheel her out of the armory to the waiting carriages. As soon as I can, I unfreeze time.

Fatigue hits me like a tidal wave. I only held time for about twenty seconds, but it feels like I haven't slept well in six months. I wince and bear it, forcing myself to remain upright as time tries to drag me down.

Sora blinks, looking around. She, of course, has no idea what just happened. Royo didn't, either, when he fell into the boat, but he also hit his head. With Sora, it's different. One second she was in the armory, and now she is outside in the rain that started falling heavily once I let go of the amulet. She stands up and shakes her head.

"What just happened?" she asks.

"No time to explain. Get in," I say. Even my voice sounds weary.

The confused valet races to open the carriage door for us. I don't know whose carriage this is, and it doesn't matter.

"Bring the lady to the Gray Shore Inn. She is in distress." I hold my head high as I settle onto the seat and issue the command like I'm nobility. Like of course this coachman will take me anywhere I demand.

But it works. Looking and acting upper class takes you far. Even in this land of supposed equals.

The carriage begins to roll away. I breathe a sigh of relief and lean against the plush blue velvet. The fatigue in my bones makes it difficult to breathe.

"I don't understand—how did we go from inside the armory to outside?" Sora asks.

It's night, but with the huge monsoon moon, I can see her clearly. She looks thoroughly confused when her head tilts and her eyebrows knit.

"You don't remember?" I ask. I always have to act as surprised as anyone. "Hmm, I guess you don't. You fainted, and I rolled you out on the dessert cart. Sorry it wasn't more dignified, but I couldn't carry you."

It's as good an excuse as any.

"Oh," she says, smoothing her dress.

She allows herself to accept my answer because no one ever

thinks it's etherum. Magic is never anyone's go-to explanation.

"Thank you, Aeri. I really..." Her voice wobbles. "I really appreciate it."

Sora stares blankly out the window and twists her hands in her lap. I know that distressed, shocked look. I've seen it in the mirror.

"Do you want to talk about it?" I venture.

"Not just yet," she says.

Then she starts to cry.

CHAPTER SIXTEEN

ROYO

THE NORTHERN PASS, KHITAN

I t's real fucking awkward riding on a three-man sled with two lovers who aren't talking to each other. I thought they were okay when I fell asleep, but I guess they had another fight. I dunno, I passed out.

I didn't think I'd sleep when I laid down, but the next thing I knew, they were waking me. It's still dark out, but it's Euyn's turn to rest. He got me up and went in the back. They haven't said a word since.

Mikail sits next to me as I drive the sled. It's not hard to steer, since the animals are tied together with a leather harness. But it is hard to see the road with all this snow.

"We just keep heading north 'til we get there?" I ask.

Mikail nods. "Yes, the lake is a little northwest of the old capital, but we can use this pass until we're almost there."

Easy enough, since a compass hangs next to the lantern on the sled.

Mikail gets quiet again, which is weird for him.

"You okay?" I ask.

He goes back to being casual. "Just running through possibilities."

"Of."

He sighs. "Success. What it means. Baejkin rule. And other mysteries."

"What about Baejkin rule?" I ask.

The plan has been to put Euyn on the throne from the beginning. I don't get what he's confused about. The country can only be run by Baejkins, and he's the last prince left.

Mikail motions his head in the direction of the back seat. I glance over my shoulder. It's gotta be three bells in the morning. Euyn has been asleep for a bell. Or at least he's pretending. I guess Mikail doesn't want to risk it.

"Okay," I say. "What mysteries?"

Mikail pulls a key out of his pocket. "I stole this from the ambassador."

I keep one eye on the road but glance over at the key. I've never seen one like it. It looks like it's made of pure jade and gold. It's real fancy with a lot of nooks, which means it fits a complicated lock. Definitely not one Aeri could pick with hairpins.

Oh good. I'm thinking about her again.

I shake it off. I don't need that right now. "What's that go to?"

"That's one mystery," he says. "It's no ordinary door—that's for certain. I've seen thousands of keys, and none look like this."

I think about what it could be for, but I've got nothing. I'm not the brains of this outfit anyhow.

"How are we going to get into an underwater temple, anyway?" I ask.

"That's another mystery," he says. "There has to be a way in, as there wouldn't be enough air in a glass dome for anyone to survive the six months it's buried. It's a matter of finding access. Hopefully a door."

"Maybe that's the key to it," I say.

Mikail raises his eyebrows but then slowly smiles. "You know, you might be right. I've never seen keys to a Temple of Knowledge. That, of course, would beg the question of why the ambassador, a man not particularly known for his intellect, has one. But that's a mystery for another day. If he were somehow a priest, it would also explain why he knew about the murder. Although, the body was found in Trialga Square, so it's not exactly a secret. It could all just be a scheme to send us to the temple. The key in his office was rather convenient—maybe too much so." He pauses and stares into the distance. "Why keep it under a medal of valor if he wanted me to find it, though?"

His thoughts make my head hurt. They spin so fast in so many directions. I don't know how he deals with it.

"It could be an ambush," he finally says. "Zeolin knows we are not with the girls. He knows that I need to find an exception to the Rule of Distance and that I would go to the Temple of Knowledge to seek that information."

My stomach sinks at the mention of Sora and Aeri.

"You mean Aeri is in danger, or *we* are?"

He shrugs. "Could be both. Euyn said we were being watched. I thought he was just being paranoid, but maybe he was correct."

He's so casual, it takes me a second to realize what he's saying. Anger and worry fill me as heat flushes my cheeks. Did I leave Aeri when there was a threat?

"Are you fucking—"

Mikail's head suddenly snaps to the right. He holds up a hand for quiet, but I'm about to turn this sled around. We need to go back for Aeri and Sora. Fuck this frozen-temple thing.

But he's so alert, so still, that I scan around, too.

It's all white snow, and then it's pitch black where there's woods. I'm not sure what is up with this guy. There's nothing out there.

I grit my teeth. "But Aeri—"

"Shh!" he hisses.

My hand balls in a fist. No one tells me to shut up. Not ever. Tension fills my body like a crossbow being cocked. I don't really like Mikail, and at the end of the day I don't trust him. I still don't get why he tried to destroy the crown. I still don't think he's telling us everything.

I'm ready to knock him out, and then I see them: eight eyes

shining just past the tree line.

Zaybears.

I uncurl my fist and rake a hand down my face. Ten Hells. We're fucked.

CHAPTER SEVENTEEN

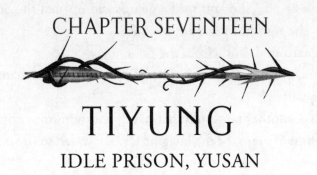

TIYUNG

IDLE PRISON, YUSAN

It's hard to tell if it's day or night, but I lean back against the stone wall and cross my arms to go to sleep. I rest a lot to maintain my strength and to pass the time. I sleep sitting up, of course—the straw bed is laden with vermin.

Sometimes, when I'm very lucky, I get to dream of Sora. Her laugh. Her smile. Her voice. I get to be in her presence again. I imagine dining with her at that table in Aseyo. Her gorgeous face and her brave spirit that would stand up to the God of War himself.

The next thing I know, we're back in her room in the Fountain Inn in Tamneki. I know it's a dream because I can freely kiss her, make love to her, and I can't do that in reality—not when her body is likely poison. Still, we were able to satisfy each other that one beautiful night, to be more intimate than just tumbling into bed.

In this version, she smiles and asks me to stay with her. I do, even though somewhere in my mind I know it's the morning we are supposed to kill the king.

A sound pulls me back to reality, back to the dungeon floor. I shake my head. No. I'm not getting woken from this for some stale bread. Not this dream.

Then I realize it's not the sound of a meal tray. It's the door opening again.

I come to and slowly open my eyes as Hana walks in.

"That'll be all," she says to the guard who opened the door. Her tone says she significantly outranks him.

The guard nods and closes the door.

Zahara, she called herself. She gave herself a new name along with a new life.

She has another lantern in her hand, and raindrops cling to her cloak. I think it's rain. I can't imagine it's lake water, so the monsoons must've started.

Hana observes me for a moment, then sighs and tosses down a cloth sack. It falls open on the ground in front of me. Food! Inside, there's cured meat and cheese bursting from paper wrappings. It's enough calories that I won't starve for days, maybe a week.

She is keeping me alive.

I would think that she was trying to poison me, but she wouldn't need this much food to do it. She could put tabernacle in my water, and I would be dead in seconds. I want to scramble to the sack, but I hold myself in place. I'm certain this gift comes with strings. What does she want in return? My stomach groans, my hunger not caring about the conditions, but I won't do a thing that will hurt Sora.

"Why are you doing this?" I ask. "Why are you being kind?"

A cold stare greets me. "Because I'm not like your bloodline."

She doesn't demand information or anything else. She just watches me.

"I… Thank you," I say.

I tear into the paper, unwrapping the rest of a sausage and hard cheese. My body is so eager for sustenance that my hands shake.

I gnaw bites right off. The food plays like a symphony on my tongue, and I go back for more. All the amazing meals I took for granted in my life were not as good as this one. I know if I eat too fast, I'll get sick, but I can't seem to slow down. I suppose this is why Euyn eats the way he does. He was starved once in here as well. Deprivation clings to you while excess gives up the moment it stops.

Hana eyes me. "You know, I find it odd…"

I wait for her to continue, but she casually strolls around the cell. I can't tell if she's giving me a chance to eat or letting silence sink in. Either way, I rip off a chunk of bread. It will help cut the richness of the food.

"What do you find odd?" I finally ask.

She comes to a stop. "That you haven't mentioned saving my brother."

I choke on the bread and have to take a moment to drink some water.

How does she know? Nayo was the first indenture I bought. Hana's death was fresh on my mind, and her brother was the last child sold by my father and therefore the easiest to locate. I'd worried that Nayo had been purchased by my uncle's pleasure houses. It would've been much more difficult and expensive to buy his freedom from a place like that, but he was sold as a private pleasure boy to a nobleman in Leep. Nayo was there for around a month before I finally negotiated a price for him.

The boy was never told I bought his freedom. I was specific about that. I never wanted the sale traced back to me.

How does she know?

Hana rolls her eyes and sighs. "How many people do you think have the means to free a pleasure indenture? And it certainly wasn't out of the goodness of his owner's heart."

She curls her lip, and I'm quite certain that the noble who bought him is now dead. I try to find sympathy for the murdered man, but there's only one kind of person who would be the highest bidder for an indenture sold by my father—no one worthy of pity.

"Nayo was given a gold bar worth a thousand mun and put in a carriage to Tamneki," Hana says. "Why?"

She sharply focuses on me, her hands behind her back.

I'd worked through an intermediary to maintain anonymity, paying with my generous annual allowance. My instructions had been to give Nayo enough money to start a life somewhere far from the southern region. I didn't want to risk my father finding him. I thought he'd naturally flee to Khitan, but after he was freed, I didn't inquire. For the first time, I felt good about something I'd done, so I moved on to finding the next indenture.

Not long after I bought out the second contract, my mother discovered what I was doing. She is the one who helped me hide it from Seok and locate three others—the last being when I was in Rahway. She said if I was going to do something so foolish, I should at least not be foolish about it. But I could tell that she was proud.

Hana waits for an answer.

"To free him," I say.

Her eyes scan from side to side. "For what purpose?"

I shrug. "That was the purpose."

Her expression hardens. "What was the real reason?"

She thinks I'm trying to deceive her because I am Seok's son, and therefore I must have another motive. There is no goodness in my bloodline in her mind.

She's not terribly wrong. We have been rich and powerful for centuries, and no family stays that way without dirtying their souls.

"What is the play? What do you want?" She steps closer. "What is Seok planning?"

"Hana, Seok doesn't know," I say. "The point was to free Nayo and give him some money to start over again. I couldn't ever replace what was taken from him, but I believed that his sister was dead and that he would needlessly suffer in Leep. I wanted to help because I could."

Hana exhales, hard eyes narrowing on me. She swoops down and picks up the rest of the food. I want to tackle her and rip the sack from her hand, but I hold myself back. Barely.

"When you're ready to be honest, we can try again," she says.

Panic floods me. I need that food. But also, I need answers.

"Where is Sora?" I ask.

Hana whips around, anger transforming her beautiful face

into something truly frightening. But she contains herself at the last moment. She stands straight. "Khitan. And you might want to cooperate if you care about her at all."

"What?" I ask. "Why do you say that? Is she in danger?"

A million thoughts race through my mind. What is she doing in Khitan? She wouldn't have run with Daysum being held by my father. So she must have been sent there.

"She's been in danger since she was nine years old," Hana says. "And now she has to steal the Golden Ring of the Dragon Lord or she will die."

She has to take the Golden Ring of Khitan?

"Why?"

I barely get the word out before pain knocks the air from my chest and my stomach revolts. I groan, dropping my last piece of cured meat.

Hana smiles as I grip my sides. "You of all people should know what men are willing to do for power."

Pain like I've never felt before courses through my body. Poison.

I collapse onto the floor, sweating and shaking, rolling onto my side. I moan like the iku, unable to stop myself.

Hana takes the lantern, steps over me, and leaves.

I wait for death.

CHAPTER EIGHTEEN

AERI

CITY OF QUU, KHITAN

Sora and I make it back to the inn, but what do I do now? I tip the coachman and thank him for his discretion, which means *keep your mouth shut about this.* But I'm so exhausted that it's hard to think straight. I drag my battered body into the inn. Sora wanders in after me.

All I want to do is flop onto my bed and sleep, but I need to take care of Sora. I need a plan. So, even though I can barely move, I bring her to my room.

As I unlock my door, I force my mind to focus. Seok knows Sora is in Quu, and I'm sure it won't be hard to figure out where we're staying. This isn't his country, but money and power have a way of transcending borders. He already tried to have Sora detained in the armory—I doubt he'll just say *oh never mind* now.

We can't stay.

But I want to. I'm so tired, and I'm not sure where everyone else is. I know they're going to Lake Cerome, but there's no telling how far they've gotten. Maybe we should stay put and wait for them as planned.

No. I pace as Sora drops into an armchair. The more I think about it, the more certain I am that we need to leave. At a minimum, Seok will try to have Sora arrested. The only reason to stay at the inn is because I'm tired.

I sigh to myself. We need to leave tonight and meet Royo, Mikail, and Euyn at the lake or along the way.

Now I need to relay the plan to Sora, which is easier said than done. Seok broke her completely. She's in no shape for a journey.

"Did you know there's an owl on your windowsill?" Sora stares out the window and gestures with a limp hand.

"Oh, um, yeah… I did," I say. "I'm not sure if she fell out of her nest or got abandoned or what, but when we checked in, this tiny moon owl was already living there. I gave her fabric for a nest, and I've been feeding her. I named her Dia."

Honestly, I don't know if the owl is female or not, but in my head she is. She is snowy white with big amber eyes.

"That's sweet," Sora says. Because even though she's in shambles, she still thinks to compliment me.

I reach into the pocket of my dress and pull out a napkin. I hid some food for Dia during the banquet. Moon owls are always small, but this one is tiny—the size of a sparrow. I think they eat moths and maybe baby mice or worms. But I don't have those, so some shreds of wild boar and crusts of bread will have to do.

Dia cautiously hops to the other side of the sill when I open the window, but I lay down the napkin and she dives right in.

Sora smiles slightly.

"Do you want to tell me what happened?" I ask.

She shakes her head and takes a deep breath, trying to brace herself. "Se-ok… He… He sold…Daysum."

Her breathing is jagged, and her eyes well with tears before she convulses into sobs.

I put my hand over my mouth to hide my gasp. Sora said Seok had threatened to sell her sister to the pleasure houses if we failed to kill the king. But I didn't think he'd actually do it when we still plan on taking the crown.

Anger at Seok, at her position, and at my father floods me, and it's hard to remember to breathe. Sometimes it feels like fire rises through my limbs and I'll just ignite. And there's no way to extinguish it. Not when men like this are still in power.

I grit my teeth as I remember that *I* was supposed to be sold to a pleasure house.

The reason I hate the cold is because I froze on the street after running from men who tried to kidnap me to sell me to the brothels. They came into my room as I was sleeping at my first boarding house. I used the amulet to flee, but I didn't know where to go. I looked sixteen, but really, I was only twelve. I wound up curling in a ball behind a sugar house. I shook in the alley, freezing all night, and tried to hold on until they turned on the ovens. My lips were blue by the time the sun came up. And now, whenever I get cold, my body remembers nearly dying.

"I'm sorry," Sora says, sniffling. She wipes at her tears.

She's apologizing for her tears. As if being sad, as if love is some kind of weakness. Love is the greatest strength. Love powered her to endure all these years for her sister.

"No, I'm sorry," I say. "I'm sorry this happened."

Her eyes meet mine. A fierce determination lights her purple irises. "I need him to suffer."

My gaze hardens. "I know. He will." I mean it with every fiber of my being. "I swear it on my mother's soul."

She nods.

I take a breath. "Do you need a minute? Because I have a plan and—"

Dia lets out a loud screech. It's a sound I've never heard her make before.

I run to the window to see if there's a predator or something. And there is. But he's not hunting Dia.

He's after us.

CHAPTER NINETEEN

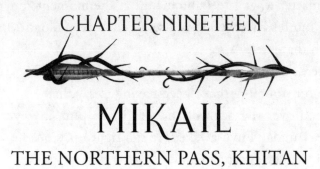

MIKAIL

THE NORTHERN PASS, KHITAN

You know, I really thought we were done with megafauna trying to eat us when we escaped from Fallow.

Apparently not.

Four zaybears stalk our sleigh from the tree line around seventy yards away. They move in the darkness of the forest, parallel to our sleigh, but they're getting closer. Their silhouettes are now visible in the snow. One would be a problem. Four is a full-blown crisis.

Zaybears are built like enormous black wolves, but with more strength and thicker pelts like bears. They're not as hard to kill as pigars, which have to be speared up close, but it's not easy. The best course of action is to simply not come across one.

Four means we have no chance of surviving.

Royo steers us straight along the pass as I weigh our options. I'm glad he finally stopped talking so I have the quiet to think. They're still a decent distance away, but we've attracted their attention and we can't outrun them should they chase us.

Zaybears are solitary hunters when grown, so these must be a mother and three juveniles. The juveniles are still seven feet long. The mother is ten.

I suppose it could be worse—a full-grown male is twelve feet.

But they stand about as tall as a man from the tips of their ears to the ground.

No matter what I feel about him at the moment, Euyn is still the best hunter I know. He is also a genocide apologist, but I can deal with that later.

If there's a later.

It's a bit troubling that I keep having to say that.

I reach over the back of the sleigh, keeping my eyes on the tree line. I nudge Euyn awake. He sits right up, since he was only pretending to be asleep anyhow.

His eyes meet mine, his stare filled with hope and curiosity. And love. Euyn loves me to the extent he can love anyone. Lately, though, I wonder if it's enough. For now, it needs to be.

"Zaybears," I say.

"Plural? You're joking." He looks around and sighs. "Are there really as many as I'm seeing?"

"Afraid so," I say.

"Gods on High," he mutters. He gets out his crossbow and belts of bolts, then slings them over his chest. He loads the bow. "All right."

"We're not gonna outrun them in this heavy sled," Royo says. "Let's get on these deer and make a break for it."

He's gripping the reins and pulling hard because the califers have just sensed the zaybears. They bolt, trying to leave the path, to get away from the threat.

The sled rocks, and I grab the front lip of the wood as Euyn thuds against the back bench.

"It won't work," I shout over the rushing wind.

Califers are herd animals. They won't stop until they physically can't run anymore. Climbing aboard them is no easy feat when they're trotting. At this speed, it's not possible. Plus, they're rigged to this sleigh and there are no saddles. At least one of us would fall off and be trampled.

Probably the one who thinks these animals are deer.

"We have to cut one free and leave it behind," Euyn says, struggling to regain his footing.

"You want *me* to cut the harness?" Royo yells, raising his eyebrows. His large hands are gripping the reins, so I'm not sure how he thinks he can grab his knife.

"No, he wants me to do it," I say.

I glance behind us, confirming what I already know—the zaybears are chasing the sleigh and gaining on us.

Euyn looks, too, and then leans forward. "Lose the one and hope the zaybears will be content with the sole kill."

I glance at him. It's so easy for him—the slaughter, the sacrifice for what he thinks is the greater good. In all the time we've known each other, I've never asked his thoughts on Gaya. Probably because I feared the answer.

But he does happen to be right in this case.

Before I can think too much about the poor creature I'm dooming, I lean forward, bracing my torso against the front rail of the sleigh. I lift my sword and aim for the leather band that holds the back harness together. I cut the right side in one motion. But there's still the other side keeping the animal in place.

I reach back to swing my blade, but just as my arm is raised, we hit a bump. Off-balance, my feet leave the floor of the sled. My sword slams into the wood of the lip, the blade sticking.

And then I'm falling out of the sleigh.

CHAPTER TWENTY

EUYN

THE NORTHERN PASS, KHITAN

We just lost Mikail.

One second, he was cutting the harness; the next, he was gone with only his sword left behind. He disappeared before I could even reach out to grab him. We must've hit an embankment, because the sled tilted and he flew off the side into the snow.

"Try to stop the sleigh," I yell.

"What? Are you serious? Where are you going?" Royo asks, bewildered.

"To save Mikail."

Or die with him, eaten by zaybears in this empty pass and left as carrion for the vultures. No hope to be with Mikail in this life or the next. However, there's no point in saying all that—and no time. I didn't die in Fallow with the samroc, and I'm not dying tonight in Khitan.

I hope.

Gods on High, this is so damn foolish.

I take a breath and leap out of the sleigh. I land and roll into the powdery snow. Mikail is about thirty yards away from me, weaponless, with two juvenile zaybears circling him. The other two continue to chase the sleigh.

With my bow to my shoulder, I aim at the first zaybear. I focus on the chest cavity for a kill shot. I home my gaze behind the right shoulder of the beast where I can hit his vital organs.

I don't think about Mikail or Royo or anything else. It's just me, a hunt, and a snowy night. My aim will be true. The beast will drop when I shoot it.

My breathing slows, my mind quieting. I exhale, and I pull the trigger.

I don't wait to see the animal fall, but I know it will. Instead, I cock the mechanism to reload the bow, put in another bolt, nock it, and bring it to my shoulder. I breathe and aim again, this time at the second beast. I look for the same place—behind the shoulder.

I fire.

A cry pierces the night. The second animal howls, but it continues to move. I don't know how. I felled the first with one bolt. That zaybear lies dying on the snow. Dark blood pools underneath it. But the second is still very much alive and making a terrible sound, because the bolt hit the rib.

A clean hit to the rib bone—it's the worst luck. And now the zaybear is injured but not dead. And very angry.

Gods on High.

I utter a long string of curses and reload to finish it off.

"Euyn!" Mikail yells. There's terror in his eyes as he stares at something behind me.

I turn. The largest zaybear is sprinting toward us—the mother. She's larger, faster, and more cunning than the juveniles. To make matters worse, I'll also have to shoot her head-on.

Mikail runs up beside me, arriving in moments. I'm worried for both of us, and it's impossible to block the world out this time. But with steady hands, I bring my bow to my shoulder. I aim for her neck as I can't aim for her chest without hitting the breastbone. I exhale and shoot. Success rushes through me as the bolt is on target.

But at the last second, she swerves.

The bolt tip misses her neck and grazes her shoulder instead.

She's bleeding, but not even slowed because I missed.

I can't believe I missed. I don't have time to reload. There are maybe eight seconds before she'll reach us. Reloading and aiming takes longer than that.

Mikail has a short dagger drawn, but he can't use that on a zaybear. He'll be mauled to death before he can do any damage. But in his eyes, there's the determination to try.

No. I won't let him. I won't let him die for me.

It feels like time slows, but last moments are always this way. There's the clean scent of the snow on the wind. I exhale a cloud of heat into the frosty air. It's a beautiful night, really—the moon is huge, so large it feels like I can reach up and touch it. And what closer feeling is there to being a god? I suppose the only thing closer has been loving Mikail. All the notes, the kisses, the nights spent in his arms. The feeling floods me.

The evening gets slower, quieter. The howling of the injured zaybear fades. I smile at Mikail. I see the boy he was and the man he became.

I've loved every version of him.

I toss my bow down and run at the zaybear. As she kills me, it will give Mikail time to escape, to find Royo and the sleigh. He'll live another day.

With hard breaths, I make it one step, two. But arms wrap around me and pull me back. Mikail's reflexes have always been unnaturally fast.

No! Foolish, stubborn, loving Mikail. He holds me as the zaybear leaps at us. We're both going to die. All I wanted was to save him, but now we will die together. I suppose that's still something—not dying alone.

Her claws are out, and her jaws are nearly on us. The smell of her breath is horrid, laced with the stench of rot and blood. I brace myself. Ready.

Suddenly, she falls from the air and careens into the snow. With a desperate cry, she rolls onto her side with an axe protruding from her spine.

Royo.

Mikail and I stare as he stands in the moonlight with his throwing arm out. A sword trails through the snow in his other hand.

Gods on High, I'm glad we made him come with us.

With the zaybear down, I scramble to grab my bow. The beast is injured, but she's not dead. The mother is not like the juvenile, who is still distracted by the bolt stuck in his side. She could attack to her last gasp. And she will, to save her cubs.

I reload the bow and take aim. The bolt leaves my crossbow and goes exactly where I aim—through her muzzle and into her skull.

She stops struggling, her head falling and her tongue lolling.

She's dead or close enough.

The last zaybear comes running toward us. I reload, ready to shoot, since he's near Royo. But instead of attacking, he runs to his mother. He sniffs her face, her body, then sits and howls.

The sound is haunting. I didn't know these animals could mourn.

Howling echoes around us, as the injured zaybear is still alive. I turn, aim again, and hit him between the ribs, this time killing him.

Then I focus on the last zaybear. I reload. For a second, I consider leaving it be, but the animal is a juvenile. Without his mother to teach him to kill, he will slowly starve to death. Or he could turn and decide to attack us. I can't risk it. I aim and fire at his heart. He falls on top of his mother.

It's silent now. Just the breathing of the three of us and the four dead zaybears bleeding crimson into the white ground.

My heart remembers to speed up, my skin prickling with the rush of the kill. Energy and a bit of euphoria flow through me from almost dying once again.

"I think we should go," Royo says. He points down the path where there's nothing but darkness in the distance.

The sleigh is gone, and Royo is right. We have to go. If we don't catch up to the califers, we may still die. Not a quick death by zaybears, but by freezing to death or being attacked by another predator.

We all take off running in the direction of the sled.

"You came back for me," Mikail says between puffs of breath. He sounds surprised as he glances at me.

Sure, now he wants to talk.

"Of course I did," I say.

He gives me a quizzical look, which is no easy feat when we're running as if our lives depend on it.

Mikail can out-sprint me—he's always been able to—so I wonder why he's not going faster. Then I realize he's keeping pace with me, to guard my flank. Because he still protects me. He'd still give his life for me until the end.

He smiles. "Every time I think I have you figured out, I don't."

"You say that like it's a good thing."

Mikail shrugs.

It's not normal, this love, but it's ours. I could never love anyone else like this. I could never love anyone else at all.

But does Mikail love me, or is it just loyalty? That was the question we never answered in Tamneki. Will he still be loyal when I tell him my plan to give Joon the ring?

I turn and scan the forest, making sure we aren't being followed by anything except Royo, who is slower than we are.

There's nothing behind the three of us aside from snow and my bolts sprouting out of the dead zaybears. Soon, they'll be covered by the storms as the monsoon continues, well buried until the next thaw. That would've been me if it weren't for Royo and Mikail.

We saved each other just in time.

But how long will time be on our side?

CHAPTER TWENTY-ONE

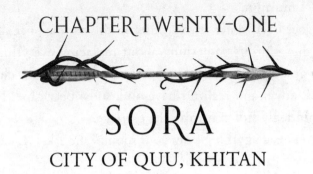

SORA

CITY OF QUU, KHITAN

Aeri is panicked and trying to speak to me, but she's talking very fast, and it feels like my head is underwater. My left ear is ringing like mad. All I can hear is Seok saying that he doesn't keep track of his brother's affairs. All I can see is his smile. And then all I feel is the fury that made me wish I had killed Tiyung myself. Ty, the man who'd tried to protect me, to free me, to love me, I wished I'd murdered him with my own mouth just to hurt his father. Just to take something, anything, away from Seok and be able to return a small part of the pain he's caused me. Just for the satisfaction of the moment.

Aeri is wrong—I am not that good of a person. I am not a good person at all. A good person wouldn't ever wish that.

Shame twists around me like a vine.

Hate can overcome and defeat goodness. Hate has the advantage of being easier. And there's no one I hate more than Seok. He took my family, my first love, all the girls in poison school, and now he took Daysum from me.

"...Okay?" Aeri gestures, arms flailing.

Oh. She was talking.

"I'm sorry, I don't understand," I say.

"We have less than a minute before guards burst in here, Sora! We need to go!"

"Oh," I murmur.

Aeri goes over to her trunk, pulls on the handle once, and then kicks it. She mutters something about replacing everything again and then grabs a velvet bag. She puts her new, heavy fur cloak back on. I look down and realize I have on a snow bear cape. I must've absent-mindedly stolen it from the carriage.

"Do you need anything from your room?" she asks. "Like, is there anything you can't live without?"

I have no idea.

Aeri groans and then takes my hand. She squeezes, pumping my fingers a few times. "Sora, I need you to focus. We have to get out of here now. We'll replace anything you leave behind, but get it together and let's go. Guards are coming in the front—I saw them when Dia screeched. They will arrest you and probably me. We need to try to sneak out the servant entrance. Now!"

I nod and follow her, but the truth is, I really don't care. I did so much. I stayed alive despite not wanting to, I endured nearly a decade of torture in poison school, and I murdered over eighteen men—all to prevent Daysum from being sold to Lord Sterling, to save her from being a pleasure house indenture. And yet it happened anyway. The very worst thing I could imagine has happened. What is the point of escaping? What is the point of living? Of continuing to struggle when nothing I do matters. I can't stem the tide of evil in this world, so why fight it?

I float down the back staircase after Aeri.

"Come on, Sora!" she whispers sharply.

I try to keep pace, because even in my haze I can see how frustrated she is. Aeri's body is rigid, and she keeps looking back at me. I make myself go faster so that I don't anger her. Plus, I really don't want her to get arrested because of me.

We go all the way to the basement. I follow Aeri as she breezes through the cold, stone space. She skirts along moldy boxes and dusty barrels, but I knock two over. Cannisters go rolling, loudly skittering across the floor. She shoots me a death stare, and I take more care. Then we go up some stairs that end at hinged metal doors. I have no idea how she knows about this exit.

Aeri unlatches the doors and then stops after she opens the right side. She waits with one hand grasping a blade and her other by her neck. Then she takes a breath before popping her head out. Her arm reaches down, and she pulls me up.

We're on the street behind the inn. I stand in the rain, looking around as she shuts the door with a soft click.

"Sora, please. You must focus," Aeri pleads.

I want to do what she says, but I just can't. I am empty. Nothing could fill this void.

"It's okay," I say. "I'm okay. Just leave me."

Her shoulders slump. "I can't do that."

"Why not?"

She gestures wildly and then slaps her hands to her sides. "Because you'll be caught. Because you and the others are like family, but not a family I've ever known. The one I've always wanted, one that actually gives a shit about me. And I'm *not* going to lose you. I lost my home once. I won't let it happen again."

It's sweet, but she's more determined and angry than anything else.

"Look, I know it's all terrible," she says. "I don't pretend like you should be smiling or anything. But Daysum is still alive. We can figure this out and save her, but in order to do anything, we have to get out of Quu. You have to snap out of it for ten minutes. Just… can you give me ten minutes? Once we find winter horses, I can lead yours, but you have to stay with me until then."

I hear her. I do. But I failed Daysum. It would be better for Aeri to go without me. Then she wouldn't have to risk me failing her as well.

I shake my head.

"Sora…" She trails off and purses her lips as if she's debating telling me something. "Seok is with the guards."

That name makes me focus. I wipe the rain from my face and dig my nails into my palms, arms trembling. Seok. The Count. I will see him suffer. I will see him choke on poisons. I will be the one to show him that power is an illusion but being powerless is real. I will be the one who tortures him to his blood-soaked death. But in order to do that, I need to escape now.

I raise my head and set my shoulders back.

"Come on," Aeri says. "He told you just to break you, but you survived. And you can't kill him if we're caught here."

She's right. I have to keep going. I have to see this through. I force all my feelings aside and become a blade once more.

I get my legs to work, and we start to run. She's very fast, even in a long dress and heavy cloak. I should've remembered that from Yusan. I struggle to keep pace with her, my legs working harder under the weight of this ball gown and fur, but I manage.

After a few turns, we get to the stables, and she slows to a walk. We saunter up, appearing calm, as if we're not fleeing, but I'm glad we stopped running. My lungs haven't been the same since Oxerbow poisoning when I was sixteen. I get winded easily now.

"Wait here," she says. "You're too memorable."

I stand around the corner from the stables. Aeri blows out a breath and then fixes her posture and strolls like a lady.

As I pull my cloak around me in the rain, I try not to think about everything that happened tonight. But as time passes, the reality of it drags on me. The energy I found in the alley dissipates. I try to focus on something, anything other than Daysum. Instead, I wonder what will become of that little owl Aeri was taking care of—Dia. I hope she will survive. But I know in my heart she won't. There are too many predators. There are too many dangers in this world to just be a pretty little thing.

I look up at the monsoon moon, and there she is. I squint. It can't be her, but what are the odds of there being two owls this small?

She followed us. I didn't think she could fly, but she's stronger, more capable than I thought.

Dia lands on the roof of the stable and lets out a small hoot. For some reason, I feel hope bloom inside me like a crocus in the dead of winter. The blossom clears my mind. Maybe I am more capable, too.

Aeri is right—Daysum is still alive. As long as she's breathing, I can't stop. I won't. Another wave of shame snakes around me for wanting to give up. But shame is only what you feel when you can be better.

A minute later, Aeri comes out with two horses. I manage half a smile at the girl, the thief, the princess who saved me. But she's not looking at me. She's staring at something else. I turn and watch smoke rise in the distance. It's coming from the direction of the inn.

"We're definitely going to get blamed for this." Aeri groans, then shakes her head. "Whatever. We'll deal with it later. Get on."

Putting my dress boot in the stirrup, I climb into the saddle and wrap my heavy cloak so it stays closed. I cast a last glance at the flames smoking in the rain. Then I spur my horse to follow Aeri into the night, hoping that no one other than Dia is tracking us.

CHAPTER TWENTY-TWO

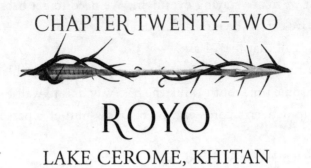

ROYO

LAKE CEROME, KHITAN

We had to plod through the snow for two fucking bells just to catch up with the sled. The stupid deer had wandered so far away that it took forever to find them. My old boots got soaked and ruined, but we got back on in one piece at least.

Now, we're at Lake Cerome—just about. We're in a small town right outside the lake. There's not much to it—a bread house, a pub, and a feed store. I'd guess about two hundred people live here. It's a good thing we stopped in Vashney for supplies and new winter gear.

"We need to come up with a plan," Mikail says, tying the sled to a tree. The tree is next to berry bushes, and the deer help themselves. We only caught them last night because they'd stopped to graze.

Now, we need to get to some books in a temple under a frozen lake, which I still don't get. None of it. Why would people devote their lives to dusty, dry pages, anyhow? I read what I had to in school, but I quit when my mother died. I'd see swells with books sometimes in Umbria, but I never understood it. Why spend the money when the same mun will keep you in bread and ale? I guess we need the information. But how are we gonna get into this temple?

We're all arming ourselves with as many weapons as we can carry. A temple shouldn't be dangerous, but we need to be prepared.

I slip another knife into the vest I bought in Vashney. Euyn takes out camping supplies. I quirk an eyebrow. It's late afternoon, almost dusk, but we're not staying overnight. We need to get back to Quu as fast as we can if the girls are in danger.

"What's all that for?" I ask.

Euyn tugs open another rucksack and shoves in a blanket. "It may take some time, but I think the best way in is to wait for a priest to come to deliver records and then follow him or…persuade him to take us."

"But what about Aeri and Sora?"

"At most they could be detained, and then I'll handle it once we're done." Mikail shrugs and casually checks his sword. It's not the flaming one he had in Yusan—the palace took that back when they knocked him out. But he's real picky about his weapons. He spent a lot of time choosing a sword in Vashney.

Mikail isn't worried, and maybe I shouldn't be, either. But I can't shake the feeling that we should go back.

"Royo, bring your axe," Euyn says. "We may need it."

I stare at him, wondering if he means we're gonna kill a Yoksa.

"For the door," Mikail adds.

Oh.

Euyn has his crossbow and four bands on him. He's gotta have over sixty bolts in total, but he reaches for more.

Seeing him shoot last night was really something. Too much had been going on in Oosant for me to notice, but in the snow, his marksmanship was on full display. It ain't easy to bring down a wolf, and he was doing it with one bolt apiece. I've never seen nothing like it. My axe throw was lucky. He has skill.

"Take the lead in and I'll cover your flank," Mikail says to Euyn. He slides a dagger into his vest.

They glance at each other.

Ever since we got back in the sled, they've been closer. Not like they were in Yusan, but it's not as tense as when we left Quu. Maybe people can move on from lies and betrayals. Maybe it brings you closer together.

Not me—other people.

"Royo, watch our backs," Mikail instructs.

I nod.

"All right, let's go." Euyn loads his bow and puts another bolt in his hand. Then he begins to trek through the snow.

Lake Cerome is at the center of a bunch of hills. Euyn chooses a path, and we walk uphill from town.

Their steps are light, silent as woodland creatures. Mine…aren't. We're ten feet in, and they both look back at me. It's not like I'm trying to be noisy, though. I'm just not a hunter or a spy. I don't normally need to sneak up on nobody. I find a guy, and I hurt him—simple as that.

Mikail stares at me as I huff along.

"Can you do that louder?" he mouths.

I try to breathe through my nose, but the air is thin. It feels like I'm gonna pass out.

We're about a quarter of the way up when Euyn stops with his hand raised. We all put our backs together and scan. He's tracking, looking for signs of other people or things. I remember it from Oosant, how he searches the ground for clues, almost like an animal. When he gives the all-clear, we walk again.

We trudge along for a while. I'm glad we picked up winter gear and clothes. My old boots never would've made it this far, but these ones are new, sturdy, and fur-lined. It's snowing hard, and this all seems like a lot of work just to get to some old books, but what do I know? Hwan used to tell me there were whole worlds in books, but I had enough trouble in this one.

The top of the hill is twenty yards away when Euyn spins around. We all shift our weapons. Even I heard that—a footstep out of sync with ours.

I hold my breath and wait. The hair on my neck stands. There's somebody behind us.

Ten Hells, how? I just checked a second ago.

Euyn raises his bow to his shoulder. I turn to look back. My eyes widen, and my jaw drops.

He's about to shoot Aeri.

CHAPTER TWENTY-THREE

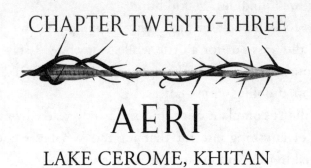

AERI

LAKE CEROME, KHITAN

I'm about to freeze time when Royo cries out and jumps on Euyn, tackling him into the snow. The crossbow goes off. A bolt flies in the air, then lands on the ground a yard from Sora's feet. She throws her arm up in surprise, but she doesn't make a sound.

The five of us all stop and stare at the bolt sticking out of the snow.

"Well, hello to you, too," I say. I exhale the tension and release the neckline of my dress.

Once the shock has passed, we all look at one another. They stare at us like we're mad, and maybe we are. Sora and I are still in our capes and ball gowns. We didn't have time to change, since we galloped all the way here. Turns out, ball gowns aren't the most comfortable choice for riding a full day through the snow. But we didn't have time to visit the shops.

It looks like they did, though.

We were going to stop overnight, but then we came across the corpses of dead zaybears. Well, first I spotted bolts sprouting out of lumps in the snow. I stopped to check what it was, praying on tiptoes that it wasn't Euyn, Mikail, or Royo. I was so nervous; it was hard to even breathe as I brushed off the snow. Then I uncovered the jaw of a zaybear. I fell back, scared to death. But the more frightening thing was thinking Royo might be under the snow, too. I couldn't stop until we found out. Found him.

So, we rode through the night, only stopping when we absolutely had to. I did pass out for a little while. Somehow, I stayed in my saddle. Sora kept us going in the right direction, and I woke up from a short nap, drooling on my horse.

Sora didn't complain once, but she barely reacted to the dead zaybear, or anything else for that matter. Whatever energy she summoned to run with me in Quu is long gone.

"Stars, where did the two of you come from?" Mikail asks, rubbing his forehead.

"The Banquet of the Sky King," I say. I look over at Sora. Her eyes are still vacant. "Count Seok sends his best."

The three men exchange glances.

"Seok?" Royo blurts out. "The guy who owns Sora and her sister?"

I nod. "The very one."

Secretly, I'm thrilled Royo is standing here, unharmed and breathing. My heart patters in my chest. It's a bonus that he's talking to me. That he seems happy to see me.

Okay, fine, he's not *happy* to see me because he's almost never happy. Still, he looks relieved to see me, too, and that's a big improvement from when he left Quu without a word.

Also, he just saved my life. But he's done that a few times now.

I move a step closer, facing him like a winter plant desperate to soak in the sun. Snowflakes land on his dark lashes and dust the hood of his coat. I hold his gaze, but then he looks away.

I swallow the hurt.

"Are you all right?" Mikail asks Sora.

She shakes her head no.

Mikail inhales. "Well, you did the right thing tracking us. But stars, your feet. You rode all the way here in those?"

"I can't really feel them," Sora says with a shrug.

Mikail studies her, his teal eyes bright against the gray sky.

"We need to get you both warm, now," he says. "Frostbite can set in fast when you're not properly dressed. And you look far too cold."

"There's a warming hut down there, close to the shore," Euyn says.

We all follow him. Once we make it to the top of the hill, I can finally see Lake Cerome. The lake is much smaller than Garda in Yusan, but it's still enormous and, importantly, frozen. The wind makes snow drift across the ice, and it picks up, swirling in small twists. It's really pretty, and I bet it's even better in warm weather. I see a few huts made of wood at the shores of the lake.

But I don't see a temple.

Mikail said the Temple of Knowledge is *under* the frozen surface, but I expected to see a dome sticking out or something. Somehow, this is worse.

Euyn goes first down the hillside. He gestures for all of us to follow as he puts his bow to his shoulder. The footing is tough. It's not a mountain, but it's hard to scale in dress boots, with fresh, deep snow.

I stumble on a hidden rock and fall forward. Before I can tumble down, Royo reaches out and grabs me. With one strong hand to my stomach, he stops me. I rebalance, but he leaves his arm out so I can use it to steady myself. My heart fills, but I try not to smile. I walk holding his biceps while he clutches an axe in his other hand.

Euyn leads, scanning the horizon. Mikail stays by Sora's side, but he's constantly looking around, too. I leave my free hand by my neck, just in case. And Royo always looks for trouble. Everyone is alert, except for Sora.

We make it inside the warming hut that's not much bigger than an outhouse. Euyn shuts and locks the door behind us.

No idea what the little lock is supposed to do, but who cares, if it makes him feel better?

There are four benches, one on each wall, and a stove in the middle with wood stacked next to it. Exactly what we need. It smells like oak and charcoal, and it's clean and dry in here.

Euyn gets to work starting a fire while Mikail takes a knee by

Sora's feet and helps remove her boots. Royo just stands in front of me, frowning at my shoes.

"I can't believe you hiked in those," he grumbles.

"I didn't have much of a choice." I shrug.

He nods and sits on the bench next to me, then pats his lap.

I stare at him.

"Gimme your foot," he says.

Surprised, I turn on the bench and put my boots in front of me. He starts trying to untie them, but he gets frustrated. He tosses his heavy gloves to the side, then undoes my laces and slides my boots off. My socks got soaked, so he removes them as well. Then he breathes into his hands and puts them on my feet.

The heat from his palms is amazing. I didn't realize how cold my toes had gotten until now. They're bright red, and I can't feel them the way I normally do. Royo massages my long, narrow feet, focusing so hard, he has lines between his eyebrows. It's so cute and sweet that I can't help but smile.

I've never been cared for like this in my life.

The fire in the stove begins to throw off heat. Everyone is quiet, but in a content way. I look at the four of them. I wish we could all stay here forever—Royo's hands on me, and all of us safe and warm. But we can't. Life is a series of fleeting moments, and this one will end soon.

We have to get inside the temple, and we need to start a war.

But for now, we have the fire in a snowstorm.

I begin to feel sleepy, the tension and worry that kept me awake fading. My head bobs, and I struggle to fight it. I made it through the worst of the amulet fatigue after my brief horse nap, but now I've also been up for nearly two days.

Drowsy, I reach down and stroke Royo's hand. He stills for a few seconds before he withdraws.

I pretend it doesn't crush my heart.

He clears his throat and sits up straight. "The, uh, fire will help."

Royo gets up and puts his gloves back on. I try not to be disappointed. He took care of me, and he didn't have to. That's enough for now. He places my boots and socks right next to the stove to dry.

I really wish he could get over me planning to betray everyone. I mean, really, hasn't everyone here? But maybe that's asking too much, too soon from him.

Then again, it would be good if I could remember that he murdered his girlfriend. He lied on the Sol when he made it seem like he wasn't responsible—they said so in the throne room. Although something bubbles in my chest. It feels an awful lot like doubt, but it's probably just hunger. I hope we find what we need quickly so we can visit that bread house in town.

I extend my feet out near the stove but not close enough to burn them. It takes a while, but eventually I can feel my toes again.

The hut only has one small window, and it faces the lake. Mikail stands by it with something in his hand. I'm not sure what, but it's green and gleaming. I think it's jade, but he's not really one for jewels, and it's much bigger than a gemstone. Yet it's polished like one.

"What is that?" I ask.

"It's a key I stole from Ambassador Zeolin," he says, flashing it at me. "We think it might be to the door of the Temple of Knowledge."

I run my hands along the lace and heavy satin covering my thighs as I think about how convenient it would be. Ambassador Zeolin didn't seem like a guy with any connection to knowledge, but I guess looks can be deceiving. Still, that's not like any key I've seen. It's almost round, but with many notches. And if it is to the temple, where is the door?

Sora glances at Mikail, her small feet out by the fire. Her feet are, unsurprisingly, perfect. But a couple of her toes look so dark red they're almost blackened. That can't be good.

"The ambassador spoke about ice fishing," she says. "He mentioned there were warming huts by a lake. I think he meant this lake."

Mikail and Euyn exchange glances. I catch Royo staring my way. I suppress a smile and pretend like I didn't see.

"Was it a clue or a trap?" Euyn asks, stroking his beard.

"It's hard to say," Mikail replies. Then he stares out the window. "We're about to find out—someone is walking out on the lake."

All of us move, grasping at weapons—even Sora picks up a dagger and brandishes it with skill. Euyn joins Mikail at the window, his bow loaded.

My stomach twists as we wait. Is it Khitanese guards? Did Seok follow us?

"It's a priest," Euyn says. "Or at least it is someone in gray robes."

I stand on the bench, peering over the heads of the others, but I can barely make out a man because the sky is also gray. I squint and look for movement. Mikail is right—someone is walking out toward the ice. I wonder how he'll get into the temple, but that's what we're waiting to find out.

We're all crowding the window except for Sora, who sat down to continue warming her feet. I think her boots were even less useful than mine. She may lose those toes, but I don't think she cares.

"We need to follow," Mikail says. "Euyn, keep him in your sights. Royo, for the Kingdom of Stars, step quieter."

Royo gestures at himself with his palms out.

"Put the outside of your foot down first and roll your step instead of bringing your sole flat," I say. "It'll help."

Royo seems puzzled, but he nods.

Euyn hands us dry socks from a rucksack, and Sora and I slip them on, and then our boots. Mine are still damp, but it's better than before with the thick socks.

Well, until we get outside. Snow immediately falls into my boot again. I sigh. I'll have to buy winter boots after this.

Euyn takes the lead, and we follow behind him in a single line on the shore. We're a good distance from the priest—fifty yards or more. I'd worry about us being spotted, but we are all wearing white fur against white hills, and it is still snowing. So long as we stay far enough away from him, the storm will hide us.

Euyn waves an arm for us to step onto the ice, I assume because the priest has gone farther in. I'm not sure how Euyn can even see him, but he does have exceptional vision.

Royo has a hard time stepping on the lake, his feet skidding.

"Just slide your feet," I whisper.

He nods and tries. It's better.

It's strange to walk on water. I keep thinking we will break through and fall into the lake, but the surface holds. For now.

Sora has a hard time in her fancy boots, and Royo can't seem to walk without stomp-sliding, but still, we make progress. We follow behind the priest, shuffling along the ice until Euyn suddenly throws himself down and lies flat. We all get down and do the same. The priest must have stopped or spotted us.

As I lie on the frozen lake, I keep my head up, and I finally see the priest. He has red hair with a bald patch. His robes billow in the wind. I think for a moment that he saw us, but he doesn't turn around. Instead, he disappears.

I blink. He just disappeared.

"Ten Hells, what the fuck?" Royo whispers.

My thoughts exactly.

CHAPTER TWENTY-FOUR

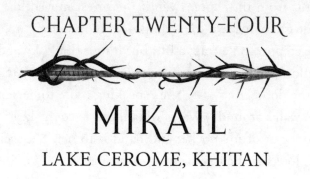

MIKAIL

LAKE CEROME, KHITAN

Well, that was interesting.

We get to our feet, armed and alert. Aeri has a throwing knife in her hand, Euyn is searching for a target with his bow, and my hand is on my sword, but there's nothing. And that's exactly the problem. How did the priest simply vanish?

We run to the spot where we saw him last, no longer worried about stealth. I'm a little concerned Royo will smash right through this ice with his heavy footsteps. It's a good thing the lake has been frozen for nearly a month now.

"I thought he stopped right around here," Aeri says. "Where did he go?"

I thought so, too, but that can't be. There's only snow and ice. We have to be missing something—people don't just disappear.

When he vanished, I thought he'd fallen through, but if that were the case, there would be a hole. Yes, the lake would freeze back over, but not instantly. I bend down and feel the ice with my hand. It's so thick that I can't see the water below. If he fell in, there would be a break, at least a thin spot, and there's nothing.

Euyn tracks along the ice, and the others continue to look around.

"There has to be something we're missing," I say.

I glance at the side of the hill in the distance. I wander toward it, but it's not possible that there's a door there. We are twenty or thirty yards from the shore. Even if the priest moved like Aeri, he still couldn't have made it to the hillside. I look straight up, thinking maybe he stepped on a trap, a lift, but it's just gray sky and snow.

"If I didn't want anyone to be able to get into my temple, I'd disguise the door," Aeri says. She's speaking more to herself than to me as she walks around. "Wait. Mikail, can I see the key?"

I take it out of my pocket and hand it to her. She weighs it in her palm, looks at the key again, and then at me.

"It's not jade," she says.

"What?" I ask.

She shakes her head. "Sorry, I thought it was jade when you first showed it to us, but it's not. It's not emerald, either—the weight and color are off. This almost feels hollow." She moves her hand up and down, and then her eyes grow wide. "It could be veritite." She holds it up to the sky. "Yes, I think it is."

Aeri raises the key in the air and then strikes it hard against the ice. Like she's trying to break into the lake.

"Gods on High, what are you doing?" At the last second, Euyn remembers to aim his bow away from her.

Just as the words leave his mouth, the ice shakes and the perfect corners of a glass door come into view, along with a green keyhole. Royo and Sora jump back. Euyn studies it intensely. I shake my head.

Stars, that's impossible.

There was nothing there before. I'm certain of it. I felt the ice— there was no crack, no keyhole. But now there's a door and a lock, clear as day.

I stare at Aeri. Her eyes are wide with wonder. How did she know to do that?

"Should I even ask?"

She glances at me, tilting her head. "You've never seen veritite?"

"No."

"Strange," she says. "Anyhow, it's a rare stone but not a gem. It's known as a truth seeker—it will reveal other stones of the same material. The lock and edges must also be made of veritite. It's really clever."

Aeri leans down and puts the key in the lock. It's a perfect fit. She exhales and turns her wrist. I hold my breath and wait for something incredible.

Nothing happens. At all.

"It's...stuck." She knits her eyebrows, removes the key, and tries again, but the result is the same. "That's weird."

I take a knee and try. I expect the key to turn, but I can't get it to move, either. I try to the left and right, and then I remove it and try again with the key upside down. It makes no difference. I wonder if the lock froze shut or if the priest blocked it.

Royo wanders over. "What's wrong?"

"We can't get the lock to open," Aeri says.

He leans down, and I move for him to try. Maybe muscle will help. If not, we'll need him to smash through the door. But at least we know where the door is now—it's in the middle of the lake.

Royo puts his hand on the key, turns it, and the lock clicks. The thick, frosted-glass door opens straight down, revealing white stairs that lead to pitch blackness.

Stars.

I take a step back, blinking hard. Then I shake my surprise.

If the priest used the same kind of key, it explains him disappearing. All we saw was ice while he went through the doorway.

But...why did the key turn for Royo? I tried it every which way.

"After you," Aeri says to me. Royo looks right at me and arches an eyebrow.

Neither wants to be first through a door in the middle of a lake, and I can't say I blame them.

I pause and consider whether Aeri is setting us up again. She knew where to meet us and figured out how to locate the door and use the key, and that all seems just as coincidental as finding the key in the first place. But we did tell her we would be at the lake. And she seemed shocked that the key worked.

No, she's just a very good gem thief.

At least, I hope.

I go down the stairs first, with Euyn behind my shoulder with his bow. Killing the zaybears united us again, the way violence always seems to. His beliefs are, at times, appalling, but they are also evolving. Or that's what I want to believe.

The girls follow, and then Royo is last. He closes the door behind us with a loud thud.

What the fuck.

All four of us stop and stare at him. Then it occurs to me that it is light enough inside to see one another, somehow.

Well, now that we completely lack the element of surprise, I draw my sword and take the marble staircase down. The stairs are slippery, but it is almost like the white stone is lit from within. The staircase continues for a great distance, slightly curving. I can't see the end, and I dislike that. It feels like an obvious trap, and hairs on the back of my neck stand up.

I'm surprised when we make it to the bottom of the stairs without being attacked. When we come out, we're inside the glass dome of the Temple of Knowledge. Which means we are in a courtyard underwater.

It's…incredible.

I never believed the myths about the gods creating structures on earth, because why would deities worry about architecture, but as I look around, this place changes my mind. While I'm certain men built the King's Arena, I can't see how people made this. I touch the glass of the side of the dome, wondering how it holds. There is dark water all around us, and glowing fish swim by, but we are dry. In front of us stands an astonishing white marble temple. Torches blaze, illuminating it from within. Small trees grow in the courtyard, lampposts light the space, and none of this should be possible.

"How?" Aeri whispers. She delights at the fish going by, and Royo nearly smiles at her joy.

Even Sora, who isn't herself, looks around, violet eyes filled with wonder.

The second I saw her face, I knew Seok must have sold her sister—or worse. I regret not telling her that the southern count was in Khitan. I should have warned her, but I didn't think he'd be at the banquet. Zeolin had said it was only a rumor. Still, guilt gnaws at me for allowing her to be blindsided.

Thoughts of Zeolin bring me back to reality. He was the one with a key to this temple, and he shouldn't have had it. It was too convenient that I found it. I snap out of it.

"Stay together," I whisper.

I shake off my awe and observe. I don't trust how easy it was to get inside the temple. Euyn would say the gods are on our side, but we've been nearly eaten a few times too many for that to be true.

We approach the temple carefully. Euyn picks up on my skepticism and scans with his bow ready. Royo has his axe on his shoulder.

All of the Temples of Knowledge have elements of the four original realms—the white marble from Wei, the gilded domes of Khitan, the fountains of Yusan, and the wooden doors of Gaya. Gaya used to be home to the tallest black wood trees in the world. At the end of the Festival of Blood, Joon decimated the ancient forest.

But these doors are older than the massacre. The black wood reaches thirty feet high and is elaborately carved, depicting the mythical tree of knowledge.

As we approach, I pull the brass handle, and we step inside. But as soon as I open the door, I realize something is terribly wrong.

CHAPTER TWENTY-FIVE

SORA

THE TEMPLE OF KNOWLEDGE, KHITAN

This temple is a true gift from the gods. I have been to spectacular places in my life, but they all pale in comparison to this.

If I were a man, I'd become a priest to the God of Knowledge and happily live out my days under this dome. And Daysum would love it, too. She loves nothing more than sitting by a sunny window, reading a book. We were poor children, so all we had was one tattered book of fairy tales, but she'd sit with it for bells as if each time reading was the first.

A sharp, twisting sadness hits me, because I know where Daysum is right now.

I sniffle, but I try not to make a sound as it's completely silent all around us. It feels wrong. These temples should be quiet, but not like this.

I genuflect as I enter the doorway. So does Royo. The others just stroll in. Aeri remembers late and kneels quickly, but neither Euyn nor Mikail pause. I suppose a demigod and a demon don't pray—Mikail being the demigod.

A large fountain sprays water in the middle of a spectacular great hall. The ceilings arch high above us with painted domes, gilded in the now familiar Khitanese style. There is a second level completely open to this one—almost like a massive balcony wrapping around the room. The floors are covered in mosaics as beautiful and ornate as the throne room in Qali Palace. The walls hold countless books and scrolls on thousands of shelves, in the alcoves of gleaming white marble. But there's a dash of red on the back wall.

I gasp. Kingdom of Hells. Is that blood?

We walk in carefully, scanning for trouble. Something about this splendid temple is all wrong.

Where are the priests?

We reach the center of the room by the central fountain and altar. From the midpoint of the great hall, two other rooms are visible—one off to the right and another to the left.

I point to the right. It looks like that room is full of scrolls from floor to ceiling, but I shiver and I want to stay away from that side. So that is where we need to go.

I hope that one day we'll be able to avoid danger, but for now we have to run through it.

Mikail and Euyn ready their weapons, and Royo shifts both hands to his axe. We creep toward the scroll room, treading along mosaic tile until we reach a dark-red floor.

I gasp. It's red because it's a sea of blood.

Scrolls litter the room, some now sopping wet. Many have been destroyed, shredded by blades.

We find the priests. They're all here. And they're all dead.

CHAPTER TWENTY-SIX

TIYUNG

IDLE PRISON, YUSAN

I am alive.

Hana didn't poison me. My stomach just rebelled from having too much rich food at once. After eating nothing but bread and water for so long, I couldn't process meat and cheese. I was in pain for nearly a day, but the discomfort went away, leaving me alive and still a prisoner in Idle.

Once I survived, I found myself waiting by the meal slot, hoping to see Hana. I pray she'll share more information about Sora. About the others. Not that all the information will be something I want to hear. I wasn't thrilled that Hana knew I'd freed her brother, and it's even worse to know that Sora is in Khitan in order to steal the Golden Ring. I assume she's with the others, but I don't know.

Although I keep constant watch, I don't see Hana. I fall asleep, then wake and wait again, but no one comes, aside from the guards bringing my trays of water and stale bread. The disappointment stings like a salted wound.

Every time I rise, I hope to see her, but then I fall asleep without any sign. The cycles of hope and depression continue until slowly, I realize that she might not return. Maybe she said everything she needed to. Maybe I don't have the information she is looking for and thus she has no use for me. Or maybe I just imagined her completely. Maybe I was so desperate that it was all an elaborate hallucination.

I clutch the letter in my pocket. No, I still have this. I let the paper dig into my palm until it hurts and I'm certain it is real. Hana was here—she gave this to me, and Sora wrote it.

When Hana still doesn't appear at the next mealtime, despair gets the best of me. Despite how I try to imagine a future with Sora, I can't seem to keep heart.

I slump on the ground and pass on the next round of bread. I'm hungry, but what is the point? Why keep going?

Keys jangle in the door, and the lock turns. At first, I figure I'm hearing things, but then the door opens and I have to scramble out of the way. My heart speeds up. Hana is back.

Or someone is coming to kill me.

I've learned to close my eyes once they open the door, and it at least helps with adjusting to the light.

I stare at the ground, and guard boots come into view. I take a deep breath, trying to brace myself, but then there are dress boots and a cape. Hana appears with a small lantern. She dismisses the guards.

"I'm surprised to see you," I say, my voice scratchy from lack of use.

I keep my tone cool, trying to hide how eager I am to talk to her. I'm not sure how long it's been since she was here last. Maybe she'll tell me.

"You've been gone for days," I add. I search her face. She doesn't deny it, so it *has* been days. I did retain some sense of time.

"I wasn't going to come back," Hana says. "And then I realized something."

"And that was?"

"You're not smart enough to lie."

She means it as an insult, but she is calling me honest, which I am, so I shrug.

That wasn't the reaction she was expecting. Hana tilts her head and then tosses down another cloth sack.

Food.

I dive onto the ground to open it, more of a wild animal than a nobleman at this point. She wrinkles her nose in disgust. Sora had once looked at me that way, her expression filled with contempt. That was before we left for Tamneki, before I finally convinced her that I care. That I am not like my father.

The thought of her makes me pause. It's only Sora that could be more important than a meal right now.

"Is Sora all right?" I ask, glancing up.

Hana nods.

I start eating, making myself chew. The meat is so delicious that it will be worth the pain, but taking smaller bites will help my stomach.

"She is alive at any rate," Hana says. "Your father is also in Khitan, though."

That's odd. My father traveled extensively when he was a young man, seeing the far corners of the world, but he doesn't leave Gain nearly as much now.

I rip off a chunk of cheese and shove it in my mouth. "Why?"

She sighs. "You aren't going to be of any use, are you?"

She sounds both disappointed and unsurprised.

"Seok shares only what he wants," I remind her. "What he thinks I need to know. You know that."

"Was he the owner of the warehouse in Oosant?" she asks.

I pause, surprised she knows about the warehouse, though I shouldn't be if she's a spy. I've wondered the same thing about Oosant. There are only four men with enough money and power to have a million gold mun in illegal laoli, and my father is one of them.

"I'd never heard anything about Oosant until I was there. It isn't on his books, but it is possible. The drugs had the royal insignia on them, though, which means they were brought in from Gaya. There would be obstacles to that amount of smuggling, but it's not out of the question."

"Unless it was for the crown." Hana refocuses on me. "I tell you what. I'll make you a deal. You tell me everything you know from before you left Gain until now, and I will bring you food to eat, light to see, and even paper to write on so you won't lose your sanity. You give me all you can about Seok and his businesses, and I will buy you time."

"Buy me time?" I make myself slow down on the fatty, dried sausage and soft cheese. She even brought me a custard bun, but I am saving that for last. "What does that mean?"

"You are supposed to die in here. I don't know when that will be. But soon."

I freeze, my heart pounding before my mind can catch up. The brie lodges in my throat. Hana said it so casually, it took me a second to fully absorb her words. "The king ordered my death?"

She nods. "I heard the order today. General Salosa said to make it look like an accident or a sickness, not an execution. I will delay the prison guards for as long as I can...but I don't think I'll be able to buy a full month."

Bile rises in my throat, and I want to vomit all the good food I just ate. If she can't get me a month, that means I will die before Sora gets back to Yusan. No matter what happens, I'll never see her again. Tears flood my eyes, and I sniff them back. It was all I wanted—just a chance at a life with her. Not even certainty, just an opportunity. And now it can never be.

I close my eyes and take a moment to mourn the loss. All I did, all I was prepared to do, and it amounts to nothing because of time. Sobs rack my chest, but I don't let them out. I suppose time makes a fool's game of all men's efforts.

"Sora," I whisper. Then I open my eyes.

Hana flinches but doesn't attack me. Instead, she studies me. Her eyes are sharp until her full mouth opens.

"Oh gods, you fell for her," she says.

I don't bother denying it—what difference would it make?

"From when I first saw her," I say. "We were only children, and she tried to hide Daysum behind her skirts."

Hana takes a step closer. I brace myself, thinking she'll strike me, but instead she leans down. "You can help me save her. The more I know, the more I can assist them. And they need all the help they can get now. This mission was never supposed to succeed. Someone is betraying them."

My heart races in my chest, but I pause. It could all be a lie, a scheme from a clever spy, but it's Hana. I know she loves Sora—that much is true. I decide to start from the beginning and pray that it will help her somehow.

Before I can speak, the moaning song of the iku shakes the cell. Hana's eyes shift toward the walls. She must not be down here much for the sound to surprise her. I'm so accustomed to it that I just wait for the echoes to fade.

"Sora's father refused to sell her, no matter what price my father offered," I begin. "Determined to take the girls, my father threatened to slay his whole family unless Chul sold Sora."

Hana puts the lantern down.

CHAPTER TWENTY-SEVEN

SORA

THE TEMPLE OF KNOWLEDGE, KHITAN

Euyn searches the scroll room for threats, but I can't take my eyes off the eight priests lying in the middle of the floor. They range in age from around twenty to over seventy. Three were women. And they all died slowly.

A shiver careens down my spine as I stare. All their mouths are open as if reciting something together, but they look peaceful. I've seen the difference between a body accepting death and one bitterly fighting it.

We leave the scroll room and search the rest of the temple, weapons drawn, because whoever did this might still be here, lying in wait. Anyone bold enough to slaughter all the Yoksa has nothing to lose and thus is wildly dangerous.

We pass a body slumped on the ground by the blood splatter on the back wall—a ninth priest. I don't understand why he's not with the others, but he is also dead with his eyes open. This one is smiling.

I shake off another chill.

All the Yoksa have fatal, painful stab wounds to their midsections. The lone priest was also slashed in the neck.

The five of us stop at the fountain altar. Aeri and I catch our breath. Seeing this much death drains your soul. And I'm so very tired. Tired from riding all night, tired of never being safe, tired of always having to persevere. But the only way to free my sister is to get to the queen. I stand straight, with my head held high. We must keep going.

We gather ourselves and search the room to the left. Luckily, there are no bodies here, but it's ransacked. The reading tables are overturned, volumes torn apart. Paper obscures the floor tiles the way blood did in the other room. I'm not sure how many books were destroyed—probably hundreds.

Gods, what Daysum and I would've done with hundreds of books as children.

Someone was searching for something. I can't imagine what or why. And it's impossible to tell if they succeeded or not.

"What do we do now?" I ask.

Mikail relaxes, sheathing his sword. "We find the exceptions to the Rule of Distance."

"How are we gonna find anything in here?" Royo asks, gesturing around.

It's a good point. There have to be a hundred thousand books and five times that many scrolls in this temple. If I remember correctly, the temples house not just the history of Khitan but also Wei, Yusan, and Gaya. The four original realms of the Dragon Lord—a complete history of the thousand years of human rule.

I look up and around. We could spend the entire monsoon season reading and still not find what we're looking for. Our plan always depended on the priests being alive and willing to help us.

My ear chimes, my fingers growing icy. We don't have time. Every second we waste is another second Daysum and Ty suffer. Another moment where I could lose one or both forever.

"Why don't we ask him to help?" Aeri points up above us.

Cowering on the second floor, under a library ladder, sits a priest. He has the same bald spot as the one we were following, which explains how he is still alive.

He just got here.

Mikail speaks in Khitanese to the man, asking for help and

promising safety. It's funny how language suddenly comes back, even when you haven't heard it in years. It's like picking up a conversation with an old friend.

Though he doesn't speak a word, the priest eventually climbs down the spiral staircase. He is a middle-aged man of medium height with a timid air. He's a priest of knowledge, not a warrior or a blade—that much is certain. Even Euyn realizes he is not a threat and lowers his bow.

Mikail talks as the priest stands at the bottom of the stairs, clutching the gilded railing. There's no response. He tries again in Yusanian.

"If he ain't talking, I can make him talk," Royo offers, shifting his axe.

I wonder why the priest isn't saying anything, and then from some corner of my mind I recall that they cannot speak inside of the temple.

"He can't talk in here," I say. "It's part of their vow."

The others all turn to me, but the priest nods. Mikail waves him to the door, and then they disappear into the courtyard. A few minutes later, they come back inside.

"Our new friend, Luhk, is willing to assist us in exchange for helping him release the souls of the dead priests," Mikail says.

The priest nods. Unsurprisingly, he understands Yusanian just as well as any of us. I imagine he speaks all languages fluently.

Euyn and Royo seem less than eager to agree, but it is a fair trade. Though I'm not sure where we can burn the bodies. Certainly not underwater.

"Royo and Euyn, I'll need your help carrying the priests out, where we can build a pyre," Mikail says.

"Great," Royo says. He doesn't mean it.

Mikail turns to the priest. "In the meantime, show them where to find the exceptions to the Rule of Distance." He points to Aeri and me.

Luhk nods and gestures for us to follow him. Women are respected here, so he doesn't find this odd. It's only Aeri and me looking at each other, surprised to be tasked with something so important.

Euyn whispers his objections to Mikail.

"We're trusting them with this?" he asks.

Mikail ignores him.

I expect the priest to take us to the ransacked room, but instead he brings us upstairs. As Euyn shifts his complaints from us to the mess, I wonder when the priests were killed. I've never been around my victims for long, and the girls who died in school were burned before their bodies went cold. But it doesn't seem like they've been dead for more than a day at most.

Luhk goes to a random spot on the wall and pulls out two large, leather-bound volumes. I thank him in Khitanese. Even though he speaks Yusanian, it is always kinder to greet someone in their native tongue. He smiles, and we go back to the main floor.

"We also need all the information you have on the relics of the Dragon Lord," Mikail says between deep breaths. He's hauling a large priest by the shoulders while Euyn carries the legs.

I look away from the blood dripping on the floor.

Aeri turns toward Mikail. "Why is that? I thought we weren't stealing the ring."

Euyn pauses but Mikail keeps walking. The body's long legs drop with a thud.

Mikail frowns. "Because Joon might be trying to reunite the relics."

I'm not sure what that means, but Aeri's fingers worry the side of her cloak, so I doubt it's anything good.

The priest goes toward the room on the left but not inside it. He takes an armful of scrolls and a volume from the third shelf down. Then he goes to another wall. And then another.

As he moves around, his robes swishing, I am certain that we never would have located this information without him. Because of that, I doubt that the people who murdered the priests found what they were looking for, either. The slow murders were likely punishment for a lack of cooperation. The serene faces were because the priests had won in death.

There's a small comfort in that.

Aeri and I bring the books to a reading table far from the bloody scroll room. Luhk deposits ten other volumes on the table alongside the many scrolls.

It's a lot.

Aeri opens a book on the Rule of Distance and frowns.

"This is in Khitanese," Aeri says. "I can't read it."

She hands me the second volume while she opens a scroll. Luhk comes back with five more volumes on the Dragon Lord relics. I begin to read. I don't speak enough Khitanese to decipher all of this, so I will have to wait for Mikail or Euyn, but I skim what I can and mark places I think will be relevant. I don't want to prove Euyn right.

Some of the scrolls are written in Weian and old Gayan, and I'm not sure if even Mikail will be able to read them. But we have to try.

Aeri and I quietly read. It's almost peaceful, except for the shuffling out of bloodied bodies and Royo cursing between grunts.

CHAPTER TWENTY-EIGHT

EUYN

THE TEMPLE OF KNOWLEDGE, KHITAN

I never expected to haul as many corpses as I have with Mikail. We bring the priests out of the temple, up the stairs, and onto the ice. It's easier said than done with their robes, wounds, and the winding staircase. It takes a while, but we get all nine onto the shore.

Now we have a new quandary of creating a funeral pyre in all this snow. The four of us stand, puzzling over it, but I keep looking around. We need to move. We're too exposed out here, and I can't shake the sensation that we're being watched.

"Can't we just use the books as kindling?" Royo asks.

I think the priest might faint from the suggestion. He shakes his head vigorously, and his breath comes out in spurts.

"I mean the ones they tore apart…" Royo adds and then trails off, kicking at some snow.

The priest continues to shake his head, a man of few words even when he's not under his vow. I assume he's going to salvage what he can and rewrite all the materials that were destroyed—if he lives that long. Something tells me he will not.

"We can take apart the warming hut and use it," Mikail says. "It might just be enough." He stares down the shore and then at me. "Euyn, cover us. The priest says he hasn't been here in a week. It's hard to say when the others were killed, but I estimate it's been less than a day."

"Yours in this life and the next," I say, lifting my bow.

He doesn't say it because he is busy directing Royo and the priest. Or at least that's what I want to believe.

I thought we were back to normal after the zaybear attack, but we are not. I can feel him pulling away from me, like the tide slipping through my fingers, and it's maddening.

Regardless, I will always protect him. I take up a position on the side of the nearest slope and build a quick snow wall in front of me. I crouch behind it and wait with my bow on my shoulder. It's cold and uncomfortable, but I am used to sitting like this from my hunting days. My legs are deceptively strong from crouching for bells and bells—it's how I was able to lift and carry Mikail in Fallow.

Who would've thought that would be a simpler time?

The other men get to work on building a pyre. They bring the benches, firewood, and even drag the stove out of the hut. The stove is clever. It will help get the fire hot enough, since all nine bodies will have to burn together.

Royo lumbers back to the shed, stares at it for a moment, then rips the door off with just his gloved hands. Mikail shakes his head, laughing to himself as he carries the wood over to the pyre.

Royo swings his axe and hits the corner of the hut. The entire structure begins to buckle. A few swings later, it's in manageable pieces.

They work efficiently, but it's solidly dark by the time the pyre is ready. I keep a sharp eye out for any signs of danger—a lantern, a glimmer of steel, a clang of armor. Mikail estimated a day since the killers were here. I think it's less than that—half a day at most, given the state of the bodies. I expect to see shadows creeping along, spies or assassins hiding. The hair on the back of my neck stands. But the only thing of note is a tiny moon owl circling the lake multiple times.

The priest brings a torch and a vase of oil out of the temple. He says prayers to Lord Yama for each of the priests, even the female ones. He then says another prayer to the God of Knowledge and one to the Sky King. I start to get antsy, tapping my foot as he begins yet another prayer. We really don't have time for a full funeral, but a deal is a deal.

I just don't understand why Mikail agreed. We had the muscle to force his hand.

Finally, the priest pours all the oil on the bodies and lights the pyre. With so little wood, the oil will help the bodies burn. In Yusan, we consider the souls released as soon as the bodies catch fire. I imagine it's the same in Khitan.

Once the souls are released, we head back down the blood-splattered stairs. The priest asks us to wait at the doors of the temple.

"What if it's a trap?" Royo asks. His eyes dart around as he voices my paranoid thoughts.

"Unless he has an army hidden back there, I think we can handle it," Mikail says.

But I keep my bow ready.

The priest comes back with a cloth for us to clean our boots. Royo is the first to sheepishly comply. The priest passes us, heading to wipe down the stairs.

When we get inside the temple, the girls are still at the reading table, only now it's covered in open books and unfurled scrolls.

They stop and look up at us.

"What did you find?" Mikail asks.

"Well, there's good news and bad news," Aeri says. "Which would you like first?"

My stomach sinks. Of course there's bad news. "The bad."

"The good," Mikail says at the same time.

He and I pause and exchange glances.

"Well, that was weird." Aeri looks from me to Mikail. "Anyhow, the good news is that there appear to be two exceptions to the Rule of Distance. But neither of us speaks enough Khitanese to figure out what they mean. They're written strangely."

"Easy enough." Mikail saunters over to the table.

"Wait, what's the bad news?" I ask.

Aeri pales a little. "Well, the thing is…we figured out why the king wants the ring so badly."

I raise my eyebrows, waiting.

She opens a scroll. "It's right here. 'The use of multiple relics amplifies their powers as man merges with god,'" she reads.

Mikail runs a hand down his face as my stomach sinks. Joon has the Immortal Crown, the Flaming Sword, and now he wants the ring, which would make him the most powerful being in the world.

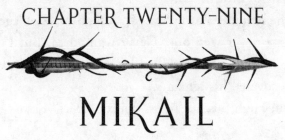

CHAPTER TWENTY-NINE

MIKAIL
THE TEMPLE OF KNOWLEDGE, KHITAN

Under no circumstances can we let Joon get the ring. Succeeding here just became that much more important, and it was already life-or-death.

I take a seat at the long, varnished table to read about the exceptions to the Rule of Distance. Aeri and Sora are on either side of me, and Royo and Euyn stand across from us. As I finish reading, I wish I hadn't. I sit back, and Sora's violet eyes are on me. Actually, everyone is watching me.

"It's not good, is it?" she asks, the corners of her mouth tilting down.

I run a hand through my hair. "Well, it's not easy."

That's putting it lightly.

"Give it to us," Royo says. He's been standing there, waiting. I'm sure he can read, but he's no scholar. While everyone else has flipped through a book or unwrapped a scroll, he's been content watching Aeri read—when he thinks no one is looking, of course.

"All right," I say. "The first exception states that the person who brings the king an egg of an amarth will be granted a villa with utmost standing on Oligarch Mountain. But more importantly for our purposes, they can dine at the table of the king."

They're all silent.

"What's an amarth?" Royo asks.

"It's a type of bird," I say.

That's the best way I can phrase it. A nightmare of legend is more accurate. I've never seen one. Never wanted to. But I've heard of them. One of our spies was killed by an amarth around a year ago. We never recovered his remains.

"Gods on High, it's not like a samroc, is it?" Euyn's brown eyes widen.

It might be worse.

"The amarth are part human but mostly bird. They have white plumes and stand roughly a head taller than a man. They are purportedly servants of the Sky God. According to this text, their queens lay black-colored eggs."

"Part human?" Aeri asks.

"The legend is that the son of the Sky King loved a woman and mated with her in the form of an eagle, producing an egg," I say. "That was the first amarth. If they are, in fact, human, I believe that makes them cannibals. They are carnivorous, with razor-sharp beaks, long talons, and the speed of eagles. But they reportedly have human features and can speak."

Euyn shudders, and I know what he's thinking. The only thing that could've made our encounter with the samroc worse would've been them talking to us. A chill runs over my shoulders at the thought.

Royo rubs his forehead. "Speak like a parrot?"

"No, I think it's closer to you and me," I answer. "But the book doesn't say."

His brow wrinkles as he tries to get his head around it.

"I really..." Euyn pales. "You said there were two exceptions. Perhaps we should try the other?"

I think we've both had all the bird encounters we can handle. But the second option is not easy or safe, either.

"The other states that the person who brings in the head of Staraheli will be granted a villa on the mountain with primary standing and will be allowed to sit at the feet of the king."

"Who or what is Staraheli?" Sora asks.

"He was the ruler of the Marnans—the people of the northwestern part of the country who did not become Khitanese. They fought with Khitan over land and water for centuries and had to retreat to the ice caves and the frozen wasteland after heavy losses. But Staraheli was a brilliant strategist who organized successful invasions. He made it all the way to Vashney and killed a prince before being defeated. But Khitan wasn't able to capture him, so they want his head."

Luhk nods from the back wall, where he's wiping away the blood splatter.

"But the last Staraheli revolt was over a century ago," Euyn says.

I nod, although I'm surprised. He must've paid attention to his history tutor, which I didn't expect. Euyn wasn't much of a student if it didn't interest him. His tutor was probably attractive.

"Then there's no head to bring to Quilimar," he says. "Even if he lived a long life, he must be ashes by now."

"The Marnans bury their dead," I say.

The table is silent as the thought of grave robbing a hundred-year-old corpse hits everyone. Like I said, it's not great.

"I kind of get wanting to display the head of an enemy, but why the egg?" Aeri asks.

"That, I don't know," I say.

"It's because of the curse," Euyn says, flipping a book to face us.

Everyone gathers around. It's an illustration of a king sitting with a knife and fork. He's getting ready to eat what looks to be a black ostrich egg.

"What curse?" Royo asks.

"The ring, like all of the relics, curses the wearer with a terrible price for its use," Euyn says. "The crown is an exception because it only protects or turns imposters to ash, although there's a thought that the cost is increasing madness. Regardless, the Golden Ring causes tremendous pain and weakens the blood of the wearer. The same as how the Water Scepter causes desiccation and the Flaming Sword causes burns. All relics pull life out of the wearer. It's written here that eating the black egg of an amarth is thought to cleanse the blood. The king was looking for a cure."

"Maybe he did die of natural causes, then," Sora says on a soft breath.

We all turn and look at her. Aeri skews her face, Royo's eyebrows come together, and Euyn blinks. Sora isn't naive, though. She believes in goodness, which is incomprehensible with what she's been through.

"Never mind." She looks away.

"Something tells me we can't just find one of these eggs at the marketplace in Quu, right?" Royo asks.

"The nearest known amarth nest is in the Light Mountains, five days north of here." I look around at everyone. "So who wants to do what?"

The only noise is the rustle of parchment as the priest cleans the scrolls.

No one wants to get either of these items, of course. That is why they are the only exceptions to the Rule of Distance and why they come with tremendous rewards. No one in their right mind would try. But we have no choice now.

"The good news is that so long as we succeed at one, it will be enough for a private audience," I say.

No one finds this to be very comforting. Probably because it's not. With no volunteers, I make the decision for them.

"Royo and Aeri, you go to the Light Mountains to steal the egg," I say. "Sora, come with Euyn and me. We will get the head of Staraheli—it should be somewhere by the ice caves of the Marnans about four days west of here. After we succeed, all of us will meet in Vashney. There's an inn called The Revelry in the center of the old city. We'll reconnect there ten days from now and proceed to Quu together. If either party doesn't return, wait for up to a sunsae from now, but then go alone. There's no reason for all of us to fail."

Everyone starts talking at once, no doubt to disagree.

I sigh and hit the table with my palm. They all quiet down. "The reason I divided us this way is because I need Sora to kill the guards quietly and Euyn to protect me while I cut off the head. It's best to use stealth to take the egg and do it quickly, which makes Aeri best suited for that task. She needs someone to protect her on the way and to fight off the amarth if it goes wrong, which means Royo. I suppose Royo and Euyn can change places, but all of you have unique talents, and neither mission benefits from additional people."

The second the words are out of my mouth, I realize why we were sent to Khitan.

"That's why we're here," I say.

The others turn to me as I stand and puzzle it out.

"Since the throne room, I've wondered, *why us?* Why would Joon go through all the trouble and risk his daughter? Why the ruse to capture us and the effort to keep us alive? And now I have an answer."

I pause, and they all stare at me.

"The Temples of Knowledge contain written histories of all four original realms. Joon must have read about the Rule of Distance and the exceptions in the temple in Yusan. He knew we had the skills needed to give the head of Staraheli to Quilimar. Shoot, poison, plan." I point to Euyn, Sora, and myself. "And with Aeri, we can steal the black egg. Once we are within a few feet of Quilimar, Sora could poison her."

It's not an answer to everything, but one mystery is solved. However, I know I'm missing something because none of that explains why he'd try to kill Quilimar before we reached Khitan.

"Does that mean King Joon killed the priests?" Sora asks.

"It might. The murders could also be unrelated to us," Euyn says. "Someone was obviously searching for something—the question is what."

We turn to the priest, who pales and sways.

"Luhk, do you know?" I ask. "What did your brothers and sisters die to keep in the temple? Was it this?" I wave at the information on the table.

He shakes his head and shyly walks over. He doesn't entirely trust us, and I don't blame him. But he puts his hand in his pocket and pulls out a tiny scroll.

I read it and then read it again. I look at the priest, raising my eyebrows to see if it's true, and he nods. This is exactly what Quilimar would kill to prevent people from knowing. I run my hand down my face.

"What is it?" Euyn asks.

I hand the scroll back to Luhk and exhale. "Your sister cannot wield the Golden Ring of the Dragon Lord."

Euyn closes his eyes slowly. Sora covers her mouth. Aeri gasps. And Royo just looks confused. I am, too. I'm not sure why Quilimar can't use the ring, but I am certain she wouldn't want the other realms to find out. Without the ring, she is weaker, and weakness will always get you killed. To keep it a secret, she faked the assassin's gilded shirt during piteua and sent soldiers to destroy the information and kill the priests. It's a shame the ring can't turn an imposter to ash—it would be one less worry.

But now, we know her secret.

We have to get out before her soldiers come back.

CHAPTER THIRTY

ROYO

THE TEMPLE OF KNOWLEDGE, KHITAN

This plan is shit.

We're all gonna split up again like we learned nothin'. Every time we go separately, it all goes to the Ten Hells. Now, Aeri and I need to get an egg from a vicious parrot in the mountains. Just her and me alone for up to a sunsae.

I'd rather deal with a rotting, hundred-year-old corpse.

I spin my axe like a top as I sit with it between my knees. I can't be alone with her for that long. Whatever I tell myself, however strong I want to be, I know I'll break. Those eyes, that smile, that carefree happiness, not that I've seen much of it these days. And more than that—the way she makes me feel. She pretends like I matter to her, like she loves me. I've managed to mostly keep my distance, and I can remind myself that she's a liar and an actor. But alone with her, I'll fall for her all over again. I strangle the axe handle. I can't do it. My heart won't survive a second betrayal.

Mikail is over by the fountain. He's in the middle of an intense discussion with Euyn, but I need a word with him. Euyn and I can swap places, like he said. It'll be better for everybody.

Okay, it'll be better for me, and what's the difference to him?

Mikail and Euyn are so focused on each other that they don't even notice me walking up to them.

"Null," Euyn says.

Mikail shakes his head.

"We *have to* kill him," Euyn whispers.

"I'm sorry?" Mikail says.

Euyn's eyes dart to the side. "He knows too much. And they will come back—they will realize there should have been ten priests. My sister will murder him like the rest of them, or torture him, and he will give away our locations. It's a kindness to kill him now, cleanly and without pain."

Mikail stares at Euyn, speechless.

"Who are we killing?" I ask.

They both turn and face me. Euyn's cheeks flush, and Mikail looks annoyed at best. Furious is more accurate, his jaw clenching, his eyes hard.

"No one," Mikail says. "I don't kill people if I promised them safety for their aid."

"Mikail…" Euyn says.

"No." Mikail's sharp voice echoes through the fine space.

Aeri flinches, and Sora pauses. I look down at my new boots like they suddenly got real interesting.

"If your sister chooses to break the edicts and spill blood in the temple, that is on her," he continues. "Be more than your family."

Euyn reddens. "I am the crown prince of Yusan!"

Mikail leans forward, his features hardening. "You are *nothing*."

Euyn stares like he was just smacked in the face. Nobody moves.

Well, this ain't the time to ask.

I go back to the table. Aeri is tracing her finger over a map of the region, and she resumes asking questions as the priest shakes his head yes or no. He's leaning a little closer to her than he needs to, if you ask me. I feel my blood rise and heat warming my face, but I clear my throat and focus on something, anything else.

Sora is closing a book on Khitanese poisons. I guess she doesn't know the ones here like she does in Yusan.

"We need to leave now, Sora." Mikail wanders over, his normal self again, as if he didn't just break from Euyn. I'd worry more about what the change in their relationship means for all of us, but we gotta survive the missions for it to matter.

Aeri jots down some notes. She thanks the priest, putting her hands to her forehead. I wonder if he knows he just had a princess salute him.

Luhk smiles and walks us out of the temple.

"We can give you safe passage home," Mikail offers.

I quirk an eyebrow. Why's everybody so concerned about this guy? Yeah, he helped us, but it's not like he wanted to. He only did it because we dragged bodies outside for him—it was a deal. That's it.

The priest shakes his head. "This is my home. With the head priest deceased, I am now the only keeper of the temple."

"But you can't stay here," Sora says, her eyes pleading.

"They'll come back," Mikail urges. "I assume this was the work of General Vikal, and she won't simply give up."

"Then I will die for my god, protecting what I love," the priest says, looking around with a smile. "There are far worse ways to go. But if I abandon what I love just to live, what kind of life is that?"

His words hit all of us. Everyone pales or flinches, thinking about what we left behind. For me, his words are a gut punch. Hwan is still locked up and may die while I'm here. But I didn't abandon him, not by choice, and I will make it right. Even if the only thing I can do is kill the man who wronged him—I will. All I might be left with is revenge, but sometimes that's enough.

"Thank you for allowing me to honor my fellow priests," Luhk says. He turns to go back inside.

"Wait," Mikail calls. "Why did the Yusanian Ambassador have the key to your temple?"

"Our keys unlock all temples," the priest replies. "It might have been this one or the one in Yusan. Or even Wei or Gaya."

I thought these guys were supposed to be smart.

"That doesn't seem real wise," I say. "To use the same key for all your doors."

"Maybe not, but it is our commitment to knowledge transcending realms that matters," the priest says. "Priests of one nation are always welcome in the temple of another. And there is a safeguard. Only those who bled on the altar of knowledge, of keeper blood, can use those keys. The locks will not turn if the key doesn't recognize the blood of the user."

Everyone turns and stares at me.

I point to my own chest. "Wait, what? Me?"

"You opened the door," Aeri says, beaming.

The priest raises his eyebrows. "I thought you pried it open after me, but if you were able to use the key, someone in your line was a keeper. One of your parents, I assume. That is your key now."

Mikail gives it to me, although he eyes me skeptically. He couldn't be more confused than me. I figured Aeri was too slight and Mikail's fingers slipped or something when I opened it. That it was just muscle. But...I didn't have to try. The key turned like my house key, and the door popped open.

None of it's possible, though. I don't know nothing about my father. And my mother died in Tamneki a decade ago. I guess either could've been a keeper like the guy said. But it don't make sense. They weren't scholars or priests. Yusan doesn't have female priests, and even if they did, my mother worked a dozen different jobs trying to make ends meet. She never mentioned anything about the God of Knowledge.

Aeri looks so happy, smiling widely.

I guess we both got blood we won't talk about now.

We get back onto the ice and close the door. I wonder how long the priest will be alive. Then again, with what we're about to do, he might outlive us.

It's dark out, with a huge moon hanging over the lake. The five of us stand on the shore in the quiet night. This could be the last time we see each other, but no one says it. Words spoken have got a funny way of happening.

"How did you two get here?" Mikail asks Aeri and Sora. He hasn't looked at Euyn once.

"Winter horses," Aeri answers. "They're tied up that way."

She points to her left. So that's how they caught up to us. They had fast horses and didn't have to run through the snow chasing after a bunch of deer.

"All right," Mikail says. "Vashney in ten days."

We all nod. The three of them leave, and then it's just Aeri and me in the snow. She shivers, and I remember she's still in a ball gown.

"We need to get you out of that dress," I say.

Aeri arches an eyebrow, her lips curling into a smile. "I thought you'd never ask."

I can feel the blood rushing to my face. I stomp off away from her, headed somewhere south.

CHAPTER THIRTY-ONE

AERI
CITY OF VASHNEY, KHITAN

Royo is determined not to talk to me as we ride into Vashney. So really, it's a pretty standard trip.

Between my lack of winter gear, the time of night, and my desperate need for sleep, we made the decision to stay in the closest city and leave for the Light Mountains in the morning.

We check into the first traveler's inn we find. I'm not even sure what the name is, but it's a small place of maybe eight rooms. We put the horses in the stable and then go into the lobby. Royo, impatient as always, rings the bell for the innkeeper. Then he purposefully avoids looking at me.

An older Khitanese woman with gray hair comes out of the back room. I think we woke her, but she smiles.

"Good evening," she says in Khitanese.

"We'll need two rooms," Royo says in Yusanian.

The innkeeper squints and shakes her head.

Oh. We didn't think about the language barrier when we split up. All the people who can speak Khitanese are on a sleigh headed to the ice caves.

Royo holds up two fingers and then says it again louder and slower, as if that will translate. I can't do any better. Although I pick up languages quickly, I don't know enough Khitanese to tell her that we need two separate rooms.

She slides across one key. Royo tries to ask for another, pointing again and putting up two fingers, but she must think he's telling her that there will be two of us in the room. She nods and nudges the key again.

He looks at me and then gives up with a sigh. He turns to the woman and makes the money sign, rubbing his fingers together.

The innkeeper tries to tell him the amount, then purses her lips and writes the number down. They use papers for money here called marks. The room is twenty marks. I have no idea what that means in terms of mun, if we're being ripped off or not, but Mikail gave us two hundred marks before he left. It won't be nearly enough for a wardrobe, but I can sell a small diamond tomorrow.

"Let's go," Royo huffs.

I smile at the woman, and she nods, then shakes her head, confused.

You and me both, ma'am.

I race to keep up with Royo, but I don't know why he's so bent out of shape. Ever since we met, we've spent more nights together than apart. Why is he acting scandalized by the idea? Plus, I saw all the times he looked at me today—all the moments he didn't think I was watching. He's angry, but he's not nearly as put out as he pretends to be.

He opens the door to the quaint room. There's a dresser, a nightstand, a washroom but sadly no bathtub, and one small bed. It'll barely fit the two of us. I laugh.

"It's not funny," he says. "It's not enough space."

I shrug. "It's better than an isle."

He looks at me like I'm the least amusing person in the three realms. Right. We're back to pretending like that never happened.

I roll my eyes. "We'll manage for a night, Royo."

I'm so exhausted that my vision is blurry. I force myself to wash up and get ready for bed. The new problem is that once again, I lost all of my clothes. And that includes nightgowns. I'm beginning to wonder if I should even keep replacing my wardrobe. I'm going to, but it's been a pain that my trunks keep getting lit on fire.

My hair is past shoulder-length now from using the amulet, but no one's noticed. People just assume they misremembered my hair length. I brush it as I come out of the washroom. Royo stands by the weapon-covered dresser. I see he's unpacked.

"Here." He holds a shirt and pants away from his body like they're contagious. "For you to sleep in."

"That's thoughtful, Royo," I say. Because it is.

He grunts and goes into the washroom. I change out of the dress and into his clothes. It's ridiculous how much more comfortable they are, even though the pants are way too big. I'm trying to figure out how to keep them up when he comes out of the washroom. He looks at me and laughs and then pretends like it was a very strange cough. But I heard it—the greatest sound in the world. My heart flutters, and I smile. He frowns harder.

"You can laugh, you know," I say. "I won't tell anyone."

I give up on the pants and let them fall as I peel down the quilt and get into my side of the bed. I hope he's not going to be weird about sleeping next to me.

He stands at the end of the bed, folding his arms.

Weird it is.

"What?" I really am too exhausted for this. I feel it in my bones. This cheap bed feels like a cloud. After being awake and panicked for two days, this room is Elysia.

"I'm angry," he says.

Never mind. It just became the Tenth Hell.

"What else is new?" I murmur, snuggling the side of my cheek into the soft pillow.

He scoffs, but there's a bit of a laugh in there, too. Enough to make me feel lighter, for my toes to curl under the quilt.

"Why are you angry?" I ask, sincere this time.

"You lied to me."

There's so much pain in those four words that my heart twists at having caused it. I had my reasons, but in the end, he's right—I did lie. I purposefully made him think I wasn't the king's daughter. Because I'm really not. Or, at the very least, he's never been like a father to me.

But I wasn't honest with Royo.

"I know I did," I say. "I wish I hadn't. I wish I could've told you the truth from the beginning. But I didn't know you had anything to do with the plan. I really thought you were just a guard. And you weren't honest, either."

Well…that wasn't what I meant to say. I meant to apologize, but sometimes *sorry* is the hardest word to pronounce. It rolled off my tongue with Sora, but it's so much more difficult with Royo. And not because I mean it any less. I suppose it's difficult because my heart is at stake.

He blinks. "What wasn't I honest about?"

"Killing your girlfriend," I say with a yawn. I do *not* mean to yawn. It just escaped because I shouldn't have gotten in bed before we finished talking.

His amber-colored eyes take on the appearance of an incoming storm. And then I know for certain: he didn't do it.

The realization hits and rakes down my guts. I dig my nails into the pillow. It had been my excuse—I was a liar but so was he. We'd both made mistakes. And that made us even. But he wasn't lying. Just me. Well, me and my father and the northern count. Really, only Royo was telling the truth this whole time.

"They lied…" I whisper, sitting up in bed. "Why did they lie? What was there to gain?"

He's breathing hard, but he shakes his head and speaks quietly. "I didn't hurt her. I never would've. I don't know why Bay Chin and your father said I did. Maybe so you wouldn't trust me. I dunno."

He stares down at the ground, wounded. It hurts so bad that my heart physically aches for him. I didn't know that was a real thing.

"I'm sorry, Royo," I say. "For all of it."

My words have never felt punier than they do now, measured against the damage they've caused.

He nods. "You swear you didn't know I was being set up? You thought I was just a guard?"

"On my soul," I say. "On my mother's."

He stares at me, and I hold his gaze because I am being honest. I had no idea.

Eventually, Royo nods again. "You're exhausted."

"I'm so far past that. I've been up for two days." I shift my shoulders. They're so sore they click as I move them.

He stares at me. "Ten Hells, why didn't you stop?"

"I saw the dead zaybear, and I needed to know you were okay. I couldn't rest until I reached you, so I rode all night."

Royo shakes his head. "You're the most foolish girl I know."

But he says it like *I love you.* Being called a fool shouldn't make my chest fill with joy, but here we are.

"I know," I say, lying back down.

He hesitates, but he turns out the oil lamp. I can still see him in the moonlight, though. Those super broad shoulders and muscled arms.

Slowly, reluctantly, he gets into the other side of the bed. I think about clinging to him like the barnacles on the fleet ship, but he might go sleep in the horse stall if I touch him.

"I really am sorry, Royo," I whisper in the quiet.

"Why didn't you say so on the ship?" he murmurs. I feel the vibrations of his voice on the mattress, and I love it. I love hearing, seeing, and feeling him.

I shrug. "I thought you wanted to kill me."

"I did…" He looks over at me and hesitates. "Because you didn't apologize. I thought you just didn't care."

"How could you think that?" I ask, my eyebrows shooting up. "You know me."

"No, I knew a girl named Aeri. Not a princess."

"Royo, all I am is a girl named Aeri. Naerium died seven years ago, and no one mourned her."

He stares at me, his eyes shining in the moonlight. Pity and then understanding flashes in them. "Don't ever lie to me again, Aeri."

"I won't." I yawn. I really hope I mean it.

He adjusts his pillow, his body stiff as can be on the bed, but at least he's next to me. I fall right to sleep, although I wish I could stay awake just to hold on to this moment for a little longer. Tomorrow, we'll leave for what promises to be certain death. But right now, I hold on to this fleeting moment.

CHAPTER THIRTY-TWO

MIKAIL
THE WESTERN PASS, KHITAN

We trek back to the sleigh. Sora doesn't complain about a single step, even though three of her toes have frostbite. We need to find winter gear for her before we reach the ice caves. Luckily, Loptra isn't far.

Loptra is a new-style city, without a single building over a hundred years old, because the Marnans burned it all to the ground on their march to Vashney a century ago.

Once we reach the sleigh, Euyn gives Sora a spare set of his clothes. He is around half a foot taller than she is, so they hardly fit. They'll work for now, though, as all she needs to do is rest.

Sora goes behind the sled and changes out of her gown. As soon as she's finished, she lies down under the fur blankets in the back. That leaves me alone with Euyn in the front.

I repaired the harness when we caught up to the sleigh, and I'm glad I did because the Western Pass can be treacherous. The road mostly winds through the mountain valley, but there are sections of narrow paths carved along the cliffs. I've taken the pass back to Yusan a few times, and I can't say any of those treks were easy.

Euyn drives through the light snowfall. He is a decent coachman, cautious and attentive. He is also, undeniably, a bad person.

To be clear, I never thought Euyn was a good person. I *did* think that removed from the opulence and decadence of Qali, he *could* be, especially after he was banished and lived among commoners in Fallow for years. But after our conversation about the priest, I see I was wrong. The Baejkins are rotten to their core.

Euyn loves me—I believe that. He'd give his life for me and has proven that several times now. But as much as I look for the good in him, it's not enough. Not enough to hold absolute power. The throne only makes immortality greater, only deepens character flaws, and he has too many to exploit. His Baejkin thinking will prevent him from ruling fairly and ultimately from freeing Gaya. He will always be able to justify suppressing others if it benefits Yusan.

His rule will only be more of the same. Or worse. Euyn being given immortal power has the makings of a disaster.

I wish I knew where that left us. I suppose we're in the same place. We need to convince Quilimar to start a war, to kill Joon, and then we'll worry about the aftermath later. If it's not a Baejkin ruler on the throne, the nobles will battle for the crown, and I can't say Seok or Rune would be better than Euyn. The eastern count, Dal, is dead, and I swear on Gaya that Bay Chin won't live long enough to see a regime change.

Stars, are there no good noblemen in Yusan?

I stare up at the sky as we ascend into the mountains. Gayans believe the stars guide us, but the snowy night obscures their light. I might as well be in Idle for all the constellations I can see.

As soon as I think about Idle, Tiyung springs to mind. Maybe Ty could be our next king. He is a nobleman with a conscience, and there are very few of those. The issue, of course, is that he'd have to survive prison first. And come out relatively sane, which is no easy feat.

Before we left for the temple, I received confirmation that he was alive, but things can change quickly in a dungeon. I will have to make arrangements to ensure his safety. When I first met Tiyung in Rahway, I never thought we would need him, but he just might be the one who saves all of Yusan.

I tap my fingers on the varnished wood of the sleigh as I think through the logistics.

Installing a new king means finding Joon and killing him first. Zahara is the acting spymaster, and she doesn't know where he went, which means he told no one. The mystery haunts me. Where did he go and why? Qali is the safest place for him. Only one assassination attempt ever succeeded there—when he murdered his own father.

I searched for answers in the temple earlier, but who knows where to look for the motivations of a king? I read scrolls on historical Yusanian rulers. Generally, they only left the palace for diplomacy or war. There is no war, and I doubt it's diplomacy, so what is Joon's reason?

The only thing pressing enough could be the Sands of Time. And Lord Yama help us if he locates that.

I shiver, but it's not from the cold wind. The crisp mountain air is refreshing. No, Joon acquiring any other relic would be disastrous.

When we reach Loptra, I will be able to gather more intelligence on Joon and send messages to my loyal spies. I also have another source there—Fallador's cousin, Gambria. I'll arrange a meeting with her before we leave.

I smile to myself—she'll love that.

She decidedly will not.

Euyn keeps glancing over at me as we ride into the night. I'm sure he's wildly confused as to the distance between us. He can't fathom why I take issue with genocide or slaughtering a priest we promised to aid.

I sigh and shift on the padded wood bench. I won't be able to change Euyn. I'm not certain anyone ever changes for the better. At best they alter themselves to fit the situation. So the question is—will he still love me if I don't give him the throne? Or will it be one betrayal too many?

We ride until we see the telltale lightening of the predawn in the distance. Against all odds, we lived to see another day. There's always hope with the sunrise that the new day might be better than its predecessor. I have to believe that, believe in hope, or there's no point to living. There would've been no reason to survive the Festival of Blood. I made it through those horrors to put an end to all of this. Euyn was a distraction along the way who I wanted to believe was the solution. It is clear that he is not.

It'll be time to wake Sora soon, and for Euyn to sleep—or at least pretend to. I'm about to suggest we stop, and then I hear it: a crack high above us. It sounds like a hundred branches breaking, but I know that's not what it is. I hold my breath, hoping I'm wrong. But next comes the distinct rumble of snow.

I glance up at the mountains as the ground begins to shake. We're going to die.

CHAPTER THIRTY-THREE

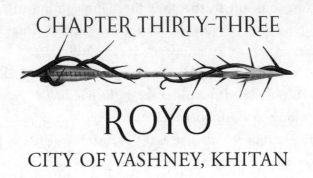

ROYO

CITY OF VASHNEY, KHITAN

I wake up holding Aeri close. I don't know how to feel about her, whether I should want her or run, but my body has an opinion.

Thick and imposing everywhere, she'd joked.

I adjust my hips away from her and lie still. I stare at the wall, thinking about hundred-year-old corpses, murdered priests, anything to take my mind off the fact that she smells good. Aeri has a gentle way of breathing, like she's sipping air. Her long neck would look so pretty curled in pleasure. That mouth should be…

I groan. Maybe I should think about the fact that I can't trust her.

After last night, though, I do believe her. Thinking back, she seemed as shocked as anyone in the throne room. Then again, I believed her the whole time in Yusan. So either she means it, or I'm the dumbest mark on the continent.

I must have moved, because she wakes up and smiles in that unnaturally happy way of hers. Warmth fills my chest like hot soup on a cold day. I missed this. I missed *her*.

"Good morning, Royo," she says in a raspy voice. She doesn't move her hand from where it rests against my chest.

I force myself to roll away, out of her reach. I throw my legs over the side of the bed and sit up. "Are you ready to go?"

"I will be soon." She sits up as well and stretches. I like her wearing my shirt, even if it's huge on her. The morning is gray because of monsoon season, but the light coming in from the window illuminates her just right. She's so beautiful. Then she turns and glances at the sill. "Oh, my goodness, Dia!"

I whip my head toward the window. What? Who's Dia?

Aeri gets out of bed and runs over to the window. My shirt barely covers her long legs. Another inch or two and…

Impulses stronger than I've ever felt rush through me. I go over to the dresser and gather my weapons, gripping the handles and shoving them into my bag. I have to do something with my hands. I want to do unspeakable things to her—all of which she'd love. But we have a job to do.

I breathe out. I focus. What is she talking about, anyhow?

"Who's Dia?" I say to the paint chipping on the wall.

"She's a moon owl I was feeding in Quu," Aeri says. "She came all this way!"

She says it like that's a normal thing to do—to have a little owl friend.

Aeri is the strangest person I've ever met.

I glance over. Sure enough, there's a tiny white owl asleep in the corner of the windowsill. Weird. But then I look at Aeri. Her bright smile. Her half-naked body.

"Can you put on some clothes?" It comes out harsher and louder than I meant it.

"Yeah," she says, unfazed. "We need to get breakfast anyhow. I haven't eaten in a day, and I want to get something for Dia, too."

"Why's her name Dia?" I ask.

She tilts her head at me. "Because I named her that. Owls don't come with name tags, Royo."

I stare, unamused, as she laughs. My stomach rumbles, and I remember I haven't eaten, either. Not since we stopped for gear yesterday.

"Fine," I say. "We'll look for breakfast for you and…Dia when you're ready."

She lights up and goes into the washroom. I finally relax once she's away from the bed. The fuck am I doing with this girl? I am definitely not favored by the gods—that's for sure.

Aeri comes back out in her ball gown. I'm not sure if it's more or less ridiculous than wearing my clothes, but at least she's covered. The green skirt of her dress goes down to her boots.

"Let's find a jeweler," she says, arranging her hair. "I'll sell a diamond, and then we can get a good meal and I'll find proper clothes."

"Mikail gave me enough money," I say.

She frowns, looking skeptical. "Probably not. I had to leave everything behind in Quu. Seok set it all on fire."

Seok, the guy who owns Sora. I run a hand over my short hair. Nobody should own somebody else.

"It'll be fine," I say. "You don't need that much."

I have a hundred and eighty marks. That should be enough to eat well and get the stuff we need. But if she wants more, what do I care? It's her diamond, and she stole it anyhow. It's force of habit to argue with her, I guess.

She better not buy a trunk, though. We're not carting a wardrobe into the mountains.

We leave the inn and ride inside the city walls of Vashney. The old capital is not as busy as Quu, but it's just as big and also filled with a mishmash of people. The buildings are carved stone, stained with centuries of runoff. In the distance, there's the frozen port. All the ships are aground because it's just a big sheet of ice stretching into the pitch black of the North Sea.

It doesn't take long to find the gem district. The town is laid out like a pie that's been sliced—everything runs off the center, where there's a colossal statue of the Sky King. The gem houses and luxury shops are together in a wedge-shaped district.

Aeri chooses a gem house and then picks a diamond from her bag. She has a bunch. The shop welcomes her. She walks up to the counter, and a man examines the stone. Then the negotiation starts. I'm not sure what he's saying, but I recognize haggling in any language. They write numbers down on a paper and go back and forth. He bargains with her just like she's a man. It's weird.

They settle on three thousand marks as I look around the store. It's a fortune for a little rock.

Aeri says something as the gem guy hands her the money.

"Wait, you speak Khitanese?" I ask.

"Not really, but I'm a fast learner." She shrugs and pockets the paper.

I don't get this language or this place at all. We pass display cases of jade necklaces and bracelets on the way out. Some are almost the color of the key in my pocket.

A lot happened yesterday. I know I turned the lock when the others couldn't, but I don't know nothing about being a keeper. I'm just a strongman.

Because of that, I go on alert as we leave the gem house. I don't have to worry about Aeri being taken here because indentures and slavery are illegal in Khitan. But pickpockets are everyplace, and a gem house is an easy mark.

"Let me hold some of your money, just in case," I say.

Aeri blinks at me, but she digs into her velvet bag. She hands over all her marks except for a hundred note.

"You don't need to give me that much," I say.

She shrugs. "I trust you."

My palms sweat as I put the money into my bag. I don't know if she should trust me. I haven't had a girl believe in me in so long. I don't know if I deserve it. But I'll do what I have to in order to keep her safe.

"Royo." She waves her hand in front of my face. "Stop spacing out and start helping me find a good tavern. I'm starving."

"Yeah," I say.

I walk with her to find breakfast. I like this little thief—no point in denying it. But if she lies to me again, I may kill her myself.

CHAPTER THIRTY-FOUR

SORA
THE WESTERN PASS, KHITAN

After being awake for so long, lying down in the sleigh is a priceless relief. I'm nearly asleep the second I recline on the bench. Surrounded by soft fur, it's easy to nod off. Even thinking about Daysum can't keep me awake. And it should. I should be unable to live, to breathe, while she suffers. After all, what is a life abandoning what I love?

Thinking about what she and Ty must be enduring kept me up through the entire ride to Lake Cerome, but my eyes drift closed, and the next thing I know, I'm in a dream. Except it's not a dream—it's a memory.

I recognize where I am immediately. This is my childhood home in Inigo. The house I grew up in was a two-room shack by a stream. Our parents had their bedroom, and the other room served as the living room, dining room, kitchen, playroom, and the bedroom for the four of us—me, Daysum, and our little brothers, Taj and Jee. Jee was two years old and had just started sleeping with us instead of in our parents' bed.

Based on the ages, this was a few months before Seok arrived and shattered my world.

Back then, I didn't know anything about Gain, or poison maidens, or counts. I knew our clapboard house and the foothills of the mountains. I was nine years old and singing a song. Daysum and the boys were dancing around the room. My mother and father were at the sink, cleaning vegetables and rinsing rice for dinner, but they were singing the chorus with me. My father two-stepped as he shelled peas, and my mother laughed. Daysum grabbed my hands, and we spun in a circle.

Warmth floods me. This was all I ever wanted and needed.

I was happy.

Suddenly, Daysum started coughing and coughing, until she turned deep red. Seconds later, she collapsed. I skinned my knee falling to catch her before she hit the rough wood slats. The cut stung as I held her. Daysum's eyes rolled back, and I just barely stopped her head from slamming onto the ground as she convulsed.

"Mama!" I screamed.

Our mother rushed over, wiping her hands on her tattered apron.

"Daysum!" she yelled. "Darling, can you hear me?"

My mother took her from me, and I sat on the floor, shocked. We went from dancing and laughing to this so quickly.

"We need a healer," Father said, wringing his hands.

Mother pursed her lips, frown lines marring her perfect face. "How will we—"

"I will figure it out," Father said, his lips set in a determined line as he slipped on his worn shoes. Healers were expensive and Daysum was often ill, but not like this.

Mother lowered her eyes and nodded. She held Daysum in her arms. "Please hurry."

My father rushed out the door.

"What can I do?" I asked.

My mother cupped my face in her hand. "Just be the good girl you are. We will take care of her."

I paced and waited by the window, and it felt like an eternity before the healer arrived. Father came in, out of breath with his brow glistening with sweat. He'd run after the healer's horse from across town.

Daysum was diagnosed with purple fever and given herbs to drink. Until that moment, I hadn't realized how poor we were. My parents' fleeting expressions when the healer prescribed red meat said it all—they couldn't afford it. Maybe, in the end, that's why we were sold.

The healer said that Daysum's illness was contagious. My brothers and I were instructed to move our sleeping mats to the floor in my parents' bedroom. I did as I was told, but once everyone was asleep, I snuck out and padded into the big room. I knew I could get sick, but I didn't care. I didn't want Daysum to be alone.

"You shouldn't be here, Sora," she said, her voice weak.

I snuggled in under her blanket, holding her fevered body as she shook. "I'm always here, little one."

"I'll love you for always," is what she said. I remember it plainly. But this time she turns to me, and her eyes go wide and alarmed. "Sora, listen to me—you need to go!"

I shake my head and sigh. "I'll be okay."

I did develop purple fever, but I was fully recovered in two days. Daysum was sick for months.

"Sora, wake up! You need to run!"

I open my eyes to a dark, starless sky. I expect Daysum to be next to me, but I'm alone on the bench of a sleigh. It's just before dawn, but there's a distinct rumbling in the distance. Icy, immediate fear spreads along my spine. I jerk upright and watch a mountain of snow careening downhill, heading right for us.

An avalanche.

CHAPTER THIRTY-FIVE

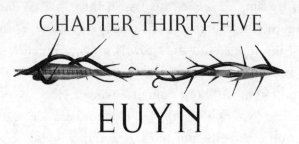

EUYN

THE WESTERN PASS, KHITAN

I steady the califers, snapping the reins to urge them to run as the snow begins to tumble down from the peak of the mountain. At the same time, Mikail goes to wake Sora, but she suddenly bolts upright from dead sleep.

"Avalanche!" she yells.

It's as bad as I thought. Spending most of my life in Qali and then the desert badlands of Fallow, I've never been in an avalanche, but I know how dangerous they can be. We've lost entire garrisons to them. Thousands of soldiers buried alive, gone in seconds.

"Kingdom of Hells," she says.

"I'll try to outrun it." I snap the reins again.

I grip the leather tight as I stare up at the mountain. The snow is spreading, but it's slightly behind us. There's only so fast we can go on this narrow cliff pass, though. The drop is hundreds of feet to the gorge and the Uulatar river on the left. One animal slips, and we're done for, but we have to try.

"No," Sora says. "We can't outrun it. We need to get out of this sled. We have to jump. Look, there's a cut up ahead."

"What?" Mikail and I yell at the same time.

Getting out of the sled is the worst possible decision.

"I grew up at the base of the mountains," she says. "Grab what you can. We need to jump."

There isn't time to argue, but I wish there was. What does she know? Chul did mention that their village was at the foothills of the Khakatan Mountains, and the snow is moving much faster than I expected, and spreading far wider.

Gods on High, we're not going to make it.

Within the span of a breath, I decide to trust her. It may be the worst decision of my life, but in that case, it will also be my last.

"Jump now!" Mikail yells. He grabs a rucksack in one hand and uses the other to push off the sled.

The three of us dive toward the mountain. I'm last out. I've just barely cleared the sleigh when snow begins to pour down. More snow than I can fathom slides off the mountain. The ground shakes, the roar deafening.

Sora pulls us into a cut in the cliff face that's maybe three feet deep. She leans with her back against the frigid stone. Mikail and I do the same.

I breathe hard as the snow begins to rise, piling up around us. Calves. Knees. Thighs. Sora was wrong. We're going to be buried alive. No chance to fight. Mikail and I could've run if we just hadn't listened to her.

My heart drums in my chest. I've been ready to die several times in my life by someone or something's hand. This, however, is nature, a larger force than I can fight.

The califers and sleigh continue on the pass until suddenly they disappear, pushed off the road by tons of snow. They plummet into the gorge as if they were weightless.

I suppose it's a comfort to know that we would've died either way.

Snow continues to rise with a thunderous groan until we're covered past our waists, nearly up to Sora's chest. My breathing is frantic, desperate. Each gasp feels like it may be my last. I want to reach out to Mikail, but he is on the other side of Sora.

I'm ready to shout my last goodbye even though I know it won't be heard over the rushing snow, but as the avalanche cascades all around us, I realize we should've been completely covered by now.

Why are we alive?

I look up. Somehow, most of the snow is shooting straight out from where we are. The cut in the cliff created a slide of sorts where the vast majority of the avalanche misses us and falls into the gorge.

Sora knew it was our only chance to survive. She saved me. And more importantly, she saved Mikail.

I look at this girl, this beautiful thing. She's staring ahead, her violet eyes wide. She has her hands on our chests, to keep us as close to the rock face as she can. It was her knowledge that put us into this small crevice of safety. The margin between life and death was about three feet.

She could've jumped out of the sled and let us fall, but she didn't. Even though Mikail and I both lied. Even though she knew I hunted her father. It's a selfless bravery, a debt I can't hope to repay. But I can at least gift her honesty.

The snow subsides. The white of the avalanche turns back to the dawn sky. The roar is replaced by perfect quiet. As quickly as it started, the avalanche is over.

We made it. We're all so relieved, we smile and then laugh. We've escaped Lord Yama's clutches once again.

Sora looks over at me. She's so beautiful, and it was her beauty that condemned her.

I take a deep breath.

"Your father never stopped looking for you," I say. "Seok had threatened to slay your entire family if your father didn't let you and Daysum go. Chul stopped fighting in order to save your mother and brothers, but he refused to sign the indenture certificates. Seok forged your father's hand in front of a corrupt magistrate. Your father later found the judge and murdered him in his chambers. But your parents never sold you."

Sora's eyes well with tears. She's sad, and yet there's some relief and maybe even a little joy in her expression. Happiness fills my chest. I gave that to her.

Then her face shifts and her cheeks color. I've only just noticed her anger when her arm comes flying at me. Her fist connects with my face, and I see stars.

CHAPTER THIRTY-SIX

AERI

THE NORTHERN PASS, KHITAN

The snow is beautiful. Deadly and cold, but it really is gorgeous now that I'm rested and wearing furs and proper clothes for the winter. And it's especially nice with Royo by my side.

He and I travel north, past glistening drifts and stunning frozen waterfalls. I stare at the icicles. The water has just stopped, suspended in air until thaw. The forests are coated, their green limbs dressed all in white. Everything is quiet and still as if I stopped time. But it wasn't me. It was just the seasons.

Khitan has an untouched type of beauty. The farther we ride from Vashney, the more pristine it is. I could tell from the maps, and the priest confirmed, that nearly all the people live in the southernmost part of the country. Khitan is largely just frozen wasteland.

We are headed to the border of that tundra. The Light Mountains mark the end of the tree line in Khitan. There is seemingly nothing on the other side.

"We should stop soon and make camp before it's too dark," Royo says.

Camp? What camp? I look around. Does he really mean sleeping outside in all this snow?

"Aren't we going to stay in a traveler's inn?" I ask.

"Do you see one?"

Okay, that's a fair question. There's a whole lot of beauty but also nothing around us. And we still have three days until we reach the mountains far in the distance.

"Don't worry," he says. "I picked up supplies to make a camp when we were in Vashney."

He said that when he got bored in the dress house. *I'm gonna get camp supplies.* But there isn't a house on his horse.

"I've got to tell you: I'm really not a huge fan of freezing to death," I say.

He nods. "I know that. I'll keep you warm."

My stomach swoops, and my heart flutters. I glance over at him.

He stares for a moment and then clears his throat. "We need to let the horses rest and gather firewood while it's still light."

The wind blows right into our faces, and I sigh from somewhere deep within me. I really, really do not want to sleep in the cold.

"It'll be all right, Aeri," he says.

Easy for him to say. He's built like a brick oven.

We continue along the Northern Pass until Royo pulls his horse off the roadway.

"This is a good spot," he says.

We have to talk about the definitions of words. There's nothing "good" about this.

He heads toward the rock outcropping. It's literally a few boulders and some pine trees.

I'm still trying to figure out what makes this good when we ride up. Apparently, what he means by good is "not covered in snow." There's a patch of bare dirt between the rocks and the pines.

"This is perfect," he says.

I arch an eyebrow. "That's not what that word means."

Royo glances at me, nearly smiling as he dismounts. "We'll be protected on three sides, making it hard to ambush us. Tie your horse to that branch. You can feed them while I get us set up."

That's right—he also bought feed bags while I was in the dress house.

I could've been there all day, but I settled for ordering just four necessary outfits when Royo came over a third time to ask if I was done. The reality is that if we don't survive stealing the egg, it won't matter how many outfits I bought.

It doesn't take long for Royo to have a very small tent set up and a fire going. Gods, I think this is what he means by a "camp." He takes out a pot and fills it with snow.

"What's that for?" I ask.

"I'm making our dinner," he says.

"Oh good—we're having snow."

I stand with my hands on my hips as he pulls out our provisions. I don't have faith in this, but it's not like I know how to cook. I'm just glad I stuffed myself full at breakfast and bought some buns, breads, and cakes at the bread house for our trip. I also picked up some dried meat for Dia.

She's sitting on the branch of the tree closest to us. I fed her after breakfast, despite Royo staring at me like I'd lost my mind. I don't tell him about how Dia warned me to flee in Quu. I don't think he'd believe me.

And it's a minor miracle that Royo is speaking to me again. We aren't nearly as close as we were in Tamneki, but I also don't have the weight of the secrets and lies keeping us apart.

The sun goes down, but I have the warmth of the fire. I'm also in pants. I was lucky to be the same size as the mannequin, so I could buy the slacks ready-made from the dress house. It feels strange to wear the same thing as a man. Some peasants in Yusan will wear rough spun pants regardless of gender, but never like this, fine and lined with soft fur.

Royo serves us dinner. He made a pot of rice and threw in some dried sausage, dried mushrooms, and seaweed. I'm skeptical, but I take a bite and it's actually quite good. He must've tossed in a seasoning sachet as well. Who knew he could cook?

He sits next to me on a log we cleared off earlier. We eat, almost touching, slurping our rice stew from two wooden bowls.

It's one of the best meals I've ever had, safe here next to him.

We are almost finished when the sky lights up. Both of us tip our heads back. It's not snowing at the moment. Instead, magnificent swirls of greens and purples trace through the dark sky, constantly moving. The stars are illuminated behind the waves of color, creating an enchanting scene.

Royo stares with wonder in his eyes and a boyish expression. "What is that?"

"In Khitan, they call them the Lights of the Sky King," I say. "I read about it. If you follow the lights to their end, they're supposed to lead to the Kingdom of Heavens, realm of the Sky King and celestial deities. We can't see it this well in Yusan, but on clear nights sometimes they're visible in Pyong. We call them the Night Rays of the Sun King."

He glances at me. "You think that's true? That the lights lead to the Heavens?"

"I think it sounds nice." I look at the sky again. "But either way, they're the most beautiful thing I've ever seen."

I lean my head back again to watch the lights dance.

"Not me," he mutters.

"Of course not," I sigh.

Royo is so guilty about whatever happened with his girlfriend that he thinks not enjoying life will somehow absolve him. But it doesn't work that way. Atonement is for the Ten Hells. Life is for living, for making mistakes and wringing the most out of good moments because the bad will always be there.

I feel him looking at me.

"You're better than the lights," he says.

I stare into his eyes. I've never been struck by lightning, but this has to be the same feeling—lit up and shocked all at once.

Royo leans forward, and then his mouth is on mine. My eyes open as wide as they can go, and then they drift closed as my lips soften against his. He kisses me, slowly at first and then faster. Sparks fly in my chest and at the base of my spine. I drop my bowl to the ground and wrap my arms around his neck as he pulls me against him. I don't know what happened—what put him under this spell. I don't know how long this will last. But I'll live in this moment before the enchantment breaks.

CHAPTER THIRTY-SEVEN

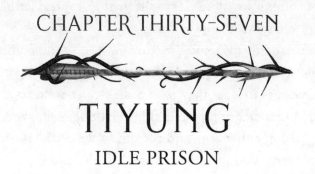

TIYUNG

IDLE PRISON

This cell isn't so bad—as sunless dungeons go. I have a lantern and a small supply of oil, thanks to Hana. She also brought me plenty of food; more than I need, really. Every time she comes in, she tells me the day and bell. These are little luxuries I never would've noticed before. She even gave me a notepad and ink to write down my thoughts and keep my mind busy.

Hana confirmed that the guards patrol and bring food randomly to disorient prisoners. It prevents escape attempts and aids in breaking the minds of prisoners when they need information.

I asked if they drain the lake every time she comes and goes. She shook her head and said there's another entrance. I wonder where it is and how she gets here, but I haven't asked. There are limits to the trust we are building.

My breakfast of stale bread and water arrives. I eat it with some meat and cheese as I wait for Hana. Even though I take my time, I finish without seeing her. I thought this was when she usually arrives, but then again, the meal could've been random.

I begin my exercise regime—Hana said it would help my mind to keep my body active. I run in place and do push-ups, sit-ups, and lunges until I'm exhausted. But still, there's no sign of her.

The guards arrive, but they silently push another meal through the slot. As they walk away, worry begins to set in. Where is Hana?

Is she not coming anymore? Have the guards stopped letting her see me? Will I die soon?

I breathe hard, my thoughts turning to my impending death. I've tried to make peace with the inevitable. Every person dies. The difference is in how they live. Still, I can't seem to accept my execution. I keep believing something, anything, will save me. I can't let go of the hope that Sora and the others will make it back. I still hope that Hana is lying, although she has no reason to.

Half a day passes, and I remain alone in my cell. Suddenly, there's the sound of footsteps in the hall. I stand, ready to see her, but guards just push a third tray through my meal slot and leave.

I pace. I wait. I eat again. And then I sit down.

She's not coming.

My chest sags as if there's a weight attached to my ribs. The fatigue and despair I'd kept at bay engulf me. She didn't come. She either couldn't or wouldn't, and I don't know which is worse.

I try to be thankful that she was here at all. Her visits were a blessing from the gods. But blessings lifted create a new type of pain.

More time passes, and my chin dips to my chest. I shake my head, blinking awake, trying to stay up. Hana not appearing today could mean that I die tonight. The guards might try to kill me in my sleep.

The worry keeps me awake, but eventually, even on the fear of death, I can't keep my eyes open any longer. I lean my head back against the wall and extinguish the lamp. I murmur a prayer that Lord Yama won't claim me tonight, and then I say the prayer that has become my daily wish.

Gods, please, just let me see Sora once again. But if you can only protect one of us, let it be her.

With that, I fall asleep. I must be out for a while because the keys have already turned in the lock when I stir. The heavy wood-and-iron door swings open and nearly hits me. I scramble to my feet, pressing myself up against the wall.

Is it Hana? Please be Hana.

It's not. It's the guards, and they carry a torchlight.

My heart thunders, and the pain behind my eyes is intense from the flame. I can't see, blinded by the fire. With my eyes tightly closed and my hand over them, I try to ready myself for my fate. I won't cry, try to flee, or beg. I've promised myself that much—to have an honorable death in the end.

I stand upright, ready to be pulled out of here. Ready to die facing my executioner.

But no one touches me. Instead, they throw someone else in. As my eyes adjust, a man trips and lands on the dirty stone floor with a groan. I have a cellmate now. I have no idea who he is. But I think he's here to kill me.

CHAPTER THIRTY-EIGHT

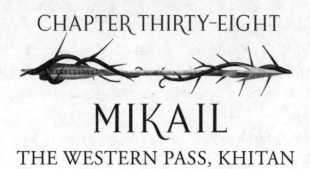

MIKAIL
THE WESTERN PASS, KHITAN

Euyn rights himself as I try to keep Sora from killing him…again. I hold her as gently as I can, restraining her at the elbows, but she struggles with all her might to reach him. If I'm honest, a part of me wants to let her go.

I need to figure out if I heard him correctly. We just lost the sleigh and barely survived an avalanche. It's been an eventful minute and a half. Did he really say that Sora and her sister's indentures were never legal? That he knew this the whole time? That—yet again—he's more of a callous monster than I imagined?

Stars, I really thought we'd hit the low already. Apparently, there's an Eleventh Hell.

Sora stops struggling and controls her breathing. From the look in her eyes, though, she's ready to throw him off the cliff, even if it means falling with him. I stay ready, because someone willing to die to commit murder is the most dangerous kind of killer.

Euyn holds snow against his jaw where Sora hit him—and he's still half buried.

"Sora," I whisper.

She exhales and looks away. I leave her for the moment, assured at least for now that she won't try to kill him. I stoop down and help dig Euyn out, using my arms like shovels.

"Tell me because I got distracted—did you just say that Sora's father never signed the indentures?" I question him as I drag the heavy snow to the side.

"That is what he told me," he says, meeting my gaze. "I wasn't able to confirm it, what with being locked in Idle Prison and all."

I study his face—he's telling the truth. Chul said this, but Euyn dismissed it.

"You didn't think to mention it while we were in Yusan?" I raise one brow.

He blinks. "What good would it have done?"

I stare at his confused expression. I can't figure out if he simply has no empathy or if there's a reason it wouldn't have mattered.

Sora comes up next to me, seething by my shoulder.

"What good?" Her hands ball into fists at her side. "I could've freed Daysum! She wouldn't be trapped in a pleasure house right now! She wouldn't be—"

She lets out a haunting scream, and I jerk my gaze up at the mountains, worried she'll start another avalanche. But Sora doesn't care at this point.

"No, she would not have been free," Euyn says, pursing his lips. At least he has the decency to look sorry.

She lunges for him again, but I catch her. Barely.

"Let him explain, please," I murmur.

She stares right at me and shakes her head, disgusted. She's going to kill him. Whether it's now or later, poison or not, her resolution is clear in her raised chin. It's going to take a lot of effort to keep him alive if I can't defuse this. And I already have too much to do.

I take a steadying breath. "You need to explain now, Euyn, and take care with your words. What makes you say Daysum wouldn't be free? You just said the indentures weren't valid."

"I believe they aren't, but with Dal dead, Seok is the most powerful nobleman in the realm." He frees his legs and backs an extra step away from Sora, which is not easy with so much snow piled up around us. "The word of a commoner wouldn't matter, especially since Chul murdered the only man who could've testified on his behalf. There's not a court in Yusan that would believe her father over Seok. Especially not when Seok can claim he paid a fair price and Chul already confessed to killing the magistrate."

As much as I disagree in principle, Euyn is correct. A Yusanian court would look at the murder of the magistrate as an admission of guilt. They would see a convicted commoner who sold his daughters for gold and who now seeks to renege. Seok would be believed without question.

"I thought it would upset you for no reason, Sora," Euyn says. "I swear—that is why I didn't tell you. I didn't want to dredge up the past because knowing the truth doesn't change anything."

He really should stop talking to her now. We all know it wasn't the only reason. He wanted to save face and not admit he hunted her father. He wanted to avoid the consequences of his actions.

She stares at him and takes a step closer. I wait, ready to restrain her again.

"The truth makes no difference to *you*," she says, voice shaking. "It means *everything* to me." She pauses, and tears well in her eyes. Then she leans forward. "I pray that every single thing that happens to Daysum happens to you, Euyn. In this life or the next."

Sora walks away, fur blanket wrapped around her shoulders. Her head is high, and she looks more regal than the prince even as she pushes through the deep snow. Euyn flinches as she passes, but she doesn't touch him. She doesn't need to.

I let her put some distance between us, and then I look Euyn in the eye. "Any more secrets that you're holding on to?"

He swallows hard and shakes his head. "No."

"Good. This is the last time I save you from one of them."

"But don't you think..." he begins. He studies my face, and something in his expression shifts.

"Don't I think what?" I ask.

He shakes his head. "Nothing."

We walk along the cliff together, even though I'm certain he's lying to me again.

CHAPTER THIRTY-NINE

ROYO

THE NORTHERN PASS, KHITAN

Aeri's mouth is on mine. I inhale her. She tastes like a treat from a sugar house and feels like the softest silk. Her flower smell blooms all around me, and I can't get enough.

The sky glows with ribbons of color as I pull her onto my lap. She straddles my hips, light like a feather. We're both in winter gear, and I wish we weren't. I want her in one of those short dresses with just a strip of fabric separating us.

Heat flushes through me, and I sweat, holding her tight. She hums with pleasure as she kisses me just as hard as I kiss her. I want to break her, devour her, and be lost in her all at the same time.

I've never desired someone like this. It's a need, not a want.

I run my hands under her shirt. Her skin is as soft as the fur she's wearing. She makes little gasps and moans when my thumbs graze her nipples. I reach up to her collarbone and then trace my fingers down. But my hand catches on something—a necklace, I think.

Aeri breaks our kiss, recoiling for a second.

But that's enough.

Ten Hells, what the fuck am I doing?

I catch my breath as we stare at each other. "I'm sorry—"

"No, I'm sorry," she says. "I— It's just—" She looks to the side.

She doesn't want this. A boulder lodges in my throat. It feels like I'm plummeting, falling from the top of a mountain as my stomach turns and my head spins.

"It's fine," I say quickly.

"It's not that…" she begins, shaking her head.

We keep talking at the same time, and it's real annoying. I move her to the side and stand. Her gaze flickers to my pants, to the bulge she was just pressed against. I clear my throat and then get busy with picking up the bowls. I need to get away from here.

"It's fine. We got carried away," I say. "It's fine."

"Royo…"

"I'm gonna bury the rest of this so animals don't come for it," I say.

I avoid looking at her as I take the empty pot and bowls and stomp off toward the roadway.

Embarrassment and the sting of rejection make me move quickly. It don't matter, though. We just got lost in it. She'd looked so beautiful, and this place is so incredible, I forgot. I forgot I'm better off alone. I forgot that I can only ruin any woman who gets close to me.

I'd say sorry for taking things too far, but she'd seemed like she wanted me. No. I must've read it wrong. She pulled back. In the end, she didn't want me.

Or maybe it's all just a game to her.

The thought is a bolt. A stab to the gut, made worse because I should've seen it coming.

Why would a princess like Aeri ever want a street thug like me?

I squat down by the pass and dig a hole in the snow. I take my time scraping every grain of the rice out of the bowls. Then I bury it all, along with my feelings. I use the snow to rinse everything clean.

By the time I'm done, my head is clear again. She was right to pull away. This is the last distraction we need. We're on the brink of war, still trying to kill a god king, and we have to get an egg from a deadly talking parrot or something.

Sex should be the last thing on my mind.

It's not.

I run my hand down my face and groan. I'd let it all go as a mistake, but when we were kissing, I'd listened for every little sigh, paid attention to every gasp. She was enjoying it. She wanted me right up until I hit her necklace.

It's gotta be the one I saw when we were on the riverboat. Simple with a yellow gem. Maybe it's a memento of something…or someone.

My heart thunders at the thought. For all I know, she has someone waiting on her in Pyong. I never asked.

I take a deep breath. Yeah, that idea doesn't make it better. Not even a little.

Now I have to sleep in a tiny tent next to her and keep her warm for the next three nights. And hopefully there's a return trip.

I should've gone with Mikail to steal that rotting corpse.

CHAPTER FORTY

TIYUNG

IDLE PRISON, YUSAN

The stranger in my cell gets to his feet as the door closes behind him. Like me, he's unchained. I fumble to light the lantern. As the flame spurts to life, he looks at me warily, keeping his distance. He's around my father's age, a little younger maybe, but this man is far different from Seok. He's a fighter, with a scarred eyebrow to prove it. He's probably been a long-term soldier from how he carries himself. And now he's a prisoner like me.

He's assessing me the same way I look at him. I keep my hands loose at my sides as I search for the glimmer of a weapon. I don't see one, but his shirt and pants are relatively neat, and he is clean-shaven. He must've recently arrived in Idle. The man has dirty-blond hair and light-brown skin. He takes in my soiled dress, but he stops and squints at my face.

"You're a nobleman," he says. Then he takes a quick look around the cell.

I nod. "Are you here to kill me?"

His eyes land on mine again. "Not that I know of."

A feeling of familiarity washes over me. He reminds me of someone, but I can't place whom.

We still eye each other, but with slightly less suspicion than before. I'm not what he expected, and he's not what I thought, either.

"Why are you here?" I ask.

"At the king's request," he says with a slight bow. "Same reason every guy is in here, I imagine."

"I meant in my cell." It comes out far more pompous than I meant. I hear my tone and internally cringe at sounding like my father.

The man sniffs. "Didn't see your name carved on the door."

I sigh and raise a palm.

The man focuses to my side, where there's the lantern and notebook, along with the sack of food I keep wrapped up. He has a certain sharpness that makes me rethink my guess of soldier.

"I don't know," he says. "The guards threw me in here. They didn't offer a choice of lodgings, my lord."

"You are not a nobleman," I suggest, but it comes out arrogant. I don't know what's wrong with me. There's no status in the Tenth Hell. And my pretentiousness is making this man actively dislike me, which could result in him murdering me even if that wasn't his mission. But I suppose I'm falling back on what I know.

"No, I was in the king's guard," he says.

Hmm, so my initial impression was correct. A small dash of pride runs through me at still having some of my wits.

I decide that it's best to stop talking. I let him get adjusted, but I keep one eye on him at all times. It seems too convenient that this man showed up on the day Hana didn't appear. It would be an easy excuse to tell my father they had no hand in my death because another prisoner was responsible.

But then again, they could say that with no one in my cell. So what game are they playing and why?

Time passes, and the man stays to the other side of the space. I had been rationing the lantern oil, but I keep it lit to observe him.

Mealtime comes, and they deliver two trays. The soldier takes his and says thank you to the guards. Those are manners I've already forgotten.

We both linger by the door. The meal is bibimbap with bread

and water. It smells decent, but I know it is not. The man sits on the ground with his tray and lifts a spoon.

"You don't want to eat that," I say.

"No?" He stares at me with challenge in his eyes. The look seems so familiar. I really wish I knew who he reminded me of.

I actually have a lantern, so I hold it up over his meal. It takes a moment, but then maggots wriggle in the rice. My stomach turns at the knowledge that I ate the same or worse my first meal. My mouth waters, and I swallow my nausea.

He clears his throat and puts his spoon down. "Bread and water it is."

I get it. I was hungry enough to consider eating congee, even after the first meal of stew made me so ill I prayed for death.

I reach into the sack Hana left and extend a chunk of cheese and a bit of sausage to go with his bread.

The man eyes me, confusion flashing on his face. I reach over and rest the food on his tray so he doesn't have to take it from my hand.

He stares at me and then at the food without touching it. "Why… why give this to me?"

"I don't know."

It's the truth. I don't know why I just did it. He's a stranger, and I don't know if or when I'll see more food from Hana. My father certainly wouldn't have given him anything. He would've called me a fool for this. And maybe it's foolish to not hoard every crumb. But the man seems hungry.

I shrug. "I suppose it's how I'd want to be treated."

He nods. "What's your name, son?"

"Tiyung," I say.

With some effort, he rips a chunk off the stale bread. He turns it over in his hand. "Should I ask why you're in here?"

"Same as you—at the king's request." I offer a rueful smile.

He raises his water bowl and drinks to me.

I like him, but he's still too casual, too clean for me to trust him.

It's too convenient that he was put in here today. I decide to appeal to his mercy.

"If you're going to kill me, please do it while I'm awake," I say.

He pauses, slightly confused, but he nods. "Seems like a reasonable request." He takes a bite of the cheese. "Thank you for this, Tiyung."

I forgot to ask his name. My mother would be so disappointed that I forgot my manners this quickly.

Don't be noble in title only, she used to say.

"What is your name?" I ask.

"Ailor," he says. "Nice to make your acquaintance."

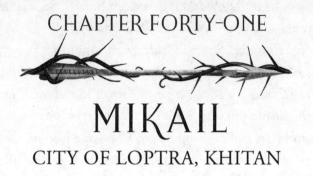

CHAPTER FORTY-ONE

MIKAIL

CITY OF LOPTRA, KHITAN

I t took three bells of trudging through the snow to make it to a trading post where we could get horses, and then another five on horseback, but we finally make it to Loptra. Our first order of business is buying winter gear for Sora. After the avalanche, I'd cut up one of the furs and wrapped the pieces around her dress boots so her frostbite wouldn't worsen. It worked well enough to get us here, but she desperately needs proper boots and fitted clothes.

She picks a simple dress house in the garment district, and the owner and workers can't help but fall all over themselves. Seduction comes easily to Sora, but she is also effortlessly charming and unfailingly kind.

Well, she'd like to murder Euyn, but she has good reason.

I can't believe he didn't mention that her parents didn't sell her, but then again, it's so utterly believable.

I already deposited him at an inn, so he's resting. Actually, I'm sure he's setting half a dozen traps and pacing while I take care of things with Sora. I suggested she sleep first, but she didn't want to. She's both not tired and completely exhausted. I understand the feeling.

"If you'll excuse me, I need to drop into the messenger house and make a few other arrangements," I say. "I'll return for you shortly."

She nods.

I step out of the shop and take a deep breath. Sora is never hard to be around—the opposite, actually. Even on the long trek here, she didn't complain once. She will quietly endure nearly anything, but the waves of grief and anger coming off her are suffocating.

The fresh, snowy air feels nice as I stroll to the messenger house through the bustle of Loptra. It's the third largest city in Khitan and the most modern and cosmopolitan. Glass and gilding gleams, and the statues are newly cut. Everyone dresses in their best, the women mostly in slacks and stylized jackets. People with new fortunes meet those with cutting-edge inventions. It even smells fresh and promising, with buildings still in construction along the banks of the Uulatar River. That's the body of water we almost fell into during the avalanche. The Uulatar runs off the Khakatan Mountains and winds all the way past Loptra to Vashney.

It's the same mix of people found throughout Khitan that navigates through the city. Food hawkers call out their regional specialties in various languages. Because of the weather and terrain in this frozen land, Khitan has always welcomed anyone who wanted to settle here. They have a level of tolerance not found in other places because they don't have the luxury of being snobs. It's one of many reasons they don't get along with Yusan.

I pass sizzling meat and fragrant rice as I scan for the telltale color of a messenger house. In Yusan, the shops are painted cobalt blue. Here, they are a loud shade of red. Messenger houses are primarily the same in any realm—half aviary and half shop, with a large stable attached for less urgent, cheaper correspondence. Messages can take a month on horseback, and I never have time for that.

I need to send coded letters to Zahara and others. But when I arrive at the Loptra messenger house, Zahara has already beaten me to the punch. There's eagle post waiting for me when I give the woman my (false) name. Two letters. I assume the other is from Gambria, as I sent a message letting her know I'd come.

With the letters in hand, I stand to the side, leaning against one of the many ledges. The houses provide paper, envelopes, and clay. I grab a pen and scratch paper to decode Zahara's message. Again, it's one word.

ALIVE

Tiyung is still alive in Idle Prison. That's a relief, especially given Euyn's latest moral failing. Ty increasingly looks like the only viable option we have for the throne. He was the one who wanted to spare the barmaid and her father in Oosant, reasoning that they were not directly involved with Sora's kidnapping. That is far better than a man who is willing to condone genocide so that we don't have to pay tribute. A man willing to let Sora believe her parents sold her for coin.

But I forget my thoughts of Euyn when I notice the second envelope is red, meaning it's also from the palace. Zahara must have sent an eagle after the first one. I wonder what was so urgent. I brace myself to read that Tiyung has died and that yet again I'll need to formulate a new plan.

I decode the letter.

SHE IS ASHES

I lean on the counter, the wind knocked out of me. My hands dig into the wood, and the horizon tilts. I open my jacket for air, but it doesn't help. It still feels like I'm suffocating. Like invisible hands are pressing on my throat and chest.

"Are you all right?" the woman asks in Khitanese.

I nod. But I am not. I have to gasp through jagged breaths. I struggle not to cry for a girl I've never met.

She is ashes.

Daysum is dead.

CHAPTER FORTY-TWO

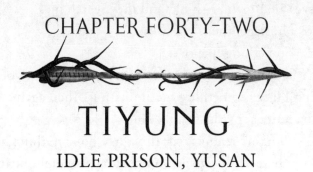

TIYUNG

IDLE PRISON, YUSAN

I survive my first sleep with a cellmate. Ailor didn't try to kill me, which, frankly, I find a little strange. I suppose he is actually a prisoner like me. Or he's lulling me into a false sense of security, into complacency.

But there's no need for that. I'm mostly a useless nobleman, even though I *am* a murderer. I've thought about the men I killed every day since Oosant. The ones I cut down without hesitation in the warehouse. I'm not a dangerous man like Mikail, though—that's a person you'd have to catch unaware.

As soon as I think it, I realize that's who Ailor reminds me of.

"Something up?" he asks.

I was staring. I lit the lantern as soon as I woke, and he can see me from his spot across the cell.

"I'm sorry. You just remind me of…someone."

He arches his scarred eyebrow. "Someone this witty and handsome? Impossible. There can't be two of us."

I laugh. He doesn't look anything like Mikail. He's shorter than Royo, maybe five foot seven and built stockier like him, but it's strange—his mannerisms are similar to Mikail's.

"You know, son," Ailor begins, "you don't seem like the type who'd wind up in this place."

"It was a surprise to me, too, I assure you."

His eyes are brown, I think, and they search me.

"You're a hostage, then?" he asks.

I nod. "Something like that."

I can't figure out if he's trying to get a read on me or if he's a spy hoping I'll say something incriminating. Then again, I've been talking to another spy this whole time.

Hana still hasn't reappeared, though. I hope nothing happened to her. It's only recently dawned on me that she might be in trouble herself. Spies are rarely safe, and neither are assassins, but I can't imagine a survivor like her or Sora could succumb to anything as ordinary as danger.

"I've been thinking about it. I figured you were noble, but I've only seen that type of big necklace on one guy—the Count of Tamneki," Ailor says.

"All counts wear collars as part of their formal dress," I say. I shift the gems that sit on my shoulders and string across my chest. "It goes back to ruling the four old kingdoms."

I touch the sapphires. The west wears diamonds, the north opals, and the east emeralds. The king wears blood rubies. The stones are all from over a thousand years ago, but they've been reset for each family.

Ailor's lips quirk. "You're a little young to be a count, kid. From what I remember, they're all older than me."

"My father is Seok, the Count of Gain," I say.

Ridges mar his forehead. "Oh, so you really *are* a hostage."

I nod. "What did you do?"

"To tell you the truth, I don't know." Ailor coughs and then stretches his legs in front of him. "I was at home, and then suddenly the palace guard arrived, and I was taken and brought here. I don't claim to be an innocent man—it could be any number of things from my past. But I'm not sure what I did to warrant Idle or why I was put in the cell with you. I take it you didn't have anyone else in here before."

I shake my head.

"I wonder why the special treatment, then. I would think it has something to do with my boy, but if that were the case, I would be dead."

"Who is that? Your son?"

He smiles. "I'd rather not say."

I have to respect that. I have people I want to protect as well.

A prisoner wails in the distance. It's a high-pitched scream that makes me shudder for how brief it was. Chills run along my arms, and Ailor turns toward the noise as well. Whatever is being done to the man is doubtlessly horrific. All prisons are a type of torture. Some are just more direct.

"I take it not every cell comes with lanterns and cheese and privacy," he says. "Perks of your status?"

"A friend on the outside," I admit.

I still don't trust this man, and I want to protect Hana as best I can. That prisoner's scream was a harsh reminder that there were other ways to get information out of me. Hana chose kindness because I saved Nayo. Although I suppose "saved" is the wrong word. Even a month forced to serve as a pleasure boy would be beyond saving for me. But he is free. "Saved from worse" is more accurate.

"Can that friend get a message out of here?" Ailor ventures.

"I don't know," I say. "Truthfully, I don't know if they will return."

"I guess we will hope they do." He coughs again and leans against the wall.

He puts it so simply that I can't help but think it's the only thing to do—to hope.

Hope is the first thing that flees from a place like this. Either Ailor is a spy or he is an incredible coincidence, because for the first time since I received Sora's letter, I feel some optimism. Like there is reason to hope. Like I might just survive. Like we all might make it.

CHAPTER FORTY-THREE

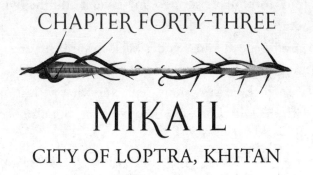

MIKAIL

CITY OF LOPTRA, KHITAN

She is dead.

I close my eyes, then inhale the pain. With a single breath, I lock away yet another tragedy to the recesses of my mind. Maybe one day the dam won't hold and I'll burst with horrors—but for now I press on. I can't alter the message. I can't change reality. Daysum is dead, and there's nothing I can do about it. I am not Lord Yama, the god of death who can send souls to be reborn. The only thing to do is to move forward. That's the only thing to ever do.

I swipe at my eyes and fling the letters and decoding paper into the fire. Then I get to work. I've been through far worse. I'll get through this.

As I planned, I code and write out my messages. I suppress all my sadness and load the carrier pouches, then slide a ten mark to the woman behind the counter. With that amount of money, she'll pick the fastest, strongest birds. The ones that fly high enough to evade archers.

The gray-haired woman slips the tip into her pocket, then ties the pouches to the eagles. She removes their tethers and hoods and releases them one by one through the aperture in the ceiling.

I pay the total with my mind clear, yet my hands shake as I take the change. I stare at my fingers. It's curious. I resolved to care more about the living than the dead long ago, but grief surrounds me, heavy as lead. Although I suppose my issue is still the living—how do I tell Sora?

I rub my forehead and wander back toward the dress house. I take the long way, hoping the words come to me. As I pass the marketplace, I pick up provisions, replacing what we lost in the sled. I haggle with the sellers because they expect it, but also because I'm in no hurry.

Once I have the goods purchased and couriered to the inn, I secure winter horses for tomorrow. There's someone watching me, a spy. Euyn has gone on and on about how someone has been following us, and I suppose he was right. But they're far enough away to just be observing.

I spin my dagger and consider spilling blood, but I'd be engaging the spy just to escape from this feeling. And I don't kill for sport.

No. I have to go back to Sora and get this over with. I gave my word, and cowardice isn't my way.

But *how*? How do I take away the one thing she's living for?

No matter what I say, she is going to fall apart. Even the sharpest blade has its breaking point. Only the Flaming Sword of the Dragon Lord never shatters.

I reach the dress house and lean against the side of the building. The pain in my chest is severe. Those same, invisible hands have me again, crushing my windpipe.

What would I want if it were me? Would it be better to know immediately or have a sister a little longer? And what words could be strung together to soften a death blow?

No one had to tell me I lost my family. I saw it myself—their mutilated bodies on the ground. I did, however, hear about my father. Ailor, who later adopted me, told me the entire rebel force had been slaughtered. No captives, no prisoners. But the Festival of Blood was such a mass tragedy, the scale so overwhelming, that the death of my birth father barely made an impact. Few sounds can be heard over an avalanche. Everyone I knew and loved was gone, and there's a limit to how much sorrow you can feel at once.

It won't be the same for Sora.

So I'll just say it—simple as that. Sometimes when there are no words, any will do.

I imagine she'll find some peace in the fact that her sister can't suffer anymore. Pleasure house indentures typically die by a patron's hand, their own, or, most commonly, laoli. The drug helps them get through their nights, and it's all too easy to overdose. Though I'm not certain how Daysum died, in the end, I'm not sure it matters.

Without another thought, I stand straight. I open the door to the dress house and stroll in. Sora is still on the platform, the workers fussing over her beauty, particularly her eyes. Khitanese royalty wears purple the same way the Baejkins wear dark red. The shop girls keep calling her eyes imperial.

I take a breath, ready to tell her. But as I open my mouth, Sora picks her head up. She smiles at me, warm and unassuming.

And I choke.

I can't do it. It's not cowardice—or maybe it is. But she will never be the same once she knows. She won't smile like that, maybe ever again. I can't take that from her right now. If it were Ailor instead of Daysum, I wouldn't want to know until my mission was complete.

It's better to wait. I swear to myself that I will tell her when we leave Khitan. When she will have time to mourn and not be in both danger and grief together.

"It's been ages," she says with a smile.

"Far too long." I smile back.

She laughs. One of the workers lifts the fur-lined hood on her new coat to show me, thinking we are husband and wife.

"Like it?" Sora asks, modeling the jacket.

"It's delightful."

I take a seat as if nothing is wrong, casually brushing snow off my pant leg. My eyes sting, but I smile. I'm suddenly glad I have twenty years of experience pretending to be something I'm not.

CHAPTER FORTY-FOUR

AERI
THE NORTHERN PASS, KHITAN

I've had time to mull it over, and I really don't think last night could've gone worse. I flinched when Royo touched the amulet, just out of shock, and everything fell apart. But it wasn't like I could explain it to him. I couldn't say "um hey, I'm not sure if my magical, time-controlling gem will know it's you touching it and not me, and I'm not sure what will happen if it does."

So I recoiled, and he got weird, and now it's a grand mess.

What makes things even better is that it's time to camp again.

I purse my lips.

We haven't talked much today. Royo has tried hard to pretend things are normal, but they aren't, which makes everything even more awkward.

We were supposed to have stopped a while ago, but we can't find a clearing like we did yesterday. The snow is deep, and he doesn't want to go into the woods because of predators. After seeing the body of the zaybear, I don't disagree.

I shudder thinking about those fangs. The memory of my fear that I'd lost Royo and maybe the others for good sends ice down my spine. Royo said there'd been four zaybears. Four. I don't know how they survived. Except that with the gods on your side, anything is possible.

The one good thing is I don't think there are zaybears this far north. I haven't seen the yaks or califers that could sustain them, and I cling to the comfort of that.

But it's nearly sunset and we haven't found a spot, which means we're going to have to make camp at the edge of the forest—exactly what Royo said not to do.

So, we ride a little longer.

"What is that?" Royo points a thick finger to the northeast.

I'm so surprised he's speaking that it takes me a second to look. The sun is setting in pinks and oranges, making it difficult to see. Not to mention the constant falling snow. But smoke or steam rises from somewhere in the distance.

At first, I think it's a campfire, but the longer I look the more I'm convinced it's steam. And steam can only mean one thing.

"Hot springs!" I exclaim.

I spur my horse and take off in the direction of the steam.

"Aeri, wait," Royo calls from behind me. "What are hot springs?"

"They're warm, natural pools, and a hot bath sounds like reaching the Heavens right now." I curl my toes, so ready for the dip.

"Aeri!"

He canters until he's next to me. I raise an eyebrow and flash a smile at him, daring him to keep up. I spur my horse harder, clicking my tongue. Royo looks annoyed at first, and then I make out the gleam of his teeth. A smile! Gods, what a sight.

We gallop through the fresh snow, racing until we come to boulders lining a hot spring. It's not terribly large—about the size of two rooms in an inn, which is perfect.

I dismount, tie my horse to a tree, and start taking off my jacket, eager for a bath. I've washed, but I haven't had a full bath since before we left for the ball in Quu.

In seconds, I amble down to the water level.

"Aeri, wait," Royo says. "How do you know that water isn't scalding?"

Honestly, I hadn't even thought of that. I scan the surface at the edges, and it seems okay.

"Because it's not bubbling. But here, pass me a piece of dried sausage," I say. "If it's too hot, it'll scald the meat."

He frowns at the water, then finally nods and climbs down. He hands me a dried sausage link. I dip it in. When I lift it out, the casing is fine, just warm. I put my hand in the clean water. It's hot, a bit warmer than bathwater. But I can't tell if it feels hot because it actually is or because the air is so cold. Easier to tell once I'm submerged.

I slip off my boots. Royo, killjoy that he is, continues to stand there.

I take off my shirt and pants, leaving on my undergarments so I don't scandalize Royo. I'd like to note that he doesn't stop me from stripping down.

"Come on, Royo," I say. "Don't just watch. That's weird."

He stares at me, unamused. I smile.

I get in carefully, because it's hard to say how deep the spring is, but there's a boulder right beneath my feet. As soon as I step in, the water feels incredible. Just hot enough to sting, but not in an unpleasant way.

I walk in a little deeper, so I'm just up to my chest. I look back at Royo. He sighs and starts taking off his boots and jacket.

"That's better," I say.

"Debatable," he mutters.

He takes his shirt off, and I'm free to ogle him—the broadness of his shoulders. His arm and chest muscles. He's not pretty like Mikail or lean like Euyn. He's something that's perfect for him.

I wait for the pants to come off, cradling my face in my hand. The second smile of his breaks through that tough exterior. It wasn't until Royo that I realized a hard-fought smile is so much better than an easy one.

With a deep, aggrieved sigh, he takes his pants down. I think about whistling, but he'd get dressed again. His thighs are thick and muscled like the rest of him. He carefully folds his clothes and rests them on a stone. I'm devastated to discover that he has on underwear.

"Feel free to continue the show," I tease.

"I'm going back to Yusan." He turns around, walking back toward his horse.

I laugh and take another step in so I can clean my hair. The boulder I was standing on is slick. My foot slips, and I wait to land.

There isn't another beneath it.

I fall before I can make a sound.

Water covers my head. I'm so shocked that it's a moment before I even try to stand, but the drop was steep. Very steep. I sink fast, but my feet can't touch the bottom.

Panic sets in, my arms and legs flailing. I claw the water, trying to reach the surface, but I've never been able to swim. Mama didn't think it was proper for a girl to learn, so I didn't.

I can't believe I'm underwater. I was fine just a second ago. One step and now I'm in mortal danger.

I look up through the clear, hot water. I go to clutch my amulet, as it's saved my life so many times, but my stomach turns. It won't help. Not when I'm drowning. Even if I stop time, I can't make myself know how to swim in the future any more than I can now.

Royo. I need Royo.

I stare up, hoping.

Please help, Royo. Please.

I scan the surface, but there's no sign of him. He's not coming. My lungs burn as I run out of air. Terror sits heavy in my stomach, and my heartbeat thuds in my ears. I'm going to die alone. Like I've always been. I thought... I thought things would be different once I met him. But I was wrong.

Desperate, I look up one more time. The last thing I see is the Night Rays of the Sun King. And then it all fades to nothing.

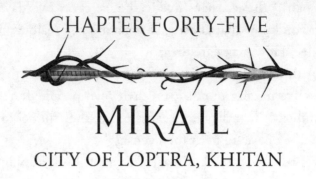

CHAPTER FORTY-FIVE

MIKAIL

CITY OF LOPTRA, KHITAN

Gambria's apartment smells of lumber and lilacs and overlooks the city of Loptra. Somewhere down there is her wife, whom she sent out for goat cheese when I knocked on their door. Gam served me tea and custard buns out of custom and politeness, but she'd rather I not be here. Not because I'm a Yusanian spy but because that's how she generally feels about me.

I lean on the wall by the picture windows and glance down at the street, but really, I'm studying Gambria in the reflection of the glass. She sits with her legs crossed in a green armchair. Her pink pants are perfectly tailored to her small frame. She's a touch over five feet tall and barely a hundred pounds, but she's as formidable as a mountain.

"Tell me about the Marnans," I say.

"Hello, it's nice to see you as well, Mikail," she drawls.

My lips quirk. There's always been a certain tension with Gambria. She likes me, I think, but she's protective of Fallador, and she believes I'm trouble. She and Fallador survived together, the last of their family, hiding in the cargo ship that took them from Gaya to Khitan during the Festival of Blood.

Gam has dark curls and light eyes, but aside from those features, she doesn't bear much of a resemblance to her cousin. I knew her on the island, too, so her poor opinion of me is entirely personal.

"What do you want to know?" she asks, too inquisitive to not take the bait. "The Marnans live in the ice caves two days west of here, but you know that already, so what are you really asking?"

I smile. "How many are they?"

"Eight thousand, maybe ten at this point. It's hard to say with how they live underground. Even their own people don't have an exact number. When they need more room, they tunnel to another location. They have no need for a census."

I have the same intel. I grimace internally. I was hoping for a far lower number, but without infiltrating their caves, it's impossible to say for certain. Gambria's wife, Lyria, is Marnan. Her mother left the caves and came to the city before Lyria was born. I assume in some kind of disgrace, but it's hard to say.

"Where do they bury their dead?" I ask.

Gambria's tea is nearly to her lips, but she puts her cup down, clanging it in the saucer. "No."

I face her. "No, what?"

"To what you're thinking," she says. "Absolutely not. It's suicide."

I arch an eyebrow. "I didn't know you'd miss me so much. I'm touched, Gam."

She inhales and stares in the middle distance like she's suffering, but amusement shines in her eyes. They are sky blue and wide set.

"I can take or leave you," she says, "but someone else doesn't feel quite the same."

I grin despite myself.

"Then help me survive—where is their burial ground?" I ask. "I doubt they keep their bodies where they live. Frozen or not, that's fairly grisly."

She sighs. "Staraheli is in a glass coffin inside a mausoleum at the cave entrance. Both the mausoleum and the cave mouth are guarded day and night."

Well, that's not ideal.

"My darling, there is a reason Staraheli still has his head," Gambria says, turning serious. "Khitan, and Loptra in particular, would love nothing more than to display it. It can't be done."

It's a good thing can't and won't are different things.

"Not with that attitude," I say.

She rolls her eyes, but the ghost of a smile lights her face. She has a quiet beauty. Fallador's whole family did. Past tense. The royal family of Gaya was slaughtered and thrown into the sea after Joon declared they had broken the colonial treaty. As if that paper wasn't signed at the point of a sword.

I stare out the window, thinking about how to get to Staraheli's corpse. Mausoleums are typically sealed, but if the body is in a glass coffin and guarded, then perhaps not. Sora and Euyn can take care of something as simple as a few guards as I smash the glass and cut off his head.

We can do this. One step closer to Quilimar. Another closer to freeing Gaya.

I watch the snow fall on the sleek buildings. There's less gilding here than in Vashney or Quu, but it's still foreign. Thoughts of Gaya, of the fields and the black woods return. It never snows on the island. Our houses are stucco and black timbers, not this.

"This place couldn't be less familiar, could it?" I ask.

She shrugs. "It's home."

I whip around. "Gaya is home."

"Oh, Mikail, it is not." She looks truly sorry for me. "We have changed."

"What do you mean?"

"You and me and Fallador—we are now from but not *of* Gaya. We are both the lands that adopted us and Gayan, but that is not the same as Gaya being our home."

I stare at her in disbelief. As much as I have pretended to be Yusanian, I have always known that I am not. I am not a part of Yusan now, nor will I ever be.

"That's ridiculous," I snap. "I am Gayan. As are you. Your cousin is the rightful ruler of the realm!"

"The former realm." She shakes her head, her curls bouncing as she stands and walks closer to me.

My eyebrows rise as she gently rests a hand on my shoulder. It's very strange, since she is not a gentle person.

"We have not been there since we were children," she says softly. "Even you haven't been back. I am certain it is much changed in nearly twenty years. We love the Gaya of our past, as we should. But that Gaya is gone. It disappeared when our boats set sail."

I try to let her words slide off me, but the barbs sink in. "I hope you're wrong."

"But that's so rarely the case." She smiles a full-lipped grin.

I'm shaken, so I change the subject. She can't be right. She just can't be.

"You know, you've never told me why you settled here and not in Quu near Fallador," I say.

"Because you can love someone and want to make your mark separate from them. I am my own person here." She drops her hands and folds them. She's both telling the truth and lying, because that's not why she really left the capital. "I hope there's a place of peace for you, my friend."

I nod. "Maybe one day."

She sighs. "You couldn't sound less sincere if you tried."

I smile. "Don't be silly, Gam. I can always be less sincere."

CHAPTER FORTY-SIX

ROYO

THE NORTHERN PASS, KHITAN

Where'd she go? Aeri was just standing there a second ago. I turned and made like I was going to walk back to Yusan, but now she's gone.

I groan. She's playing a game, hiding from me.

"Aeri," I call out. I expect her voice, but there's no answer. "Aeri, this ain't funny. Come out."

Still nothing. I hold my breath, listening, but everything is dead silent. A feeling of wrongness drapes over me. A creeping sensation up my back tells me I'm missing something.

It's nearly dark out, but I spot bubbles rising to the top of the hot spring. That's weird. Aeri had just said the spring wasn't bubbling.

My stomach plummets. Oh fuck. Aeri! She's in the water.

I jump right into the pool, and the hot water stings, but I barely notice because I'm swinging my arms wildly through the water below, my heart thundering in my chest.

"Aeri, Aeri, where are you?" I call out.

I scan the surface, but there are just the ripples I caused.

My breath lodges in my throat. Did she pass out? How could she have gone under so quickly? Then I realize: she can't swim.

That was the face she made on the Sol when the pirates attacked—she can't fucking swim. And I turned my back on her.

Frantic, I feel around the water. Nothing. I take a deep breath and dive under.

I don't remember when or where I learned to swim—must've been when I was real young. It feels like I've always known.

It's not until I'm a few feet down that I realize I don't know what could be lurking in this dark spring. But it don't matter. I'd fistfight Lord Yama to get Aeri back.

I keep reaching out, pushing deeper, and finally I feel something. It's slight. I'm not sure what it is until I hit fingers. Aeri's arm. My chest floods with relief as I pull her body to mine, then kick as hard as I can to reach the air.

We break the surface. I gasp, my lungs burning, but her eyes are closed and she's not moving. I toss her onto the snow, and then I jump out, too.

I land almost on top of her. The cold air is shocking, but so is the fact that I found her. She's okay. But she's just lying there.

Fuck my life. She's not breathing.

With my hands shaking like an earthquake, I turn her over my knee. I hit my palm on her back to try to force the water out. Nothing happens. I lean down and put my ear to her chest. I wait, hoping, holding my breath.

Silence. There's no heartbeat. Not a single one.

Cold like I've never felt before seizes me and holds me in place.

She's dead. She died while I fucking stood here.

Panic and agony take turns stabbing my chest. I could've saved her. I didn't. I failed again.

I slap my hand to her back, trying to do something. Anything. "Aeri! Breathe. Breathe."

But there's nothing. She's not moving at all.

Tears sting my eyes, and I scream. The sound shatters the twilight, echoing all around. I don't care if there are predators. Let them come for me.

She drowned. And I did nothing.

All of a sudden, a strange calm takes hold, and it's like I can see the Sol River in front of me. Then I see the bodies pulled from it. They look terrible—pale and bloated. Living on the river, I also saw half-drowned people pulled from the water. Ones who fell or jumped or whatever and people got to them quickly. They looked like this—like they were sleeping—like how my mother did when they found her.

There was one day she and I were going to the market, and we saw someone brought back to life. The memory plays out before my eyes. A woman in a gray dress knelt on the stones of the dirty riverbank. Her husband lay dead in front of her. People in hats and scarves crowded in around them, pulled toward death the way moths want to explore a flame. Then she did something weird. She held his nose and breathed into his mouth. She pressed on his chest, and it brought him back. He sat up, sputtering.

It was called a miracle.

I shake off the memory and decide to try it. I'll try anything.

I roll Aeri over and open her mouth. The mouth with the plump lower lip I just kissed last night. I don't know what I'm doing, but I hold her nose. I blow two hard breaths in her mouth, like I'm breathing for her. Then I push on her chest, trying to pump the water out. She's so slight I have to be careful not to break her. But I push again. And again.

Tears well in my eyes. Frost nips at my skin, but I'm sweating.

"Come on, Aeri," I say. "Stay with me."

I push and I push.

"Stay," I beg as I reach for her nose again.

Suddenly, she moves. She comes to, coughing. Then she leans to the side and pukes up water.

I sit back on my knees. Ten Hells. Praise to the gods!

My hands shake as I run them down my face. My whole body's quaking, and I can't seem to catch my breath.

Aeri is trembling and throwing up on the snow. But she's alive. Her heart is beating and she's breathing.

It's a miracle.

She gasps, her eyes wide, and then she stares at me. I can't believe that worked. But also, it had to work because I wasn't gonna lose her.

"You saved me." She blinks, bewildered. "I... I drowned. I know I did. How did you save me?"

I don't know. I really don't. That memory of the woman saving the man on the Sol has gotta be twenty years old, but it rushed back like it happened yesterday.

"I wasn't gonna let death take you from me," I say.

She stares at me with those big brown eyes, tears swimming in them. "Royo...you say something like that, but then you wonder why I've fallen for you."

"Aeri..." I shake my head. She can't fall for me. It's a bad mistake. But my heart swells all the same. It's everything—all I've ever wanted to hear my whole life.

"I know," she says. "You weren't going to let death take me from you but in a *just friends* sort of way."

I stare at her, suppressing a laugh. "Drowning looks better by the second."

She smiles, but then she shivers, shuddering hard as she rubs her own arms. Because she's wet and nearly naked on the snow. Her undergarments are soaked and see-through. Fuck, she's freezing. Of course she is.

I don't look. Okay, yeah, I saw, but I stare down at the snow. "I can sit you back in the water to get warm, then I—"

"I can't." She shakes her head, eyes wide.

Right, she doesn't want to get back in the hot spring. I get it. But I don't have a fire made yet. I run to my horse and grab our supplies. I pull the two blankets out, wrap them around her, and cover her tight. Then I go back to the hot spring and fetch her clothes. I climb up and hand her things to her.

She stares up at me, her hair dripping onto the fur. Her mouth is still half open as she breathes hard.

"You're soaked, too," she says.

I am, and I'm cold, but I barely feel it. I grab the dinner pot and toss in some fallen sticks. My teeth chatter as I reach in the bag for the fire starter. I need to change, but getting her warm is all that matters right now.

The twigs catch, making a small fire right in the pot. I put it on her lap. It's not much, but I can't make a campfire without a pit and wood.

I scramble back down to the hot spring, strip off my wet underwear, and throw on my dry clothes and boots. Now, warm enough, I grab some rocks. I get enough to make a fire pit up by Aeri, then I take out my axe. It's a battle axe, not a wood axe, and I had to sharpen it after taking down the warming hut, but it's fine to chop up a young tree.

There's a five-year pine that fell, rotten, not far from the boulders. I start splitting it into logs and branch pieces. I work so quickly and get so hot that I have to take the jacket off again. I stop and drape my coat over Aeri's shoulders, then rewrap her blanket. She looks up at me with those big, brown eyes. She's okay. She's alive and here with me.

I get back to work. The exertion feels good. Each swing back, each split calms me a little.

As soon as I have enough, I bring the wood over and arrange it in the pit. The fire in the dinner pot is almost out, but it's enough to start the campfire. I toss in some dry hay, and it flames to life.

Finally, I take a breath and crouch down next to Aeri. She's put on her dry clothes, but she's still as white as the snow and shivering. The fire will help, though. She eyes me, her jaw shaking because her teeth are chattering. Still, she opens the blankets to wrap me as well.

I pick her up and put her on my lap to give her my body heat, then close the blanket around us. She melts, shaking into me, as cold as ice. But gradually, she warms.

She nuzzles against me, safe now.

As I look around, I realize this isn't a bad place to make camp. We'd be protected by the hot spring, and we already have the fire going in the twilight.

"Are you okay with staying here tonight?" I ask.

She meets my eyes. "Yes, but no more dips in the pool."

I snort, and she smiles.

When she's warm enough, I leave her with the blanket and get to work on the tent. I lay some canvas on the ground. It won't be as warm on the snow as it was on the bare earth last night, but we'll manage. I'll do whatever I have to.

It's not until camp is done and Aeri hands me my jacket, insisting I put it on, that I let myself think about what happened. Aeri drowned. She died, and I lost her. I lost all of the tomorrows I want with her. But then I brought her back.

I don't understand it. Maybe it really was the gods helping us. I can't explain it any other way—how I remembered how to save someone or that it worked. A minute more and nothing would have helped. I know it in my soul. If I was just a little slower or if she'd fallen a little farther, I would've lost her for good. If there was one time for the gods to shine on me, I'm grateful it was this one.

After Lora, I swore I'd never let someone in again. I thought it was better to just be alone. So much for that.

Aeri is slowly sipping water from a canteen as I rinse out the dinner pot. I put fresh snow in and hang it above the fire on the metal stand. I can feel her staring at me, but for now she's quiet. When I met her, all I wanted was for her to take a breath and not talk my ear off, and now her voice is what I want to hear the most.

"Don't do that again," I say.

She breathes out a laugh. "Believe me, Royo, it isn't the plan."

I pour some rice into the pot. While it cooks, I reach out and tuck her wet hair behind her ear.

"It really scared me," I say.

Her eyes get glossy, and she nods. "Me too. I thought... I thought you wouldn't come."

"I'll always find you."

We stare at each other under the rising moon. I want to kiss her again, but I won't. I won't ruin this moment. She's safe, and that's enough.

Aeri gently smiles, and then she reaches into her pocket. She pulls out a napkin and unwraps the paper. Inside is a little cake. She holds it out to me.

I knit my eyebrows. The girl had cake in her pocket.

"For saving my life," she says.

She's so serious that I take half and fold the rest back into her hand. "You've saved mine."

She smiles. "Twice, but who's counting."

I take a bite. Sugar, buttercream, and vanilla dance on my tongue. It's good, really good.

"Three," I say.

She doesn't know it, but she saved me the day she planted her card in my jacket. I just hadn't realized it at the time. I was alive but not living until I met Aeri at the Black Shoe Inn.

CHAPTER FORTY-SEVEN

SORA

THE WESTERN PASS, KHITAN

There's something off about Mikail. Something in the way he's looked at Euyn and me the last two days has been strange. I noticed the same hollowness haunting his eyes before he destroyed the crown. Which can only mean he's planning something—some type of betrayal or secret. I'm not sure what it is yet, and I'm running out of time, since we're nearly to the ice caves.

It's late at night, probably one bell in the morning, when he signals for us to stop our horses.

In the distance, about a hundred and fifty yards from us, sits a towering cave sixty feet tall, maybe more, and there's a small building nestled in the entrance. Mikail called it a mausoleum. It looks like a windowless stone house.

Why you'd put a body in one of those for all eternity is beyond me. But they believe in different gods.

Maybe theirs are kinder than ours.

Euyn has ridden on the other side of Mikail since we left Loptra and avoided me when we camped overnight. I'm not sure if it's out of cowardice or respect, but he's also keeping his distance from Mikail.

I've had time to calm down and consider what Euyn said. As much as I hate him for not telling me about my parents, he is correct that Daysum would not have been free. No one would have believed a commoner over Seok. The Count of Gain remains the real problem, even though Euyn is not fit to rule.

However, one issue at a time. My mother used to tell me to just focus on the next step when the whole problem was too daunting. We need to bring the head of Staraheli to Quilimar and convince her to help us murder King Joon for the successor to matter.

My mother, who I hated for years because I thought she traded her own daughters for gold. I haven't begun to unravel all of those feelings. There simply isn't time to work through it now. But there's a thorny comfort in knowing the truth.

Euyn stops ahead of us. He dismounts, crouches closer, and scans the horizon.

"Two guards by the mausoleum," he whispers. "Two patrolling."

Taking out four guards isn't bad. Well, until you start thinking about them as people you're murdering, as stolen souls.

We found luminae in Loptra. It's a glowing flower, and the pollen can be turned into a poison dust of the same name. It's on my lips and in my pocket. Luminae kills with a slow, burning sensation as if you've been lit on fire, but it affects the mouth first, disabling the tongue. Erlingnow would've been kinder, as it is the fastest death, but I couldn't find any. Every realm has its own toxins, its own ways to kill.

I'd hoped I wouldn't have to murder anyone in Khitan other than Seok, especially not guards protecting something sacred to them. These aren't disgusting noblemen or a gang who'd devour me as soon as look at me. But if the only way to save Daysum is to kill innocent men, then that is a trade I accepted long ago.

I want to shrink from this, to run, but I don't. Instead, I steel myself and dismount from my horse alongside Mikail. We tie the horses to a tree. People have to die for Daysum to live. It's a simple exchange.

Except there's nothing simple about it. I don't want to kill these guards or steal a head that belongs to their worshipped hero. Staraheli led downtrodden people against an oppressor—something

I can relate to. A feeling of wrongness envelops me. I try to shake it off, but it clings. This isn't a mark I have to kill or a life-or-death situation. This is a prize.

And not all of us kill for sport.

Still, on Euyn's signal, the three of us approach the mausoleum from the side. We are nearly there when Euyn disappears. Strange. I glance at Mikail, but he doesn't seem concerned, so I'm sure it's fine—just another part of the plan I wasn't told about.

We go another few steps, our feet silent on the white ground, but a guard turns and notices us. I take a breath, ready to seduce him, but Mikail grabs my arm and flings me down.

I hit the snow hard and cry out. I remember too late to muffle the sound, and now we have his full attention.

Even though I felt Mikail's hand on my arm and I know he threw me, I try to convince myself that I merely tripped. Mikail is my friend and ally. He wouldn't hurt me.

But then he mutters something in a language I can't understand.

The guard runs over. He shouts something, and Mikail responds, putting his arms up. He points to me and says something again—it must be Marnan. The word he uses sounds like a Khitanese slur for the pleasure houses, though. I stare up at him, bewildered, the insult stinging. What is he doing? Who is he right now?

Mikail stares at me with hate in his eyes. And then he knocks twice on the scabbard of his sword.

The signal.

I get to my knees and focus only on the guard. He's not much older than us, even though he has a long twisting beard. His eyes are slightly too close together, but I look at him as if he contains all the hope in the world. As if I've suddenly fallen in love.

Once he locks eyes with me, I tip my head and let the hood of my jacket fall back. I don't have to speak the language for this to translate. Tears swim in my eyes, and I part my lips.

"Help me," I whisper in Khitanese in case it loosely translates.

He doesn't seem to understand me, but he knows I'm begging and at his mercy. The nobles in Yusan love this act—the damsel in need of rescue. I assume it transcends borders, but I hold my breath, waiting.

The guard hesitates but then extends his hand to me. I show nothing but gratitude as I take his arm and slowly stand.

"Thank you," I say in Khitanese.

It is a shame he won't be able to understand my last words to him.

I lean forward and kiss him, giving him a mouthful of poison. He starts choking immediately, his fingers grasping at his lips and neck.

I look back at Mikail to avoid watching the guard suffer. I brush the snow off me as the man falls to the ground. "A bit overkill, don't you think?"

He'd said he was going to pretend to be a cheated husband leaving me at the caves and therefore at the mercy of the Marnans, but I didn't expect him to throw me.

"No, we had an audience." He points to the tunnel entrance. I turn just in time to see two men collapse from crossbow bolts to the neck. "Are you all right, though?"

"I'm fine," I say.

His gaze barely meets mine before he stares at the mausoleum, his eyes all hunger. "Let's go, then. We don't have much time."

I don't know where the last guard is, but he's probably dead.

Mikail walks with careful but fast steps. With his back turned, I pause and remove a bottle from my pocket. I pour a drop into the guard's open mouth. The guard had tried to show me kindness and got nothing but pain in return. But he doesn't have to die.

I read in the temple that the antidote to luminae is actually made from the same source—the liquid in the stem and leaves of the poison flower. Like the poison, the antidote is slow acting. It stops the burning from spreading and gradually brings down inflammation. The guard won't be able to move until morning, and of course he'll remember the pain, but he will live.

It's the best I could do. We needed him out of the way, but for minutes, not forever. Mikail and Euyn wouldn't have understood why I wanted to spare him, so it was best to do it quietly on my own.

Euyn meets us at the entrance to the mausoleum. Surprisingly, there is a bronze door, patinaed green, on the cave side. I suppose it makes sense to have a door—they had to get the body in somehow. Mikail said Staraheli would be in a glass coffin, so perhaps they open the door for viewing.

Disturbing, if you ask me, but perhaps they think that about our funeral pyres.

Mikail pulls at the handle, and eventually, it begins to open. Strange that there wasn't a lock. Euyn helps him, pulling as well, and together they shift the heavy door wide enough for us to creep inside.

I brace myself for what I'm about to see.

We squeeze in, them first and me last. It's pitch black in the small room except for the ray of light coming from the doorway. But even in the dark it's clear: the room is empty. No glass coffin, no body of Staraheli.

"What now?" Euyn asks.

He takes another step inside. All of a sudden, a cracking sound echoes through the room.

There's barely a second to move before a net springs up from the floor.

It was all a trap.

CHAPTER FORTY-EIGHT

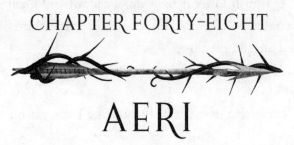

AERI

THE LIGHT MOUNTAINS, KHITAN

Dying is strange. Overall, I don't recommend it.

I drowned in the twilight. I know I did. I struggled under the surface, holding my breath for as long as possible, but eventually, I inhaled the water. A burning pain like I'd never felt before filled my chest, and then I woke up walking on the Road of Souls—the pathway that leads to the Kingdom of Hells. I only stopped because I heard Royo's voice begging me to stay. Next thing I knew, I was back. Soaking wet and throwing up mouthfuls of water. I was alive, thanks to him.

But now I'm not sure if we will see another sunset together. It's late morning, and we've reached the foothills of the Light Mountains.

We tie our mounts to trees close to the edge of, but not in, the forest. I haven't seen Dia since I fed her after supper last night, but I hope she stayed where she'll be safe. I hope she's sleeping cozily somewhere. I hope I will see her again.

Royo and I have to hike on foot to find the nests. Once we do, we have to steal an egg from a creature that will happily eat us if we're caught.

I put my hand on my throat, feeling very mortal. I can freeze time and run, but my power has limits. If one of those birds comes after us, how will I get Royo out alive?

My heart twists as I realize I won't be able to move him on a mountain. If I push him off the side, we'll fall and likely both die.

I can't chance losing him. I'll have to convince him to stay here.

"Maybe I should go alone," I say.

He stares at me and blinks a couple of times. "Are you out of your mind?"

I sigh. That went over great. But maybe I can get him to see my logic.

"I know I can move silently," I say. "Can you?"

He looks to the side and frowns. If we learned one thing from Lake Cerome, it's that, no, Royo cannot.

The amarth are nocturnal. The best chance we have is to sneak up on them during the day, when they're asleep, and then kill one quickly and steal the egg beneath it. Which, of course, won't work if one of us is stomping around like a bee-stung ox.

"I'll get you close," he says.

I guess that's the best compromise. Especially since I'm not sure where the nests will be.

The priest helped me with a text that theorized on the location. The amarth are so large, they'd need old, mature trees to support their weight, so they won't be at the summit or on the windward side of the mountains where there are scant trees. But as animals, they'd want high ground to avoid predation of their young. So the foothills are out. The writer thought that the birds build their nests not in trees but in the mountainside itself, right above the tree line.

There was no confirmation, though. Apparently, everyone who has been close enough to see the nests hasn't lived to describe them.

That's not comforting, but we don't have a choice.

I'm certain that if my father lives, he will torture and murder Royo in front of me. And I'm not going to let death take him from me—in a strictly-friends way, of course.

Royo slings a pack over his shoulder, and we start hiking. If we can't find the nests quickly, we'll have to make camp in the mountains. Which means sleeping in a tent and hoping they don't find and eat us overnight.

So, it's pretty important we find the nests well before sunset.

We trek for a while, keeping an eye on the summit. Luckily, the winter outfit I bought at the dress house is keeping me warm. I have a brand-new reason to hate the cold, but everything but my face is nice and toasty. Royo is sweating.

"Can I ask you something?" he murmurs.

We've been quiet so that we don't wake the amarth, but there's been no sign of them.

"Sure," I say.

"What's the story with your necklace? Where's it from?"

I trip on a raised root, but I'm glad for the distraction. My amulet. That's right—not only did he feel my necklace while we were kissing, but he saw it when he rescued me.

This is the moment for me to tell him the truth—all of it. To trust him with knowing who I really am and what I can do. That I'm not just a gem thief with incredible sleight of hand, but a thief of time. That I'm how we escaped on the Sol, how Mikail lived in the warehouse, and every other weird "happening" since we met.

I want to tell him, I do, but the words don't come. It's not that I don't trust him. I wish it were that simple. It's that the knowledge itself is dangerous. When we were in the temple, I read about the relics, specifically the terrible things done to possess them.

For example, my father slaughtered tens of thousands of innocent Gayans under the pretense of subduing a rebellion just to capture the Flaming Sword of the Dragon Lord.

When Gaya became a colony of Yusan long ago, part of the treaty was that Gaya would submit to being governed, and in exchange they would keep their relic and figurehead royalty. The colonial treaty held for over two hundred years. But when my father took the throne, he saw opportunity. He wanted the relic, thinking that with the sword, he could defeat Wei. He sowed the seeds of rebellion on the island with new taxes, harsh laws, and increased laoli production. He even had his spies encourage and arm the rebels. Once the Gayans killed a Yusanian garrison, he mercilessly put down the revolt. He claimed Gaya was the first to break their treaty by refusing governance.

Thirty thousand men, women, and children meant nothing to him. Who knows what he would do to get the Sands of Time, but I have to imagine he'd kill me without hesitation. And if Royo knew, it would only put him in danger.

I can't. I can't risk it. I won't risk him.

"It reminds me of my mother," I say, choosing my words carefully. "I never take it off so that a piece of her stays close to my heart."

Royo looks relieved. I'm not sure why.

"I miss my mother, too," he says. "I get it."

"Was she a priest?"

I'm thrilled to change the subject. Lying to him feels like a torch pressed to my throat. But the truth can cut like a knife even when you don't want it to.

He shakes his head. "No... Well, I don't think so. I guess somebody had to be a keeper, though, right?"

"You said she died ten years ago?"

"In Tamneki."

"What happened?" I ask.

He rubs his face. "That's the thing—I don't know."

I tilt my head. That's...weird.

His eyes take on a far-off look. "We were in the capital, and I woke in the middle of the night and she wasn't in the room. It was two bells in the morning, and I waited for her until sunrise. Then, at dawn, I reported her missing. The next day, the king's guard found her body." He pauses and looks at the ground. "They said it was an accident. That she drowned in one of the canals. But...she knew how to swim."

Royo takes a shaky breath, and I think about how awful it must've been for him to have found me drowned in the hot spring. My chest squeezes.

"Everyone just shrugged it off," he says. "She was burned on a capital funeral pyre, and I went home alone. But it never seemed right to me."

"Why is that?"

"My mother never just left without telling me where she was going and when she'd be back. And I didn't even know she'd left the room the night she disappeared. That, with the fact that she could swim, it just… It don't make sense." Then he shrugs. "But maybe I don't want it to. Maybe a mystery is better than the truth."

I walk, making footprints in the fresh snow. I can picture it all: Royo younger and unscarred, sitting in a room, waiting for a mother who never returned. It cracks my heart into pieces. But what were they doing in the capital?

"Are you from somewhere near Tamneki?" I ask. "I thought you were from Umbria."

"No, I'm from Umbria. We went to watch the Royal Tuhko Championship. It was…" He pauses and clears his throat of the emotion clogging it. "It was a birthday gift. She'd saved up for years to take me."

The guilt in his voice rings clear, and it wrenches my soul. Royo blames himself not only for what he does, but also when people he loves are harmed. Which makes no sense, but it's one of the most endearing things about him.

"That was very kind of her," I say.

The lump in his throat bobs. "She was kind."

Mine…wasn't.

Mama was charming, and I loved her completely. I missed her for so many years, and all I'd ever wanted was to have one of her perfumed hugs again. But just because you love someone, especially as a child, doesn't mean they're perfect or even good. I'd managed to overlook the bad. Like how she used to call me a "little unloved girl" when I was young. That she'd want me out of sight any time she found a man she liked. That she didn't mourn me after she thought

I'd died.

Over the years, I created a perfect mother, cobbling together select good moments. And that is who I remember—the charismatic beauty striving for a better life for us. But there were more bad memories than good.

I duck under a tree branch as we continue up the mountain.

To some extent, she blamed me for being born female. Then again, to some extent, every girl in Yusan is cursed. It wasn't until I got to Khitan that I realized it's not the same everywhere. And it wasn't until Sora—how she cares about her sister and how she cares for me—that I realized I shouldn't have been made to feel bad for my birth. You can only lie to yourself about being loved for as long as you don't know what real love feels like.

Royo would rather not love anyone, but his love is deeper than the West Sea.

The bells pass, and we continue up the mountain, keeping an eye out for nests and amarth. Mikail said the animals are white, so it will be difficult to spot their plumes with all of this snow.

We keep going, and I start to wonder if we're even on the right mountain. The texts referred to the mountain range, and we chose the central, largest one, but maybe they inhabit a different mountain. I wonder if we should go all the way to the summit to get a better view. We are quickly losing daylight, and we'll have to make a choice soon.

"Do—" I begin. Royo clamps his hand over my mouth, his palm on my lips.

I stare at him, confused and surprised. And then my surprise turns to fright. His eyes are wide, his muscles rigid. His hand is locked against my face, and he's looking at something past me.

What could scare him like this?

I follow his line of sight. He's staring at a nest—or more aptly, the sleeping amarth on top of it.

Chills run through me, my shoulders trembling. Good gods,

what is that?

A bird taller than I am stands with its back to us, its head tucked into its wing. I brace myself, ready for an attack, but it's asleep, steadily breathing. Then I look up at the trees.

I *really* wish I hadn't done that.

There are at least a dozen more sleeping in the branches. And I can't tell how many more are in the trees farther along the mountain, but I'm guessing a lot.

The sheer terror of it hits me at once. We are outnumbered and exposed. If any wake, we will be eaten before we make it a few feet. I realize how foolish I was to think I could easily kill one of these things. As if it was the size of a chicken.

Every muscle in my body wants to turn and run, but we've come this far. I take a breath. I have to see this through. Alone.

I signal for Royo to wait. He silently argues with me until I point to his boots. Then he balls his hands into fists but reluctantly nods.

On silent feet, I hold my breath. I go a little closer until I can smell the bird. Gods, it reeks of rotting meat and death. I try to focus and breathe through my mouth, continuing until I can peer inside the nest.

This is easily the most absurdly dangerous thing I've ever done. If I survive, I should rethink my life choices.

The nest is about waist-high to me, carved into the mountainside and lined with sticks, rocks, and spit-covered down—that's probably why it smells. But inside the nest are black eggs, including a solitary one at the edge.

That's it. That's what we need! And I won't have to kill an amarth to get it.

It's strange that the amarth is not sitting on this egg. Either she abandoned it or she rotates the eggs for warmth. I don't know, but it doesn't matter. I won't second-guess a gift from the gods.

I grab my amulet and freeze time. Then I lean down and pick up the egg. It's half the size of my torso and ice-cold. It must've been abandoned, which is oddly comforting. I unfreeze time and start running.

I only held time for a few seconds, but I'm already exhausted. I force my heavy-feeling legs to work, my body to run down the path. Royo picks up on the hint and starts sprinting, too.

Full speed ahead, I don't look behind us. I can't. It feels as if the amarth will stay asleep so long as I don't turn back. I run in front of Royo, who took out a dagger, but he sprints holding it.

We go so fast and I'm so light on my feet that I pray he doesn't fall trying to keep up. Fleeing for your life with the love of your life gives you a strange amount of energy even when you're dead tired.

I just keep looking ahead. I try to believe that everything will be okay. That Royo and I will make it.

But I can't help it. I glance over my shoulder. I have to make sure he is with me.

Royo's a little behind me, but he's staying in my tracks. It's clever.

I face forward and barely avoid slamming into a tree. I muffle a scream as my face comes within inches of an oak.

Lesson learned.

Heart pounding, I pay attention. I steady my breathing and focus on carving as straight and safe a path as I can, but it's sharply downhill from here. This is not the way we came, but it's the fastest route off the mountain. I don't worry about my steps or balance, because the second you overthink it is the moment you fall. But I can't tell Royo that. We need to continue in silence. We need to just keep going.

It took us five bells to reach the nest. It takes less than one bell to hit the foothills.

But we do make it.

We pause at the base of the mountain, where the ground finally levels out. We aren't safe yet. We won't be until we get on our horses and ride far away, but we're off the slopes.

We've done it. We got the egg before sunset.

I've run with the egg cradled in my arms this entire time, and I readjust to make it more secure against me.

Royo nods at me, breathing so hard he's red-faced and wheezing. I don't think he runs much—he's more of a stand-and-fight kind of guy.

I let him catch his breath. I'm relieved that our horses are still tied to the trees. We might actually make it out of this. If we gallop, we can put two miles, maybe three, between us and the mountain before sunset. I'm not sure about the birds' hunting radius, so the more distance, the better.

Royo stands straight, ready to run again. We take off a little slower than I'd like, but I stay with him, matching his speed.

We're halfway to the horses when the wind swirls. I squint, throwing my arm up to shade my eyes as white falls from the sky. I think it's a snow squall, but then I realize it's not snow. It's…down.

Feathers rain on us. Then I see giant wings. And claws.

An amarth lands in the snow. It is powerfully built like an enormous, white eagle, except for its gruesome, humanlike face. Its sharp brown eyes home in on the egg I'm cradling.

Gods, we're dead.

CHAPTER FORTY-NINE

EUYN

THE ICE CAVES, KHITAN

Gods on High, we're trapped. I struggle, twisting my body, but Mikail and I are in a net, pressed to the ceiling of the empty mausoleum.

I barely felt the loose stone underfoot before the trap sprang shut. Impressive, but the entire place is a snare designed to catch thieves looking for a prize. There's no glass coffin, no body of Staraheli in here. I wonder if it was all a setup, a bad source who lied to Mikail and led us to our deaths.

I hold my breath and wait for the Marnans. They are known to impale intruders on spikes. There were half a dozen snow-covered skeletons on pikes as we approached. They don't burn the bodies here. No, instead of being released, our souls will be left to rot for all time.

A fitting end for me.

But even though I listen for the slightest sound, no one comes.

I exhale. Mikail must simply have had old information. Still, we're now stuck in this net.

"Kingdom of Hells," Sora whispers. "What just happened?"

I look down and see that Sora is free. She was last inside and closest to the door, so the net must have missed her when it swept us up.

She tilts her head, her eyes moving rapidly.

"I'll cut the rope," Mikail says. He takes out a dagger because there isn't room to wield a sword in this spiderweb.

I free my dagger as well and try to cut the net. From the feel of it, I can tell it won't work. I sever a few threads, but then I hit metal. It must be rope meshed with steel. I didn't think the Marnans knew how to make such things. This is shockingly advanced.

As I feel the metal mesh, I realize it must have been made by Weian forgesmiths.

Because of their common enemy, the Marnans have had a long alliance with Wei. Staraheli's revolt against Khitan was thought to be financed and armed by the island nation. But I was never sure if that was true or just Khitan wanting to save face as their cities burned.

Now, I think it is.

After a few more tries, it quickly becomes evident that we can't cut our way out of the net.

"Sora, you'll have to find a way to disable the trap," Mikail says.

She looks around and then up at me. I can just barely make out her face in the sliver of light, but she has hate burning in her eyes. She doesn't move; instead, she seems to be weighing her options. If she leaves us here, we are dead men. That much is certain.

Mikail must realize at the same moment that she's thinking about leaving us behind.

"Sora…" he says.

Her expression goes from hard to softening. She looks away and takes a breath.

I can't honestly say I would've done the same if the situation were reversed and she'd hunted my father.

Carefully, she tiptoes to the other side of the mausoleum. Her steps are small as she edges along the wall, avoiding the center tiles. I wonder what she's doing until I realize that each tile must spring a trap of some sort. I happened to step on the one that triggered the net.

There is a stone sticking out of the wall—the counterbalance.

She presses on it with her hands, but it doesn't budge until she leans on it with all her weight. The net falls on one end, creating a rope ladder to the door. Mikail tumbles down and lands gracefully on his feet. I...am not as smooth.

Sora meets us by the door. I wonder how she knew how to disarm the trap, as she's just a girl and has no training as a spy. I also wonder why, in the end, she let me go. Alliances don't last forever, especially not among killers.

Perhaps she wouldn't sacrifice Mikail just to get even with me. Or she feared him hunting her if we survived. Maybe she simply believes she can't save Daysum without us.

But she can.

Sora has the ability to seduce and poison her way to Quilimar's hand with or without Staraheli's head. There's just more left to chance. But my sister is no more immune to beautiful women than anyone else in my family. With Quilimar dead, Sora could give the ring to Joon and claim all the spoils.

The realization is a bolt that sends my pulse pounding. Any one of them could betray us and take the ring to Joon. They seemed like they were all on board with Sora's plan to start a war, but so did I.

And now, because Mikail decided we should split up, Royo and Aeri could succeed, get to Quilimar, and bring the ring to Joon themselves. She's his daughter, and Royo would follow her to the ends of the South Sea. Perhaps Joon was planning on exactly that— all of us double-crossing each other again. Maybe he didn't send a team of killers, but five separate assassins with one prize. And among them was his daughter, because she has the best chance of winning.

My thoughts of betrayal spiral until they're interrupted by the tolling of alarm bells.

My heart races in my chest, and my stomach sinks. The Marnans know we're here, and they're coming.

CHAPTER FIFTY

ROYO

THE LIGHT MOUNTAINS, KHITAN

What the absolute fuck *is* that thing?

We'd done it. We'd taken the egg and made it off the Light Mountains, and now this…*thing* is in front of us. It's focused on Aeri and the egg, but then it cocks its head at me and, yeah, that's worse. Primal fear streaks through me, twisting my guts. This has gotta be an amarth, and I really wish I hadn't seen its face.

This thing has human eyes, but they're enormous. A disturbingly sharp eagle's beak is where a nose and mouth should be. Instead of hair, it's got white plumes that stand straight up, but the face is round and eerily human, even though it's coated in short feathers.

I'm gonna see this in my nightmares—if I live long enough to dream. That doesn't seem likely, though. Not when the talons of this thing are six inches long at the base of legs twice as thick as mine.

Aeri cradles the egg in one arm. Her other hand is by her neck. I shift my palm to the hilt of my sword, but I have a feeling it won't do much good.

"Thieves," it says.

Says isn't right. It's not talking. The voice is echoing inside my skull.

Am I hearing shit now?

"I am speaking through your mind," it says. "But I can call out to my brothers if you prefer me to vocalize."

The fuck does that mean—speaking through my mind? It's in my brain? How?

"We mean no harm," Aeri says. "The egg was abandoned."

The amarth moves its head suddenly, more like an eagle than a person. It stares at the egg. "It is not yours to take, Princess Naerium."

Nope, okay, that's much worse. How does it know Aeri? Why?

"Your kind are not complicated to know, Royo," it says. "Son of Snaw."

My heart lodges in my throat. How the fuck did this get weirder? How does this bird thing know me? Then the name Snaw tears through me like a salted blade. That was my father's name—the man who walked out when I was a toddler. The man my mom kept a plate for at every dinner table until she died.

What is happening right now?

"We need to take this to the Queen of Khitan," Aeri says.

Honestly, she's too calm, considering we're having a conversation with a seven-foot-tall bird. But I guess that's the princess part of her—always ready.

"The Queen of Khitan cannot wield the ring," it says. "You are on a fool's errand. As are your friends."

Aeri turns pale, and her eyes shoot over to me. She looks for help, like I'm the one in control of this.

"War of the realms and the rot of death come as fools try to become gods," it says. "You have your roles to play, especially you and the Son of Vengeance. Leave the egg, and I will allow you to escape with your lives."

"Perhaps a trade," she says, gripping her necklace. "For the egg."

The bird closes its eyes in a way that I somehow know means no.

"Our kind serve the Sky King. We cannot break the treaty of the Dragon Lord. And the bells are useless for another while your heart still beats."

I have no idea what any of that means, but Aeri looks stunned. My spine stiffens. Whatever it is ain't good.

"Leave the egg," it says. "That is your final warning."

Aeri looks at me, torn. She wants to flee and try to make it, but we both know I can't run as fast as she can. Which means that even if she could escape, I won't.

Fuck it. It's an easy decision.

I shift my weight and put one leg out, dropping into a fighting stance. I'll keep this bird busy while she gets away. I open my jacket, revealing the throwing knives in my vest just as a gust of wind blows. My heart pumps hot, but I'm steady. I've got no nerves at all. The forest and the mountains are beautiful, the air crisp and clean. I'm ready.

There are much worse ways to go than protecting what you love.

Fuck, now I finally get what the priest was saying. Better late than never, I guess.

"No, Royo." Aeri puts her hand out for me to stop. "No."

She leans down. She's going to leave the egg so that we can escape. So that *I* can escape.

I open my mouth to argue, but a shriek comes out of nowhere.

Our time is up.

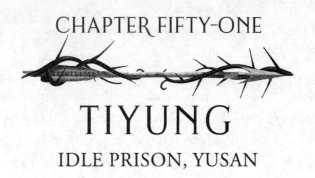

CHAPTER FIFTY-ONE

TIYUNG

IDLE PRISON, YUSAN

Ailor tells good stories, and he hasn't tried to kill me, which makes him my best friend in a place like Idle Prison. Well, we're friends inasmuch as cellmates can be friendly. I like having him here, and I don't want anything bad to happen to him. I've come to believe that he's not a spy. I think he simply happened to be thrown in with me.

I should say: I'm sure someone powerful has something planned by putting us together, but I don't believe Ailor is in on it any more than I am.

Ailor is forty years old and from a city near the Strait of Teeth. He has a grown son, a wife who died long ago, and a donkey named Sticks, whom he misses. Since he retired from the king's guard, he primarily spends his time growing lemon and olive trees and trying to forget what he saw and did as a soldier. The last part is speculation. I've told him I have done things I'm not proud of, and he just said, "Kid, you have no idea."

We've been exchanging stories in the dark because the oil for the lantern ran out long ago. There's been no sign of Hana for twenty meals—which I think is somewhere between five and nine days, but it gets harder and harder to keep track.

The food she left ran out a while ago, and my stomach has been clamoring ever since. It roars like the iku, and I wrap my arms around my waist.

"What I wouldn't give for another block of cheese," I say.

"It'd be nice," Ailor says casually.

I can see his form but not every expression. I've become skilled at reading his tone, though.

"Been through worse?" I ask.

He nods. "You're probably too young to remember the famine around twenty years ago. I would've happily eaten this prison food if I could've gotten my hands on it. I had more than most because I was a soldier, but that's not saying much. We had some rice provisions, and we were left to fend for ourselves for anything beyond that."

He's right—I don't remember the famine. I was a year or two old when it happened. But I'm sure even if I had been older, I'd barely recall it. I'm certain my family didn't experience any hardship. Those at the top never do.

But I am no longer a noble. And I don't think Hana is coming back to help. The thought twists a knife in my side. Or maybe that's hunger pangs, too.

Our meals come, and once again I think about chancing it for some spicy pork and glass noodles. How infested could just the noodles be? But I also don't want to soil myself in front of Ailor or make the cell reek. Instead, I just have the bread and water.

Hana explained that prison food is left over from what the palace kitchens feed the many servants in Qali. What isn't eaten is brought here to feed the guards, and then finally left out until it's dished to the prisoners. That is why it smells good. Some meals will be edible, and some will be well-spoiled by the time the food makes it to our cells.

A little after our trays are taken away, keys jangle and turn in the lock—someone is here.

Ailor and I both startle. I scurry, while Ailor steps back in a dignified, ready fashion. I think we're both expecting the guards to pull us out. He still hasn't told me what he did to be in here, but I haven't been forthcoming, either. We've told detailed past stories, particularly about the antics of his donkey, but vague recent ones.

"Put your hands over your eyes," I say. "It will help you adjust to the light faster."

The door opens, and someone comes in. I brace myself for the bright torches of the guards, but instead it's a small lantern.

Hana?

I remove my hand and squint in her direction. It *is* her.

Joy races through my body, my heart filling. I hadn't realized how worried I was about her until she just reappeared. Maybe it's all for selfish reasons—for the help she gives me—but I don't think it's ever a bad thing to want to see someone alive and well.

My happiness, though, is snuffed out by the haunted look on her face. She seems like she was tortured. She's still beautiful, of course, but there's a hollowed-out gauntness to her. Something about her seems changed for the worse.

I can only imagine one thing that could throw her this much: Sora is dead.

My mouth goes dry, and my head feels light and woozy, but I keep my composure. I brace myself to ask. I don't want to, but I have to know.

"What happened?"

My pulse beats, pounding in my neck as I wait for her to tell me that all hope is lost. My heart thuds like it wants to leap out to get the answer faster.

Hana shakes her head and sets down the lantern. Then she takes a deep breath, puts her hood down, and faces us. She looks collected, more like someone who simply didn't sleep well last night. But it's an act.

"Is Sora all right?" I press.

She nods.

I breathe out a sigh of relief, but that reprieve is short-lived before worry sets in again. Because if it's not Sora, then who? Why does she look this way?

"I see you've met." She gestures to Ailor and me.

"It took me a while to find him, but eventually we did," I say.

The side of her mouth turns up. "Do you know who he is?"

271

"Ailor," I say.

I glance over at him and see that he's studying Hana. He doesn't know her. The way she asked the question means that he's someone important to me or her. My face flushes and I feel immensely foolish because I don't actually know that much about him. He's been in here with me for probably a week, giving me all the time in the world, and I didn't ask the right questions.

"Who are you, miss?" He stands very straight, attentive to her. Ailor, like most men, is apparently swayed by beauty.

"I am Zahara—the royal spymaster."

He smiles, running a hand over his hair. "That's impossible."

She tilts her head, but it's clear she was expecting that reaction. "And why is that?"

"Because my son is the royal spymaster."

Oh gods, that's why he reminded me of Mikail—Ailor is his father. He's young to have a twenty-four-year-old son, but things happen. Mikail's mother must have died when he was only a young child, since Ailor said he lost his wife twenty years ago.

"You're Mikail's father?" I ask, turning toward him.

He raises his chin, evaluating me. Then he nods. "I am. You know him?"

"I… I do."

He frowns. "Then I doubt either of us will make it out of this alive."

"King Joon ordered Tiyung's accidental death the same as he ordered you to be placed in custody," Hana says to Ailor. "I thought that together, you could help me save the people we love."

"And how do I know you're not just trying to trap my son?" he asks.

She shrugs. "You don't. You'd be foolish to trust me at all. The king saved me from Tiyung's family and gave me a life of prestige. Because of Mikail's betrayal and fall from grace, I've now, temporarily, taken the position of royal spymaster. It's something most commoners can't ever hope to achieve. Therefore, you can believe that I love someone and something more than this exalted position…or not.

It's your choice."

Ailor is silent, stroking the short, brown beard that's grown in his time here.

"Where have you been?" I ask.

She draws a breath as if the words will be painful. "I was spreading Daysum's ashes."

Daysum's…ashes. No. Oh gods, please no.

I shake my head, denying it, but I know in my core that it's true. My cheeks tingle as blood drains from my face. That was the look Hana had when she came in. She knows what Daysum means to Sora. Daysum was her reason for living, and now, without her…

I pray she doesn't know, but someone like Hana will tell her. She loves Sora too much to hide the truth.

"They said Daysum died of a laoli overdose in one of your uncle's pleasure houses," Hana says quietly. "I had to arrange for an investigation while her body was preserved and rushed here. I burned her myself and said the prayers."

My uncle's…? Kingdom of Hells, my father sold her. He sold Sora's sister as a pleasure indenture.

Daysum had told Sora that she thought she was dying, so she might have simply passed—a kindness from the gods. But it's equally likely that my uncle killed her. They give out drugs in his pleasure houses, so an overdose is possible. Lord Sterling loses many indentures to drugs and violence. His houses advertise new indentures weekly, the girls and boys replaced like fresh horses.

But gods… Daysum. The cell feels like it's spinning. I try to get my bearings, but I can't.

"Your uncle is also ashes," Hana says.

That catches me off guard and grounds me. I raise my eyebrows.

"He was found in his bed with a blade in his neck." She speaks with all the passion of a shrug.

I would think Hana killed him, but even by fleet carriage it would take a week to reach Gain and another to return. She simply didn't have the time.

"From whom?" I ask.

She shrugs. "We aren't sure. As you can imagine, there are over a hundred likely suspects. Including Daysum."

I try to find some sympathy or grief for my uncle. He never did anything wrong to me, but he was far from a good man. If Daysum killed him, it was well deserved. Now I have a new mystery, in addition to why my father is in Khitan, why the king planned his own assassination, and why he needed Sora. I suspect the king knew about Sora because of Hana, but why would she put Sora in harm's way?

Ailor has been quietly observing us. "You really know her," he says to me.

I nod. "From when we were children."

"Can I trust her?"

I hesitate because I don't know. I had nothing to lose, but he does. His death wasn't ordered—just his captivity.

"Oh, I forgot to bribe you. Here," Hana says.

She takes out a cloth sack twice as large as before. I think about diving for it, but she won't take it away so long as I cooperate. Ailor remains standing still, skeptical.

Instead of tossing it to the ground, she hands the food sack to me. I can smell truffle oil through the cloth.

"I'm sorry I couldn't come for a while, Tiyung," she says. She looks sincere. "There was much afoot. More than just Daysum and Lord Sterling's deaths."

"Such as?" I ask. It takes all my reserve to follow her conversation as my stomach churns. I want to tear through the bag, and I've noticed Ailor's eyes have landed on it more than once.

The moaning sounds of the iku shake the walls, and she leans in between us.

"Soldiers are on the move," she whispers.

"To where?" Ailor asks.

"North," she says. "They are headed north."

CHAPTER FIFTY-TWO

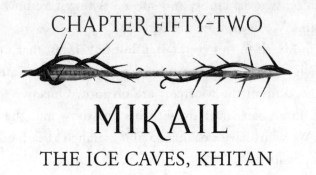

MIKAIL
THE ICE CAVES, KHITAN

Bells signaling the alarm and our doom ring out into the snowy night. I may kill Gambria myself, if I survive this. She gave me bad information either because she didn't know—which in that case, she should've said that—or on purpose, to protect her former lover, and then I swear I'll have my revenge.

Assuming I'm not impaled.

Sora, Euyn, and I run from the mausoleum toward where we stashed the horses. I look back, and a guard with a twisted beard is being tended to by two men. He can't walk, but he's breathing.

That is the guard Sora kissed. The one she was supposed to kill. He's alive and sitting under the alarm bell.

She follows my line of sight, and her mouth drops open. Then she stares straight ahead as if she didn't notice.

"Something you want to explain?" I ask as we sprint.

"Not any more than you," she says.

I stare at her, puzzled but also running full speed. This isn't the time to ask, but we will need to have a conversation about this later. If we survive. Hopefully, it's not with our last breath as stakes go through our bodies.

Stars, I'd really like it if we could stop running for our lives.

Now clearly isn't that time as dozens of armed Marnans pour out of the cave mouth, the alarm still echoing behind them. They have maces, swords, clubs, and spears. A few have bows—that's concerning. We need more distance.

I push myself to run even faster, but not so fast that Euyn can't keep up. It shouldn't matter soon, though. The horses are beyond that ridge, and all the Marnans are on foot. Once we reach our mounts, Euyn can cover us with his crossbow and then get on himself. We won't have a chance to find Staraheli's head, but we can live to try again.

We crest the hill, and there's nothing. Just snow and the tree they'd been tied to. My stomach drops. The horses wandered, or, more likely, they were taken.

What now?

I look for a solution, but I don't see one. And the Marnans are gaining on us. Their war cries echo louder.

Arrows fly up into the sky. I duck and roll out of the way of two poorly aimed shots. I use my scabbard to shield my head and neck, but nothing lands near me.

They should really know to plant their feet before they fire.

Suddenly, Euyn cries out. His scream chills me, and he falls forward. He's been hit.

I run to him, diving into the snow. I pull him out of the way as a well-aimed spear hits where he just was. He's alive, but now he can't run because of an arrow lodged in the back of his left thigh.

This won't be pleasant for him, but I grab the arrow shaft in my fist. In one smooth motion, I yank the bloody arrow out of his leg.

Euyn lets out an animal cry, but I had to do it. It was better not to warn him because he would've tensed up and made the pain worse. I couldn't leave the arrow in because it would've sliced the muscles of his leg apart.

It's done now.

All I need to worry about is Euyn losing too much blood. Oh, and also how to get away from three dozen armed Marnans without horses and with Euyn limping.

Not ideal.

I stand, looking around, desperate, but I quickly realize from the terror in Sora's eyes that there is nowhere for us to go. No way to get out of here. This is it. Lord Yama will collect from Euyn and me tonight. I can't help that. But I can still save Sora. I can keep my promise to her.

"Run," I say to her. "Live a long life."

I take out my sword. I can occupy enough of them to maybe give her time to get away. Euyn sees my determination and understands it's hopeless for him, for us. But we can take as many Marnans to the hells with us as possible. He stands and readies his crossbow despite bleeding steadily down his left pant leg.

Sora stands, terrified and torn.

"I'm sorry, Sora," Euyn says. "Now go."

His eyes meet mine after he just apologized to a common girl. Surprising until the very end.

"Yours in this life and the next," he says, grimacing.

"Yours in this life and the next," I say.

The Euyn I once knew would've tried to save himself without looking back. Now, he stands his ground, shooting so that an indentured girl can live. Prince, criminal, villain, hero. Liar and unfailingly true. He is all of that and more. There is no easy way to describe Euyn, and maybe I've always loved that.

Sora gathers herself and runs.

The Marnans close in, falling back where Euyn shoots but constantly gaining ground. I'm ready with my sword, but three sharp whistles pierce the night. I whip my head to the side. I know that shrill, birdlike whistle. I remember it from the fields of Gaya.

I look behind me. There, a few yards away, Gambria sits in a sleek, black sleigh with her wife next to her.

"Well, are you going to just stand there and die?" Gam asks, gesturing crudely.

Sora is already halfway to the sleigh. I run, helping Euyn as he hobbles. He turns and shoots haphazardly, making the Marnans stay back a bit.

We jump into the sleigh as Gambria whips the horses. As we fall into the high-sided sled, spears thud against the back. Euyn lies on the floor, and Sora curls into the bench where the arrows and spears can't reach. But I don't duck and cower. I stand, protecting Gambria's back.

Lyria suddenly stands as well.

"Death to the traitors!" she yells in perfect Marnan. Then she repeats it again and again.

The Marnans pause, baffled by a woman who looks and speaks like them. Their confusion lasts long enough for Gambria to coax the horses into a gallop.

All of us fall silent as Gambria urges the four winter horses faster, out of range of the Marnans.

I kneel and check Euyn's leg. I will need to cauterize the wound or stitch it up when we get to safety. For now, I tear a blanket apart and tie it tightly around his thigh. He'll live.

Or we'll all die, and then sutures won't matter.

We've outpaced everyone on foot, but three Marnans pursue us on horseback. Those horses look suspiciously like the ones we lost.

One of their riders has a bow. I notice it just as an arrow whizzes by my ear. He's apparently a decent shot.

"Euyn," I say. "An archer."

With a pained grunt, he gets to sitting and then to standing. The archer has ridden up, gaining on us because his horse doesn't have to pull a sleigh with five people. The Marnan doesn't aim at us, though. No, he's focused on our horses. Clever. If he takes one out, we will be sitting ducks.

Euyn is unsteady, leaning on the side of the sled, but he brings the loaded bow to his shoulder and aims. He fires. With one arrow, the archer drops, hit in the neck. The Marnan falls from his horse, toppling into the snow.

Euyn then collapses onto his knees. Too much blood lost.

There are two more riders behind us, still in pursuit. I grab Euyn's bow. I don't have his aim, but it's better than nothing. Before I get the bow reloaded, though, the other riders fall back. I stare with the crossbow to my shoulder. What just happened? Why did they give up?

I watch them gallop back toward their caves. Then I realize why they stopped: they won't risk being far from the caves with Khitan looking to eliminate them once and for all. Although the Marnans would like to kill us, we didn't actually succeed in getting Staraheli's head. They can let us go.

We failed but made it out alive. Somehow, fate saw us through another night. Well, fate and Gambria.

Then again, she also put us in this situation. I suppose it's a wash.

"Thanks for the hot tip," I say in old Gayan.

No one else can follow us in this language. Lyria speaks Khitanese and Marnan. Sora speaks Yusanian and a surprising amount of Khitanese. Euyn learned all four major languages, but his ability in Gayan never improved over that of a small child. He called it dead, since once Yusan took over hundreds of years ago, they made Yusanian the official language. Old Gayan died out for the most part—or so the empire thinks.

But Euyn is also lying on the floor of the sleigh, distracted by his blood loss and the pain in his leg.

Still, I speak at a normal volume to not encourage him to listen in and try his hand at translating.

"You're welcome for saving your ass," Gambria says, picking up on my language choice. "Who are these two?"

"They are a long story. Why did you help me?"

Gambria is direct and only respects others who are the same.

"After you left, Lyria told me I'd given you old information," she says. "That they moved the body years ago and you were walking into a death trap. I tried, but I couldn't get a message to you—you'd already left Loptra. And if you're asking why I helped you in a broader sense, you already know why."

She turns back to face me and arches an eyebrow. Then she stares over at Sora because everyone stares at Sora. Gambria is curious and will definitely ask me about her later. But even I can't fully explain her at the moment.

I sit back on the bench and speak in a low voice to Sora. I watch my feet, though, since Euyn is trying and failing to get comfortable on his stomach on the floor.

"Are we going to talk about why the guard was still alive?" I ask.

Her lashes shade her eyes, but she doesn't respond. She pets the fur blanket covering her lap. "Poisoning is complicated."

It's a truth that's also a lie.

"You made an antidote," I murmur.

She stiffens just a touch. That's exactly what she did. Because she's kind. Because she's merciful.

"It worked much faster than expected," she says. "I don't have the experience with cures the way I do with toxins."

She sighs as if my issue is with her craftsmanship, not her altering the plan. Or the fact that her mercy almost cost us our lives.

"You weren't honest about it," I say.

She stares into my eyes under the bright monsoon moon. "Mikail, let's not pretend like you're honest. You're hiding something. More than one thing, I'd wager."

I try to keep my mind blank, remembering the read she has on me, but my thoughts immediately turn to Daysum. To what I'm not telling her.

"Mm-hmm," she hums. Then she looks out the side of the sled, and there's nothing more I can say.

CHAPTER FIFTY-THREE

AERI

THE LIGHT MOUNTAINS, KHITAN

I give up. Taking the egg isn't worth losing Royo. I'll leave it here and hope that Sora and the others have better luck with their mission.

Or maybe they won't because the amarth said it was a fool's errand. But it doesn't matter. Nothing is worth this price. If they fail, too, we'll find another way.

I've nearly placed the egg on the ground when there's a cry and something flies in at full speed. Dia. She's shrieking like she did at the Gray Shore Inn, and she's aimed directly for the amarth. Fear makes my heart leap. I know she's just an owl I happened to find, but I love her. I don't want her to risk herself for me when she's so outmatched. But she's like Royo, ready to battle monsters to protect me. And I don't want them to sacrifice their lives. Not for me, not for anything.

"No," I say.

Dia, of course, doesn't understand me. Instead, she continues to fly until she pecks at the neck of the amarth. I expect him to kill her, but the creature doesn't attack. He doesn't react much at all aside from looking quizzically at the little owl.

Dia flies up and swoops down at his head before stopping, nearly frozen in front of his face. I don't know what the creature is doing, but with one small bite, she will be dead. He has a long, sharp beak that would make quick work of a winter horse. A moon owl doesn't stand a chance.

"Please don't hurt her," I say. I don't know if amarth have human mercy, but I hope they do.

"I am calming her," he says. "Why does she protect you?"

"I'm not sure. I found her abandoned in Quu and gave her some food. She's followed me since."

Dia flies over to my side and hovers in the air. The creature's eyes go from her to me and back again. He blinks and nods as if he understands something.

"Go now," the amarth says. "Before the other sentinels come."

I think he means that I can leave *with* the egg, but I'm not sure. My mouth is dry, and I don't want to ask because I don't want him to second-guess his decision. But also, I don't want him to kill me.

"Selfless kindness to ours doesn't go as unnoticed as it does to yours," he says. "I will care for your owl. Flee now, princess. You have an unenviable choice of love ahead of you."

He takes off into the air, his wings causing a blast of wind. Dia goes with him before I can even say goodbye to her.

I'm still looking up at the sky when Royo pulls my arm. Shaken, I remember it's not time to bird-watch. He let us go, but we still need to escape.

We start running.

As soon as we get to the horses, I hide the egg in my saddlebag. I don't know if these creatures will still be able to sense it or if they'll be able to read our thoughts as we pass, so we gallop away from the mountains as fast as possible.

"That was..." Royo begins, but he doesn't have words.

"I know," I say.

We ride in the quiet of another surreal place and another incredible encounter. We've had a bunch since we met.

"What did it mean—a choice of love?" Royo asks.

I shake my head. "I have no idea. I guess they're oracles. But I don't get what he's referring to."

I really don't. There was nothing in the texts about amarth being able to see the future, but something tells me he wasn't making it up. His pity at my impending choice chills me to my core. But a choice of love could only mean choosing between Royo and something else, and that's simple—I'd choose him every time.

I shake it off as we ride through the snow, desperate to get away. The sun continues to lower in the sky, and the amarth begin to wake.

CHAPTER FIFTY-FOUR

TIYUNG

IDLE PRISON, YUSAN

The army marching north can only mean that war is coming. Ailor seems to reach the same conclusion, if the tightening in his jaw is any indication. Good gods. Yusan is about to declare war on Khitan...again.

Yusan and Khitan battle each other at least once a century. Thousands of people die, homes and lives are destroyed, children get orphaned, and atrocities are committed—all for the border to shift slightly or sometimes not at all. A truce or an everlasting peace is brokered and then soon forgotten because the rulers lose nothing.

Ever since Hana told us about the soldiers, I've been pondering the war. It cannot be a coincidence that King Joon sent Sora and the others to Khitan at the same time he is mobilizing an army. Hana said that the king wanted them to steal the Golden Ring of the Dragon Lord, but perhaps they were merely a decoy, a distraction for Queen Quilimar. But why? I am convinced that this is tied to the laoli in Oosant, but I'm missing a key piece of information. And it's driving me mad.

"You seem to wish you were with them," Ailor says.

I must've been staring off into space again. "I mean, not that I don't enjoy your company, but yes. I'd rather be with her."

Ailor laughs, and then he coughs. He's been coughing more and more since he's been in here. The damp cold and lack of sun will do that. I've only stayed healthy because I almost never get sick and Hana has been feeding us.

Finally, Ailor stops coughing, and then he spits. A glob of red lands on the floor.

Blood.

He just coughed up blood. I stare at the spot on the ground, and he does as well.

"Is that…new?" I ask.

He shakes his head. "It comes and goes."

I'm no healer, but that can't be good.

I'd ask Hana to bring him a healer, but I doubt they have any here. Also, Ailor hasn't told her much. I don't know if he doesn't trust her or if he really doesn't know what Mikail is up to. He was surprised by our plan to kill the king—or at least that I was a part of it. He thought I should've gone free, since I am the son of a count, but I knew the risk. I wanted to help Sora get her freedom no matter what the cost.

"You love this girl, huh?" he asks.

I nod. He's heard a lot about Sora during our time together. I've told him everything from my family's sordid dealings to me punching a king's guard to try to save her in the arena. My hand only recently feels better.

"I grew to love them all, really," I say. "Mikail included. But yes, Sora is the one I'm thinking about."

He smiles. "It's a beautiful thing to be in love—dulls the atrocities."

My eyebrows rise at the last word. "Which atrocities?"

Ailor shakes his head, as he's done whenever he's mentioned bad things. I understand not wanting to talk about it, but we're coming to the end of our time together. I doubt I'll live long enough to spill his secrets. So I might as well share mine.

"I've killed a man," I say. And then I remember the second man in the warehouse. "More than one. I know you must see me as a soft nobleman, but I don't think you can shock me."

The corner of his mouth turns up just like Mikail. "Believe me, son, it's different when your victims weren't all grown men."

He means either boys or women, or maybe both.

Ailor takes a wet-sounding breath. "I killed a family. The little girls, and then the mother, so they wouldn't have to watch their parents die first. The father went last, and their bodies were thrown into the sea. Not even burned and released."

I grimace, looking to the side. I don't mean to judge him, but I also can't stop myself.

"Awful, isn't it?" he says. "I was following orders—even received a medal of valor for it. But the funny thing is, the acts that haunt me aren't even what I did, but what I permitted. What I didn't stop."

He leans his head against the wall. He coughs again, but quietly.

The truth of his statement shocks me. Isn't that the feeling I have about my father? I didn't stop him from putting a sword to the throat of Sora's father. Yes, I was a child, but so was she. And she was hiding Daysum behind her to do what was right. I didn't stop him from poisoning her or nineteen other girls. I didn't stop him from selling their siblings. I didn't stop my uncle from running the worst pleasure houses in Gain, invested in by my father and therefore by me. I didn't refuse to have anything to do with my family once I knew what they did, where the money came from. I let him do it all to expand my inheritance. I thought it was because I loved him, because I was loyal to my family. But now, I don't know. General cowardice and complacency seem to be the more accurate reasons. I permitted it all.

"You'd be surprised at how much I can relate to that," I say.

He eyes me.

"You know, kid, I believe you."

We're silent for a minute. It's the comfortable quiet of two men who are different but have come to understand each other.

"Do you believe in redemption?" I ask.

He strokes his beard. "In the eyes of the gods, or in your own reflection?"

I swallow hard. What a question. "Both, I suppose."

He smiles. "I hope the gods who made us judge our faults and our kindnesses as products of themselves. Do I believe in redemption for myself, though? No. There is nothing I can do in the future that can atone for my past actions or inactions."

Ailor states it so plainly—not sugar-coated or couched. I'm having trouble believing someone with a silver tongue like Mikail came from Ailor. He must be like his mother.

"How do you live with that?" I ask.

"Well, son, I'm in a prison cell right now, and I'm not too upset about it." He looks around and shrugs. "I figure I deserve what's coming to me. I work hard to not deserve more."

I shift against the wall, my shoulders feeling tight. "I haven't made the same kind of peace with it."

I haven't at all. There are far worse men—my father being one, Bay Chin being another, King Joon being chief among the kind who have done terrible things en masse and who are not facing death and torture. Who are free to commit more atrocities.

"But you have the rest of your life to atone," Ailor says. "I don't have much time." He gestures to the spit on the floor.

I shake my head. "My death is ordered. I have less time than you."

"We'll see," he says. "The important thing is that you want redemption. That alone makes you better than most."

He folds his arms the way he does when he's about to rest, so I turn out the lantern and also lean my head against the wall. There was something oddly comforting about how he said *we'll see.* I suppose he is right—with war coming, anything can happen. And it does matter that I want to do better, be better.

The thought allows me to rest well for the first time in a while.

But sleeping soundly in prison is always a mistake. It takes me entirely too long to wake up. And that could cost me my life.

CHAPTER FIFTY-FIVE

ROYO

THE NORTHERN PASS, KHITAN

We ride hard until we gotta stop and make camp. I find a spot that'll work for the night, and I make a fire while Aeri…digs a hole in the snow. I stare at her because if she's digging a toilet hole, it's way too close to where we're going to eat and sleep. But she just keeps digging with the stirring spoon.

"What are you doing?" I ask.

"Burying the egg." She says it like *of course I am*.

I can feel my forehead wrinkle. "Why?"

She pauses for long enough to tilt her head at me. "We don't want to risk predators getting at it, and I definitely don't want amarth to see it from the sky."

Both solid reasons.

She buries the black egg deep in the snow and then covers it, patting it down until she's satisfied.

By the time she's done, I've got the camp set up. The fire's going, and a log is cleared for us to sit for a meal. She perches on the log, and then she starts laughing. I stare at her while sharpening my axe. She's the oddest person I've ever met, but I don't think I'd have it any other way. The strange thing is she's not just laughing, she's crying.

"Are you…okay?" I ask.

She sniffles and wipes her eyes, still crying and laughing at the same time.

I stop what I'm doing, stone on the blade. "Aeri, what's wrong?"

She gestures around and laughs again. Then a weird thing happens. For some reason, I start laughing, too. There's nothing funny. Not even close. But we're alive and safe and we shouldn't be. I tried to save her, and she wound up saving me instead. Well, her little owl saved us both.

Which…was fucking weird.

I'm happy, afraid, exhausted, awake, sad, and relieved all at the same time. Too much conflicting shit.

I laugh until tears run down my face. I'm not crying like Aeri, but my eyes leak. I sit next to her. She leans into me, and I brush her tears away, rubbing my thumbs under her eyes.

The next thing I know, her mouth is on mine. She moves so impossibly fast. Her arms wrap around me and she's kissing me before I can even react.

Then I do.

I kiss her hard, like she may fade away.

I like it so much—kissing this girl under the monsoon moon. I've wanted her so badly. But alarm bells ring out in my head. I try to ignore them, to just shut off my brain and enjoy her, but the warning bells chime like a fucking gong. Her kissing me now is like her laughing and crying. It's just because of everything we've been through, all the emotions boiling over like a rice pot. It's not love or even lust. Not for her. If it was, she wouldn't have pulled away when I touched her.

"Aeri," I say.

I go to remove her arms, but she has me in a vise grip.

All right, fine—I'm not trying that hard. I like her around me, even if I know better.

"I don't think…" I begin.

"Good, don't think," she murmurs.

Her lips are on mine again. Her taste is like fresh honey. It's a cirena song, making it hard to think straight. All I want to do is dive in and drown in her. But I hold on to my last bit of control.

"I don't want to hurt you," I say.

She stares into my eyes. "Then don't." She smiles. "Or do, and maybe I'll like it."

She's playing with me again, and I've had just about enough of this game. I thought her hair was a lot shorter when we met, but it's shoulder-length. I grab it as I kiss her.

Then I pull her hair so she looks me in the eye. "Do you want me?"

"For tonight," she says. "And tomorrow. And tomorrow. And tomorrow."

Feelings swell inside me, and I can't stop them. I lift her up. Her eyes open in surprise, and then she sinks into me.

This is the stupidest shit I've ever done. Easy. But I rip the blanket out of the tent and lay it down by the fire. Then I lay her down on top of it.

CHAPTER FIFTY-SIX

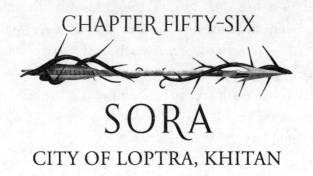

SORA
CITY OF LOPTRA, KHITAN

"Royo and Aeri will betray us!" Euyn yells. He slaps his hand on his side, frustration oozing from him.

As we rode toward Loptra, Euyn worked himself into a full meltdown about Royo and Aeri taking the ring to King Joon. I'm listening but also not. This has gone on for a while as he's spiraled into an elaborate conspiracy theory.

I'd be concerned, but as far as I can tell, it's based on nothing.

I'm still shocked that Euyn apologized and tried to save my life by the ice caves. It's no small thing for a man like him to say he was sorry, to put a common girl's life before his own. Is it enough, though? He can't take back what he did in the past—no one ever can—so is it enough that he feels sorry? I don't know. I've pondered it for bells now.

Everyone else has slept on and off in the two-day trip to Loptra, but the thing that's kept me up nearly the whole time is how making the antidote, showing mercy to the guard, was a mistake. Mikail was right—it almost got us killed. By trying to spare one soul, I nearly took five.

When I was in poison school, Madame Iseul used to say mercy was a luxury that girls like us couldn't afford. I used to argue that she was wrong—that kindness was the only way we could afford to keep our humanity.

Now, I'm not so sure. I would think this was just unfortunate, that mercy only failed me this one time, but maybe it would always end like this for someone like me. Maybe mercy is a privilege of the powerful.

We deposit the sleigh in a stable in Loptra. I stretch and yawn. It's nearly midnight.

"We should leave," Euyn says.

Mikail and I both look over at him. Gambria and Lyria stand a few yards away, waiting by the stable entrance.

"I am taking a bath, and you could use one, too, to prevent an infection," Mikail says. He stitched Euyn's leg together when we stopped for water. It was a nasty-looking wound.

Euyn wavers. "All right, then immediately after that. We need to beat them to Quu."

Mikail utters a long-suffering sigh. I don't think Gambria or Lyria speak Yusanian, but they're staring over here.

I wonder what the relationship is between Mikail and Gambria and why Lyria, a woman who is ethnically Marnan, helped us. But I don't speak any Marnan, and I don't entirely trust Gambria for some reason, so I can't ask.

"I think Euyn is right," I say. "I think we should head to Vashney tonight."

Mikail stares at me, puzzled, and Euyn looks taken aback as well. I agreed not because I think Aeri and Royo will betray us. I don't think that at all. Aeri has accepted that her father is a bad man, and Royo has too much integrity. None of us want to hand another relic to King Joon. I hope they've succeeded and are on their way to meet us.

No, I want to leave as soon as possible because each sunset is another night my sister is forced to work in the pleasure houses. Yes, I could use rest in a proper bed, but what is my comfort compared to what she is enduring? If we get to Quilimar just one day sooner, that is one more night of freedom for Daysum. And a greater chance

Ty will be alive in Idle.

"Euyn?" Gambria asks as she approaches us. She's much shorter than I thought when I first saw her. Smaller than even Daysum. But her presence looms larger. She stares at Mikail with startling intensity.

I feel like I said something wrong, but I can't imagine what. Then it occurs to me that Mikail hasn't said Euyn's name since we got into the sleigh. He was keeping his identity a secret.

Mikail gestures. "This is Euyn Hali Baejkin, Crown Prince of Yusan."

He says it in Khitanese, but I can follow.

Gambria and Lyria stiffen. Gambria's cheeks gain a cherry hue, and Lyria looks like she'd rather be somewhere else.

"Tell me why I saved this son of a demon," Gambria says.

I think that's what it translates to. I might have the creature wrong, but the sentiment is the same.

"He is part of the plan," Mikail says.

Her eyes narrow. "To?"

"To kill King Joon," he says.

Euyn blanches even more, which is surprising given his blood loss. He limps closer to Mikail and whispers. "Mikail…are you sure we can trust them?"

"They literally just saved us, so yes, even you should think so," Mikail says.

Gambria arches an eyebrow. "*You* are going to kill the god king?"

There's something about her that reminds me of Mikail. Perhaps they've simply known each other a long time.

"Our plan is to kill him with the help of Quilimar," Mikail says.

The wives exchange glances in an unspoken language—their connection is deeper than words. Suddenly, I'm reminded of Hana—my first love. We used to be able to speak through a look in school. I turn away, feeling so homesick I could cry. But I'm longing for a home that I lost two years ago. It's just another thing that's gone.

Another soul.

I shake off the disappointment and heartbreak. At some point, I know it'll all be too heavy to ignore, but I'll make Seok pay first.

Mikail walks over to Gambria, and they speak in hushed tones.

I'm left standing in awkward silence with a woman I can't communicate with and a man I am unsure about.

Eventually, Mikail and Gambria come back.

"We are going to bathe and change, and then Gambria is going to come with us to Quu," Mikail announces.

Euyn's eyebrows nearly hit his hairline. "And why is that?"

"Because Gambria has...history with Quilimar," Mikail says. "It could prove useful if Royo and Aeri were unsuccessful."

Lyria's eyes volley as she tries to absorb what Mikail is saying in Yusanian. Gambria says something to Lyria in Marnan, and her wife's face gets stormy. Then she stomps off in the other direction.

Gambria's face falls, but she takes a breath and then gestures over her shoulder. "Come with me."

We follow, but my shoulders sag. Apparently, we're going to ruin everything and every relationship around us.

But sometimes, losing everything is the only way to get what you want.

CHAPTER FIFTY-SEVEN

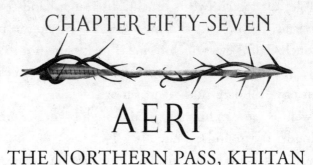

AERI

THE NORTHERN PASS, KHITAN

I'm lying on a soft fur as snow falls gently all around us. I stare up at the billion stars and the waving haze of the Night Rays of the Sun King.

And, best of all, Royo is on top of me.

He kisses me, savoring my mouth while he cradles my neck in his hand. He's taking his time, whereas I've been on a mission to get his clothes off. My legs are wrapped around him, but we're both sadly still fully clothed.

I sigh.

Finally, he gives in. A little. He slides off his jacket and then a vest that contains a shocking number of knives.

For the first time since I can remember, I don't think about stealing a weapon. I don't think about anything other than him.

Royo takes his shirt off, and I do as well. But I leave on my camisole, so I don't scandalize him just yet.

He stares down at me. "Ten Hells, you're beautiful."

His compliment flushes through me, and then his weight is on me again. I run my hands over the broadness of his back and shoulders. His skin is scarred but so much softer than I expected. I'm savoring every place I get to touch, every bit of him that he's allowed to be exposed. And yes, fine, I'm also trying to push his pants down. In fairness to me, though, I've thought about this *a lot*.

But I get distracted by his touch. His rough hands roam over me—my arms, my breasts, and my waist. He's trying to be gentle, but his touch claims every inch of me. I make sure not to flinch or recoil, and he doesn't graze my amulet again. I really don't care about time right now, though. All I want is more of this.

All I want is more of him. Yet even though his desire presses into me, he doesn't try to undress me.

I take it back—he's killing me. I'm aching for him. The throbbing between my legs is intolerable.

I slide my pants down, and he stops kissing me and pulls back, away from me.

Oh no. Gods. My stomach flips. I could not have ruined this again. Embarrassment makes me want to curl in a ball. He pulled away again. I should've taken things slower, just allowed them to unfold.

I am the court jester of trying to get Royo to bed me.

He sits on his knees, then reaches into the tent. His hand comes out with the other blanket, and he lays it over me. It's the brown fur one he wrapped around my shoulders after he saved me from drowning.

"What's this for?" I ask.

"I didn't want you to get cold." His face is so pure and thoughtful. My heart flutters. It literally feels like a caged butterfly.

"Come keep me warm, instead." I push the fur aside. I'm naked except for my camisole, so I take that off, too.

He groans, and his eyes change. Something in him, that last shred of reserve, breaks. We've finally kicked off our boots, and he slowly takes down his pants and his underwear.

Worth. The. Wait.

He slides his body over mine, but instead of kissing me he makes a trail down the center of me. Each place his lips hit leaves my skin feeling aflame. It's nearly the same sensation as when I'm furious—a burning at my core, racing through me, until I feel like I'll ignite.

But this time it's so pleasant. All the sensation converges between my thighs, molten and waiting.

This isn't my first time, but it's my first time wanting someone so desperately. He's made it down to the pit of my stomach when I start shamelessly begging.

"Please, Royo." I moan. "Please."

He smiles, looking up at me. "Please what?"

I groan. Terrible man. He knows exactly what I want.

"I'm going to pass out and explode at the same time," I say.

Royo laughs and shakes his head. And gods, that smile. "Impatient little thief."

He shifts my leg, bending it up, then kisses by my knee. I grab at the blanket as his lips tease the delicate skin of my inner thigh. I'm going to pull every piece of fur out of this if I'm not careful. I shake from anticipation, my hips arching, begging.

"You're ruining me," I say.

He stares into my eyes. "I'm about to."

Then his mouth is on me, and I gasp, seeing stars.

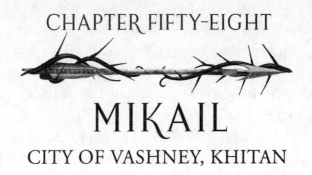

CHAPTER FIFTY-EIGHT

MIKAIL

CITY OF VASHNEY, KHITAN

Stars, if I have to hear another of Euyn's conspiracy theories, I'm at risk of losing my own sanity. I opt to take a long walk to the Vashney messenger house, but really, I'm just trying to get away from him.

Because you can love someone and want your own space.

That's what Gambria said. Although I continue to debate my feelings for Euyn, Gam had distinct thoughts on my relationship with the crown prince. It's not as simple as she pretends it is, though. She calls him a colonizer and a bloodletter, among other colorful phrases, but he was a child, just as I was, during the Festival of Blood. And holding children responsible for the acts of their elders always leads to atrocity.

Still, she isn't completely off base about him. He did want to kill the priest in the Temple of Knowledge under the guise of mercy. And then there are his thoughts on the pragmatism of sinking Wei.

I sigh deeply.

When we left the temple, we gave Royo and Aeri a sunsae to meet us in Vashney. It's a ten-day journey round-trip, and that's *if* they were able to locate the egg immediately. It is now day ten.

A little fear chills me on the snowy walk. Not because I think Aeri and Royo will betray us, but because they might fail. And then what? We couldn't find Staraheli, and I doubt the Marnans have made it easier to access his body. We are running out of time, and what's worse is that I still haven't figured out Joon's master plan. I keep probing and winding up at loose ends. But perhaps we can get to Quilimar even without an exception to the Rule of Distance. Maybe she will see Gambria—that is why I asked her to accompany us, as my backup plan.

When Quilimar first arrived at Khitan, she, of course, met dignitaries, and Gambria was by Fallador's side. Both direct, ambitious women, they became quick friends and more. Quilimar was long thought to only be attracted to women—something not allowed for royal women who must produce heirs. Gam was a favored lady of the court, but she left when Quilimar became pregnant with Prince Calstor. I never learned why, but I always suspected Gambria fell in love and was devastated when it turned out Quilimar was bedding her own husband. I highly doubt she had a choice, though, knowing the King of Khitan. It is equally likely that the king himself banished Gambria from Quu.

It's worth mentioning that Gam sees no hypocrisy in falling for Joon's sister, who is also a colonizer and criminal under her definition. To Gambria, however, Quilimar had no power because even though she was a princess, she was a girl in Yusan. It remains to be seen what she thinks a little boy could have done to prevent the Festival of Blood. But hate doesn't have to follow logic.

I arrive at the messenger house after taking the outer loop. I give the woman at the desk my fake name, and there's an envelope waiting for me. Zahara is almost excessively clever. I'm glad she is on my side...if she's on my side. She doesn't have a reason to help me—not one I can discern. Therefore, I need to be cautious with what I tell her and what I believe.

After I tip the woman, I decode Zahara's message, and once again the seemingly long code translates to one word.

WAR

War. Yusan is about to declare war on Khitan. Not the other way around.

I grip the hilt of my sword as everything falls into place. I'd nearly had it figured out in the Temple of Knowledge. Kings leave the safety of Qali because of diplomacy or, more likely, war. That is why Joon left the palace, and that means we were sent here as a distraction for Quilimar and nothing more. We can't wait any longer. We have to get to Quu and somehow arrange an audience with the queen. Even if we have to shout "war" from a hundred feet away.

Stars, I hope she still loves Gambria.

With no time to spare, I hurry back to the inn.

The Revelry Inn is a white, marble-faced building, stained partially gray with age. But the patina fits the five-hundred-year-old inn. It's four stories tall in the gilded, ornate Khitanese style. Euyn, being used to luxury, loves this inn. I think it's a little too conspicuous, but it doesn't matter anymore. We need to leave now.

As I walk into the lobby, I spot two familiar faces. Relief floods my chest.

"You're here?" I ask.

Aeri tilts her head. "Where else would we be?" Then her large eyes scan the painted, domed ceiling. "Well, I guess we could've been dead and eaten by amarth… But no, we made it back. Did you succeed?"

I shake my head. "There was a complication. Did you?"

"We got it," Royo whispers.

Something is different about the two of them, but I'm not certain what. Maybe nothing is new. It could just be Euyn's constant conspiracies altering how I view them.

The most important thing is that they have the egg, which will allow us to dine at a table with Quilimar. We will be able to tell her about the impending war and Joon's plan to take her relic. Yusan attacking should only aid us in forming an alliance with the queen. Very simply, she won't have a choice. And then we will organize a mission to ambush Joon and take his crown.

Energy and a little hope surge through me. This could all work.

"Come up," I say, walking to the stairs. "There have been changes, and we need to leave immediately."

"We have some...information as well..." Aeri hesitates.

I debate between asking what it is now and waiting. I decide anything they say will just have to be repeated to the group, so it's better to wait.

We get to the third floor. I gather Gambria and Sora, then proceed to the fourth floor, and I knock on Euyn's door. His room, of course, is a corner suite. I had to bribe the innkeeper with a hundred marks to move someone else's reservation. Euyn was already on edge. I didn't want to make it worse with him not receiving his preferred accommodation.

I knock twice, and then we wait for Euyn to take down all of his traps. Royo eyes Gambria, and she stares right back at him.

"Who's this?" Royo asks, pointing a thumb at her.

"This is Gambria. She's an...old friend of Quilimar's."

Gam knows much more Yusanian than I expected. Enough for her to comment on Sora's unexpected mercy of sparing the guard as soon as we were alone and to arch an eyebrow now at me for my remark.

I suppress a smile.

The door opens, and Euyn's eyes become as wide as tea saucers when he sees Aeri and Royo. He has the decency to look a little ashamed, which shows a shred of conscience. After all, he did spend the last few days railing against them, calling them traitors and disloyal. And that was a terribly unfair character assassination of Royo.

"Did you succeed?" Euyn asks, gesturing for us to take a seat.

Aeri and Royo look at each other and then both nod. She blushes, smiling at the ground. I was correct—there is something different about them. If I had to guess, they finally figured out they were in love.

Good for them.

"Should I ask how you did it?" I raise one brow.

Sora smiles, looking as happy as the two of them. "She's an incredible thief. I bet they never saw her coming."

Aeri grins back at her. "Thanks…but, um, we did get caught."

Euyn and I exchange looks. If they were caught by an amarth, I don't know how they're standing here. Royo could take one down with an axe, but from my understanding there are a hundred in the mountains. They should've been torn apart.

"One swooped down and talked to us," Royo says with a shrug.

The room is silent.

"It *spoke* to you?" Euyn asks.

He nods. "It was the weirdest shit ever."

"How did you survive that?" Sora asks.

"Because Aeri was kind to an owl," Royo says. He looks over at Aeri, admiring her.

Gambria stares as if she isn't translating the words properly. Sora's mouth breaks out into a true smile.

"Dia!" she exclaims.

And now I'm not sure I'm translating this, either. What are they talking about?

"The creature liked that I helped an orphaned owl," Aeri explains. "I think that's why we were allowed to take the abandoned egg."

Sora nods, seemingly thrilled that someone's kindness was rewarded. Gambria and Euyn look confused at best. Royo, however, stares at Aeri as if she hangs the monsoon moon.

"Anyhow, the birds can talk, and I think… Well, the thing is… they can predict the future," Aeri says.

All of us stare, absorbing the information with varying levels of skepticism.

"What makes you say that?" Euyn's tone makes it clear he doesn't believe her at all.

"The bird thing said all of us were on a fool's errand," Royo says. "It knew Quilimar can't wield the ring, and it said that a war of the realms is coming."

His words are a bolt through the room. All I can see is the word *war* that I decoded. But a war of the realms is much more than Yusan marching on Khitan.

From the look in Gambria's eyes, she knows exactly what it means. Euyn pulls at his beard and adjusts his bandage. Sora looks uncertain.

"What did the amarth say exactly?" I ask Aeri. "Word for word."

I silently pray that Royo is just misspeaking.

"He said a war of the realms and the rot of death were coming," Aeri says. "And that we have our roles to play as fools try to be gods. Also, that I'd have to choose between love. I'm not sure what he meant by the last part—neither of us are."

"Gods on High." Euyn raises a shaky hand to his brow. He's broken out into a cold sweat, and I feel the same, even though I don't show my reaction.

Aeri looks around. "What? Isn't that a good thing? It means we will succeed in starting a war with Yusan, right?"

I wish it did.

I draw a breath. "A war of the realms means all four original realms at war. In this case, Yusan, Gaya, and Wei would all attack Khitan at once."

The room is silent. No one moves.

"We need to get to Quilimar as fast as we can," Euyn says, and I nod. He limps around, packing up.

"Why?" Gambria asks. She'd been leaning against a windowsill but steps forward now.

Euyn doesn't answer, so I do. "Because if what we think is happening is actually happening, then we're all fucked."

CHAPTER FIFTY-NINE

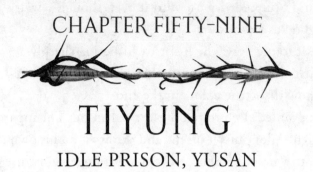

TIYUNG

IDLE PRISON, YUSAN

I'm sleeping against the wall of the cell when I stir. Ailor is shaking me awake.

"What—"

"Shh," Ailor whispers.

Hushed voices echo outside the door. It's not Hana—that much I know. The voices are male. But I'm groggy and miss some of the conversation. It could be guards, judging from the light bursting through the transom window and tray slot. More likely, it's assassins.

"But which one is it?" one asks.

"What do you mean? There's only one target in there," another voice whispers.

"I see two."

"No, this is Tiyung's cell. It should only be him in there."

I swallow hard and sit up straight, now fully awake. This is it. The night I die. Hana bought me as much time as she could, but tonight I'll walk the Road of Souls.

I quickly pray to the gods to spare Sora. I pray that what I told Hana was enough to save all of them and not information I never should've given to a spy. I pray that Lord Yama has mercy on me for my failings and allows me to see Sora again in my new life. I pray that her next life will be kinder to her than this one.

"Give me your collar," Ailor says.

"What?" Stunned, I grab onto it even though jewelry won't do me any good as a dead man.

"Give it to me now!" he insists, whispering sharply.

I didn't think jewels meant that much to him, but I suppose people show their true colors in the end.

Disappointed, I go to remove the collar, but I'm apparently not fast enough. Ailor pulls it off me and throws it on his own chest. He sits close to where the door will open, leaning against the wall like he's resting. The lantern is off, but I can see him clearly from the light of the meal slot.

"What are you doing?" I whisper.

"Tell my boy I love him," he says.

Before I can ask what he means, the door opens and light bursts into the cell. I duck onto the floor to protect my eyes. The pain is intense because there's not one torch but two. If they're supposed to make this look like I died in my sleep, they're failing miserably.

As I lie on the ground, I wait. I expect a blade through my back or hands around my neck. I should've stood like a man, but instead, I can't get my limbs to work. I stay on my belly, waiting to be dragged out. Or to be stabbed and die like a pig in this cell. I only hope it's a quick kill shot.

I hold my breath, trying to find peace in my last moments. Boots shuffle around. There's hard breathing and the scrape of metal as a blade is drawn.

Sora. Her long black hair. Her smile.

She is my last thought.

But then the door swings shut and locks. By the time my eyes adjust again, the assassins are gone.

What in the gods' names just happened?

"Ailor," I whisper. "What happened? Where did they go?"

No response.

An ice-cold chill runs through me. No. No, no, no. It can't be.

"Ailor? Ailor!" I yell out. I don't care about being heard. Where is he?

With shaking hands, it takes me a couple of tries to light the lantern. Finally, I get it lit and pick it up.

There's no one across from me. No one in the straw or by the latrine.

All that's left of Ailor is a smear of blood on the stones near the door.

Stunned, I stand staring at the wet blood. It takes me entirely too long to realize that Ailor chose to sacrifice his own life to save mine. That he'd planned it out. That's what he meant when he said "we'll see" about me living longer than him—he must've already decided that when the time came, he'd pretend to be me. That whoever they'd send to kill me would know me not by my face but by my cell, and with two of us in here, both grimy and bearded, they'd choose the one with a noble collar. And that's why he said to tell Mikail he loved him.

I gasp, shuddering. I cover my mouth with my hand.

Ailor's true colors did come out at the end, and those were of a man willing to give his life for a stranger who showed him kindness. A man who thought of his son with his last breath.

Tears sting my eyes, and I sniffle. My first impulse is to hold them back, hold the emotion in. To not disgrace myself, my rank, by crying. To be a man and not risk Seok's disgusted backhand because of my reddened face or tearstains. But a man I barely knew was just murdered, chose to pay the ultimate price, to buy me a chance at surviving. He is worth the tears that beg to be shed.

I lean against the wall, and I cry softly at first. Then deep sobs rack my chest, and I cry and wail and thrash.

I sob on and off until keys turn in the door. And by then, I'm ready for whatever fate has in store for me.

CHAPTER SIXTY

EUYN

THE NORTHERN PASS, KHITAN

We race the Northern Pass back to Quu, eager to reach my sister. I take a seat up front in the sleigh between this Gambria woman and Mikail. Sora sits in the back with Aeri, Royo, and a trunk full of clothes. Somehow, Aeri found the time to acquire a new wardrobe. She and Royo are noticeably closer than when we left the Temple of Knowledge, but I no longer believe they're plotting against us.

Mostly.

I do feel a twinge of guilt for accusing them, but I had my reasons. Trusting Aeri would be a fool's game when none of us are beyond betrayal. Especially not her.

However, no one has mentioned my theories to them. Everyone is far more concerned with a war of the realms and what it will mean for each of us and Yusan.

"Are you going to tell me why you think we're all fucked?" Gambria asks Mikail. She's speaking in Khitanese. Her accent is slightly off for a native speaker, but I can't place where she is from.

"If there is a war of the realms, what happens?" he asks.

Gambria glares at him. "Are you a tutor now? It means Yusan, Khitan, and Wei go to war with one another."

"And Gaya," he adds.

Her eyes pray up to the snowy sky, and she sighs. "And Gaya."

Once she says the name, I realize this woman looks Gayan, not Khitanese. That's probably the reason for the occasional word sounding off. I was woozy at the time, but I think they were speaking Gayan the night she rescued us.

Mikail has never mentioned Gambria before. At first I thought they might have been lovers, but there's so little chemistry between them that I don't think she even likes him as a person. Which makes saving us a puzzlement.

She must be one of his Gayan sources. Yusan keeps constant secret and overt tabs on the colony. With all the laoli we found in the warehouse, I'm sure he's been looking into it.

Still, it seems like there's more to the story. They are too familiar for her to just be a source.

"A war of the realms would also mean that all of the relics of the Dragon Lord *could* end up in the same place at the same time, wouldn't it?" Mikail says.

Gambria sits, considering it.

"No," I say in Khitanese. "The Sands of Time was lost long ago."

"But what if Joon found it?" Mikail asks.

I shake my head. "That's not possible. There's been no sign of the relic for centuries—it was lost in the deserts of Fallow a thousand years ago when the Dragon Lord ascended."

"All 'lost' means is that someone wanted people to stop looking for it," he counters. "Joon wouldn't advertise to Wei that he has it. He wouldn't want anyone to know until Yusan was locked in battle. My sources say he left the palace right after we were sent north."

I stroke my beard as we sit in silence. Joon has the Immortal Crown and Flaming Sword—the relic Gaya would've brought to a war of the realms centuries ago. Quilimar wears the Golden Ring. Uol, the priest king of Wei, has the Water Scepter to command an unsinkable navy. If Joon found the Sands of Time, he would have three relics. He wouldn't need the ring or scepter to win a war. However, winning a simple battle might not be the point. He may be trying to take the last two and *become* the Dragon Lord before the end of the monsoon season.

The thought is ridiculous until I remember Joon's ambitiousness. Then a cold chill spreads over me.

He must've murdered the priests in the temple. He knew everyone would assume it was Quilimar, and the ancient edicts call for a war of the realms on any ruler who spills the blood of a Yoksa. By framing Quilimar with killing the priests, he guaranteed a war on Khitan's soil. Wei is so assured in their constant victory, they would accept any provocation to gain more tribute. And he controls Gaya.

But it's equally likely that it was, in fact, Quilimar. I'll need to ask my sister directly to figure out if she did it. Hopefully, as I take her ring to give to Joon. If he *is* starting a war and has three of the relics, the ring just became that much more valuable to him. It would be enough to pardon our group and give us the spoils he promised.

He, very simply, has bigger concerns than six people committing a little treason. With the odds stacked against us, it's the only way we'll all survive.

I'm about to point that out when Gambria speaks.

"Skies," she says. "We can ask Fallador if he's heard anything about the Sands of Time."

"I have, and he hasn't," Mikail says.

I turn my head because that's a name I *do* know. Fallador is one of Mikail's sources—one I have always suspected he was in love with. It's something in the way he says his name, a look in his eye—just a small tell. Mikail says I'm paranoid, but being paranoid doesn't mean I'm wrong. Not all the time.

"Where is Fallador?" I ask.

"In Quu," Gambria says. "Unless you've heard otherwise."

I glance at Mikail. Of course—that's who he went to see the second we docked in Khitan. He looks to the side casually, as if it doesn't matter. As if Fallador isn't the reason he hasn't visited my bed since we left Yusan.

Jealousy flames inside me, corrupting my thoughts like poison. "No, I haven't," I say.

I grit my teeth. I'm so furious I could scream. Then I remember that helping Joon will mean I'll soon be crown prince of Yusan again. I won't have to worry about being betrayed at every turn by the ones closest to me.

I steady my breathing and put my mind to making a plan to steal the ring, whether the others agree or not.

CHAPTER SIXTY-ONE

TIYUNG

IDLE PRISON, YUSAN

Keys turn in the lock, and I'm ready. Time has passed slowly since Ailor was murdered. I assumed the assassins would realize their mistake and come back for me, and here they are. It just took far longer than expected.

Half a day has to have passed since they killed him. The blood on the stones has dried, and two meals have been served. But every moment has been excruciating.

The door opens, and I stand. I don't want to die sitting or lying down. I need to show more bravery than before, which isn't a high bar. I'm glad that I have this second chance to die with honor.

I brace myself, but Hana runs in, holding a torch. She's breathless, looking around. I squint, but the torch doesn't hurt much, since I'd been sitting with the lantern on. There was no need to conserve the oil anymore.

"Gods, you're alive?" She sounds relieved and very surprised. Then her shoulders slump as she realizes Ailor isn't here. She closes her eyes, shakes her head. "No time for that now."

She's talking to herself. I admire how she can pivot so quickly, but also, it's inhuman.

Hana takes a bag from under her cloak and extends it to me. "Here. Put this on."

I blink at her. "What?"

"They think you're dead," she says in a hurried whisper. "Do you want to have a conversation, or would you like to escape?"

I've run many scenarios in my mind since they killed Ailor. This wasn't one of them. Mainly because escape from Idle Prison is impossible.

"Move," she says through her teeth. "Put those *on*."

She stomps her foot in frustration as I continue to pose like a shop mannequin.

I open the bag. It contains a jacket and pants like the guards wear—a spare uniform. I change quickly as she wipes off my face and hands with a rough, damp cloth. She sprays me with cologne, then brushes my hair, which has grown to my ears. She combs my beard and hands me a sword. I put it in the holder at my hip.

She looks me over and sighs. "Your beard is terrible, but we don't have time for you to shave. This will have to do. I hope you're more useful than you seem."

"Won't they realize?"

Hana shakes her head. "Not unless you act suspicious. Guards are changed all the time. Unless they're a captain or higher, they don't stay down here for long. I think you can imagine the dungeon isn't a coveted position."

As soon as I'm ready, she hands me the torch and picks up the lantern from the ground. I take a breath, steadying myself as we walk through the door.

Hana winks at the guard who'd opened the cell and fixes her long, thick hair. He's so distracted by her that I step right past him.

My heart pounds and my breathing hitches—it couldn't have been that easy.

Hana proceeds down the hall, and I walk beside her. Half a step behind, actually, because I have no idea where we're going. Torches cast vicious shadows on the stone and earthen space. I try not to look around, but it's hard not to as prisoners moan and call out.

Hana was serious when she said my cell was "royal

accommodations." The other cells have bars, not walls. The stench and squalor are intolerable. The other prisoners are also all tied in place by chains that are six or ten feet long.

And then there is the torture.

I understand the random wails now. We pass hideous-looking devices. I can't imagine what some of these do, and I don't want to know.

We reach an open space, and I take a breath. The halls were almost tunnels and terribly claustrophobic. But my relief dies quickly. This is a torture chamber. Screams echo in the vaulted space, but the quiet between them is almost worse. Close to my right, a tall prisoner hangs by his arms from a rack. He must've been there for so long that his thin shoulders broke and he passed out from the pain. Another hangs upside down, screaming. And then his scream becomes a cry as the smell of charred flesh fills the room.

I'm going to be sick.

I don't want to look, but I do. The guards have pressed a red-hot poker to his bare stomach, burning him. Meanwhile, a well-dressed person sits on a chair, calmly eating a sandwich.

"Perhaps now you remember who else was involved?" he asks the prisoner.

Bile rises in my throat—that could be me being interrogated.

Hana nudges my wrist, and that gets my attention. I manage to settle my stomach. We keep moving, but as we round the corner, there's a head on a pike. Just the head with bloody tendons hanging off it. My heart leaps, and I fall back against the wall.

"Watch your steps," she says.

I look at her, fully nauseous again. I knew men weren't all good, but I didn't think they were capable of this... Not on this scale, not on a regular basis.

Hana lowers her eyes quickly and meaningfully to tell me to look at the floor instead of what's around us.

We continue, and I focus on the dirty floor tiles. I try to ignore the screams and pleas for death, the streaks of dried blood. I don't look into the foul-smelling pit. I don't want to think about who or what is down there.

Instead, I get myself together. I breathe. I count my steps. By keeping my gaze on rough-hewn stone tiles, I avoid the atrocities, but the added benefit is that the other guards can't get a good look at my face.

We pass a few, skirting to the side in the tight corridors. I hold my breath, certain I'll be recognized. I'm convinced there will be alarm bells and then a dagger in my back.

Or maybe we'll both be dragged to the torture chambers.

I sneak a peek at three guards as they pass us, but they're not looking at me. Hana has kept her hood down and her cape open to draw their attention. It works. They're too busy staring at her red lips, long lashes, and curves to even glance my way.

A heady high fills me. We might actually make it out of here.

Hana takes a dizzying sequence of turns, and it seems like we're constantly walking uphill, but it could be that I haven't walked this much in weeks. My calves burn; my thighs feel like lead pipes. I've exercised in my cell, but this is different. I can't imagine how weak I'd be if Hana hadn't been feeding me or if I'd been chained.

Eventually, we find ourselves at a heavy iron door at the end of a hall. Two guards stand to either side of it, but they wear a different uniform. They are palace guards, not prison ones.

Hana glances at me, telling me to be prepared. This must be the other entrance she mentioned. And it must lead directly into Qali.

I take a deep breath and keep my stance loose. I know I can kill if it comes down to it, but I hope it doesn't because palace guards are far more lethal than I am.

"Identification," one of the guards says. He's tall but young, with brown hair and eyes.

Hana smiles slowly, flirtatiously. "You don't know me, Jimi?"

She adjusts her cape to show off more of her body. Both guards notice, but discreetly. They are more professional than the prison guards.

"I was talking to him," Jimi says, gesturing to me.

I brace myself.

She looks back at me, waiting. "Well?"

I pat my jacket and my pockets. Unsurprisingly, I don't have any papers on me. I don't know how Hana even had the time to steal the uniform.

"You don't have it?" she asks.

I give her a hapless shrug.

She draws a long-suffering breath and rolls her eyes. "The gods have cursed me, Jimi. Just sign him out, please. I need to get the smell of this place off me."

He frowns. "You know I need to see his identification, Z."

"A little difficult when he is a new guard who forgot it." She tosses me a withering look.

"I will need to get the prison supervisor," Jimi says.

"Go ahead." She steps up to the other palace guard, who has been eyeing her. Hana engages him in some small talk. He has a mustache and a jaw that's nearly square. He also has fifty pounds on me.

I'm not certain what I should be doing while I wait, so I stand here staring into space.

Jimi opens the first set of bolts to the door with his key. Then he looks at the other guard. "Ral."

Ral stops flirting with Hana for just long enough to unlock the second set of bolts with a different key.

But there is still a third set.

Jimi turns and bangs on a windowed door that faces the exit. It blends so well I hadn't even noticed it before now, but it looks like a door to an office.

"Captain," he says loudly. "Identification check."

A minute later, an older man lumbers out of the doorway. He's incredibly tall, with salt-and-pepper hair and a gray mustache. It seems like he just woke from a nap. "What is the issue?"

"A new guard and Zahara leaving, but he forgot his identification," Jimi says.

"And I'm in desperate need of a bath," she adds with a slow smile. Her voice drips with suggestion.

The captain looks Hana up and down and then nudges Jimi. "I suppose I can overlook it just this once."

"Yes, sir," Jimi says.

The captain takes out his keys, but his eyes sharpen as they land on me. "What is your name, soldier?"

I...didn't think to come up with one. He holds my gaze, and every name I've ever heard leaves my head. The captain's expression shifts. He opens his mouth, and my stomach drops. He's about to call out an alarm.

CHAPTER SIXTY-TWO

ROYO

THE NORTHERN PASS, KHITAN

Day breaks over the snowy horizon, and Aeri is still asleep on my chest. She passed out not long after we got into this sleigh, dead tired from traveling so much. We didn't get a lot of sleep at the traveler's inn or the night under the stars. I'm tired, too, but I've also never been more awake.

Okay, she's not exhausted *just* because we've been traveling. I've never felt the kind of bottomless hunger for someone the way I do for her. And I've never felt needed the way she needs me.

Aeri looks so sweet in sleep, her breathing soft, but I know what she looks like when she wants me a second and a third time in a night. When she arches back in pleasure. When she clings to me like a vine, shaking and moaning.

Sora glances over at her and then at me. She smiles to herself.

"What?" I ask.

"Oh, nothing." She grins, shrugging her shoulders. I guess everybody can tell.

I can't help it—my face breaks into a smile. Sora raises her eyebrows. I don't think she's seen me smile more than once since we met. It feels weird on my face, too, but I'm getting used to it.

"You both deserve to be happy," Sora says.

"Do we?"

Aeri does. But I don't know if I deserve this—from how good it feels to have her asleep on me to the crackling energy inside my chest. Do I deserve for the sky to seem brighter, the food tastier, the ale colder? I've hurt, and I've maimed, and I've killed for coin. I failed the one girl who relied on me and her father who was kind to me. I think most people would say I don't deserve shit.

Fear beats in my temples, and my past screams that this won't last. That I'm only kidding myself. I don't deserve no one good. I will fuck up again and lose this, lose her forever, because in the end, I don't deserve to be happy. And then it will be like Lora all over again, and I'll wish that I'd never met Aeri. I'll regret our time together because of the lifetime of hurt that follows.

My palms get clammy, and I rub them on my pants. I haven't been scared like this in my life.

Sora looks at me, tilting her head thoughtfully. "Maybe 'deserve' is the wrong word, because that makes it seem like love is a reward. And it's not."

"It isn't?"

"We don't deserve love any more than we deserve air. It's just something we need."

My throat feels dry, and it's not the cold air from the sleigh. I swallow hard. "But what if it stops?"

She shrugs. "I don't know. I've never stopped."

That's right. She had a lover she lost a while ago. She don't talk about them much, but Seok killed them.

"How do you do it?" I ask.

"Do what?"

"Live. What makes you keep going without them?"

She stares into my eyes, and her expression changes, hardens. "Vengeance. Settling the score is what I have left. I can't and won't stop until I get it."

Sora is real pretty, but something about her face puts a blade of fear deep in my spine.

Ten Hells, these broads are terrifying. And we're supposed to meet a queen who makes King Joon run for cover.

I glance down at Aeri, wondering how she's Baejkin. How she can be related to a man who hunted people for fun or a king who said he'd torture the people we love if we don't bring him the ring? How is she related to her uncle, who was hurting little girls and who they thought murdered her? Did they all start off like Aeri—sweet, loving, and caring? Or is she different from them?

I settle on her being different. She's gotta be. But who was the bird thing calling the Son of Vengeance? Me? What does that even mean? So much was going on that I didn't even think to ask.

Aeri wakes up as I'm staring at her. She smiles brightly, still unnaturally happy the second she opens her eyes.

"Good morning, Royo," she says. "Ugh, sorry I drooled on you. That's so unattractive."

She scrunches her face as she wipes at my jacket. I couldn't care less.

She looks around. "We're almost there, aren't we?"

I nod. The snow is changing over to freezing rain as we come closer to Quu.

"Sora, are you sure this is going to work?" she asks. "I mean… telling the queen about the king's plan to get her on board?"

Sora stares ahead. "It has to. Especially with war coming." Then she looks at Aeri. "But remember what I said about the crown and who is fit to rule."

Aeri looks down, fiddling with the hem of her jacket. Her nervous habit. But what's she nervous about?

"We're going to bathe and change, right?" she asks. "Before we see the queen?"

Sora leans forward and says something in Khitanese to the woman driving. I still don't really get who this Gambria woman is or how she's involved in all this, but Sora nods and sits back. "Yes, we'll stop at a traveler's inn before we go to the palace."

"She wants to change her outfit?" Euyn asks over his shoulder.

"And is that foolish?" Sora replies. "It's a royal reception. You should as well."

He turns to face forward, his shoulders stiff.

I don't know what happened with the three of them while we were getting the egg. I don't get why they failed—it doesn't seem like Mikail *could* fail. But something's different with Euyn. And most of all with Sora.

I can't shake the feeling that none of us should be trusting Mikail. He didn't betray us before, but that doesn't mean he won't now.

Oligarch Mountain lies in the distance, looming like a beacon of hope...or a cirena of death. I just wish I knew which one.

CHAPTER SIXTY-THREE

AERI

THE PALACE OF THE SKY KING, KHITAN

The Palace of the Sky King towers over Trialga Square, perched at the top of wide marble stairs. Gambria pulls our sleigh right up to the base.

So, I guess we're not going for stealth.

As soon as we stop, a dozen guards train their eyes on us. We're foreigners, but at least we're formally dressed, bathed, and perfumed. Fancy clothes always make you feel different. We carry ourselves better, and I, at least, feel more prepared to meet my aunt.

Although, if I'm honest, I don't know what to expect. My father and uncle fear her; Mikail respects her, which means she's a formidable opponent; and yet Gambria loved her and Sora insists there's more to the story.

"She's more than you think," Gambria says to Mikail as we get out of the sled.

Sora walks next to me. Of course, she looks like she could be the Sky Queen in a fine dress and fur. Even the constant drizzle won't dampen her beauty.

It's not until we get under the portico that we reach our first roadblock. In this society, anyone is supposed to be allowed into the palace if they have business with the crown. But after the assassination attempt, everything changed. There are still official royal offices inside, but access is severely restricted.

The huge gilded doors sit open with people milling about inside, but most are mingling on the massive portico.

"Halt," one guard says. Her red hair is pulled back in a bun under her guard's hat. "State your business here."

"I am the royal spymaster of Yusan," Mikail announces in Khitanese, lifting his chin.

He really is fluent in all languages. He speaks without an accent or hesitation. I've picked up the language from listening to him, Gambria, and others. I miss a word every now and then, but I understand much of it.

The redheaded guard and a male guard exchange glances.

"I'm here to see Queen Quilimar," Mikail adds.

"No one sees the queen now," the female guard says.

Mikail waves his hand. "Tell her we brought an exception to the Rule of Distance. And also, her youngest brother would like a word. See if that changes her mind."

Unsurprisingly, his words cause a commotion. The nobility and military wandering around the portico start whispering to each other. Everyone looks our way, subtly or otherwise. Mikail has created a stir—just as he planned.

It isn't long before General Vikal comes out of the palace. This time, she wears a type of military dress. She has on beige crepe slacks that flatter her long frame and chest armor. Hers is obsidian black, compared to the silver of the other guards. It covers a long-sleeved white silk blouse. It's the best outfit I've ever seen, both feminine and warlike. I want one. Her curly hair is pulled back in a dignified twist.

"What a surprise," she says in Khitanese, eyeing Mikail.

"You meant to say, 'What a pleasant surprise.'" He grins and intentionally looks down at her, because even though she is tall, he is taller.

Vikal stares. "No, I spoke correctly the first time."

He smirks. She looks from him to Euyn. "And what a surprise to see you alive, Your Highness." She inclines her head, but just.

Once again, she leaves out the word *pleasant*.

Euyn nods stiffly. "General."

Then she looks at Gambria and draws an irritated breath. Her composure cracks slightly. "I see the surprises continue today."

Gambria holds her head high. "I am simply their driver."

They really don't like each other. Gambria is probably a foot shorter than the general, but you'd never know it from the way she carries herself. Her posture is perfect, her face unaffected.

I stop slouching, and I'm just in time because the general looks at Royo and me. But she pauses on Sora. She must remember her from the banquet where Seok made the scene. Even if he hadn't, it's impossible to forget Sora.

She could never be a thief.

"I am told that you have an exception to the Rule of Distance," General Vikal says in Yusanian. "Who brings it? The assassin, the dead prince, or the spy?"

She points at Sora, Euyn, and Mikail in turn.

"Actually, we were able to steal it as a team," Mikail says. "A group project, if you will."

The general shakes her head. "You can all live in the villa together, if that's what suits you, but only one of you may pass."

Mikail gestures to me—the signal, in case we were refused entry.

I take the egg out of the saddlebag, holding it up so everyone can see. "From an amarth nest," I say loudly in Khitanese.

Even the general is taken aback, shifting on her heels with her eyes wide. It's not every day people see an egg as big as an ostrich's that's a deep, black color. The crowd stops what they're doing to remark on the egg, the legends of the amarth, and the Rule of Distance. Their whispers and gasps fill the space, echoing around us.

General Vikal blinks for a second too long, annoyed at being outplayed. We have public attention, and now, if she refuses us, it will make the queen look weak. They can't afford that after a nearly successful assassination attempt. Not when she's only a regent.

"We took this as a team, so we will see the queen as a team," Mikail says, switching back to Yusanian.

"Absolutely not."

"Then I suppose she doesn't need this," I say.

Royo opens the bag again, but I pause. I place my hands on the top and bottom of the egg and raise it, as if I'm considering smashing it on the white marble. We hadn't discussed this, so Sora audibly gasps. Strangers around us do the same. I catch the glimmer in Mikail's eye—he approves.

"Should we let people know she refused, and they can speculate as to why?" he asks.

Vikal raises her chin and stares coldly at Mikail, but there's a hint of respect in her expression. She's impressed that he knows Quilimar's secret.

"A five-minute audience," she says. "We will prepare a table, and there will be an abundant amount of guards present. If any of you bring in a weapon, all of you will die."

"Sounds like a deal," Mikail says.

She takes a step away and then pauses. "Your driver can wait here with your arms."

With that, Vikal turns on her heels and leaves with her personal guards.

"You make friends everywhere," Mikail says to Gambria. He takes his sword off his belt and hands it to her. Then he removes two blades from his boot, the knife tucked in his interior jacket pocket, and three throwing stars.

"You know this is a trap, right?" Gambria asks.

"I'd be disappointed by anything less," he answers.

Gambria stares at him, unamused. "You need to be careful, Mikail."

He smiles. "Always am."

She lets out a long-suffering sigh. "Don't...don't hurt her. She is who she had to become."

Mikail pauses, staring at his friend. "Aren't we all?"

My chest tightens at his words—what have we all become? There's no time to consider it, and maybe I don't want to. I start pulling knives out of my cloak and handing them to Gambria. Everyone else does the same. Soon, she has a small arsenal at her feet. Bolts, knives, swords, an axe, and the list continues. Royo takes the longest, continually pulling knives and daggers out of nowhere like a magician.

I hesitate, but I part with my last throwing knife, hidden in the waist of my dress. I leave my hair dagger in, though. It's small but deadly sharp. I doubt they'll find it inside the decorative clip that holds my hair back.

"*Is* this a trap?' Euyn whispers to Mikail.

Mikail shrugs. "We're about to find out."

Royo and I look at each other. That's not exactly comforting. But we don't have long to think about it. A palace servant bows elaborately to us and asks us to follow him. I take Royo's hand as we walk in under the watchful eye of twelve swords.

It's time.

CHAPTER SIXTY-FOUR

SORA

THE PALACE OF THE SKY KING, KHITAN

We enter a stunning palace. The palace at Qali is also beautiful, but we had hoods on when we were brought into the throne room, and then we were dragged out, dazed and in chains. But now we are escorted inside as honored guests. Nobles and dignitaries—even Ambassador Zeolin—stand to the side to watch our procession. He gapes with his mouth open as Aeri passes him, holding the bag that contains the egg.

It is said that the palaces of the four original realms were made and lived in by the gods, and I can see it. This one is filled with white marble, deep-purple rugs, gently fluttering lilac-and-white flags, and gold. Tons of gold—from flecks in the floor, to the eagles on the center of the flags, to the massive chandeliers, to the carved decorations on the walls, to even the banisters on the dual, central staircase. With its high ceilings, open domes, and columns, the space has an airy feeling. It truly seems like the Sky King could have walked these halls himself.

The palace servant stops at doors not far off the grand entrance, but we're all taking our time following him, not outpacing Euyn, who walks with a limp. Plus, there's much to see. Elaborate tapestries, sculptures, and paintings celebrate the grandeur of the Trialga rulers. Gilded and bejeweled flowers sit in solid gold vases around the halls.

Aeri's eyes are keen.

"No," Royo murmurs.

She pouts and then smiles at being caught eyeing things to steal. My heart fills as I watch them. This world is brimming with unkindness. It takes a brave hand to carve out a small piece of happiness and to stand ready to defend it.

We're shown to a banquet room that makes the gilded armory look shabby. The ceiling must be three stories high, and it's painted with frescos of the sky at different times from the stars to midday. And, obviously, there is gold everywhere. The room has a gold dome and a gold fountain in the center that collects the rainwater falling from the oculus.

It's a little unsettling that only one table at the far end of the room is being set right now. The walls are mirrored, but not behind the dais. On that wall hangs the largest painting I've ever seen. It depicts the founding of Khitan by the Sky King. A god's hands extend from the clouds to the country, pulling mountains from the soil.

We take our seats at the king's table, facing the varnished painting, as we wait for the queen regent. She will occupy the throne opposite us. Queen Quilimar. The woman Euyn and King Joon say is vicious, dangerous. Will she be as they say, or will she be the soft mother I caught a glimpse of? A woman misunderstood in a place like Yusan but accepted here? Is she heartless or merely who the world forced her to be, as Gambria said?

I don't have to wait long for an answer. Sixteen guards enter in gray steel armor with the gold eagle of Khitan emblazoned on their chests. We all stand as trumpets blare. Queen Quilimar and General Vikal make their way into the room, the queen on the general's arm. The queen wears a fitted light-purple dress and a white-and-gold sash. She's thirty-three, but she looks younger. She is striking, really, not beautiful as much as distinct. She is around my height, but interestingly, she doesn't resemble King Joon or Euyn. She has tipped, wide eyes, but she also doesn't look like Aeri.

The golden crown of Khitan shines atop her long ebony hair. Where Yusan has a blood ruby, Khitan's crown has numerous golden peaks studded by diamonds and a large teardrop diamond in the center.

Still, even with her looks and the splendor of her crown, the Golden Ring of the Dragon Lord is her most noticeable feature. It's impossible to miss the relic. The ring has a giant gold orb that's around the size of a lime, and rough-cut rubies and diamonds surround it. It looks both ancient and powerful.

"Well, this is a surprise," Queen Quilimar says in Yusanian, looking around at the table.

Everyone seems to be leaving out the word "pleasant" today.

Her eyes land on Euyn first, and her brow wrinkles slightly. "Brother, you're alive."

She seems annoyed by the fact, but there's something in her aura that is far softer than I expected, given that King Joon fears her.

"To Joon's chagrin, I assure you." Euyn bows formally. "Sister."

He smiles, and she gathers a breath. Then her gaze falls on Aeri, and her icy expression warms.

"I hear you are my long-lost niece, Naerium," she says.

"Lost is one way to put it." Aeri stands straight, looking down at her aunt, then bobs a curtsy. "Highness."

The queen raises her eyebrows. "You look so much like Soo Lin, but you act nothing like her. You have a spirit and a spine. I'm sure my brothers will do their very best to crush both."

"They have already tried," Aeri says.

One corner of the queen's lips turns up. "The role of women in Yusan is to be underfoot. You must be steel to survive. I wish you welcome to a place where you can stand on your own."

She takes a seat on the golden throne facing the five of us. Once she is seated, we all sit down. Tea, wine, and an array of cakes and pastries are served. I suppose this counts as dining at the table of the king. The dignitaries who'd been in the grand hall watch from far outside the open doors. I can almost feel their jealousy.

"To what do I owe this unusual audience?" Queen Quilimar asks.

"We heard you were searching for an egg of the amarth," Mikail says. "We thought we'd deliver it."

Aeri takes that as her cue and places the egg on the center of the table, crushing some beautiful cakes beneath it.

Queen Quilimar smiles, wistfully looking down at her ring. A spacing band keeps it in place, as it is far too large for her finger. "We both know that's not the case. My husband sought the egg, but he is deceased. Then again, I'm sure you heard that before you went to all this trouble."

I like that she speaks plainly. I'm also certain she murdered her husband, but from what Mikail said, she was at his mercy until she produced an heir. I know better than most that a man willing to slaughter innocent villagers just to claim a prize wouldn't have much mercy. She lived as a prisoner in a gilded cage, and her husband held the key.

As the queen is direct, I decide that perhaps she'll respect the same.

"The king of Yusan sent us here to steal your ring," I say.

General Vikal stiffens, her hand moving to the hilt of her sword. The sixteen guards also react, shifting at our backs and by the doors. Queen Quilimar eyes me from her seat.

"Well, that makes sense, as Naerium is the only one able to wield it." The queen points to Aeri. "I'd been wondering why Joon would risk his only child, but that does explain the gamble."

All eyes turn to Aeri, who knits her eyebrows, confused.

"I don't understand," I say.

"Bloodlines," Queen Quilimar says with a sigh. "You must be of royal blood to wield the relics. No one else in this room is royal by blood, so I assume that is why Joon sent his daughter."

Mikail coughs into his water glass. "I beg your pardon? Aren't you forgetting someone?"

The queen stares at him and blinks slowly. "Mikail, you are supposed to run the games, not be taken in by them. No wonder you were replaced." She shakes her head, then meets his eye. "I thought *everyone* close to the throne knew that Joon and Omin were the only legitimate children of King Theum. He stopped sharing the great queen's bed not long after my monstrous second brother was born. The Lesser Queen had a great many bedmates, but…the king wasn't one of them. A hunting accident rendered him unable to have more heirs before Euyn was even born."

The room falls absolutely silent, and Quilimar plays with her ring.

"Neither Euyn nor I possess Baejkin blood," she adds.

My breath catches in my throat. The realization ripples through the table. Euyn is not Baejkin. Which means he never could've worn the crown of Yusan.

No, that can't be right.

I stare at Euyn, and he pales. Mikail seems like he wants to leap out of his seat and slaughter the clouds of the frescos above. I study the queen, waiting for a tell, but there is none. She's speaking the truth. Euyn is not Baejkin.

He never could have been king. And if his pallor is any indication, he's always known but kept it a secret from us this whole time.

A cold fury washes over me, and my stomach twists. I reach for the dagger that I gave up earlier. All I touch is my sleeve. We all risked our lives for him, risked everything for him, time and time again. We bled for promises he made to us, to Ty. Ones he never intended to honor.

"Oh, Euyn." Queen Quilimar tsks. "You keep secrets even from your lover and your closest friends? Where is your honor?"

She sips her tea as the secrets tear us to shreds. She doesn't revel in our turmoil the way Joon did. Queen Quilimar has hardened herself to feeling anything, as many women do to endure this world.

That's when I realize that everything we heard, the good and the bad about her, is correct.

CHAPTER SIXTY-FIVE

EUYN

THE PALACE OF THE SKY KING, KHITAN

I'm getting a little weary of my family reunions.

I had no idea Quilimar was also illegitimate. She was our father's favorite—at least that is what I always heard and what I vaguely remember. But I was so young when he died that perhaps I just believed the rumor. Her illegitimacy explains so much, including her molten anger toward me. We are both bastards, and yet I was pampered and crowned and she was sold off to the highest bidder. She had to allow the king of Khitan to bed her until she had a son. Such is being female royalty.

"Tell her the truth," Mikail says.

For the first time since the throne room, he actually looks shocked. He scans me, his eyes moving rapidly. He wants me to deny it. I can feel the waves of emotion coming off him, how badly he needs me to say it isn't true, to deny what my mother told me on her deathbed.

The truth eats at me as the lump builds in my throat. I want to say out loud that I've known for years that the old king wasn't my father, but I can't. I've gone entirely too long living this lie. I've built our love on it, and I can't pull out the foundation now, or the house will crumble. Mikail will never view me the same, and his love has already waned. I can feel it. I'd decided long ago to take the secret of my blood to my ashes. There is no reason to change course now.

With a breath, I try to gather myself. I'd like to sip water, but I won't eat or drink anything in this room. Quilimar isn't above poisoning us all, and even Sora isn't touching anything.

"I-I am the king's son," I say.

The room is silent, aside from rain trickling into the fountain. The audience outside the banquet hall is also quiet, desperately straining to listen in. But they can't hear us from so far away. A golden thread constantly marks a hundred feet from Quilimar, and everyone needs to remain farther than that.

Except for us.

The four others stare at me, their gazes burning into my skin.

"Right," Quilimar says, raising her eyebrows. "Well, we are nearly out of time. Obviously, I won't give Joon the Ring of Khitan but do send him my best. My apologies that you came all this way for nothing."

"He is starting a war of the realms," Mikail says quietly.

That gets my sister's attention. She's halfway out of her seat when she pauses.

"Here?" she asks.

Mikail nods. "Either he killed all the Yoksa or you did. Either way, the edict was broken here. The amarth said a war of the realms is coming, and my sources tell me the same. I'm not sure if we were merely a decoy or if Joon thinks he can actually take the ring, but the other three realms will be here within a matter of days."

Quilimar retakes her seat and curls her fingers, mindlessly tapping the ring on the arm of her throne.

I can't tell if my sister murdered the priests. Her expression is unreadable. My gut feeling is that she did not, but unlike me, Quilimar has always been an exceptionally good liar.

Finally, she meets Mikail's eye. "Why are you giving me this information? What do you want?"

He gestures with his hands apart. "We wanted you to invade Yusan so we could steal the Immortal Crown and place Euyn on the throne, but with the war of the realms coming, and for…other reasons, there are complications to that plan."

Mikail glances at me. He didn't believe me because I am twenty-three and still can't lie.

"We are seeking an alliance," Sora says. "We have a common enemy and a shared goal."

She is speaking out of turn, but Quilimar doesn't seem to mind. She has always preferred women.

"Now I understand why you needed an audience badly enough for that." Quilimar points to the egg. She draws a breath and sits back. "I assumed you came to try to assassinate me. What terms are you offering if I help you put my pretend brother on the throne?"

Sora's eyes dart over to me and Mikail. Now she waits for guidance, unlike before when she ruined everything by revealing that we wanted to steal the ring.

"Favored trade partner status, relaxed border tariffs, a removal of the lost indenture tax, and, of course, Euyn would owe his crown to you," Mikail says. "We'd also sign a new alliance of peace, although those always seem rather short-lived. The best term, however, is putting an end to Joon's life. I assure you that none of us here want him breathing a moment longer."

She considers it. She looks over at Aeri, who holds her gaze.

"Except the obvious issue is that Joon's crown makes his death impossible," Quilimar says. "You're well aware that I have tried."

She has. Before her wedding, after the wedding, before she became pregnant, and I assume after the prince was born. There might've been another time I'm missing—probably a failed attempt during the nuptials, if I had to guess.

"We are here because we stole the king's crown," Sora says. "However, we didn't understand it was all a setup. He had the real Immortal Crown on his arm when we tried to assassinate him."

"Who was able to remove it?" Quilimar asks. "Certainly not you." Her eyes land on me.

I raise my eyebrows at her petty insult, but she is correct. It was not me.

"It was me," Aeri says.

Everything, their entire plan, hinges on whether Quilimar believes her. I'm not sure what she will think of a silly girl who looks like Soo Lin.

As for me, my plan to take the ring will depend on what Quilimar does next.

Suddenly, we're interrupted by the insistent beating of drums. The percussion rattles the room from the chandeliers to the silverware. The nobility in the grand hall gasp, and the guards begin to shift around.

I close my eyes. I know that sound—war drums. The country is under attack.

Joon has arrived in style.

We need to get him the ring immediately, or he'll slaughter us all.

CHAPTER SIXTY-SIX

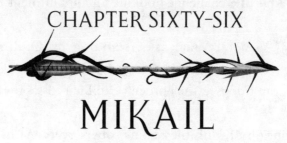

MIKAIL
THE PALACE OF THE SKY KING, KHITAN

There's never a dull moment.

Everyone at the table looks around as the palace vibrates with the beating of drums. Some of them seem confused, but there is no mistaking the sound of war drums. I will never forget the first time I heard them in Gaya. They marked the end of life as I knew it.

Khitan is under attack.

I sigh, swallowing my annoyance with myself. It took me entirely too long to figure out Joon's plan. But we can still best him—if we can form an alliance with Quilimar. The Gayan troops, even the Yusanian army, won't fight if Joon falls. We have to get to him. It's as simple as it is impossible.

Twin messengers with long braids run into the grand hall. They're older girls—sixteen, maybe seventeen. They kneel on the floor far outside one of the sets of doors to the room. Each holds a card. They're both breathing hard, their pale skin rosy. They ran all the way here from somewhere—the border of Yusan, if I had to guess. Khitan is so mountainous that in some places runners would be faster than horses.

A gray-haired palace guard takes the cards and brings them on a gold tray to Quilimar. She reads the notes and frowns. "I suppose you were correct, Mikail. Although I could've done with more warning than this."

"It was a bit of a challenge booking an appointment to see you," I say.

"Yusan?" General Vikal asks, standing by Quilimar's right shoulder.

"And Gayan troops at the border." Quilimar tosses the cards onto the table.

The mention of multiple realms sobers everyone in the room. For Gayan troops to already have arrived, Joon must have called for them as soon as we left. Possibly before.

"I have to attend to the country." Quilimar stands. "General, see Prince Calstor to safety, then meet me in the war room."

They exchange a lingering glance, and then Vikal salutes her. The general hurries out of the room, taking two guards with her.

Interesting that the prince is Quilimar's priority. I never thought her maternal. But then again, he is her only claim to ruling. And, apparently, he is her only claim to royalty at all.

"We will see where the war leaves us," she says, glancing around the table.

We failed. Spectacularly. The war of the realms has begun, and we lack an alliance, but the absence of Wei is puzzling. Their navy should have arrived in Quu Harbor before the troops reached the border. One of their major advantages in any conflict is that with the Water Scepter of the Dragon Lord, their navy can go from docked in Wei to our doorstep within a few bells. Not to mention that their ships are unsinkable with the scepter controlling the currents.

Maybe the amarth was wrong. Stars, I hope so.

Quilimar is nearly out the door when she stops. "Guards, detain them."

My stomach sinks as the palace guards salute her.

"On what grounds?" I ask. Of course I had thought of the possibility of capture, but we've committed no crimes, and we are here under the Rule of Distance.

"The beautiful one attempted to assassinate General Vikal at the banquet, and I assume the rest of you colluded with her. Euyn is a wanted criminal, and as to you specifically, you've murdered since you've been here, or at least you have in the past. We'll find out during interrogations."

My heart races in my chest. How did I not see this coming? I've become so accustomed to my status protecting me, I didn't think I was vulnerable. I am no longer the royal spymaster under the Yusanian flag, and thus she is free to arrest me. To arrest all of us. She can't kill Euyn or Aeri, as they are members of the royal family and treaties protect them, but the rest of us are fair game.

Hubris. I fell due to nothing more than hubris.

How unoriginal.

I have my poison pill, and I've been ready to die since I was a child, but I'd rather greet Lord Yama trying to fight my way out. I move my hand to my sword only to touch my pocket. I have no weapons. And if I fight, I risk everyone else being slaughtered with me.

What do I do?

Euyn studies me, his face pained. Then he stands, pushing back from the table.

"I offer you a wager, Quilimar." His loud voice echoes through the room, and I'm sure he can be heard in the hall, even over the drums.

She pauses and blinks. "What was that?"

He raises his chin. "You seem convinced that I am illegitimate."

She stares at him. "Because you are. You look and act nothing like Father, and your mother was a common pleasure house girl."

That's simply untrue. While Theum might not have been his father, his mother was the eastern count's oldest sister. The insult lands as intended, though. Euyn reddens and his hands ball into fists, but he exhales and smiles.

"Then I'm sure you would be willing to gamble the ring on it," he says.

What is he doing?

"Wager a relic of the Dragon Lord on your parentage?" She arches an eyebrow, but she hasn't left the room yet. Whatever Euyn is up to, it's buying me time to think. To come up with another way to escape, to defeat Joon.

But how?

Aeri can wield the ring, and she is fleet enough to steal it with a diversion. If we had the ring in our possession, we could broker terms—whether with Quilimar or Joon. But there is still the matter of getting out of this palace alive. Yes, we slaughtered a room full of men in Oosant, but those were far different odds.

"Let me attempt to wield the ring," Euyn says. "If I am a bastard, as you say, nothing will happen, and then you will be proven right. I will return the ring disgraced before your nobility and my lover. However, if I am royal and I can wield the relic, the ring will belong to me."

She laughs, amusement shining in her eyes. "And why would I ever agree to those terms?"

He takes one step closer. "Because you believe in your weak, inferior female brain that you are right. And I am willing to wager my life on it. If I fail, you can kill me."

The room is stunned silent—me included. Euyn didn't discuss this with me. And now I, like Quilimar, am trying to figure out his goal. If he thinks he can steal the ring and run out of here, he's wrong. Even Aeri couldn't pull that off. If he believes he's royal, then he's become an impressive liar. What is he doing?

Quilimar's gaze darts around, and I'm sure she is calculating the same thing—Euyn's intentions and the likelihood of him surviving.

"You heard me, *sister*," he says, limping a step closer to her. "If I fail, you can send my head to Joon. You can collect on the bounty or just broker peace with it. I've heard the rumors of how you love to gamble with your opponents' lives. Accept mine."

Quilimar stands there, lost in thought, or maybe she is doubting herself. I've never heard of the hunting injury to the old king, but that would've happened long before I was even born.

"Come now, Quilimar," Euyn says loudly. "You were so confident a moment ago, slinging your baseless insults about my mother and myself. And now, when you have to back up your claims, are you really nothing more than an undignified whore, like Joon said? Frankly, I expected better. Even if you are just a woman, you're still royalty. You owe me an apology." He gestures to the grand hall, to all the nobility listening in.

Fury lights her face, coloring her light-brown skin red. Euyn is succeeding in goading her, but how does he think this will end? The treaty of everlasting peace between Khitan and Yusan protects royal children and family traveling through both realms, but with war on her doorstep she could just as easily disregard the treaty and kill him where he stands.

"I owe you *nothing*," she seethes.

I step closer to him. A guard holding an axe immediately shifts, mirroring me. Quilimar knows me well enough to expect me to be dangerous. But I'm not trying to attack her. I'm trying to save Euyn from himself, because I think I've figured out what he is doing.

"Euyn, no," I say.

He hears me, but he doesn't take his eyes off Quilimar.

She smiles a vicious grin. "All right, then, brother. I accept your wager and your terms. If you turn the egg to solid gold, you may keep the Golden Ring of Khitan and your head. Fail, and you lose both."

"And you let everyone else go," he adds.

Quilimar hesitates, but she can't resist the bait. "Agreed."

Euyn nods before I can object. "You are all witnesses."

Her guards salute as one, pounding their fists to their chests. Euyn isn't looking at them, though. He's staring at the dignitaries in the hall, including Ambassador Zeolin.

"Yours in this life and the next," he whispers to me.

No. A chill runs down my spine, fear like I've never felt before gripping me. I got it all wrong. He's not trying to steal the ring... Euyn just offered his life to save the rest of us.

CHAPTER SIXTY-SEVEN

ROYO

THE PALACE OF THE SKY KING, KHITAN

The fuck is going on right now?

The fancy people in the hall murmur, crowding by the front set of doors. Well, as close as they can get. They're a hundred feet back because of the Rule of Distance. Still, they jam in together, trying to get a peek at Euyn. He's about to turn the egg into gold with the Queen of Khitan's ring. I hope. Because if he can't, she'll chop off his head.

Did I even hear that right?

I rub my forehead. I feel like I'm losing my fucking mind. Everyone in the banquet room is moving around, guards taking positions and Sora and Aeri nervously shifting their weight. Euyn and Queen Quilimar stand next to each other by the throne.

He didn't say nothing about this. Or he did, and I'm the only one in the dark.

I look at Aeri, but she and Sora seem just as puzzled by what's going on. Sora keeps holding her breath and then realizing it and letting out long exhales. The queen wanted to arrest us all and now… this.

The only one I can't get a bead on is Mikail. He doesn't ever show what he's thinking. Even when he's about to betray us. But I don't think he knew about this, either.

So what is happening?

And why does the queen hate Euyn so much?

When I was younger, I really wanted a little sister, or anybody so I wouldn't be all alone, but I've never seen siblings hate each other like this. Euyn knew exactly how to get under her skin, and it worked. But what's his plan? And is he actually Baejkin or not?

I keep Aeri close because I have a feeling this is about to go to shit. And if it does, we've got no way out.

As soon as I think it, the little hairs on the back of my neck stand. Something is up. It's the same feeling as when I catch someone following me or when the gang was waiting to attack us in the alley in Oosant.

My skin prickles. Nothing good is going to come out of this. There was no reason for the queen to take the gamble when she had us trapped. I wish I had my axe—or any weapon. I eye the guards. Two have axes, but they're far away. One has a bow. Most have swords. They keep their blades on their left hips, and they wear chest armor. I could reach the sword next to me if I had to, but the armor will make it harder to kill them.

"Ready, brother?" the queen asks.

Euyn nods.

Queen Quilimar slowly slides the ring off her finger and then extends it to him. All the guards have their hands near their weapons, ready, but Euyn keeps his eyes solely on his sister. He extends his palm, and the ring lands in his hand.

"Do you feel that?" Aeri whispers.

I don't got a clue what she means, but she's staring at the ring. And yeah, I do feel something, but it's the vibration of the drums that are still beating, softer now, but still warning everybody to get inside the city walls. I don't think that's what she means, though.

"That?" Aeri says, searching my face. "You don't feel it?"

This really ain't the time for her to be weird.

I shake my head, watching Euyn. He's sliding the ring down his finger. He gets it past his knuckle, and then he looks at the egg. His forehead shimmers with sweat.

"Are...are there words that need to be said?" he asks.

"The king would simply touch something with the ring, and it would turn to gold," Queen Quilimar replies. A couple of the guards nod, but we can't trust them.

Euyn looks at Mikail, now not as confident. His hand shakes a little.

"It's intention," Mikail says. "The etherum in the ring works based on what the wearer wants. The wielder has to desire something to be turned to gold; otherwise, it doesn't work. But I think you've taken this bet far enough. Give her back the ring, Euyn."

The queen holds herself straighter and shakes her head.

"We made a wager," Queen Quilimar says.

"Nothing worth his death," Mikail responds.

She shrugs. "That is his issue. This is a fair and legal bet."

I look over at Aeri, but she's staring straight ahead. She couldn't be thinking about stealing the ring. I follow her line of sight.

Ten Hells. Yes, she could.

"No," I whisper.

She blinks at me like I interrupted her thoughts.

"The egg," Queen Quilimar says, gesturing to the center of the table.

She presses her lips together, clearly eager to see him try. I think she's even more eager to see him fail. The queen shifts her arm to brush back her long hair, and there's just a little glimmer at the end of her sleeve. It's a blade.

There's a saber hidden up her sleeve, and I don't think anyone else has noticed.

"Euyn, no!" I say. "She—"

"Silence!" The queen's voice echoes over the drums, bouncing off the high ceiling. The guard next to me moves a step closer, the threat clear. Then she turns to Euyn. "Well? Do you concede?"

"He hasn't tried yet," Aeri says.

The queen sighs, her shoulders lowering. She regains her composure. "Do be quick about this, brother. We're at war, and I will need your head."

Euyn takes a breath, then reaches his hand out, straightening his arm.

"Turn to gold," he whispers.

And then he touches the ring to the egg.

CHAPTER SIXTY-EIGHT

TIYUNG
IDLE PRISON, YUSAN

We're caught. We're at the exit of the prison, but we're going to fail right here.

The captain of the prison guard opens his mouth to call out an alarm, but there's no sound because Jimi grips him by the throat.

Everything happens quickly. Hana kisses the second guard. His eyes bulge in surprise and then pain. I freeze because I wasn't told about any of this. Why is the palace guard attacking the captain of the prison guards? Why did Hana just murder a palace guard? What in the world am I supposed to be doing right now? I stand with my hands out, shifting from side to side.

Jimi wrestles the captain to the ground, straining to hold him and keep him quiet. Ral clutches his own throat and chest, collapsing onto the floor. Then Hana rushes over to Jimi. She leans down and locks her poisoned lips with the old man.

Within ten seconds, both men are dying.

Hana stands straight, eyeing her handiwork.

"Throw him in his office. It'll look like a heart attack," she says, adjusting her cloak.

I think she's talking to me, but I honestly don't know. She's all business, like she didn't just kill two people.

"Tiyung, I dare you to be more useless," she mutters. She runs her thumb by her lips, adjusting her lipstick.

I snap out of it, pick up the captain, and drag him into the office. He's lighter than I expected for someone so tall.

I get him through the door. His office is large with windows overlooking the pit. I don't look down there. I consider leaving the captain on the floor, but there is a couch against the wall. I put him on the sofa and arrange him so it looks like he's taking a nap. When the guards find him, they'll hopefully think he had a heart attack in his sleep.

Once I'm done, I stand in the doorway. Hana opens the last set of bolts and then tosses me the keys.

"What are these for?" I ask, catching them.

She shakes her head. "I cannot deal with him."

"For you to put back in the captain's pocket," Jimi answers.

I nod, shove them into the breast pocket of the dead captain, then leave the office and close the door. Hana stands waiting.

"What do we do now?" I ask.

"Slit that one's throat," she says, pointing to Ral. "And then we just need to take care of Jimi."

I look from Hana to Jimi and back again, and I gulp. I don't want to hurt a man who helped us, and I'm also not sure I can best a palace guard. Hana folds her arms, staring at me.

I draw my sword, facing him, and they both tilt their heads in the same direction.

"Oh gods, he *is* useless," Jimi says.

She nods. "I told you so."

"I know you did, but...how did he ever find me and arrange to buy my freedom?" Jimi asks.

"I assume someone else handled all of the legwork." She sighs. "He was simply the coin purse."

I finally put it together, feeling remarkably slow. The palace guard is Hana's brother. The one I gave freedom to and sent right here to Tamneki. But the last time I saw him was years ago. I simply didn't recognize him.

"Nayo?" I ask.

Nayo and Hana look at me with identical blinking eyes. I could not feel more foolish if I tried.

"What did you mean by take care of him, then?" I ask.

"Knock him out so he can claim he was attacked by a prisoner," Hana says. "We need to create a puzzling scene, but one that also immediately exonerates him, so by the time they do figure out that he assisted in your escape, he can be long gone."

It…makes sense. There are three sets of keys to the door, making escape nearly impossible, even if someone overwhelmed the palace guards. The captain will be found dead with his keys in the office. If they realize I am missing and not dead, they'll assume I'm hiding somewhere in the prison.

"Gods, Tiyung," she says. "We will never make it to Khitan if you are this slow." She slaps her side, tired of me already.

She takes Ral's sword out and slits his throat. Then she places it next to his body, so that's one less thing I can mess up.

I'm about to ask if we're really going to Khitan, but that would just prove her right. Instead, I put my sword back into my scabbard.

"I can put him in a sleeper hold so there's no pain," I say.

"No, he needs a bruise," she says. "Hit him with the hilt. You know, preferably *before* we're caught."

I face Nayo. He's very nearly my height—maybe an inch shorter. It feels strange to hit a man who is standing still, waiting for it.

"It's okay," Nayo says with a smile. "Thank you for my life, Tiyung-si."

He kneels at my feet to make it easier, lowering himself to help me escape. Guilt hits me like a sucker punch. I wish I could've done more for him. More for all of them.

There will always be more that I can do, more I can atone for, and maybe that's why the gods are giving me a second opportunity. Or maybe the gods have nothing to do with it and it's all Hana and Nayo and Ailor. Maybe good people matter more than the gods.

Nayo smiles at me. I raise my sword, and I knock him out.

CHAPTER SIXTY-NINE

EUYN

THE PALACE OF THE SKY KING, KHITAN

I've never been more nervous in my life—not when I was waiting in the catacombs of the King's Arena, not when I was in Idle Prison, not when I was buried alive in the Amrok Desert. And what I feel is nothing compared to the look on Mikail's face. But I have it. I have the ring. Now, the trick is to make it out of here with all our lives.

I saw a way out right before I offered this wager, when I realized Mikail had been outplayed and we were headed to Quilimar's dungeons. I'd thought I would merely die to free everyone, and I'd accepted it, but I think we can all escape if the gods are on our side.

My sister has made the grievous mistake of underestimating me. This time, she put me in a room with a bow. She was a champion fencer, but she's forgotten my skill as an archer—probably because she called it a coward's weapon. The guard over by the corner of the table has a crossbow loosely hanging at his side. If I can reach it, we have a chance. The armor of all these guards exposes the neck, sides, and legs. They're targets the size of a barn for a good shot.

We can do this if everyone else is ready—or at least Mikail.

But if the gods turn their backs and I can't make it out, at least Quilimar will have to release the others. I owe all of them that much, even Aeri, who in the end didn't betray us. Well, this time.

I can't focus on the crossbow because it'll give me away, but I hope Mikail or Royo notices. Aeri could easily steal the bow. I look at her and then at Mikail. But my sister is losing patience. Quilimar keeps pressing her lips together. She is having difficulty containing her enthusiasm for my death, which is a bit disquieting. I was aware that she hated me. I remember her face as she passed by my bedroom when Joon would tell me stories. She'd look so disgusted, then go to her quarters with the slam of a door. However, I didn't think it went this far. I was never to blame for her being forced to marry or anything else that's happened to her. But somehow, I've taken the fall.

However, right now, I have to at least try to turn this egg to gold. I sigh. Even the sentence in my head is ridiculous. A human being can't turn an egg to gold. But then again, the amarth and samroc aren't real, and yet they are. Joon should have died any number of times, but the Immortal Crown saved his life. I suppose anything is possible in the three realms.

I touch the ring to the egg.

"Turn to gold," I murmur.

I look at the egg with an onyx black shell. It would be something amazing to see it turned to solid, expensive gold.

Suddenly, pain like I've never felt before careens down my arm—so much that it is hard to keep my hand extended. I yell out and steady my arm with my right hand. The agony is as bad as when the arrow hit my leg. No, as when Mikail pulled the arrow out without warning. It feels like my arm is splitting apart.

But it is not.

The ring begins to glow. It shimmers against the shell of the egg, and then I forget my pain because of the golden halo in front of me. The light bursts and then fades in a twinkling, leaving a solid gold egg on the table.

Gods on High.

My heart stops, and my mouth falls open. I did it. I wielded the ring.

Everyone stares, and no one moves, because I really am royalty.

Oh, my whore of a mother. I gnash my teeth. I would kill her all over again if I could. Theum was my real father…or one of his sons fathered me.

I have had the passing feeling more than once when I remember Joon telling me bedtime stories, and I considered it again after Mikail said he refused to order my death. The Lesser Queen wasn't much older than Joon when she married King Theum. And Joon is twenty-two years my senior—old enough to have fathered me. But I hadn't dared to even think it until now.

Joon or Omin was my real father.

My arm drops uselessly at my side, the pain still radiating through me. I tuck it into my vest, and I remember my plan to take the bow.

"Mikail!" I glance meaningfully at the guard with the crossbow. He follows my line of sight, and the realization dawns on his face.

"Weapon!" one of the guards shouts. I look around, realizing too late that they think I'm reaching for a blade in my clothes.

Quilimar rips a saber from her sleeve. Her face contorts in rage as she aims right for my chest.

Weaponless, I have no defense. I take my arm out in a feeble attempt to protect myself, like I did in the ambush in the Tangun Mountain pass. Then I remember the ring.

Turn to gold, sister.

I touch the ring to her breast. Incredible pain, twice as great as before, shoots up my arm, and the ring glows. Quilimar lets out a piercing scream.

Nearly the same moment I reach her with the ring, her blade finds a home, cutting through my flesh. The glow of the ring disappears as her saber goes through my ribs and cuts into my heart.

We both fall to the floor. I think. I hear a thud of a body hitting the ground, and I assume it's Quilimar, but I can't move.

"The queen!" guards yell out. "Save the queen!"

I want to see if she's dead, but all I can do is stare up at the ceiling—the painted stars and clouds. The rain falling into the fountain makes a musical sound, and the percussion of the drums is fading. There's a beauty to the quiet.

Mikail dives onto the floor by my side.

"Euyn," he cries. "Euyn! Euyn, what did you do? What did you do?"

I see his gorgeous face, but he's staring down at my chest. I don't have to look to know her saber is lodged in my heart. Strangely, though, I don't feel pain anymore. I don't feel much of anything.

I hear my name called, but the voice is not human. It must be the Soul Reaper calling me to the Road of Souls, and there is no declining his command.

"Yours in this life and the next," I whisper.

Mikail shakes his head, eyes wet with tears. "Yours in this life and the next."

He's rocking me, I think. Either way, I feel him all around me.

I'd feared this for so many years—dying, being killed by a violent hand. Now it's here, and all I can see or think about is Mikail. I feel his love surrounding me like a warm blanket on a cold day. I was so lonely before I met him, wandering the massive palace halls by myself. No father. A mother who'd beat me before deigning to hold my hand. Siblings who dismissed me. What an incredible thing it was to have found him. To have had his hand brush mine in the garden all those years ago. What a gift to have loved him every day since. And to have had his love, too.

It is such a blessing to think of love in the end. I feel nothing but gratitude.

I love you, Mikail.

I try to say it. I think I do. My vision is fading, but I hold on to the image of his face as long as I can. My first love. My last.

CHAPTER SEVENTY

AERI

THE PALACE OF THE SKY KING, KHITAN

Quilimar just murdered her brother.

It all happened so quickly, the guard yelling "weapon" and the queen pulling a saber. Euyn turned her breast to gold just as she struck him in the heart. The queen released the blade, her jaw dropping in horror when she saw Euyn was empty-handed.

Quilimar was immediately surrounded by guards and carried out by four of them. But now the doors have slammed shut. There is a guard blocking each of the two doorways to prevent us from escaping. The remaining eight slowly march toward us, swords drawn.

We are trapped in this grand banquet room. Now we will join Euyn in the Ten Hells.

Sora, Royo, and I back up behind the king's table, but Mikail, the deadliest of us, is on the ground. He's cradling Euyn's body in his arms and stroking his hair, but the light has already left Euyn's eyes. Quilimar struck a fatal blow, and he was dead within seconds.

I am not ready to die, though. Not when I have Royo. Not when I want so many tomorrows with him. I want to fight for us, but the only blade we have is the saber lodged in Euyn's chest. I do have a hairpin dagger, but what is that against ten heavily armed guards? There's my amulet, but with the cost escalating for each use, I'm not sure I can get us out of here.

Certainly not four of us.

"You have all colluded to assassinate the Queen Regent of Khitan, mother of the true king," the guard says. I think he's the captain. He is the older guy who took the messages to the queen earlier. "You have been judged guilty and sentenced to death. Surrender the ring now, and we will grant you merciful ends."

That's right—the ring. Euyn died with it on, and I can wield it! I kneel by Euyn's body and turn his hand. Nothing. It's gone. I scan his other hand, but there's no ring. Is it somewhere on the floor? Did Quilimar manage to take it?

I'm about to ask Mikail if he has it when his face contorts. He changes from his normal careless expression to one of pure rage. Then he stands and lets out a soul-shattering wail. The drumming has stopped, but the room shakes from his cry. The vibrations make my spine rigid, an unholy terror flowing through me. And he is on our side.

"You want the ring? Come get it," he says.

He sounds every bit a demon.

Two of the guards hesitate, falling out of step, but the other six continue toward us in the vast room. I run my hand over my hair and take my clip down. I unsheathe the small dagger. It feels impossibly tiny versus swords and axes. Sora shifts something out of her pocket. I'm not sure what it is—a vial, I think; maybe lipstick. But she'd have to kiss a guard to use her poison, and we don't have that kind of time.

We're all so screwed.

I reach over and hand the little blade to Mikail. It's not much, but it's what we have. He won't disturb Euyn's body to take the saber. I get it. I wouldn't be able to if it were Royo. Still, heartbroken or not, I know any weapon is best in Mikail's hands. He closes his fist around the hilt of my small blade and nods.

The guards approach us in a semicircle with the captain in the center. He gestures to us with his sword.

Without a word, Mikail pitches the hairpin dagger at the captain.

My small blade flies through the air. One second. Two. Then it lands in the man's eye. It's an impossible shot, but the captain falls to the ground and starts convulsing.

Mikail and Royo use the confusion to flip the king's table on its side, creating a barricade between us and the guards. Plates smash, wine spills, and desserts roll.

Royo slides to the floor next to Euyn's body and bows his head. "Forgive me, my prince."

He rips the saber out of Euyn's heart. More deep-red blood gushes down Euyn's already soaked chest. Bile rises in my throat, and I look away, but at least Euyn didn't feel that.

Mikail watches Euyn's body out of the corner of his eye, but then he leaps over the table and gestures for the guards to come to him.

My stomach twists as four approach at once, their swords raised. Two guards follow a few steps back. One stays behind, trying to save the captain. Mikail is empty-handed, waiting.

Royo pushes me back toward the painting as he stands partially in front of me, wielding the bloody saber. He moves from side to side, visibly torn between guarding me and helping Mikail.

I wait, breathless, my hand by my necklace. Mikail is looking to die, and I don't know if I can save him. His calm is eerie as he stands with his arms out, like he's ready to embrace Lord Yama.

The guards continue toward him until they can nearly cut him down. The men and women of the palace guard seem keen to do away with the spymaster, to claim the accolade of being the one to kill him. Their gazes are sharp; one is even smiling. And maybe Mikail is looking to be with Euyn—I don't know, but it's terrible to just stand here and watch this.

"Turn!" Sora yells.

Mikail spins around, his expression puzzled. She opens her palm. He takes one look at her hand and then ducks his face into the crook of his arm. I wonder what he's doing until Sora leans over him. She takes a deep breath, then blows the pile of rose-colored dust into the faces of the guards.

All six of the guards suddenly start coughing and wheezing. The four closest to her clutch their throats and fall to their knees, silently choking. The other two move back, covering their faces.

Poison. She created an aura of death by blowing poison at them.

Mikail looks up at her, stunned and grateful. It's the most genuine I've seen him be. She places her clean hand over his.

"Kill them all," she whispers. "For him."

"Stay here," Royo says to me.

He's coughing, but he pulls his shirt over his mouth and nose, moving forward. Even though Sora blew the dust in the other direction, there's still enough poison in the air to burn my face. I put my sleeve over my nose and mouth, but my eyes sting.

Royo leaps over the barricade and grabs the sword off the nearest guard—the one on his hands and knees, dying from the poison dust. He tosses it to Mikail before reaching down and slitting the guard's throat with the bloody saber.

The spymaster comes alive with a sword in his hand. He swings it and nearly decapitates the guard who rushes at him with an axe. The guard crumples, his head lolling grotesquely to the side. Mikail kicks the axe out of his hand and sends it skittering on the marble floor over to Royo.

Before Royo can get it, though, another guard swings a sword at him. Royo ducks, and the guard hits the table instead. The palace guard is beet red, choking, and off aim. I flinch as the sword dents the wood, and I move back a step. Royo punches his face, his fist landing with a solid crack, and then he takes the guard's sword and finishes him. Royo stoops down and picks up the axe.

I hold my necklace, watching, ready to freeze time to protect Royo and Mikail, but neither needs it. Once they have their preferred weapons in their hands, it's a chaos of blades, blood, and screams. Royo grabs the last two guards who were closest to Sora and are nearly dead. He bashes their heads together, their skulls hitting with a sickening sound of bone striking bone. Then he kills them with a final stroke of his axe.

Sora sneaks out from behind the table and grabs a sword that fell a few feet from her. I'm about to do the same when two guards attack Mikail right by the blade I was eyeing.

"What did we talk about?" Royo shakes his head at me as he passes.

I hate just standing here, feeling useless, but I can't kill like they can. Royo puts two hands on his axe, running to back up Mikail, but the spymaster simply waits, sword casually hanging by his side. Then the first guard gets close enough that Mikail can grab his wrist. He gets ahold of him and suddenly twists, bending the guard's arm at an unnatural angle until it breaks. A wail of pain echoes through the room. Using the man's body as a shield, Mikail attacks the second guard. That woman swings, but her sword gets stuck in the first guard's neck. In her shock, she releases the blade. It's a mistake. Mikail arches back and then headbutts her unconscious. Then he slits both guards' throats, pulling their hair to create deep gashes in their necks. He moves at the frightening speed I remember from the warehouse, fluid and deadly accurate.

"Is this all you have?" he roars. His sword drips blood. "Is this all?"

He screams with the pain of losing Euyn, of taunting Lord Yama himself.

No one attacks. The guard who was standing at the far door has thrown down his axe and is desperately trying to pull the doors open.

I think he's soiled himself. His pants are suspiciously darker in the front. But the doors remain locked. It doesn't even dawn on him to use the axe to open them.

Mikail takes a second sword from the ground and strikes them together. He runs full speed at the guard and then launches into the air. I gasp as he impales the man on the doors, shoving the blades through the man's lower abdomen, where the chest armor doesn't protect. It's a painful, horrible way to die.

The only two guards left alive are on the floor in the middle of the room. There is one kneeling next to the captain and the captain himself. The latter is still convulsing on the ground. Mikail walks up to them, slowly, intentionally, but seething. He stares at the captain for a second, and then he raises his boot.

"Who is sentenced to death now, captain?" Mikail mutters.

He stomps the hairpin dagger all the way into the man's skull. I grimace at the sound of bone breaking, but the man stills, dead underfoot.

Mikail then faces the last guard, who puts his sword on the ground with his head bowed. He raises his empty hands.

"Mercy," the man says.

I hold my breath, waiting to see what Mikail will do. Sora and Royo are watching as well.

Surprisingly, Mikail nods.

"Thank you, spymaster." The guard bows his head again.

Mikail's expression changes, hardens. A chill runs through me right before he reaches out. He takes the guard's head between his hands and twists hard until there's a snap. Mikail lets go, and the guard's body falls limp onto the ground.

The room is silent. Mikail just killed a man he agreed to spare.

But I guess this isn't the time for mercy. The same way it wasn't for the barmaid in Oosant.

Only, if not now, then when?

CHAPTER SEVENTY-ONE

ROYO

THE PALACE OF THE SKY KING, KHITAN

I'm coughing and sweating as blood trickles down the mirrored glass and pools on the floor. Even though we just killed pretty much all the guards in here, we're fucked. Euyn is dead, and we still have the rest of the palace guard to deal with. I'm not sure how we'll make it out of this, but we gotta try.

"What happens now?" Aeri asks. She stares at me with her big brown eyes, and I wish I knew.

I cough some more. "Good question."

"Wait, come here," Sora says. "I can help with the poison, at least."

We walk to the table where she's standing, and she reaches into her pocket and pulls out a little vial. She puts a drop on Aeri's tongue and then Mikail's as her stare keeps darting over to the door. She gets to me and empties the vial in my mouth. I grimace. It's bitter as shit. But then I blink, and I can see better. I can inhale without it feeling like my nose and mouth are on fire. It's an antidote. And she's just gone through the last of it.

"What do we do now?" I ask, wiping my face. We stare at Mikail.

"We need to build a pyre," he says. He's weirdly calm, even though he looks at Euyn with unspeakable sadness in his eyes.

Ten Hells, we do not have time for a funeral.

"Here?" I ask, gesturing around. "Now?"

Mikail nods. "I won't have him be a trophy."

My stomach sinks as I realize he's right. Khitan wanted the dead guy's head from a hundred years ago. They'd display Euyn, too. We need to get his soul released and do it fast. I look over at the doors. They're gonna figure out soon that we're alive and the guards are dead.

I glance around the room. There's no fireplace or hearth, but we can use the king's table for a pyre. Except that burning a body inside will smoke us out. I look up at the gods for help but notice the opening in the dome. I start pushing the table to the center of the room. The ashes and smoke can leave out the top without choking us.

Everyone else takes the hint, moving quickly. The girls start wrapping Euyn in tablecloths. Mikail walks over to the enormous painting and pulls it down. The frame cracks and splinters, landing on the ground with an ear-splitting crash. He breaks apart the frame as if it's paper and starts building a pyre.

Once we're ready, Mikail carries Euyn's body over and gently lays him down. All wrapped up, he just looks like he's sleeping. Mikail must've closed his eyes.

We say the prayers to the Divine Kings, to Lord Yama, and to the Dragon Lord. We ask for the gods to forgive Euyn's crimes and guide his soul to redemption. Even Sora bows her head and says the prayers.

Mikail leans down and kisses Euyn's forehead, his lips lingering for a moment. "I'll meet you in the garden again."

Emotions clog my throat. For Euyn. For the fact that it would've been me saying goodbye to Aeri like this if I hadn't brought her back. She glances at me, and I reach out and take her hand.

Mikail smashes a vase of oil under the table, then lights the pyre. The bonfire sparks to life in the middle of the room and consumes Euyn's remains. Within minutes of us slaying the guards, Euyn's soul is released.

Mikail watches Euyn's body burn, the flames dancing in his eyes.

The drums suddenly beat again, but this time bells chime, too. It feels like they're ringing every single bell in and around the city of Quu.

"What fucking now?" I say.

"Is that because of us?" Sora asks.

"No," Mikail says, still watching Euyn burn. "Wei must've arrived in the harbor."

"Wei?" Aeri repeats.

Mikail nods, barely able to care. Sora stares at him and then takes a deep breath. She stands straighter, raising her chin.

"Armor," Sora says. "We need armor."

We all look around at the dead and dying guards. We're gonna have to take it off their corpses, which is fine—they don't need it. But if I'd known that was the plan, I would've been cleaner.

We walk around, sizing up our closest fits as the bonfire continues to burn. I wipe some blood and bone off the one that's closest to Aeri's size. She gives me a small smile, and I help her get the armor strapped to her body. I grab my closest match, but these guys were all built like Euyn or Mikail. The chest armor barely fits my shoulders, and it's not like the metal gives. Fuck it, though. It's better than nothing.

Bells chime so loud, it's hard to think. It feels good to have armor and weapons, but we still have to get out of this palace. I pick up the axe, ready to chop our way out of here.

"Shouldn't we try the doors?" Aeri asks. "Maybe they're distracted with Wei and we can slip out."

"But the guards couldn't get them open." Sora points to the guard Mikail impaled with two swords. He's still alive and moaning.

"Maybe the captain has a set of keys," Aeri suggests.

Mikail strolls over to the body of the captain. "It's a good thought."

I watch him like a hawk. He can't be this okay—he just can't be. But I've never understood this guy. Maybe he really is fine, or maybe grief looks different on everybody.

Mikail rifles through the captain's pockets and reaches into his breastplate. He holds up a set of keys and then flips them to Aeri.

"Give those a try," he says.

She nods and begins to work on the lock.

Sora walks up to Mikail as Aeri tries one key after another. She's been staring at him, too.

"Are you…okay?" she asks.

He breathes out a laugh. "No, and I won't ever be, so there's no sense in dealing with it now."

I guess that's fair enough. There just ain't the time. Sora stares, tears in her eyes, but she nods.

"I'm really sorry, Mikail," she says.

He nods. "I… Me too."

Aeri gets the door unlocked with a click. Once she has it, I cup her soft face in my hand. She looks at me, her lips parting in surprise. I lean in and kiss her. Because if I'm going to die, it's going to be with her kiss on my lips.

Then we both turn and look at Sora and Mikail. We're ready.

"The ones we hate die first," Sora says.

Mikail nods, lifting his sword to salute her. I bang my axe on the ground, and Aeri inclines her head.

I move in front of Aeri to be the first one out the door. Fuck, this sucks. I take a breath before I turn the knob. This is it. There ain't no way we're all just walking out of here, but at least I'll go down protecting Aeri. There are worse ways to go. Worse ways to live, too.

I throw open the door, muscles rigid but ready. I come through, swinging my axe, expecting to hit blades and bodies, but there's… nothing. Not a thing. I look around. There's nobody inside. Not one guard or a servant. No stuffy swells. No one.

"What the fuck?" I whisper, then shudder. Where is everybody?

A cold breeze blows through the empty great hall, making the flags flutter, but there's not a breath or a sound aside from the three people behind me.

Mikail is over my shoulder, and I feel his confusion. I thought the entire palace guard would be out here waiting for us. I don't want to meet them, but where'd they all go?

Sora and Aeri peek out behind us.

"I don't understand," Aeri whispers.

"Is this because Wei has arrived?" Sora asks.

Mikail's sharp eyes scan around. "I assume so, but be alert. Royo, protect our back in case it's a trap."

Mikail starts walking, clinging to the wall, his sword in hand. Sora and Aeri follow him, and I take the rear, ready for a surprise attack.

We stay tightly grouped, slowly making our way to the open front doors as one unit. Two steps, three. The quiet is unsettling as fuck. I don't know how, but it's almost worse than running straight into battle. At least we know what to prepare for when we can see our enemies. But this…this feels like willingly strolling into a trap.

We reach the golden doors, and then I get why there was no one inside—they are all in Trialga Square, standing in the rain. There have to be five thousand soldiers in the space, including two hundred palace guards in gray steel. Queen Quilimar and General Vikal sit on white horses in front of the army. Rather than hide her golden breast, Queen Quilimar has ripped off that part of her dress to put it on display. I guess it makes her seem more like Khitanese royalty. But none of them are looking at us.

Everybody is facing the harbor.

I've never seen a navy before, just boats on the Sol. And I ain't never dreamed of anything like this. There are one hundred warships facing Oligarch Mountain. All with the blue sails of Wei—except for one boat in the center. That one flies the red flag with a black snake. It also has red sails.

King Joon's ship.

"I've got a dumb question," I say.

"What's that?" Mikail is staring at the king's ship, hatred burning in his eyes.

"If we win..." I begin, but then I stop because I doubt it'll be a problem. And we have to win to worry about who'd rule Yusan. But with Euyn dead, I dunno who that would be.

It don't matter, though. General Vikal has spotted us. She stares and leans toward the queen. Queen Quilimar turns and looks.

"Never mind," I grumble.

I shift my axe in my hands, ready.

CHAPTER SEVENTY-TWO

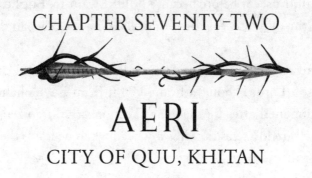

AERI
CITY OF QUU, KHITAN

It's the four of us against the might of the four original realms. Not the best odds, even though we have swords and armor and I have my amulet. One relic and four people against a hundred ships, five thousand Khitanese soldiers, and untold numbers of Yusanian and Gayan forces at the border isn't winnable. But there aren't three people I'd rather have at my side than the ones with me right now.

Queen Quilimar looks up at us, but really, she's staring straight at me. I hold her gaze. My aunt. The woman as disposable to my family as my mother was, as I am. Disrespected by her brothers, sold in marriage to a merciless foreign king she didn't love, and now she's barely holding on to the throne for her young son. I understand her rage and her struggle, but she was going to torture us and she killed Euyn. I won't give up what I have to let her win.

"I want to see tomorrow." I turn to Royo and stare into his eyes. "And tomorrow. And tomorrow. With you." Then I look at Sora and Mikail. "And if I can't have that, I want to make sure they don't see it, either."

Mikail stares at me like he's seeing me for the first time. His eyes dart over to the queen and then back to me.

"It ends here." He nods at the harbor. "One way or another."

I don't know how we'll pull it off, but I nod. Win or lose, we make a stand here. No one I love is safe so long as these rulers have power. I didn't see it before because I didn't want to. But I can't unsee it now—the only way for the four of us to have a place in this world is to change it.

Mikail reaches into his pocket, and then he pulls out the ring of the Dragon Lord. I thought he'd taken it from Euyn's hand, but so much happened after he died that I'd honestly forgotten about it. That same buzzing sensation fills my head when he holds the ring out.

"They all end here," he says.

Gods, he actually trusts me.

He presses the ring into my hand.

The second it hits my palm, it feels like lightning courses through me. This is what I was feeling when Quilimar gave Euyn the ring— the energy from the relic finding a person who can wield it, but ten times stronger, since I am the one receiving the ring—and I already have one other relic.

Power flows through my body like the tides, not unpleasant but bursting to be free.

I gather myself and slip the ring onto my left hand. I close my eyes. Once it is in place, heat burns at my clavicle and finger, warm metal against cold skin. The relics are fusing to me. I try to move the ring, and it doesn't budge—it's a part of my skin now. The amulet must be the same.

I am one with the Dragon Lord relics. Somehow that feels both more secure and more dangerous. I open my eyes again.

"Aeri... Your eyes." Royo stares at me with a furrowed brow. He looks intently from one of my eyes to the other.

"What?" I ask.

"They are...golden now," Sora says, blinking.

"I don't... Did this happen to Euyn?" I ask, looking around. I don't think so, but maybe I didn't notice.

Mikail shakes his head. "No."

The difference must be that I have two of the relics of the Dragon Lord. I was able to sense Euyn's ability to wield the ring because I had the amulet. And now the relics have changed each other and me.

No.

The blood runs from my face, my cheeks tingling. If I felt the ring on Euyn, was my father able to feel the Sands of Time on me? Is that why he made all of those promises at my mother's funeral pyre? Was that why he kept tabs on me and had the assassin protect me in Yusan?

No, the crown must work differently. If he knew I had the amulet, he would've killed me and taken it from me, or at the very least kept me locked in Qali. The last thing he would've allowed was my freedom. He wouldn't have risked one of the counts or Quilimar getting their hands on the Sands of Time.

My father has the Flaming Sword, but the texts in the Temple of Knowledge said that Yusan did not wield it against Wei. I thought Yusan had just lost the war, but maybe the sword never bonded to my father. Which doesn't make sense.

How does nothing ever make sense?

Royo reaches out and caresses my cheek.

"I love your eyes no matter the color." He smiles, thinking the aesthetics are what trouble me.

I smile back because I adore him. Because I love what he is saying. Because it's amazing to be loved by him. I exhale as the truth hits me: the only way to keep Royo safe is to kill the rest of the Baejkins.

CHAPTER SEVENTY-THREE

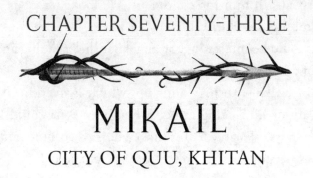

MIKAIL
CITY OF QUU, KHITAN

S ora stares at me, worried not because of the army in front of us, or the navy below us, but because I lost Euyn. Her gentle heart knows mine just broke. But I'm all right. Or at least I am completely numb right now. I'm hollowed out, nothing but a blade, and that's exactly what we need.

Sora reminds me that I am still a human being, but just barely.

I almost told her about Daysum's death before we left the banquet room, but telling her would've been to ease my burden, not for her. We'll likely die before it will matter, and if so, she'll see her sister again in the Ten Hells. I can spare her the endless grief and useless rage I feel right now. I can do that much for her.

"They die first," I say.

The three others nod; Aeri is last because she's staring down her aunt. Aeri might be the biggest surprise of anyone I've met. She seems like she's nothing more than a carefree and bubbly girl, but she is unbreakable steel in a ball gown.

Soldiers shift below us, and we stand ready. A man in a suit is pushed forward by a guard.

Oh, good, it's my old friend, Ambassador Zeolin.

He stops in front of Quilimar's horse and then bows on his knees with his head to the wet stones. Surprisingly, she doesn't kill him.

That's a shame.

She speaks to him for a moment. He looks up at us and then starts climbing the stairs.

This should be interesting. Strange that she's sending an emissary instead of a battalion.

Zeolin walks with his hands up, which is overkill. No one is worried about him being armed when even Aeri could kick him down the stairs. His gray hair is slicked darker with the rain, his face worried as he stops a step down from the portico. This close, I can see his limbs shaking.

"What is it, Zeolin? I'm a little busy right now," I say.

"Queen Quilimar desires a truce," he says from about ten feet away. He'd rather get rained on than come any closer, which is laughable. I could easily slaughter him from this distance.

"You know, she has a funny way of showing it." I gesture to the blood on me.

He sighs and frowns. "It was a misunderstanding between the prince and the queen. But the queen has greater issues at the moment."

"Really? Such as?" I ask.

Ambassador Zeolin looks around, confused. "The navy of Wei and the might of Yusan have descended on Khitan."

"You forgot Gaya," I say.

"I did say Yusan," he says.

I dislike him more each time we talk, which is saying something. "Get to it."

He clears his throat, taking on a pompous air despite quivering. "The queen says she accepts your terms of alliance."

I raise my eyebrows. I can feel the surprise and skepticism in the sharp inhales of the others. "I might be more inclined to believe her if she hadn't sentenced us all to death. But more to the point, isn't it treason for you to do her bidding?"

He looks down his nose at the four of us. "I highly doubt any of you will survive long enough for it to be relevant. What is your answer?"

I smile. What an unfortunate time for him to discover a spine. "Give her my regards."

He nods and then turns to walk away. "Euyn got what was coming to him, and so will you."

He should've quit while he was ahead.

"Zeolin," I say, stepping forward.

He faces me. I swing my leg out and kick his chest. He goes flying down the stairs.

Maybe I should've chopped his head off, because he knows very well who was behind killing the Yoksa. The same ruler keeping tabs on us through Khitan—King Joon.

Zeolin continues to roll dramatically down the steps. Quilimar barely spares him a glance. She faces us, waiting.

"We accept!" I yell out.

She nods.

Now we have a truce.

Quilimar is stunningly pragmatic—the Baejkins always are. She realizes that with Joon colluding with the priest king of Wei, we will need everything and everyone we have in order to survive. She can't afford to waste any more resources trying to kill us. Aeri is the only one in the country above the age of four who can wield the ring; therefore, her niece is the only route Quilimar has to keeping the relic and holding on to the throne of Khitan.

I'm certain she will try to murder Aeri the second the threat has dissipated. But we can settle everything else, including Quilimar paying for Euyn's life, after we defeat our common enemies.

Allies...for now.

CHAPTER SEVENTY-FOUR

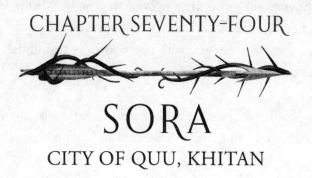

SORA
CITY OF QUU, KHITAN

In a curious turn of events, we are riding on white horses, marching with the army of Khitan to the harbor. It feels as inevitable as it is confusing. Mikail is up ahead, talking strategy with Quilimar and the general. I'm behind them, riding with Aeri and Royo.

Our procession is slow, but Mikail said Wei will not attack before a parley—that is the term for a talk of truce between the realms. It's a custom as old as the four original realms themselves—a last effort to prevent a costly war. Obviously, it is not the kings and queens at the parley, but their representatives.

All our weapons were returned to us by Gambria, who either was spared or ran in the aftermath of Euyn's wager. She now marches with us on foot to the right of my horse. I have my daggers, but I wish I had more poison on me. I had to use it all in the banquet room, and I can't say I regret it. It saved Mikail's life.

I am not sure what the plan is now, though—how we can survive this. Honestly, I hadn't expected to make it out of the palace. I also hadn't expected Mikail to kick the ambassador. I'm worried that he is not in his right mind, but I suppose none of us are. We are all warped by rage, by revenge, by the past. But for two of us, there are also thoughts of the future.

I stare at Aeri and Royo on their horses. I don't understand why Aeri's eyes turned golden. It feels like I must be missing something, because Euyn's eyes didn't change even after he wielded the ring. But there are many mysteries. One of which is how Mikail can put aside Euyn's murder and strategize with the woman responsible. I wouldn't be able to do the same if Seok were here.

But he is gone.

Mikail told me that the southern count ran back to Yusan right after I told him Tiyung was in Idle Prison. I can only hope he freed his son and then was imprisoned himself, but I doubt it. These men never pay.

But Euyn did. Maybe that's what it takes—a woman willing to risk death itself to even the score. And I am that woman.

Gambria also seems like that kind of person as she walks alongside my horse. Formidable and focused. But there's something off about her, something dishonest. I just can't place it.

A handsome soldier with brown skin and green eyes comes up to her. He bumps his shoulder into her. Gambria looks over, annoyed, and then turns again, surprise written on her face.

"What are you doing here?" she whispers sharply.

I remain facing forward, like I am not paying attention, but they are on my hearing side. I was right—she's hiding something. I'm not sure what the secret is, but I felt nearly the same about Aeri. Which means I have to figure it out.

Gods, let's hope Gambria isn't also King Joon's long-lost daughter.

"Why so surprised, cousin?" he murmurs. "You thought I didn't hear the invasion bells, or the war drums, or the rumors?"

"Go before he sees you," she insists.

The man nods and then disappears. I want to look back to see who that was, but I can't reveal I was listening. The only "he" Gambria could mean, though, is Mikail. She is keeping something from him.

An icy feeling spreads across my chest, and I grip the reins.

Kingdom of Hells, what else is there?

CHAPTER SEVENTY-FIVE

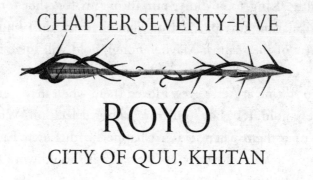

ROYO
CITY OF QUU, KHITAN

We march down the winding road to the harbor—the four of us and an army of five thousand. I'm wearing a dead guy's armor, and it's too tight. I roll my shoulders as I ride on a horse. It's uncomfortable as shit but still better than nothing.

Khitan has gotta have more soldiers than this, but Mikail said most are at the border or assembling in Vashney and Loptra. Five thousand good soldiers protect Quu, and normally it's enough.

It ain't enough right now.

Each Weian warship has got a hundred men. Which means there are ten thousand Weians in Quu, and who knows how many Yusanians and Gayans at the border.

Mikail holds up his horse and falls back in line with the three of us. "Quilimar is going to send Aeri with General Vikal for the parley."

"Like hells she is," I say.

Mikail looks over at me, unsurprised. "You can go, too, as her guard. I already said she wouldn't go without you."

All right, that does make me feel a little better.

"What's a parley?" I ask.

"It's where the leadership of the realms meet to negotiate a truce. To avoid war."

I don't see how there could be a truce here aside from Khitan surrendering, and they won't. Wei and Yusan didn't come to Khitan for nothing. King Joon didn't put all of this together for a treaty. And annihilation ain't peace. But what the fuck do I know about the politics of the realms? Maybe enough gold will solve it. Seems to solve everything else.

I keep staring at Aeri's eyes. I loved them when they were brown. I love them gold, too, but something about it feels off. Why would the ring turn them when it didn't happen with Euyn? I mean, it's god magic, so who knows, but it feels like it should work the same on all the Baejkins.

I grip the reins as a chill spreads over me. It feels like she's hiding something again. But she swore no more lies, so maybe the cold spot is just this armor. We didn't release the spirits of the guards, so maybe this off feeling is just the dead guy poking at me.

"What about you?" I ask Mikail. "Are you going to the parley?"

He shakes his head. "I was flatly refused."

"Why?" I ask.

"Something-something, I'd be too antagonistic. Cowards." He stares daggers at the queen and the general in front of us.

"Not Sora?" I ask.

She turns her head at her name.

"Interestingly, also refused," he says. "I think that has more to do with keeping our little group separated than anything political. We did manage to kill a roomful of their palace guards when we were unarmed. They'd rather not have us all together."

True enough, but we aren't nearly as dangerous without Euyn. I breathe a heavy sigh for the fallen prince. Gods guide his soul.

We ride quietly to the sound of boots and hooves clomping along the wet cobblestone road.

"Where are they doing this parley thing?" I ask.

"It's supposed to be on neutral soil," Mikail says. "Obviously, there isn't any of that in Quu, so I'm not sure. I'm certain we'll find out, though."

"Where is the priest king?" Aeri asks.

Mikail points to the largest, fanciest ship. "He is always on the same ship as the Water Scepter. He is seated on the throne under the awning. The relic is being wielded on the prow by the person in the blue robes."

If I squint, I can see somebody on the front of the ship with a gold staff, wearing cobalt blue.

"Wait, the priest king doesn't do it himself?" I ask.

"No," Mikail says. "Wei uses the scepter to constantly magic the waters of the islands, and the scepter, like all the relics, has a cost. The bearers only live around two years in the Temple of Divine Waters."

"Two?" Sora blinks.

He nods. "The longest known bearer survived for four years. No one lives longer than that, and as you can imagine, switching leadership every four years would be disastrous for any realm."

I stare at him. "So random people sign up to take that job?"

"Royal Weians," he says. "Anyone wielding a relic must be of royal blood, or it won't work, as we saw with Quilimar. In Wei, the priest kings have multiple wives and dozens of concubines to produce heirs of royal blood. And those children, along with the whole nation, believe it is the greatest honor in the land, and the most exalted death, to wield the scepter. The bearers have every luxury and comfort for the years they bless the waters."

"But if the king doesn't have the power..." Aeri starts, eyeing the ship.

Mikail glances at her, a little respect shining in his eyes. "I know what you're thinking—why not usurp the throne? It has happened a few times in the past, and believe me, we've tried to facilitate a change in leadership, but Uol, the current king, has the country in an iron grip. He is worshipped as a god on earth. It's excessively clever to create a cult around yourself when you fear a coup."

Weird to worship a regular guy. At least the Baejkin kings are immortal with the crown.

We're almost at the base of the mountain by the time I absorb all that.

"Coming out!" General Vikal yells.

Everyone stops at once, weapons aimed.

A small, narrow boat is lowered from the Yusanian ship, and one also comes down from the Weian ship. They have oars, not sails, but they are fancier than any lifeboats I've ever seen. Probably escape skiffs, to save the kings if the battleships sink.

I still don't know what the plan is, but the boats suddenly stop in the harbor. Meeting on the water is kind of neutral.

General Vikal approaches us. "Time to negotiate their surrender."

I can't tell if she's serious or joking.

Mikail, Sora, Aeri, and I ride with the general and the queen to the shore. I guess we're getting on a boat, but I don't know which one.

We're almost to the docks when all of a sudden, the water in the harbor splits. I don't know how else to say it. There's a collective gasp that ripples through the entire army as a walkway appears on the sea floor. I blink. What the fuck? There had just been dozens of feet of water, and now there's not. The muddy, debris-filled harbor is exposed because the sea water now flows into the air, like invisible hands are holding it back. At the end of the path is a rock outcropping right by the escape boats.

I look at the main Weian ship. The person with the scepter created this.

Ten fucking Hells.

"What is all that?" I ask.

Mikail smirks as he points to the little island of black rocks. "That is neutral land. Controlled entirely by Wei, of course."

"That's where the parley will be?" Aeri stares at the walls of water with her golden eyes.

The general nods.

Of course it is. But hells or high waters, I'll protect her until my last breath. My heart drums steadily—not nerves but the beat of war.

"Don't kill anyone, Royo," Mikail says.

I snap my head in his direction. "Why not?"

"Because it would start a war," General Vikal answers. "The parley *must* be done in peace."

"Do we have to leave our weapons, then?" Aeri asks.

"Gods no," Vikal says.

"But if—" Aeri begins.

The general cuts her off. "Just because we're not going there to kill anyone doesn't mean they're not going to try to kill us."

Great. Let's fucking go.

CHAPTER SEVENTY-SIX

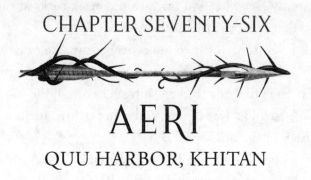

AERI

QUU HARBOR, KHITAN

"Be safe, my love," Quilimar says to General Vikal. She covers the general's hand with hers.

"I'll return to you," Vikal says.

The queen takes her eyes off the harbor for long enough to exchange a loving glance with Vikal. The general salutes her, then rides with Royo and me to where the path begins on the shore of Quu. Queen Quilimar really loves her. Does that make my aunt better or worse, or does loving someone not affect our value at all?

I don't have time to think about it, because we've reached the shore. I grip the reins of my horse so hard that my knuckles go white. We pause before entering, and that gives me a chance to feel how my pulse is pounding in my neck. This really couldn't feel more like a trap. Every fiber of my being wants to turn back, but there's nowhere to go but forward.

Yet even General Vikal takes a deep breath before shaking it off and spurring her horse. Royo and I follow, our horses taking their first hesitant steps onto the mucky path. I tense, waiting for the East Sea to descend on us, but the water walls hold.

A few yards in, I stop waiting for the water to crash down on top of me. A few more and I'm able to marvel at the miracle surrounding us.

It's…incredible to be riding through a harbor. The dry space is around twenty feet wide and leads to the black rocks at the end.

Gods, that's like the isle in the Sol.

As soon as I think it, Royo looks over at me. He rides beside me, guarding me, but also staring up at the water towering far above our heads. The prow of a sunken ship sticks out of the water over to the left. We pass lost traps, nets, and other debris, including rusted swords stuck in the muddy sand.

I have stopped time, but I have never experienced anything this amazing. I reach out and touch the wall of water. I can't help but smile as my hand comes away wet. The sea is constantly flowing fifty feet into the air, yet the only drops that land on our heads are from the monsoon.

I force my wonder aside and remember that I can't swim. I swallow the lump in my throat. If this goes wrong, I die. Again.

How in the three realms does this keep happening?

I vow to learn to swim if I live through this. It doesn't look like swimming lessons are in my future, honestly.

We ride toward the rocks where five other people wait—two from Yusan and two from Wei and one other. Although I see their clothes and robes, I can't make out their faces from this far away. The seafloor dips down. We had a better view from the shore.

Once we reach the rocks, we dismount and scale the twelve-foot boulders of the isle. Royo gives me a boost. My hands slip on the wet stone, but I make it to the top. The first two people I see are General Salosa and Bay Chin. Salosa wears his armor, and Count Bay Chin is in a suit with his noble collar over it. They stand under the banner of Yusan.

Shit.

Short of my father himself, Bay Chin is the worst possible person to stand in this parley. My stomach turns, my fingers icy—Royo's going to kill him.

Royo reaches the top, and I put my hand against his chest for him to stay a step back. He looks down at my fingers, but then he stiffens when he sees Bay Chin.

Two people also stand under the Weian flag. I don't know who they are. One wears white-and-blue robes, so I assume he's a priest, and one wears elaborate armor. The last person on the isle wears gray robes—a priest. I look at his face and his red hair. It's Luhk! Joy fills me that he survived. He must be here to record this moment and translate.

"Generals," Vikal says in Khitanese. "And others unwelcome at our shore."

"Vikal," General Salosa says.

The Weian person in armor bows with a hand to their torso. They are a mix of genders. Mikail said some people in Wei are not male or female and instead go by xe.

"Vikal," xe says.

What comes next is a mess of ritual and translation. Everything needs to be spoken in all four languages, despite no one being Gayan on this rock.

I'm not sure why I'm here, and that is a problem. Quilimar had a purpose in sending me, but I haven't figured it out yet. I would think Vikal was supposed to murder me, but then Royo would not have been allowed.

No, from the way Bay Chin and Salosa eye me, Quilimar wanted them to see that I have the Golden Ring of the Dragon Lord and yet I am on her side. She wants them to know we have chosen to ally with the queen rather than give my father the ring.

As the men stare at me, I realize we won. We did exactly what we had set out to do. Quilimar is on our side, allied with us against Joon. But Euyn is dead, a war of the realms has started, and apparently, I'm going to have to choose between loves.

We won, but at the same time, we lost.

My father stands on the prow of his ship, wearing the Immortal Crown and watching the parley from sixty yards away. The priest king of Wei, however, sits on his throne in the middle of the imperial warship. I can just make him out. I think he's ten years older than my father, and he's being served grapes. Snacking as all of these lives are about to be lost.

"No terms can be reached," Luhk finally says in Yusanian. "Return to your armies and prepare for war."

I'm many things, but I'm not surprised. Bay Chin turns to leave.

"Bay Chin," Royo says.

My eyes volley to Royo. He can barely contain his rage, the muscle in his jaw ticking. General Vikal notices as well, coming a step closer as Royo begins to pull his sword. He can't do this right now. Not when we're trapped on this rock in the middle of the harbor floor.

"There is to be no violence at the parley," Luhk says.

Royo hesitates, but he lets go of his blade. "I will smile at your corpse before this is over, Your Grace."

Royo issues a mocking bow.

"Boy, you have no idea who you're dealing with," Bay Chin says. "You'd best crawl back to the sewer you came from. Like your father and mother before you."

No. I widen my eyes as Royo turns red. He marches the short distance to Bay Chin. I think he's about to attack, but he stops two feet away.

"Pick up a sword," Royo says. "Or let's finish this with our bare hands, man to man."

Bay Chin smiles. "I wouldn't dream of it."

"Coward!" Royo yells. "Fight me now or get on your knees and beg forgiveness for your crimes."

General Vikal watches, but she doesn't interfere, content to see how this plays out. I'm not. Not when General Salosa watches him with keen eyes. Royo has chest armor on, but his head and neck are exposed.

"Royo, please." I step closer to him.

He's breathing hard, ready to swing regardless of whether Bay

Chin consents to fight, but then he finally looks at me. Royo sighs, some of his anger fading. He spits at Bay Chin's feet and then turns around.

My heart swells as he takes a step toward me. He is choosing love over his chance at revenge. He is choosing me.

But there's motion behind him. General Salosa unsheathes his sword while Royo's back is turned. And Bay Chin is smiling.

No!

The sword rises. I go to grab my amulet, but it's fused to me. I don't know how to stop time now. I don't know if I even can.

I throw my arm out for Salosa to stop. Fear pools in my stomach. I can't do anything. I'm going to watch him cut down Royo. He's going to die in front of me. I can't save him. I can't kill Salosa or Bay Chin, as much as I want to. And gods, how I want to see them dead.

All of a sudden, the ring glows. A bright gleam of gold fills my eyes, illuminating the entire isle. General Vikal and the priests shield their eyes, but it doesn't bother me. Because I realize what is happening.

I hear the screams I want to hear. And then the quiet of nothing at all.

When the glow fades, Bay Chin stands with his hands out and General Salosa with his sword swung back to strike, but they have been turned into solid gold.

Royo drops to his knees, trying too late to get out of the way of Salosa's blade, but it's not necessary. They're already dead.

He looks behind him. Shock and horror wash over his face, and then he stares at me. But I don't feel a thing. I did what I had to do, whatever it took, to save him. I'd happily do it again.

Power surges through me, more than before. It feels like the relics are begging to be used again. I don't feel exhaustion or the pain that Euyn obviously experienced. This is something else.

But then the ground rumbles as the sea begins to fall.

My mouth falls open as water starts flooding the space that had been dry, beginning at the entrance to the harbor. They're blocking off our means of escape. By now, everyone must realize that I have the ring, and they are coming to take it. Even the Weian general and the priests turn toward me.

And then I realize my mistake: by saving Royo, I may have just doomed us all.

Instead of feeling panicked, though, I am calm.

"A single step closer and you will wind up like them," I say.

Luhk translates.

The Weian general puts xer hands out, and the priest takes a step back.

I look at the soldiers running around the royal warships and the Water Scepter wielder who is closing off the path. I tilt my head.

Aren't they at all tired of being powerless?

I am.

I am so tired of not being safe. So tired of being a player in a game I didn't design. I feel Quilimar's rage, Sora's. Mine.

My father leans on the railing, jaw slackened at the scene in front of him—the men who had been his pawns are nothing more than gold statues now. I stare back at him. Even the priest king of Wei stands. He is the same kind of man as my father. Ruthless, pretend gods. All of this didn't start with them, but it ends with them.

Fury builds as I stare at the kings. Then I extend my arms.

Drown.

Power radiates down my limbs and out of my hands. A golden glow fills the harbor. Then I don't remember a thing.

CHAPTER SEVENTY-SEVEN

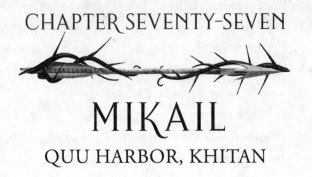

MIKAIL
QUU HARBOR, KHITAN

An enormous halo of golden light, ten times larger than the first, fills the harbor. I shield my eyes and squint. But the light quickly fades into the most incredible sight I've ever beheld. The hulls of the imperial ship of Yusan and the ship of the priest king of Wei are now made of gold and sinking fast.

Aeri just sank their ships.

Quilimar gasps with her mouth open. Sora puts her hands over her lips. I stare, as do the soldiers of three realms.

The world has never seen anything like this.

The shoreline is almost silent as we all try to process what we just saw. I'm sure the people on the royal ships are screaming, but we can barely hear them from here.

As the ships go down, I realize that it's not possible for the ring to have done that. The ring requires touch. What Aeri just did was a power far beyond one relic. And yet it happened. And since one relic can't do that, and all the other relics are accounted for except one, that can only mean…

She has the Sands of Time.

I draw in a sharp breath, trying to hide my surprise as the pieces all fall into place. That's how she was able to steal the million-cut diamond in Pyong from right under everyone's noses, to save me in the warehouse in Oosant, to survive. Aeri has had the Amulet of the Dragon Lord this entire time. And if I had to bet, that's how she survived Prince Omin.

She doesn't have incredible sleight of hand. She has etherum. Now, with the ring and the amulet, her power is unmatched.

And she's never been in more danger.

"Stay here," I say to Sora.

I spur my horse down into the harbor. It's dry again because the scepter wielder diverted the water around the royal ships to save the people on board. Weian boats are flat-bottomed, so the priest king's boat sits idly on the seafloor. Joon's boat has tipped onto its port side.

This is my chance to kill Uol *and* Joon. And I'm not the only one who senses the opportunity. A vicious smile lights Quilimar's face as she charges into the harbor next to me and calls for her army to follow her. But I need to get to Aeri before anyone else does. Quilimar would want to capture, not kill her, but I can't say the same about anyone from Yusan or Wei. Either realm would become unstoppable with the two relics Aeri holds in addition to their own. Either of those kings would become a god.

Half of the Khitanese forces follow us into the harbor. The reserves hold to the shore. Weian dignitaries who, no doubt, felt safe aboard their unsinkable navy are scrambling through the muddy harbor, trying to get to the safety of dry land. A cadre of Weian guards runs, surrounding the priest king. They're trying to reach the shore…or Aeri, who is halfway between us.

Royo stands in front of her body with his sword out, as does General Vikal. I'm not sure if Aeri is even still alive, but they stand guard as if she is. I'm awfully glad our interests align with Khitan for the moment.

I'm galloping as fast as this warhorse can go. I'm almost to the isle when I realize that in this chaos Wei left the Water Scepter bearer nearly unprotected on their ship. I can get to him and kill him. And if I do, the sea will fall and all of them will die—Joon, Uol, and Quilimar.

All debts will be settled at once.

But then Aeri and Royo would be forfeit, and Sora, too. She's slightly behind me, more careful in the debris, but she followed the moment I took off. I wish she hadn't. In fact, I'm positive I told her to stay behind, but she didn't listen.

Now, by killing my enemies, I'll also kill my friends—the closest thing I've had to family since Ailor took me in.

It's a surprisingly easy decision, but one I fear I'll regret for the rest of my life.

CHAPTER SEVENTY-EIGHT

TIYUNG

THE KHAKATAN MOUNTAINS, KHITAN

I didn't think we'd actually make it here. I was certain Hana and I would die escaping from Idle Prison, and then I thought we would surely be killed in Qali Palace, and then I knew we'd be eaten alive rowing a very small boat over Idle Lake. I was proven wrong every step of the way. Even on horseback traveling here, I thought Hana would murder me or a gang of highwaymen would get to us, but somehow, we made it to Khitan.

Well, I think we are in Khitan.

It's hard to tell because we've been walking through this cave system for bells and bells. This underground space meanders beneath the Khakatan Mountains. I was well lost a few minutes in, but Hana plods forward. She moves her lantern to check carvings on the wall, and then she keeps going.

I follow.

We had to take this way in because the king's guard occupies the main road to the border. War is descending on Khitan, where Sora and the others are trying to steal the Golden Ring. If they're still alive. I blow out a heavy breath. Please gods, let them still be alive.

"Should I ask how you even know about this?" I whisper because my voice echoes in the cave.

"Do you think spies go through the customs harbor every time we enter or leave?" she asks dryly.

That's fair enough.

We keep going. Finally, daylight shines at the end of the cave. I unclench my clean-shaven jaw and breathe a sigh of relief. After Idle, darkness crawls and grates on me. I now sleep with a fire going. I doubt I'll ever be comfortable in the dark again.

The sky is a painfully bright gray when we come out near a small, picturesque town. This far into monsoon season, everything is covered in deep snow. I put my hand over my eyes to shield them from the snow's reflection. We pull our hoods up and trek into town.

Hana keeps glancing up as we walk. I'm not sure what she is searching for until we arrive at a messenger house.

"I need to stop inside," she says.

I nod, then hold the door for her.

Bells chime as we walk in, alerting the eagles on their perches and the man behind the desk.

"Good morning," Hana says in perfect Khitanese. "Are there any letters for Nabhi of Kur?"

I'm confused for a moment, but then I realize that must be her alias. I know the four original languages, having had tutors my whole life. I'm not sure where Hana learned Khitanese—probably from Madame Iseul, but she might be self-taught.

The man hands Hana a red envelope. The kind that comes from the palace. Someone in Qali knew where we were going? Maybe Nayo.

She cracks the clay and slices open the envelope.

All of a sudden, the ground shakes. I grab the ledge closest to me. Is it an earthquake? An avalanche?

"What is that?" I ask, looking around.

"War drums," she says casually.

She reads the card in her hand. It's a mix of symbols. I have no idea what any of it means, but she takes out a pencil and starts decoding it.

"I must begin to close up now," the man behind the counter says.

"Seek safety."

He moves around behind the counter, adroitly slipping hoods on the birds and putting them in cages. This close to the border, his shop is at risk. He will be one of the first who must leave everything behind to flee farther inland. One who has to pray that something will be left when he returns. A commoner lost in the shuffle of war.

But Hana isn't paying attention. She's staring at the card in front of her.

"We have to go back," she says in Yusanian.

"Excuse me?" She can't mean back to Yusan. We just got here. We need to get to Sora. We need to help the others—that's been our goal from the beginning. Nothing on a card could change that.

She hands me the message.

I read the words she translated, and the paper falls from my hand. I'm sure my face is now as pale as hers.

My father has seized Qali Palace.

CHAPTER SEVENTY-NINE

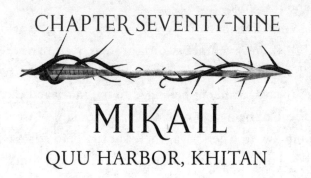

MIKAIL
QUU HARBOR, KHITAN

I spur my horse to a gallop until I reach the black rocks of the sunken isle.

"Give her to me," I yell up to Royo.

He looks down, over his shoulder. He hesitates, and frankly, we don't have time for this.

General Vikal has already used the chaos to kill the Weian general and is currently running her sword through the Weian priest. I'm not sure what her next play is, but a Yusanian soldier is scrambling up the rocks, carrying a flaming sword.

My fucking sword.

I stop arguing with Royo and snap the reins. I know exactly who that is. I recognize his ridiculous mustache—it's Thom, Salosa's eldest son. He's more useless than his father, but he was promoted through the ranks and constantly catered to because of his father's status. General Salosa is, of course, now a sand decoration. But his brat was given my sword.

I ride close to the rocks, hold my arm steady, and aim my blade. I grip the hilt with two hands and ride until I connect with Thom's legs. I mow him down at the ankles. He falls, his feet nearly sliced off.

As he screams, I stand on the saddle and leap onto the isle. I hate to lose the mount, but I'm getting my sword back. Thom, undeserving as he is, still clings to it as he cries out for his gods.

He's about to meet them.

"You're embarrassing yourself," I say. I kick my blade out of his hand and then put my other sword through his throat.

Once he's dead, I lean down and pick up my flaming sword. The sword has always felt like it belonged to me in a way I can't express. It reminds me of being a boy in Gaya, of home. I must've seen the real Flaming Sword when I was there shortly before it was stolen.

"Ready?" I ask Royo. I strip the scabbard from Thom's body and put it on.

Royo is silent. He's staring at Vikal, who has her bloody blade out. He shifts to block Aeri's body. I can't tell if she's thinking about killing him, Aeri, or both. She must have, at minimum, thought about taking the relics to Quilimar.

I raise my sword, settling on her wanting to kill both of them.

"The queen!" the palace guards yell out. "Save the queen!"

Vikal looks over her shoulder. The Khitanese guard has stopped to surround and protect Quilimar because even though the Yusanian and Weian troops are fleeing for their lives, they are still trying to kill the queen on behalf of their kings. Vikal has the same choice to make—kill what you hate or protect what you love.

It's harder than it sounds.

"Until we meet again, then," she says, sheathing her sword.

I nod, cutting down a soldier who is trying to climb up. Then I slice through another and then a third. With higher ground, it's fish in a barrel, but Royo isn't helping. He still has his sword aimed at the general.

Vikal takes three steps backward and leaps off the isle. Then she sprints on foot to Quilimar, blade out again. Soldiers try to attack her, and she slices men apart at full speed. She's not wasting time to ensure the kill. She's just trying to move past them to get to Quilimar.

Royo looks at me, somehow still struggling for words. "I just..."

"Can we go now?" I ask.

This is not time for a heart-to-heart. We'll be lucky to get Aeri to safety in this free-for-all. The longer we take, the more forces can regather and align themselves against us. Royo doesn't trust me because he doesn't trust anyone, and that's fine. We can discuss it later.

He picks up Aeri. She is breathing. Shallowly, and she's unconscious, but at least she's still alive. I'm not sure what toll it takes to use the two relics, but I have to imagine it nearly killed her. Our gods don't give without taking.

Sora rides up on her horse.

"What do we do now?" She stares at Aeri and then the walls of water.

"Get to dry land," I say. "Like I said before."

I turn and focus on the gold Weian boat sitting on the floor of the harbor. Only a handful of guards and the scepter wielder are still on the ship. Fewer than I even first thought.

"Watch out," Sora says as she points to my left.

Another soldier attempts to scale the black rocks. I decapitate him and wonder why the scepter bearer is not fleeing with the king. Then I remember the focus Euyn needed to wield the ring. If the bearer breaks focus, the sea will fall and drown everyone in the harbor—including King Uol. In choosing to create dry land, the scepter had to be separated from the king.

But it's taking a while for Uol to reach the shore—far longer than expected, I'm sure. Wei's forces are colliding with the Khitanese army in the harbor, and Quilimar is out for blood. The reserves have been called in to prevent the foreign troops from reaching dry land. And it's taking a tremendous amount of power to keep this harbor dry.

The Water Scepter has never been this vulnerable, and I doubt it ever will be again. If I had the relic, Gaya would be free. I'd give it to Fallador, and we could push away any navy. I knew it before and I chose to stop and save Aeri. But now I can do both.

"I'm going to take the Water Scepter," I say.

Sora and Royo exchange glances. They don't think it's a good idea—that much is written on their faces. But they look resigned.

"We're coming with you," she says.

I blink in shock. "What? No, take Aeri and get to dry land."

"And what? You think they'll just let us pass by with her?" Royo asks.

"We're safest together," Sora says. "We're with you for better or worse."

Royo nods, and then he places Aeri across Sora's lap. Without hesitation, I climb down a boulder and get on Sora's horse behind her. Royo meets my eye, then nods again. He's trusting me with the person who has his heart—the greatest trust you can bestow on someone.

I won't betray him. But now I have to figure out how to get all of us out of this alive.

I hold Aeri in place, and then Royo jumps down and smacks the horse's flank. He runs through the muck behind us.

Nearly all the people who'd been on the royal Weian ship have already abandoned it, but two Weian palace guards climb down as we approach. We ride another step closer, and an arrow pings off my armor. Apparently, they also left an archer on board and he's a decent shot.

"Stay out of their reach," I say, dismounting. Sora nods, circling wide but holding on to Aeri.

I unsheathe my sword, and it flames to life in my hand. The fire thaws something inside of me—something that froze when Euyn died.

"No quarrel with you," I say in Weian to the guards. "Flee now."

I mean my offer. There's no reason to kill them, and it's just a diversion from getting to the scepter.

"Spymaster," one says.

They both stand ready to battle.

Well, there goes that idea.

The first guard swings his blade and meets my sword. The Weian royal guard is better than any of the other realms. Their armor is thought to be impenetrable, the steel cooled with the magicked waters of the islands.

I'll put it to the test.

I swing my sword, and it clangs off the side of the first guard's armor. It's better than I expected. As I recoil, I dodge a blow from the second guard. They attack in tandem, and I strike the weakest point at the shoulder joint. My jaw slackens as it does nothing. Not even a scratch.

A guard slices right above my head, and I duck. I swing out, kicking him to the ground. He gets back to his feet with speed that nearly matches mine.

I parry blows until sweat slicks my skin. They aren't as fast as I am, but there are two of them and they are not falling. I don't know how long I can keep this up. Frustration courses through me, and I strike harder and faster, now aiming for their faces, hands, and knees. Every moment I spend on this skirmish is one where more troops make it ashore. It's another minute where Joon might escape with his life. Where Uol could make it to dry land, and then we'll all be drowned.

"Left!" Royo yells out.

I roll just as his dagger flies by my nose. Another inch and it would be embedded in my face. I went to my left, not his.

Stars, Royo, use east or west!

But for his lack of directional skill, his aim is spot on. His blade strikes one guard in the face. I land safely, but I'm not even to my feet when I realize I miscalculated. I'm in striking distance of the second guard. He smiles, victory shining in his eyes. He has me.

No.

He raises his blade. I don't have time to react. I can't move my sword fast enough. This is where I die.

All of a sudden, the guard falls straight forward, a blade sticking out of his neck.

I scramble to my feet, look up, and there's…Fallador, standing in front of me. I blink hard because it can't be him. Those are the same green eyes, but there's no reason for him to wear a Khitanese soldier's uniform.

"There's never a dull moment with you," he says.

Yes, it's definitely him. Anger immediately flows through me.

"What are you doing here?" I ask, standing straight. "Get to safety, right now!"

Stars, it hadn't even dawned on me that he'd be at risk. He should be in his villa on Oligarch Mountain, sipping tea, observing this spectacle, not on the harbor floor with us.

"You're welcome," he says with a smile. "For saving your life."

It's truly terrible to talk to someone so much like me.

I look up and find that the archer hangs dead off the bow of the ship. Did Fallador kill him as well?

"Gods, he's so ungrateful," Gambria says. She comes around the ship with a crossbow in her hand.

Wait, she killed the archer. She's not a marksman like Euyn, but Gambria could get the drop on nearly anyone when we were children.

I don't have time to get explanations of what they're doing here. Instead, we race up the ladders onto the golden ship. Now I have even more people to see to safety. Fallador and Gambria are the last of the Gayan royal family. If they die, no one is left with a rightful claim to the throne. They shouldn't be here at all. But *shouldn't* is meaningless, apparently.

The only Weians on board are one royal guard and the scepter bearer he's protecting. Two guards lie dead near Sora, who stands on the ship armed with a bloody sword. Two priests lie dead by the scepter—that could've been anyone, including the relic draining their lives.

Royo climbs up to the deck with Aeri slung over his shoulder. She moans. She's still somewhat with us, but she's very weak.

"Flee now," I say in Weian to the guard.

He shakes his head and holds his sword in both hands. Another person willing to give his life for a lie—for a king who'd kill him as soon as look at him, for a false god. Another sacrifice to power, for the right to commit atrocities. Another man willing to die for the privilege of treating others as less than themselves.

Enough.

The guard engages me, but I spin and cut with a slashing motion. My fury drives my sword through his armpit and into his chest. I pull out the blade, and he falls to the ground.

He lands next to the last escape skiff, which fortunately is wooden and not solid gold. The Weians must have left this for their scepter bearer to escape. But now, we all have a real way out.

My heart skips. Survival is an actual possibility. If we do this right.

"Everyone get inside the skiff," I say.

For once in my life, everyone does what they are told. Royo lays Aeri inside, and then Fallador and Gambria get in. Sora is last with a glance at me, but everyone is ready.

I take another step toward the Water Scepter bearer. He looks over his shoulder at me.

Stars, he's maybe sixteen. He doesn't try to fight or flee. He's holding the scepter steady against the water, and he's praying, I think.

Let's hope his gods listen.

I shove my blade through his back, right into his heart. At the same time, I grab on to the staff. A rush of energy flows through me, but it could just be the power of the sea that begins to cascade down. The ship quakes, and the screams are deafening as soldiers start drowning. I can only hope that both kings and the queen are among them.

I don't have time to watch. The water rises above the prow of the ship in seconds. I jump onto the escape boat and barely make it. Once I get inside, I have to sit and hold on tight while also securing the scepter. I lie on top of it as the waves of the falling water rock the boat as if it's a bath toy.

All of us slide. The skiff tilts. Stars, we're going to capsize. I hang on as the horizon goes vertical.

Please, gods, see us through this.

We stay on the precipice of flipping. One heartbeat. Two. Then, degree by degree, the skiff lowers. But then we spin and the other side starts to rise. I feel queasy, and my fingers are as slick as when I nearly dropped Zeolin out the window. But I hold on with the scepter pressed between my body and the boat. We rock from one side to another. I can't tell if we lost anyone just yet, and that is the worst feeling of all.

In a nauseating set of movements, and after what feels like a year of time, we finally make it up to the surface. I count. One, two, three, four. Sora, Aeri, Royo, and Fallador. And then there's Gambria. We've all made it. We're all drenched but floating in the harbor.

Everyone breathes hard, relieved to have survived. But we won't stay alive for long if we stay here.

As soon as we level out, I hold the scepter out to Fallador. I take a knee.

"Fallador, my prince, wield us to Gaya," I say.

He and Gambria exchange glances. Sora tilts her head like she didn't hear me correctly, and Royo was simply not paying attention, focused solely on Aeri.

"Mikail." Fallador looks down and to the side. Guilt clouds his expression.

We really don't have time for whatever this is. I can't seem to get the people I love to understand urgency outside of, apparently, drowning in a harbor.

My eyes dart all around, frustration making me choke the scepter. "What? What is it?"

"I can't," Fallador says sadly. He looks sorry for me, and I don't know why.

"I can explain, Mikail," Gambria says.

"All right, but can that be while you wield this?" I ask. "We aren't safe here."

The Weian navy is engaged with Khitanese warships, and some of the soldiers who'd been on the seafloor are flailing in the water, having survived the deluge. But we have been spotted by the boat nearest to us. They are turning their sails because our little skiff happens to have three of the five relics of the Dragon Lord. We won't be safe anywhere other than Gaya. And even that will be a challenge until all of these rulers are dead.

"I can't use it, either," Gambria says with a frown.

What is she talking about? Why are they doing this now? Anger and impatience rise through me.

"What do you mean, you can't?" I yell. "You're the royal family of Gaya!"

"Oh, Adoros," Gambria says, then purses her lips. "We aren't. You are."

EPILOGUE

AERI

I wake up in another world. The last thing I knew, I was standing on a rock on the seafloor of Quu Harbor. But one look, and I can tell that this is definitely not Quu or Khitan. I'm in a boat, I think. But I'm on dry land.

For a second, I think I'm dead as I stare up at a gorgeous azure sky. The air is warm, and the breeze is gentle. Is this Elysia? But then there's Royo's concerned face looking down at me. He's frowning, and my head is in his lap. If he's unhappy, I must still be alive.

"Good, you're up." Royo moves away from me, sliding on the bench, and then he climbs out of the boat.

Definitely not in paradise.

Confused, I sit up quickly, then put my arms out to steady myself. I'm not sure how long I was out, but my body aches and my head spins. Then I remember what I did. It doesn't feel real, but there is the Golden Ring of the Dragon Lord on my hand. I killed Bay Chin and General Salosa by turning them into statues. Then I wanted to sink the boats belonging to my father and the Weian king. But all I remember is numbness like I'd never felt radiating through me until I passed out. And Royo saw me do it—turn men into gold without touching them, which I couldn't possibly do with only the ring.

"Wait, where are you going?" I ask.

Royo stops, his shirt rippling in the sea breeze and his shoulders tense. He turns and faces me. "You lied to me again."

He's angry, but he's not staring at my face. He's looking at my chest. Or my neck.

I look down, and my armor is gone. And there, exposed, is the amulet burned into my skin, the chain long gone.

"Royo, I can explain…" I begin. Even though I don't need to. It's pretty self-explanatory. My stomach sinks. He already knows.

He shakes his head. "I asked about your necklace on the Light Mountains—"

"I know I—"

"You looked right at me and lied." His voice breaks with sorrow, with hurt. I close my mouth. He sighs. "I would've loved you through anything, anything you did, anything so long as you were honest."

"Royo, please…"

"You're a liar." He stares at me, and then he shakes his head. "I shouldn't of given you a second chance."

He turns and walks away, and my heart shatters into pieces as small as the grains of sand on the beach.

I stay sitting on the boat because I can't catch my breath. My stomach is twisting, and my chest feels like it's been cleaved in two. And there's nowhere to go. I think about chasing after him. I want to. My muscles ache to move, to climb out of this boat and run after him. But what is there to say? Everything he said was true. I lied to his face on the Light Mountains. It doesn't matter if I did it for him, because he warned me to never lie again.

I made my choice and broke my own heart. I want him to forgive it, but that's not up to me. The truth is, if I had to do it all over again, I would lie again to keep him safe. And there can't be forgiveness without regret.

"He'll come around," Mikail says. He walks up on the white sandy shore and stops next to the boat.

"No, I don't think he will." The words come out shaky and raw.

I'm not sure how I'm sitting here having a conversation with

Mikail. I'm not sure how either of us is still alive, or how I'm still breathing when it feels like I've been gutted.

"How did we escape?" I finally ask, looking around. "Where is Sora? Is she okay?"

"It's a very long story," he says. "But Sora is fine. Come with me, and I'll tell you everything."

He gestures, and it's only then that I realize he has the Water Scepter of the Dragon Lord in his hand. I can feel the energy radiating off it. It's hard to focus on anything, even my broken heart, with how strongly I can sense the scepter. Something deep inside me wants to reach out and possess it. I ignore it even though the impulse knocks on me like a drum.

"Mikail," I say, breathless.

If he has the relic, it can only mean we defeated Wei somehow. But if that's the case, why aren't we in Khitan?

"Where are we?" I ask.

"Gaya," he says. "My home."

The island. The colony of Yusan. The fourth realm that was once independent but then was absorbed, slaughtered, and weakened by the empire. By my bloodline.

Mikail just called it his home.

I look at Mikail and the staff in his hand. Then I put it together. The energy radiating off it is coming from him. I felt it when he handed me the ring.

Mikail is Gayan royalty.

We are on the colony island with three of the relics of the Dragon Lord. It's not possible, but somehow it is.

"Now what?" I ask.

"Now," he says, helping me out of the skiff, "we rest. Then, we seek our revenge."

The End For Now

ACKNOWLEDGMENTS

Thank you to the amazing, brilliant Liz Pelletier for championing my work. I could write 500 pages on my gratitude for all the ways you've changed my life and made me a better writer, but let it suffice for now to just say thank you from the bottom of my heart. None of this happens without you, and I'm so blessed to work with you. Thank you also to Jen Bouvier for your ideas, feedback, and for making this series possible.

Thank you to everyone at Red Tower for your tireless efforts in shaping this series. Thank you to the amazing edit team including: Mary Lindsey, Rae Swain, Hannah Lindsey, Claire Andress, and Jessica Meigs. Thank you to the incredible art team including: Bree Archer, Juho Choi, and Britt Marczak, but especially Elizabeth Turner Stokes. Thank you to Curtis Svehlak and Viveca Shearin in production. And thank you to the fantastic publicity and marketing team including: Ashley Doliber, Meredith Johnson, Heather Riccio, Brittany Zimmerman, and Lizzy Mason. Thank you to Nicole Resciniti for bringing this series worldwide.

Many thanks to my agent and agent assistant, Lauren Spieller and Hannah Morgan Teachout, for your notes, guidance, and support!

Thank you to my four children, who inspire and delight me. I am blessed to call you my family. Thank you to my mother for instilling hard work and dedication and leading by example. With every page, I hope to make you and Dad proud. Thank you to my sister, aunt, and cousins for your excitement and love.

Thank you to my friends who've been there for me through the highs and lows of this wild author ride, especially Karen McManus, Alexa Martin, June Tan, Sabina Khan, Rachel Van Dyken, Matt

Weintraub, Jessica Norgrove, Susan Thibault, Kiana Nyugen, and my sprinting buddy, Carissa Broadbent. Thank you to Jenn Kocsmiersky for your beautiful art.

Thank you to all the influencers, booksellers, reviewers, and most of all readers for making this series an international bestseller!

Last, but most importantly, thank you to John Coryea for showing me what love is, for being my rock in this storm, and for giving my heart a home. I was alive but not living until I found you. Tomorrow and tomorrow and tomorrow.

RED TOWER
BOOKS™